MOON CURSED COMPLETE TRILOGY

ALEXIS CALDER

ILLARIA PUBLISHING

This book is a work of fiction. The names, characters and events in this book are the products of the author's imagination or are used fictitiously. Any similarity to real persons living or dead is coincidental and not intended by the author.

Cover Artwork by Covers by Aura
Editing by EAH

WOLF MARKED

MOON CURSED BOOK ONE

1

THE WIND RUSTLED the paper calendar hanging on my wall and I glanced at the crossed off days. Six days left. I was so close to freedom. Pulling my jacket tighter around me, I walked over to the window and peered outside. The sky was steely gray and the clouds looked like they might bring a tornado. It was late spring and the weather this time of year was unpredictable.

Maybe I'd get lucky and it would hit my mom's shitty trailer and I could get out of here permanently. I had a feeling I wasn't going to get out of here that easily. Whatever witch magic they'd used to seal us in pack lands seemed to also keep the worst weather away. It also prevented us from self-harm. Not that it kept anyone else from beating the shit out of me.

I supposed if I really wanted out, I could have pushed Tyler and his entourage a little more. The penalty for killing another member of the pack was death, but I had a feeling nobody would mourn me. And it wasn't like they'd lock up the next alpha for getting rid of the broken wolf.

I closed the window. While we were unlikely to get a

tornado here, we did get rain and I didn't need the water coming in and ruining my few meager possessions.

The duffel bag sitting next to the folding table that served as my desk was already packed. It had been for three months. Waiting until the night the magic would free me from this prison. On the first full moon after my nineteenth birthday, I was supposed to shift, and with that magic, I'd gain the ability to leave the magical border around our town. I already knew I wouldn't shift, but the magic should break, letting me finally escape from the hell that was my life.

For the rest of the pack, that barrier was our savior. It kept us hidden and protected. Away from feral wolves who hunted other shifters for sport. Away from humans who would kill us on sight. Most importantly, it kept us away from witches. At least that was what they taught us. For me, it kept me away from freedom. I'd take my chances with humans and feral shifters any day over the shit I dealt with here. Witches and magic freaked me out more, but I'd cross that bridge when I got to it.

Fucking magic. Fucking witches. They were the cause of all my pain. The reason I was trapped in a town where I was abused daily. The reason my mom spent her days on her back with whatever pills she could find to dull her pain. I didn't even know who my dad was but I was sure he was an asshole. Just like my mom's dad. He was the one who pissed off a witch, resulting in the curse that follows my family. No shifting for us. Practically human with a dormant wolf shifter gene. If only my mom had fled while she was pregnant with me and let us live as humans. Instead, she'd stayed here, pining over the fucker who knocked her up. He never came back, and I got stuck here.

"Lola, did you grab cigarettes at the store?" Mom yelled.

"Yeah, Mom. They're on the table." I shouldn't indulge her habits. It was gross and it cost me a small fortune, but it kept her off my case. She didn't ask where I went or what I did as long as there were cigarettes on the table and food in the fridge. All paid for by my after-school job at the pack grocery store.

It wasn't a glamorous job, but it was helping me save something for when I finally got free of this hellhole.

I took a peek in the mirror and gingerly touched the bruises from my latest black eye. Another gift from the male who would one day be the pack alpha. If Tyler Grant had treated me with indifference, maybe I'd have stayed here. Instead, I got daily reminders that I was unwelcome. One of these days he was going to go too far and I intended to be long gone before then. Huh, how about that? I guess I didn't have a death wish, after all. My desire to survive was barely hanging on by a thread. It would be easier to roll over and give up. Thankfully, I had the reminder of my mom and what her life was like. I refused to become like her.

I considered applying some concealer to cover my injury, but it wouldn't hide it much. The rest of my classmates would be healed by now, but since I didn't have the wolf inside me to aid in that, I healed like a human. The purple and blue made my eyes look even more green than they were. Apparently, I had my father's eyes. Most of the pack had brown or amber eyes. The green in mine was another thing that made me stand out. Add in the red hair and it was impossible for me to hide.

Quickly, I pulled my hair into a low ponytail to get it out of the way. I grabbed my backpack and slung it over my shoulder. *Six more days*. That was all I had to do. Just a few more days of school, a few more days of work, a few more days of ignoring the over-acting of my mom's moaning through the paper-thin walls of her bedroom. I shuddered. No kid should have to hear their mom engaging in that. I didn't judge how she earned her money but I sure as hell didn't want to listen to it.

With one last glance at my packed bag, I left my room. The thought of leaving was the only thing getting me through the motions. Chin high, I reminded myself that I was almost there. I'd made it this far. I could make it six more days.

Students mingled in the grass in front of Wolf Creek Community College when I arrived. I glared at the building, which was right next door to Wolf Creek High School. Sometime when I was a small kid, they'd expanded the school requirement to make all of us take at least one semester of college while waiting for our first full moon. Most kids who grew up here dropped out as soon as they had their first shift and settled into some mundane job in town. Few left because we all knew being a wolf without a pack was challenging. I wouldn't ever turn into a wolf so I wasn't worried. Being alone would be better than being here.

It was the twenty-fourth of May and there were only a couple weeks of school left before summer break. But I wouldn't be here to finish the year. My birthday was last week, which meant the full moon in six days was my ticket out. I was so close, I could taste it.

As I neared the entry, I realized that a small group of guys was waiting by the front doors. My heart pounded and I froze. Tyler and his crew were gathered there despite the fact that most of them had already had their first full moon. Tyler was one of the few wolves who stayed enrolled in school after his first shift last month. I figured for sure he'd be out of here since his future was set. As the next alpha, it didn't matter if he had any actual skills aside from being able to throw people around. He could do whatever he wanted and nobody would bat an eye.

Quickly, I changed direction and started walking toward the side of the building. There were other doors I could use and I wasn't in the mood to get the shit beat out of me today. It wasn't like I was a pushover but there was nothing fair about three dudes against one non-shifted chick.

I slipped into the side door and walked down the tile hallway. Kids I'd known my whole life glanced at me and quickly looked away. That was how it was for me. When I was younger, it hurt that I was so alone. Now, I was grateful for their indifference. Ignoring me was better than the alternative.

When I finally took my seat in my Calculus class, I breathed a sigh of relief. I'd made it in without sporting a new black eye. *Six more days.*

Professor Ortiz started writing on the white board and the four other people in the class were already taking notes. I had no deep love of math, but I was good at it and Tyler wasn't. Another not as proud moment. My schedule was based on things Tyler hated. I reminded myself that it wasn't like I'd even get the credit for the class since I'd be out before the term was over. It was pure survival at this point.

Soon enough, I was sucked into class, too focused on the numbers to worry about anything else. Okay, so maybe I liked that about math. It forced me to shut out my other worries.

I went through the motions for the next two classes, doing

enough to keep the professors from noticing me and not engaging enough to draw attention to myself. It was a balancing act I'd perfected over the years. Keeping to myself and making myself nearly invisible were the only ways I'd made it this far.

The hallways were packed. There were only a hundred of us in this school, but since we all had the same lunch, it got busy when it was time for a break. I walked into the crowd, keeping my gaze down to avoid confrontation. It was especially important this close to a full moon.

Someone ran right into me, their shoulder slammed into mine, shoving me aside. I looked up, ready to find a way out, but when my eyes met Tyler's, I knew I was fucked.

"Where have you been hiding, little wolf?" He stared at me with his amber eyes, a vicious smile on his lips. His fingers dug into my bicep as he held me tight. "I waited for you at the front door but you didn't come. I thought maybe you were playing hooky."

"What and give someone else the chance to beat the shit out of me? You know we're exclusive." Missing school was worse than attending. Tyler and his friends might use me as a punching bag, but the torture that came with being truant was far worse. I'd tried a few times in high school, but it wasn't worth the pain.

He pushed me forward into the women's bathroom. The door swung open and two girls standing by the sinks screamed.

"Out. Now." Tyler growled.

"I don't know why you waste your time with her," Tenny, a tall blonde who was a few months older than me said.

Every female at school wanted Tyler. He was going to be

the next alpha, after all. Even without the promise of power, his looks would buy him a lot of attention. He was over six feet of solid muscle. With wavy black hair, piercing amber eyes, and a strong masculine jaw, he was like a walking wet dream. Thankfully, his good looks were wasted on me. He'd been an awkward kid and by the time he resembled a fucking Greek God, I knew what kind of person he was.

"Ditch the loser, Ty," Tenny said in what was probably supposed to be a seductive tone. "We haven't had a tumble in my back seat in a while."

"I said, *out*," Tyler repeated.

"She probably doesn't even know what you like," Tenny whined.

"What exactly do you think he's doing with me?" I asked. "Because I promise you if he put his dick anywhere near me, I'd bite it off."

Tyler's hand made contact with my face, slapping me so hard it nearly knocked me on my ass. The sting made my eyes water and I forced myself to clench my jaw and hold my breath rather than cry out. I'd learned long ago that when I reacted, it made things worse.

Tenny giggled. "Well, since she's not meeting your needs, you know where to find me if you want a real wolf."

"Out," Tyler repeated.

The girls left the bathroom and I pulled free of Tyler's grip. "What do you want, Tyler?"

"You shouldn't be here," he said. "My father should have kicked you and your whore of a mother out the day your grandfather crossed that witch. Better yet, he should have let you starve in the caves."

I swallowed hard. The worst punishment in our pack was

being locked in the caves on the south end of town, right near the border. Locked in without food or water with other criminals meant that wolves often went feral and fed on each other. It was gruesome and had only been used once in my lifetime, but the threat was always there. Only, this was the first time Tyler mentioned it. He'd told me I shouldn't be here in previous encounters, but he'd never talked about the caves. Ever since his first shift, he'd been more emotional and less stable. I was grateful he wasn't the alpha yet.

"Don't worry, I'll be out of here soon and you'll never have to look at me again." I glared at him.

Before I saw it coming, his hand was around my throat and he pushed me back, slamming me against the wall. I heard the cracking of my head as it made contact and hoped it didn't mean I had another concussion. Pain blurred my vision and I winced despite myself.

He was faster and stronger than he was before his first shift. When we were younger, I had a chance against him. As we got older, he got stronger, feeding off the energy of his wolf. I didn't have that advantage. It was hard to tell if the beatings had gotten worse or if he'd gotten stronger.

When we were in elementary school, he teased me but by middle school, things turned physical. In the last year, I had learned I didn't stand a chance fighting back anymore. What I wouldn't give for some of the strength and power that came along with a shift.

Tyler scowled at me. His expression reflecting pure hatred. I never knew what I did to make him so mad, but it had gotten worse recently. Beating me up had always seemed to be a sport, something he did with a laugh to show off to his friends.

That's when it hit me that we were totally alone. My heart pounded faster. In all the years of dealing with Tyler, he'd always had others with him. There were always witnesses. He liked the audience and there was always someone to pull him back if he took things too far. We'd never actually been alone before. For the first time during one of our little torture sessions, I was worried. This wasn't just a game anymore.

"Let me go," I demanded.

"Like I said, you shouldn't even be here, little wolf." He squeezed harder, making me gasp for air. My vision blurred, growing darker around the edges. For a moment, I wondered if this was it. If he took me out, I would be free of this place, done with the pain. I considered it for a heartbeat. A flicker of anger urged me forward, I wasn't ready yet.

Risking retaliation, I kicked Tyler right in the nuts. He let go, groaning, as he grabbed his manhood. I sidestepped him then bolted for the door, sucking in air as I fled. The hallway was empty. His friends nowhere in sight. Whatever Tyler had been after, he didn't want any witnesses. If he hadn't already had his mind set on murdering me, he probably did now. I might have just signed my own death warrant. *Fuck.* Surviving for the next six days was going to be harder than I thought.

2

KICKING Tyler in the nuts was probably a really bad idea but in all the years of abuse, he'd never come at me alone like that. And he'd never put his hand around my throat. I wasn't sure what snapped to cause him to up the ante, but I wasn't going to stick around to find out. Maybe it was the thought of losing his favorite victim that was pushing him to the edge. Maybe he didn't want me to be happy and figured he'd kill me before I could leave. Worse, what if his shift had unlocked some kind of violent streak? I mean, he'd always been violent, but this was insane. I had no desire to see what he would be like with power. The whole pack was fucked when he took over as alpha.

Whatever the reason, Tyler had crossed a line I didn't even know existed. I couldn't let him get me alone again.

"Lola, those boxes aren't going to unpack themselves," Jud, my manager called.

I shook myself out of my reflection and got to work pulling cans of beans out and putting them on the shelf. I'd managed to avoid Tyler the rest of the day, but my head was still fuzzy and achy from our encounter. I probably did have a fucking concussion. Asshole. At least I hadn't thrown up this time. Maybe I was getting better at hiding my symptoms. Ugh, my life sucked so hard. There was no way leaving this place was going to make my life worse.

Working my way through the boxes of beans, I moved on to corn and beets. I wrinkled my nose. How did we sell enough beets that we had to restock them every week? Did wolf shifters develop a secret craving for beets? It was the oddest thing. I'd never had them in my life but every week, I had to restock them.

The mindless work was a good distraction. None of the customers made eye contact with me or engaged me at all. I was the broken wolf and I was used to being treated like I was contagious. I suppose it was better that way. There were absolutely no ties to this place for me to break when I left.

The hours passed quickly as I emptied boxes and stocked shelves. Finally, I was caught up and it was time to haul out the recycling. I broke down all the boxes and stacked them up so I could carry them out. The cool spring air had turned cold now that the sun was gone and goosebumps spread across my bare arms. I usually lingered out here for a few minutes to enjoy the open air, especially this time of year when the dumpsters weren't stinking from heat, but it was a little colder than I expected.

I tossed the boxes into the bin and then wiped my dusty hands on my apron before turning back to the door. A solitary figure was blocking my entry back into the store. There were no lights back here and my vision wasn't any better than a normal human but I could make out the familiar shape.

Tyler's six-foot-four frame was difficult to miss. Even in

the dim light, I could tell it was him. This was a first. He'd never shown up to my work before and he certainly had never cornered me in an alley before. Was this payback for the kick in the bathroom? It wasn't the first time I'd landed a hit in the family jewels, but it had been a while since I'd been that desperate. Or stupid.

After all my escape plans, I had not seen this coming. My pulse raced but I wasn't about to let him know I was scared.

Crossing my arms over my chest, I faced him, chin held high. "Move out of my way."

"I could kill you, you know. Nobody would even miss you. I wonder how many days you'd sit back here with the rest of the trash before they found the body." He took a step away from the door, moving toward me.

I held my ground, unwilling to yield to him. This was beyond normal bullying. "I didn't realize you'd moved on to stalking. How nice to see you think so highly of me that you had to go out of your way to see me."

"You know exactly what this is about," he hissed.

"Why don't you enlighten me? Clearly, I wasn't part of the group text about whatever the fuck this is," I said.

"You shouldn't even be here," he said.

"Yeah, yeah, you tell me that daily." My fear was easing. This wasn't anything new. This was the same old shit he always pulled. Maybe he just didn't get enough today.

"I mean it, Lola," he said. "You can't be here."

"Well, as I tell you every day, I'm happily out of here as soon as I can. Unlike you, I'm stuck here." I moved my hands to my hips. "Hey, I have an idea. Why don't you leave for a week and when you come back you won't have to see my face ever again."

A low guttural sound came from Tyler. The growl was primal and sent a shiver down my spine. I'd never heard a sound like that. Involuntarily I took a step backward.

Tyler moved toward me, his whole body tense, teeth bared, eyes bright. Too bright. As in he was fighting the change. Or trying to bring it on.

"Calm down. You don't want to do that here." I backed up again. This was too far even for Tyler. He was a brand-new wolf. He'd shifted for the first time a few weeks ago and unless he had ridiculous control, he likely hadn't shifted again. Most wolf shifters were forced into the shift on the full moons for the first few months. Or they'd shift if they were threatened or emotional. Once they gained control of their wolves, they could shift on command and weren't beholden to the moon. But Tyler wasn't an experienced shifter. This shouldn't be possible. He was letting his emotions run wild.

"Tyler, back the fuck up." I was against a wall now. I hadn't even realized I continued to move away from him. On my right, the dumpster blocked my exit. On my left was a chain link fence that divided the alleyway. I was boxed in. *Fuck*. This had to be the worst day of my life.

He advanced, his body seemingly vibrating with energy. Teeth bared, he growled again.

I wouldn't survive if he attacked me in wolf form. Shit, he'd tried to kill me earlier today in his human form. He'd been stronger than me since we were twelve. It wasn't fair that puberty brought out so many wolf qualities. I worked out as best I could to keep myself strong, but I wasn't a match for him.

"I won't stay in your pack if that's what you're worried about," I said, my voice a little shakier than I wanted it to be.

That's what this had to be about. He'd be alpha in a few years and I guessed he didn't want someone like me bringing down the pack. Not that anyone else seemed to even notice me or my mom. We lived on the outskirts of town with the other rejects. Though, we were the only ones who couldn't shift in our little run-down trailer park.

"Just back off before you do something you'll regret." I kept my voice steadier this time, feigning confidence.

"I should kill you," he said.

"No, you're not a killer." Tyler was an asshole, sure. He beat the shit out of me on the regular, but he never went as far as he could. Not that it excused him for anything. He still deserved to die slowly from some venereal disease from whatever crazy bitch he rolled around with.

"Don't pretend like you know me. We're not friends."

"As if I needed reminding of that, dick," I snapped.

I was flush against the wall now and Tyler boxed me in with a hand on either side of me. My breathing grew rapid and I kept my eyes fixed on his. Tyler's pupils were huge and a vein in his forehead looked like it might explode.

"You're fighting it," I pointed out. "You don't want to change here. You don't want my blood on your hands."

"You don't know what I want." He leaned so his face was nearly touching mine. Then he breathed in as if smelling me.

My whole body tensed. *What the actual fuck?*

Tyler lowered one hand and set it on my hip, sliding it up my body until he reached my breast. His touch was gentle and to my horror, my body responded. A little shiver of lust rolled through me.

Oh, hell no.

This was not going to happen. This was never going to happen. With all the force I could muster, I lifted my leg and stomped hard on his foot.

Tyler howled as he backed away from me. I pushed past him, but he grabbed me, throwing an arm around my chest to pull me against him. I struggled to break free of his grip, but he held me tight.

"Let me go, asshole!" I threw my elbow back, trying to hit his stomach. Tyler forced both my arms to my side, pinning me against him. He pulled me even closer to him and I could feel his hardness pressing into me.

I knew wolf shifters had a practically insatiable sex drive, but there were so many willing partners. Why would someone who hated me go through all this trouble?

I felt his nose by my ear, his hot breath on my neck. He was panting and I wasn't sure if he was in control or his wolf was. Whatever was happening, it wasn't going to end well for me if I couldn't get out of his grip.

"Let me go, Tyler. Or I swear to the gods I will slit your throat in your sleep," I hissed.

His large hand grabbed my chin and roughly forced my head to turn so I was facing him. "You will be a ghost until the full moon. I don't want to see your face. As soon as the magic lifts, you're gone. If you stay, I will finish what I started."

He pushed me away and I stumbled forward, landing on the ground on my hands and knees. Shaking and terrified, I risked a glance behind me. When I realized that I was alone, my shoulders slumped and I let out a breath of relief.

I had no idea what just happened but I had no problem following his suggestion. It was already my plan anyway.

Cursing myself for my weakness, I pushed myself to standing and brushed the dirt off my hands and knees. I wished I could fight back. I hated that I wasn't strong enough. It wasn't fair being a human surrounded by these powerful creatures who could snap me in half without even trying. The sooner I could get away from all things magic, the better.

3

Of course I saw Tyler everywhere. In the halls, at the store, even walking down the fucking street. As asked, I faded into the background, hiding behind other people and even once ducking behind a tree. It wasn't like I was being stealthy, he saw me, but to his credit, he did his part to look away. And unless I was imagining things, he even distracted his friends a few times to keep them from seeing me.

None of it made sense. Years of being slammed into lockers in the hallway or being elbowed in the stomach for no reason left a mark. The broken noses, black eyes, and cracked ribs left behind were strong enough memories for me to take his warning seriously. Every time I hid, I felt like a failure. I'd made it this far on little more than mother-fucking-moxie and fleeing from a literal big bad wolf was shit on my self-esteem.

But it was almost over.

The only thing keeping me going was that nobody knew I planned to attend a human college. I was on my way out of here and going to make something of myself. Sure, my measly savings wasn't going to go far, but I'd figure it out. I was smart. Even if my teachers were too afraid to ever show kindness to me, they'd still taught me. Wolf Creek might be a magically hidden town, but the high school still printed off transcripts for me.

Surprisingly, I was a little sad when I left the school on Friday. I'd planned on leaving for as long as I could remember. Actually walking off the campus I'd attended school at for my entire memory was different. My chest tightened as the reality of leaving this behind struck me. It was a lot to process even if everything about Wolf Creek had been miserable.

Fighting against the unwelcome anxiety of starting over, I walked the familiar route toward the store. Another place I was leaving after tonight. No more stocking shelves or ringing up customers who glared at me and never said a word. Though, I supposed those who pretended I didn't exist were better than the ones who treated me like trash.

I could see a small crowd outside the store as I approached and decided the less time with others, the better. Turning, I walked toward the back of the store where the dumpsters and back door were. Balling my hands into fists I fought back against the images flooding into my head from my encounter with Tyler.

Thankfully, the alley was empty and I was able to get into the store without issue. Backpack stashed, apron on, I clocked in for the last time. This time, flutters of anticipation and a feeling of glee surged through me. There it was. The exact emotion I was hoping for. I was going to be free of this place tomorrow. Thank the gods.

I finished breaking down boxes while it was still light and

after a quick peek in the alley, I dragged the boxes out, then rushed back inside. No lingering for me tonight.

There was no way I was going out the back door in the dark. Not just because of what happened with Tyler, but because tomorrow was the full moon. Everyone past puberty would be restless tonight, feeling the call of the moon. While the wolves didn't shift until nineteen, the wolf began to stir more as they aged. I wouldn't know. I've never felt the wolf because I'm broken. The curse on my family prevented me from ever reaching my inner wolf. While I had a really great sense of smell, I was basically human. Fucking curses. What I wouldn't give for the power to put Tyler in his place.

They say our ability to shift was also a curse. We were human once. The ability to shift was the result of very complicated magic. Lots of human stories talked about werewolves being used to protect vampires, but that was a myth. We didn't get along with vampires enough to ever work for them. As far as I knew, we stuck to ourselves in our packs, and left the vampires to their own devices. Witches, on the other hand, were tightly connected to our history.

Hundreds of years ago, we were created by witches who needed protection on the nights they performed their most complicated spells. Thus, the reason our shifts aligned with the full moon. A large coven of witches cursed an entire human village to turn into wolves every full moon. The wolves would roam the woods, keeping witch hunters occupied while they did whatever black magic they wanted. Nice, huh?

Eventually, the shifters rebelled and started fighting back. They abandoned their homes and fled, hiding around other humans and making sure they were in the woods on the night of the full moon. That original curse turned out to be spread over generations, and more shifters were born as the original shifters bred with humans.

Over several generations, we'd evolved beyond the initial curse and could shift at will once we gained control. Though, the first shift always aligned with the full moon closest to your nineteenth birthday. How it managed to coincide with nineteen, I had no idea. All I knew was that witches were assholes and you shouldn't cross them. At least we'd been able to break their control over us eventually.

Before I knew it, all the stocking was finished and my last shift was coming to a close. It seemed to fly by tonight. I walked into the back of the store and took off my apron, then tossed it in the bin. It felt pretty amazing to stick my timecard in the machine for the last time. Not that Jud needed the stamp for today. He knew this was my last shift and I'd asked for my final check to be ready today. There was something symbolic about finishing the shift in the same way I'd started here. Clock in, clock out. Nearly every day for the last six years.

I took a deep breath, feeling satisfied with the work I'd done. When my mom couldn't provide, I'd stepped up and taken care of myself. It was reassuring that I could do that considering I was about to start over somewhere new.

I walked into the empty, dim store. Jud was closing down the register for the night.

"You have my last check, Jud?" I asked. "My apron is in the back along with my name tag."

Jud grunted. "You really going through with it?"

"You say it as if you're surprised," I said. "I told you when you hired me I was out the day before the full moon."

"Yeah, but nobody ever leaves. Even your ma came back," he pointed out.

"I'm not my mom," I reminded him.

"That's true, you're not." He pulled an envelope out of his pocket. "Figured it might help if your last check was in cash. There's some extra to help you get started but don't you dare tell anyone I helped you."

"I'd never dream of it," I said. "Everyone knows you're an uncaring asshole."

He grinned. "That's exactly what I am."

I accepted the envelope from him. Jud really was an asshole, but in the same way most single wolf shifters were. He was gruff and unfriendly, but he wasn't hurtful or mean. He didn't sugar-coat anything and he had zero empathy. On the flip side, he was the only one willing to hire me when I started looking for jobs at thirteen. I'd started a few hours a week sweeping then moved up to stocking and register. Thanks to Jud, I had a good chunk saved for my escape from this hellhole.

"Thanks for everything, Jud," I said.

He nodded. "Can I give you one piece of advice?"

"Sure."

"Never come back. Stay away forever." His tone was dark and I could hear the warning in it.

Swallowing hard, I nodded. It was good advice, honestly. I'd seen this place destroy my own mother. She'd been a decent mom when I was young. Then something inside her snapped. I always wondered if it was the whole denying the inner wolf the ability to shift. They said my grandfather went crazy and killed himself because not shifting was too much. I never let myself put too much stock in those rumors because I didn't want to believe it could happen to me. Maybe staying away would help slow it down or prevent me from following the same path.

"Get out of here," he said.

I stuffed the envelope into the waistband of my jeans and covered it with my shirt. Damn girl jean pockets were too fucking small to actually fit anything. "Thanks, again."

He grunted as he picked up a broom and started sweeping. Our conversation was officially over. My throat was a little tight as I walked to the front door. Jud wasn't nice, exactly, but he had shown me kindness in his own way.

The night air was cool and clean. The scent of lilac filled the air. Summer was the best time of year in Wolf Creek. Warmth, sunshine, no school. It was the time of year when I could avoid the bullies. I smiled as I realized I was about to avoid them forever.

The walk to my mom's trailer seemed longer than usual tonight. Maybe it was because I kept pausing to take everything in. It was my last night here, after all. Despite my attempts to stir up nostalgia, every memory I recalled was bad. By the time I reached home, I was more than ready to leave.

My mom's door was closed and grunting sounds escaped the thin walls. I wrinkled my nose and quickly made my way to my room, closing the door behind me. I was not going to miss that. I flipped on the light switch, but nothing happened. *Dammit, Mom.* She must not have paid the power bill again.

Looked like my last night here was going to end with a cold shower. Somehow, it seemed a fitting end to this stint in hell.

Using a flashlight, I double checked my bag. It was a

surreal feeling packing your whole life into a duffel bag. Thankfully, I didn't have a lot. The clothes that weren't too worn out, money from my job, a folder with my transcripts from school, and my two favorite books. That was it. My whole life in a bag. It was a little sad when I realized this was it. No photos, nothing sentimental. Even though this had been my life for a while, I knew it was wrong. It wasn't any way to live. I was going to break free, though. Even if I went nuts and ended it all, I'd give myself a few good years first.

After a quick, cold shower in the dark, I locked my bedroom door then crawled into bed. As my eyelids grew heavy, I wondered where I'd be sleeping tomorrow. It didn't really matter as long as I was far from here.

4

A DOOR SLAMMED and I sat up, fully awake, heart pounding. A man yelled, then my mom yelled and something crashed against a wall. I scrambled out of bed and unlocked my door. Just as I stumbled into the living room, the front door to our trailer slammed shut.

My mom was standing in front of her open bedroom door in a ratty bathrobe. Her red hair was a mess and she had lipstick smeared on her mouth. The streaks of her mascara running down her face gave away the tears even if she wasn't crying now.

"You okay?" I asked.

My mom turned away from the door and looked at me. Her eyes widened as if noticing me for the first time. We often went weeks without speaking about anything other than her cigarette stash. It was like we were roommates rather than mother and daughter. It suited me fine. She'd given up on me and herself sometime around fifth grade. I'd tried to pull her out of the funk for a while, but eventually I gave up and got a job and bought my own groceries. Shortly after the power went out for the first time, she started having male visitors over and the power went back on. I knew enough not to ask questions. She'd shut me out and she wasn't the same mom I had before.

"Mom? Did he hurt you?"

"No, it's fine, everything is fine. It's a full moon tonight. You know how they get," she said.

"Yeah."

"How's work?" She tied her robe closed and walked into the tiny kitchen.

"Fine." I wasn't sure what she was playing at. We never talked about anything anymore.

"Coffee?" She picked up a bag of grounds and held it up.

I nodded then stood there in silence watching her go through the motions of adding the filter, scooping grounds, and filling the pot with water. I knew she made herself coffee every day, but I was usually at school when she did. When I got home, I'd drink the leftovers over ice and dump the grounds.

"You're leaving tonight, aren't you?" she asked without looking up.

The coffee pot gurgled and sputtered as it percolated. I tore my eyes away from the appliance to look at my mom. She was a mess and it hurt a little to see her like this. I'd gotten good at blocking it out and reminding myself about how badly she treated me the last few years. But there was something about knowing it was time to say goodbye that made you view things differently. I felt sorry for her. She'd been handed this life without choice. She wasn't the one who fucked up, but I couldn't stay here. Not even for her. There was nothing I could do.

"I'll leave as soon as the magic lets me out," I said.

"Good," she said.

"Will you be okay?" It was a question I'd wondered about a few times but always stopped myself from asking. She wouldn't be okay and we both knew it. She'd have to start taking better care of herself and I wasn't sure she could.

"Don't worry about me," she said.

"I'm not going to come back after I go." I wasn't sure why I told her that, but it seemed like she should know.

"I hope you never do." She forced a smile then turned to the cupboard and pulled down two coffee mugs. She set the mugs on the counter and then pulled the coffee pot off and filled each before handing me one of the cups.

Just like her, I drank my coffee black. Probably because milk and sugar were luxuries that weren't really necessary when you had a limited budget. It took a while for me to adjust to the bitter taste when I was younger, but now it was a staple in my life. One of the things we had in common.

"You were never meant to be in this place," she said. "You're too good for all of these wolves. I'm sorry I got you stuck here."

My brow furrowed. "What do you mean?"

She let out a long breath. "Your father wasn't from around here. I left, I had a life. A good one. But after I got pregnant, I was scared and I came back. When I arrived, my dad was a mess so I stayed to help. I never planned to stay but you came early, and the magic took hold of you. If I left, you'd have been stuck here."

"I don't understand," I said. "I thought you'd always been here."

"It doesn't matter. The fact that I returned erased any good I had from my time away."

"You've never spoken about my father before," I said.

"He's probably long gone. He didn't even know I was pregnant with you."

"Was he a shifter?" I asked.

She nodded. "He never knew our secret. I was scared he'd find out you couldn't shift and he'd disown you."

"It couldn't have been worse than growing up here, Ma," I said.

"Trust me, there are things worse than Wolf Creek and the suffering we had here." She sipped her coffee. "You're better off without him."

"That doesn't make any sense. He wouldn't have even known I couldn't shift until I was nineteen. I'd have had a whole lifetime to feel loved and safe. How could you deprive me of that?" All the good feelings about my mom were gone now. Why would she do that to her unborn child and how had she kept this from me all these years?

"He would have known far sooner and things would have ended badly for both of us," she said. "Promise me, you will never go looking for your father. He'd bring you nothing but pain."

"How could I? I know nothing about him," I said.

"Good." She walked out of the kitchen and paused in front of her bedroom door. "Be safe out there."

I was still standing in the kitchen with my untouched coffee when she closed the door behind her. "That's it? No goodbye?"

It wasn't like I expected anything touching or memorable, but

I expected something other than this. What was I supposed to do with this information? Why tell me about my dad now? And how the fuck could living with a father and mother outside of this shit hole be worse than having the crap beat out of me every week?

Furious, I set the cup on the counter and stormed back into my room. It was time to go. I wasn't sure when the magic barrier would let me pass but I wasn't going to wait here. My guess was sometime after moonrise, I could walk right out of here but I could use any head start I could get.

Quickly, I made myself a peanut butter sandwich and grabbed a bunch of snacks to get me through the next couple of days in case Wolf Creek was a longer walk from civilization than I knew.

That was another shitty thing about this place. I had no idea where we were geographically. I knew we were in the United States and that we got mild winters with some snow and hot summers, but other than that, I was clueless. I could be days away from a hotel or I could walk right into a bustling metropolis. No matter how many adults I asked, nobody would tell me the details.

I was done with the secrets. Done with the magic. I was going to find my way out of here and start living my normal, boring, human life.

When I stepped out of my door, I was greeted by three familiar faces. Tyler, and his two best goons, Julian and Kyle, were waiting right out front of my trailer.

"How am I supposed to avoid you when you show up at my house?" I demanded. "I'm not in the mood for any of your games, Tyler."

"I had a feeling you might do something like this. You're going to run," Tyler said.

"I told you I was going to run. That was always my plan. You knew that. You're the one who told me to do it." I glared at Tyler, totally confused and super pissed about the way he was behaving. What was going through his head? He told me to get out of here. And he told me to avoid him. Yet, he shows up at my house first thing in the morning on the day of the First Moon Ceremony. Every interaction I had with Tyler was getting more confusing by the second.

"My dad says everyone has to be at the ceremony or it'll displease the gods. I'm here to make sure you attend." Tyler, to his credit, looked like he would rather be anywhere else but standing here playing errand boy for his dad. I wished the same could be said about his friends, but their grins and tense body language told me they were hoping I wasn't going to go down without a fight.

I had two choices. Try to fight all three of them and lose badly, or agree to go along with it. There was a possibility I could still run if they didn't stick around to babysit me.

"Fine." I took a step back, giving some distance between the three of them.

"I'm supposed to bring you tonight. You're the only one that might ruin it." Tyler moved closer to me, his expression serious.

"After a week of warning me to stay away from you, you want to spend more time with me? What is it, Tyler?" I probably should have kept my mouth shut but in my defense, I was already out of this place in my head.

"What is she talking about, Ty?" Julian asked.

"Keeping me away from your friends, too. What the fuck is going on, Tyler? Is this really about your dad?"

"Don't push me, Lola." Tyler growled.

"Tyler, teach her some manners," Julian said. He inched closer to me and I could practically feel his wolf pacing. The thought startled me. I couldn't communicate with the pack the way the others could. I'd heard we could sense wolves, feel emotions, connect in ways humans couldn't. But that was never an option for me.

I shook my head, trying to send the confusing thought away. It had to be in my imagination.

"If she's unconscious, she can't participate. My dad was clear that she has to be there. All the new wolves do," Tyler said.

"She's not a wolf. She's not even a human. She's an abomination and she shouldn't even have been left alive," Julian said.

I'd heard the words my whole life but they stung more today for some reason. I was so close to getting out of here and this was exactly why. Usually, I could use the hatred thrown my way as fuel, but today there was already so much unwanted nostalgia.

"I told you, she's still connected to the pack," Tyler said. "My dad said she can't be killed before the ceremony, or it could threaten the pack."

My brow furrowed in confusion. We'd had tragedy in our pack before. A few years ago, a few kids from school had drown in the swimming hole. They were seniors and I was a freshman. Of course I knew them, but we weren't friends. Not that the age difference was the cause of that but that's not the point. The point is, they died within months of their first moon ceremony and nothing bad had happened. I remembered the older folks talking about how tragic it was that they were almost to their first shift. Most people seemed to think they'd have survived if they had bonded with their wolf.

Tyler was lying. They've never needed all the wolves before. Besides, there were only two of us who were shifting this month. Aside from me, only one other classmate had a May birthday and turned nineteen right before tonight's full moon. And I knew for a fact, she would not care if I wasn't there. She'd likely prefer the spotlight.

Something was going on and I needed to get out of here before it went down. "Alright. I'll hang out here and meet you at the barn at dusk. Work for you?"

"Sure." Tyler walked over to the shabby porch swing in the dirt next to a dozen abandoned pots and containers that used to hold flowers before my mom snapped. He sat down. "We'll wait."

"You're kidding me, right?" Then I realized I could sneak out the back door if he was camped out here. "You know what, not my problem. I'm going to take a nap. You assholes knock yourselves out."

I walked back into the trailer and glanced toward my mom's room. Her door was still closed and there was no sign that she was aware that I'd been outside talking to anyone. I rolled my eyes. What had I expected? Her brief moment of lucidity this morning was the deepest conversation we'd had in years.

Making sure my bag was secure behind my back, I walked for the back door, taking care to open it slowly. The hinges creaked and I winced at the sound. I didn't get a foot out the door when I realized Julian was standing outside staring at me.

"Unless you're coming out here to offer to blow me, I'm not letting you leave this place," he snarled.

My upper lip curled in disgust at the thought of doing

anything remotely intimate with him. Julian was attractive, sure. He had long brown hair, warm brown skin, and deep amber eyes. He was the kind of male most of the girls in school would do just about anything to get even one night with. Especially after he shifted. He was marked as a protector, one of the highest ranking wolves in a pack. The crescent shaped tattoo had appeared on his shoulder the night of his first shift. He'd be in Tyler's inner circle when Tyler took over as alpha; he might even be his beta one day. Julian had shown everyone who walked by the mark after his shift, eager to impress even lowly nobodies like me.

He'd only calmed down after the next full moon, the one where Tyler had his first shift. Julian was first, then Tyler. Everyone expected Tyler to get the mark of the alpha. He never said if he did or didn't, but he didn't go around showing off anything after his ceremony and Julian stopped showing off his mark.

It was something I'd poked Tyler about at first, even though it cost me a few beatings. It had been worth it to find out the truth. Tyler, next in line to be alpha, hadn't been chosen by the gods. If he had, he'd have shown everyone his moon and star tattoo. It was a mark that would appear when an alpha was chosen. Not all alphas got one, but that mark outranked an alpha without one.

That meant, one day, another shifter could get the mark and rise to take Tyler's place as leader of the pack. A marked alpha didn't even need to fight to the death; they would just take their place and demote the previous alpha.

In my lifetime, I'd never seen that mark. I was fairly certain Tyler's dad didn't have it either. I used to wish someone would challenge him so Tyler's status would drop, but I gave up on that long ago. It wasn't my problem. By the time someone did challenge him, I'd be long gone.

"What's it going to be?" Julian said, moving closer to the door. "How wide can you open your mouth?"

"You're disgusting," I said.

"Why else would Tyler ask you to stick around if you're not putting out?" Julian asked.

"I'm not fucking Tyler." I wasn't fucking anyone. Like there was anyone in this pack I was willing to get into bed with. Sure, I had desires just like everyone else, but they were mellow compared to shifter libidos. I'd walked in on classmates in the library more than once. While I might get myself off on occasion, I could wait until I was home and my door was locked.

At least that was one good thing about this curse. I couldn't imagine having sex with any of the assholes around here. We didn't have the concern of STDs like humans did, but I wasn't about to risk pregnancy.

"There are other things a woman can do besides fucking," Julian said. "I'm sure you learned a lot of tricks from your mom. My dad says she's like a wolf in the sack, even if she can't shift."

Heat filled my chest and I balled my hands into fists. "Don't talk about my mother, you piece of shit."

"I can talk about your mother all I want. In fact, maybe I'll take a turn of my own. I was hoping you'd join the family business and I could finally wipe that smug grin off your face with my cock, but you mom would work, I suppose."

"Go home and fuck your own mother," I snapped. "At least my mom is honest about what she does. Your mom is the one hiding in alley ways and sneaking around. We all know she keeps the alpha's bed warm while your father is alone."

Julian charged so fast I didn't have time to slam the thin door in his face. His six-two, muscular frame was on top of me, knocking me to the ground. My arms were pinned to the floor, his knee on my gut. I squirmed, trying to angle myself better so I could kick him in the groin, but I couldn't budge from his grip.

"Let me go," I hissed through gritted teeth.

"Not without something for you to remember me by." He switched his grip so one of his large hands was holding both of mine, freeing his other hand. He traced a finger down my cheek to my jaw before his hand closed around my neck. "You mutter so much as a single sound and I will snap your tiny, human neck."

"Julian, get off her. Now." Tyler's voice had all the command of an alpha. Even I couldn't help but look up at him.

Julian's hand left my neck and released my wrists. He jumped to his feet, turning to face Tyler.

I sat up. "This is what you had planned? Let your friends throw me around one last time?"

Tyler didn't look at me, his gaze was locked on Julian. "I told you not to hurt her. I told you we needed her in one piece."

"I wasn't going to hurt her," he said. "I was just having a bit of fun."

"You touch her again and I will break all of your fingers," Tyler said.

"So you're the only one who gets to hurt me, huh, Tyler?" I don't know why I said it, but it was like something had snapped. I was on my feet now and Tyler still wasn't looking at me. "You bastard, answer me."

He looked over at me and I could see the anger in his eyes. He was furious. The look was enough to send a little shudder of fear through me. There was a warning there that I hadn't seen before.

I recoiled and took a step back. "Leave me alone. Both of you."

Tyler grunted. "Out, Julian." He pushed his friend toward the door before turning back to look at me. "You stay here and you don't leave. I will take you to the ceremony and then you won't be my problem anymore."

Julian and Tyler walked out the door, slamming it behind them. As soon as they were gone, I took a breath, letting my guard down a little. My whole body was shaking and I was near tears. This was never going to end. As long as I was here, I was a target. I was going to end up just like my mom or worse. I had to get out of here but I needed to do it on my terms. I had no idea what game Tyler was playing, but I wasn't sure how much more I could push him.

I had no choice. I'd wait here and go to the stupid ceremony and when everyone else shifted and ran in the woods, I'd run the other way.

5

My skin felt itchy and I had to fight against the claustrophobic feeling of being trapped in the shitty trailer I grew up in. Restlessness seeped into every inch of me, making me feel like I needed to claw my way out of this place. The minutes seemed to crawl by. I'd waited so long for this day and I had a plan. I wanted out the second the moon rose high enough to break the wards that kept me prisoner here. Instead, I was faced with showing my face at the stupid First Moon Ceremony.

I stood, my ancient bed creaking and groaning as I rose. Running my hand through my hair, I paced in the tiny space. Waiting was a hiccup, but it didn't change my plan. I was still getting out of here as soon as I could. It just delayed me a few minutes. A few hours at most. As soon as the others shifted, I felt confident I could leave without issue.

I'd never attended a First Moon Ceremony but I had some information about what to expect. Only those who were making the first shift or already shifted pack members were allowed to attend. The Alpha and Beta always attended, along with the new members. Their family usually came to experience the first shift with them and sometimes friends or other pack members would join. It was technically open to anyone who had shifted but from what I'd heard, it was generally a small group.

With a ceremony every month, it wasn't a big deal for the whole pack but it was for the family of the newly shifted. I'd heard about how humans threw big parties for significant birthdays or graduations. We didn't do that here. When we finished high school, they handed us our diploma at the end of the day on the last day of school. No ceremony, no party. Just *see you in the fall*. The only thing that mattered to the pack was the ability to shift.

So you can imagine how useless a wolf who can't do that one thing is. And nobody here let me forget it. My mom and I were alone in this curse, the only members of the pack unable to shift. It was a terrible way to grow up. When I was in middle school, I'd spent hours at the library reading about possible ways to break the curse. I'd wanted to fit in so badly. There were very few suggestions on breaking the magic. Finding a witch to do it was possible and there were people who thought that completing a mating bond might be enough, but none of my research seemed strong enough to follow up on. It was all theoretical.

By the time I reached high school and saw kids I grew up with go through the change, I realized I didn't want to stay. Bonding with your wolf was supposed to be this great gift. It amplified your strengths. I noticed it also amplified your weaknesses. Kids who were assholes before the shift were even greater assholes after. People with high sex drives pre-shift were now sneaking into the bathrooms between classes to have a quickie. Those who were already loud never seemed to shut up post-shift. You get the picture. Amplified strengths and weaknesses. A bunch of horny, angry dickwads running around. Why would I want to be like them?

A door creaked and I stopped pacing, my heart thundering in response. Had Julian come back in against Tyler's wishes? I grabbed the baseball bat I kept on the floor next to my bed and crept toward my door. Thankfully, I kept the hinges on my door well-oiled and it opened quietly. I peeked out just in time to see my mom close the door to her bedroom.

My throat tightened and I closed the door, leaning back against it. She didn't bother to come out and help me when I was fighting against a shifter, but she ducked out in the quiet. Likely to re-fill her coffee. It was probably good that I wasn't planning to return here. She wasn't worth the risk. I was better off without her.

It seemed like the shifters outside were going to follow Tyler's orders to leave me be. There was nothing to do but wait. I laid down on my bed and closed my eyes. Maybe I could at least get a little extra rest.

Somehow, I managed to fall asleep. I wasn't normally a napper, but I suppose it was easier when there was literally nothing else to do. I looked around my now dim room and rubbed my eyes. The red numbers on my alarm clock showed that it was already after five. How the fuck had I managed to sleep all day? Maybe it was the stress. I guess it was helpful since I'd now be able to stay up all night if it took a while to find a place to crash.

I grabbed my bag and ventured out of my room. My mom's door was open. I supposed she'd left at some point. For the first time all day, I didn't feel upset or hurt by her lack of concern. I'd accepted it for what it was and was fully ready to get the fuck out.

No sense in trying to avoid my jailers by sneaking out the back. I walked right out the front door to find Kyle waiting alone. He was sitting in the dying porch swing and jumped to his feet when I approached.

"Where'd the rest of the idiot triplets go?" I asked.

He shrugged. "They just told me to wait for you."

"Do we have to wait for them to return or can you handle walking me to the barn yourself?" Three of them really was overkill. Kyle was the weakest of the three but even the weakest shifter had the strength of at least three humans. A little flicker of jealousy rose inside me. I wanted that strength. If I shifted and bonded with my inner wolf, I could fight back and actually have a shot at protecting myself. Maybe even inflicting the same kind of damage they did to me. It would be amazing to be able to defend myself and kick some ass. But that wasn't possible.

First on my list when I could afford it was to join some human fighting classes. I couldn't fight off shifters, but I could at least make sure I wouldn't be the weakest human when I settled in my new home.

"You got everything you need?" he asked. "I assume you're running after."

I lifted my bag. "I'm ready. Let's get this over with."

Kyle and I walked silently away from the trailer park toward town. The ceremony took place in a wide pasture area next to a barn that was more ruin than actual barn. It was a prime location for shifting because it was right next to the huge wooded area that covered the entire south side of the magical barrier.

I had wanted to make my exit on the other side of town, away from the wolves, but I could decide more once I saw which way they ran. I knew there was a good chance the guests attending would shift and run with the new wolf. I still wasn't sure why Tyler was insisting I stayed for this.

"Hey, what's really going on here?" I asked. "Why does anyone care if I attend the ceremony tonight?"

"I just know the alpha wants you there," Kyle said.

"Don't bullshit me. The alpha doesn't care where I am or what I do. This is Tyler. Why?"

Kyle shrugged. "You know what I know. He told us there was something about needing all the pack members who had birthdays before this moon to be in attendance."

"You really don't think for yourself ever, do you?"

"You don't know what you're talking about," he replied.

"Sure, I do. You're the tag-along. Julian got the mark. He'll be a Beta one day or an enforcer at the least. You? You're nothing. You hang around Tyler hoping his status will lift yours but without him, nobody even gives you a second glance." It was true. Kyle had been the weird kid, only a step above me when we were younger. Sometime around the end of middle school, he'd suddenly been welcomed into Tyler's group.

"What exactly do you provide to the group? I know they didn't have you join for your fierceness or strength."

"Shut your mouth, reject," he snapped.

"I struck a nerve, didn't I?" I lifted a brow. "For real, though, I've never understood it. You aren't the same as them."

I used to think he wasn't so bad. That changed as soon as he made friends with Tyler. While his fist hit me less often than Julian's or Tyler's, Kyle had done his share of throwing me against walls or knocking my books out of my hands. He was as bad as the others, I just missed it at first.

"Stop talking, Lola. You're going to make this so much worse with that mouth of yours," he said.

"Your friend Julian seems to like my mouth," I said.

Kyle stopped walking. "For real, Lola. For once in your life, stop pushing back and maybe they'll go easier on you."

I stopped and stared at him, my brow furrowed as I tried to read his expression. What was it exactly? Was he scared? Nervous? Angry? It was a mixture of emotions I couldn't read. What I wouldn't give for that wolf ability to read people right now.

"What do you know?" I asked.

"I can't, Lola. You don't know what they'd do to me if I keep talking. The only thing I can tell you is that you need to watch it." He started walking again.

I hurried to keep up with him. I felt like he'd given me some information but it was so vague, I couldn't do anything with it. I wondered if it even mattered. Whatever I was walking into, it was probably going to suck whether I opened my mouth or not.

6

Ace Grant, Tyler's dad, and our pack's alpha, was standing outside the barn with a small group of other shifters when we arrived. I quickly found Tyler, Julian, and Marion Reed, my classmate who shared the same birth month. In addition to them, I recognized Marion's parents and the other shifters present. It was a small town after all, and even if I was an outcast, I still knew everyone's name.

Jenny Ortega, the high priestess, was the only person in the gathered group smiling at me. She'd always been pleasant with me, but never kind. Of all the adults in town, she was the only one who might have been able to speak up on my behalf and go against the alpha. She never did. To make matters worse, everything I knew about the moon goddess and general shifter religion came from what I read in books. I wasn't allowed to attend other ceremonies since I wasn't considered a full wolf. Not that I fought hard against that. Most of my classmates complained about how boring they were. But, it was another one of those things that showed how I didn't belong.

"Why are you here?" Ace asked as he walked toward me. "I thought you'd be long gone."

I cocked an eyebrow and turned my gaze to Tyler. "Why am I here, Tyler?"

"She's a broken wolf, but she's still pack. She needs to be here for the ceremony," Tyler said.

"She doesn't belong here," Ace said.

"I'm happy to leave right now," I said.

"What if the curse breaks? What if she shifts? We should know if there's another shifter out there from our pack," Tyler said.

Ace narrowed his eyes and seemed to study me for a minute before looking back to his son. "You suspect the spell wore off?"

Tyler shrugged. "You want to risk losing a wolf when we're on the decline?"

That was news to me. I knew lots of younger wolves chose to leave, but I didn't know they cared. "You don't want me and honestly, I've never once felt the wolf stir. The curse is solid and I'm an embarrassment. Just let me go."

"You are mighty anxious to leave, little one," Ace said.

"Gee, I wonder why? Everyone here has treated me like dirt since birth. You think I want to stick around?"

I ignored the gasps from the onlookers. Sure, I was risking pissing off the strongest wolf here but I was done. And honestly, it wasn't like he could do much worse to me than his asshole kid had been doing for the last decade.

"You stay. If you don't shift, you leave and never return." Ace glared at me as if this was some kind of dark punishment.

"You got it, boss," I said, with far too much sarcasm in my tone.

Ace's upper lip twitched, but he turned away from me. I wondered if he figured I wasn't worth the effort.

It was better that way for all of us. He didn't want me here and I didn't want to be here. Tyler was delusional. I peered over at him and caught him looking at me. He turned away quickly and pretended he hadn't been watching me.

I rolled my eyes and bit back the huff of frustration. Whatever he was playing at, it was successful at pissing me off. That was probably his end game. Beating me up and letting me leave wasn't enough. He wanted to really torture me. Which meant, make me sit through the dumb ceremony. I supposed he thought I'd be all weepy watching everyone shift when I couldn't. He didn't know how glad I was to be getting away from all this. I wanted nothing more than to live a normal, boring, human life.

Standing off to the side, I waited as everyone made small talk and avoided the spot of grass where I was standing. The sun was low in the horizon, painting the sky a gorgeous orange and blue. It was a stunning sunset but I was far too impatient to appreciate it. *Come on, moon, rise.*

Finally, the sky was dark enough and even I could feel the pull of the moon. It was tiny, but it was there, calling to the wolf buried and bound deep within me. I couldn't feel the wolf, but I could feel the moon. It was a strange sensation and it made me a little sad. Fighting back, I send the feeling away, sending it deep down inside me. Fuck that. I was about to embark on my journey to be a full human. All of this would be behind me.

"It is time to welcome a new full wolf to our pack. Tonight, we embrace our twin soul, our wolf, and run with our new sister as she begins the bonding process." Ace was in the middle of the group of shifters. They seemed to gravitate toward him as he spoke about the first shift and its significance.

I wanted nothing to do with any of it. Keeping my distance, I ignored the pretty speeches and applause. Instead, I focused my attention on the moon. Had the magic worked to break me free of this place? In theory, it should, even without a shift. I just wouldn't know until I crossed out of pack lands.

Someone grabbed my arm and I jumped, returning my attention to the present. Tyler's large hand gripped my upper arm. I tugged my arm away, trying to free myself from his grip. "Let me go."

"So you can bolt the moment the spell breaks? I don't think so." He pulled me toward the group. "You wait here until everyone has shifted. You don't leave a moment sooner."

I knew there was a good chance his wolf would force the shift as soon as he reacted to the others. He was new to this and while he was strong enough to resist the moon, he probably wasn't strong enough to resist seeing his alpha shift.

Jenny lifted her hands into the air, sending dozens of gold bangles sliding down her wrists and pooling near her elbows. They made a melodic sound as they shifted and moved with her motions. The others were silent, staring at her. Even I found myself more focused on her than Tyler's grip on my arm.

"The goddess shows us favor this night," Jenny said. "The wolf born of tonight's moon will be a powerful force in the universe."

Marian looked smug and she batted her lashes in Tyler's direction. I resisted the urge to hurl. Every woman around our age wanted to be the next mate to the alpha. It was enough to make me lose my lunch. Wait. I didn't eat lunch today. But I still felt sick at the thought of anyone being permanently stuck with Tyler. Nobody deserved that kind of eternal punishment.

"Pack, family, new wolves, it is time to connect with your soul's twin, your inner form freed." Jenny lowered her hands. "It is time to shift."

Whoops and cheers rose from the group and everyone started to strip. I'd been raised around shifters my whole life. I'd seen most of my classmates naked. I still wasn't a fan of it. Probably because it tended to accompany something awful like gym class or naked tag or gods knew what else. When people started getting naked, it was my queue to leave. I didn't need to be the only one in human form around a bunch of wolves.

"Go on, then," Tyler said. "This is your chance to try. See if you can do it."

"Are you serious?" I stared up at him. In the moonlight, his eyes looked silver and his handsome features were even more stunning. Of course they were. Of course the world's worst human being would get all the attractive genes.

The sound of breaking bones, cracking and snapping sounded louder than usual in the silence of the evening. I winced, then forced myself to look Tyler in the eye. "Go shift with your family. Leave me be."

"You don't belong here," he hissed.

"Yet, you're the one delaying my departure," I replied.

Howls exploded around me, echoing into the starry night sky. They were staggered at first, then came out unified as the pack synched up.

I turned away from Tyler to see that we were the only

people in human form. The rest of the members present had shifted. With a single howl, a huge black wolf took off, bolting toward the woods. Ace's wolf was guiding the others away, into the woods, where they'd run until dawn.

I expected to see all the wolves give chase. I even expected to see Tyler break down and join them. I didn't expect to see two wolves linger behind, moving closer to me with careful steps.

"Julian, Kyle, nice to see you," I said. "I suppose you're stupid enough to follow this asshole around even when you're in your mutt form."

The wolves growled at me but didn't advance. I tugged at my arm again, trying to pull away from Tyler but he held fast. *Stupid shifter strength.*

"Well, this has been fun, but as you see, I can't shift. So if you don't mind, I'm going to leave and never see any of you again." I tried to pull my arm away again. Tyler's fingers dug deeper into my arm and it started to hurt. I was going to have new bruises in the morning. "Tyler, you proved your point, now let me go."

"I would love to let you go, but there's a problem with that," he said.

I was out of patience. "I'm done with your games. I get that you won't have anyone to throw around anymore when I leave, but it's time to move on. Buy a punching bag, join a gym, take up meditation. Do something else to get out these anger issues."

"I wish I could. I wish I could do anything else but hold on to you right now. You're pathetic but I thought just maybe, if you shifted, I could feel something other than disdain for you," he said.

"Why start now?" I tugged at my arm again, just in case. Still stuck. "Look, we've had a good run. Let's keep hating each other and end it."

"When I had my first shift, I started feeling the pull but I ignored it. The more I ignored it, the worse it got. I thought for sure, it couldn't be true. But then, every time I pushed you or hurt you, I felt the pain as if I was abusing myself. Fate is a cruel mistress." Tyler shook his head.

"What the ever-loving fuck are you talking about?" Tyler had snapped. All these years, I thought he was just hateful. Turns out he was insane. Wonderful. I was so close to getting out of here and the crazy future alpha was going to be my undoing.

"Don't you get it?" Tyler was screaming at me now.

For the first time since he grabbed me, fear gripped me, making my chest feel tight. I looked over at the two wolves standing next to us, awaiting orders from their leader. If they wanted to take me out, there was nothing I could do to stop them. I didn't even have a hope of out running them.

"Tyler, please," I whispered, trying not to rile him up. "Let me go."

"I know you can't shift, but I thought for sure you'd feel it. I guess this will make things easier for me to break." He seemed to be talking to himself rather than me, but his tone was calmer now.

I waited, afraid to say or do anything that might result in my neck being snapped or a wolf's jaw clamped down around an important artery.

Tyler grabbed hold of my chin, turning it so I was facing him. His eyes seemed to look into my very soul. "You are my mate."

7

It wasn't possible. There was no way the fates were cruel enough to put the two of us together. He had to be messing with me. Besides, our pack took mating bonds very seriously. If a wolf was lucky enough to form a bond, it usually meant increased strength and other perks. Things like possibly even breaking curses.

He had to know that myth. He was trying to get one last dig at me. "That's a fucked up thing to joke about, even for you."

"I wish it was a joke," he said. "I wasn't certain until this past week. As we got closer to the time you should have shifted, my wolf made it pretty fucking clear we're supposed to be together."

My insides twisted as my emotions went to war. There was a tiny glimmer of hope trying to fight through the other negative emotions. I hated Tyler and I wanted nothing to do with him. The thought of being intimate with him made my skin crawl. But there was that rumor about the bond breaking the curse. I'd given up long ago of ever feeling my wolf rise to the surface. I'd long ago resigned myself to a human existence free of magic.

What if he was telling the truth? What if there was a way to get my ability to shift back? "You're sure? You're not messing with me?"

His smirk was vicious and I took a step back without thinking. He finally released his grip on me. I knew that look well. It was the same self-satisfied half-smile he wore every time he beat the shit out of me for fun.

"You're lying to me." Even as I said the words, I feared it wasn't true. Tyler was a lot of things, but I didn't think he would use something as sacred as a mating bond for sport. It was rare to find your mate at all. It wasn't something most wolves would be willing to joke about.

"Now, I'd heard the rumor that a mating bond could break a curse. I mean, you're attractive enough, you're a little too mouthy, but that could be fixed with a few beatings." He moved closer to me and Kyle and Julian stepped closer as well, closing me in.

If Tyler thought I'd willingly choose to be his mate with a speech like that, he was insane. "I'd never submit to you."

"It doesn't matter. There's one thing about you I could never overlook. You're broken. You won't be any good to anyone without the ability to shift," he said.

I kept my mouth shut. He was clearly enjoying listening to himself speak and I'd rather get this whole charade over with.

"If bringing you here tonight on the full moon around your mate and all the others didn't force the shift beyond the confines of your curse, nothing will. So, you're useless to me," he said.

"So that's why you brought me here. To test your theory?"

The moment of hope was long gone. Even if being with Tyler meant freeing my wolf, it wasn't worth it. Nothing was worth enduring being shackled to this asshole. "Well, it failed. So if you don't mind, I'll be on my way."

"That's the other odd thing about mating bonds..." Tyler stepped away from me and Kyle and Julian moved even closer to me, one on either side, boxing me in. Both wolves had their hackles up and they growled at me.

The hair on my arms stood on edge. Something was very wrong here. Tyler had me surrounded by wolves and we were alone. "Just let me leave and I'll never return. Like you asked."

"I'm afraid I suggested that before I knew that in order for me to be free of the bond to you, you have to die. And here's the really funny part: I can't kill my own mate."

"There are other ways to sever a bond," I said. "You know I don't want to be mated with you. I'll do what it takes."

He shook his head. "And risk you getting a second chance with a new mate? Or worse, having everyone know I formed a bond with a broken wolf? I don't think so."

I didn't wait to hear what was coming next. I took off at a run. What choice did I have? Tyler wasn't going to see reason with this. Cursing myself for not hiding in the woods last night, I raced forward, eyes on the tree line ahead.

In the distance, I heard a wolf howl and several howls responded. My heart raced faster. There were wolves all over these woods and I knew Kyle and Julian had to be right behind me. I was insane to think I'd ever get out of this place alive. Now that I was so close to freedom, I wasn't ready to give in to the eternal sleep of death. I wanted to know what it was like to not feel like I was a walking target at all times. I worked my ass off to make it this far and I sure as hell wasn't going down easy.

That's when I felt a jaw close in on my calf, teeth breaking the flesh, sending burning pain with the force. I was pulled back, landing face first in the dirt. I was able to break my fall with my arms, but my right hand twisted on impact and I heard the snap as my wrist broke.

Searing pain made my vision go black for a moment and I cried out in agony. My leg felt like it was on fire from the bite and my wrist sent shooting pain through my arm. "Oh, fuck!"

Grabbing my injured wrist, I rolled over to face my assailant. In the nearly pitch-black darkness of the forest, I could just make out three huge wolves looking down on me, panting and growling. Tyler had joined his friends in wolf form. Drool from one of the beasts landed on my cheek and I wiped it away with my good hand before returning to cradling my injury.

I tried to scoot away from them, but the movement sent a fresh wave of pain through the bite on my leg. I winced and hissed. "If you're going to kill me, you might as well get it over with."

One of the wolves, a dark gray wolf, who was the largest of the three, took off, leaving me with the other two.

"So he's making you do the dirty work?" I asked. "That'll go over well when your grandchildren ask for stories about your youth. Like, hey, remember that time we killed your Uncle Tyler's mate? You two are pathetic." I spit at the wolf nearest me.

The creature growled, then went for my arm, biting down. I screamed and tried to pull away but each movement made the pain more intense. Suddenly, the second wolf clamped down on my other arm and my vision blurred as the pain crashed through me. The wolves started to drag me, pulling me over the rocky and rough terrain.

Rocks tore up my back, thorns caught in my flesh, chunks of hair caught on the ground but the wolves pulled me on, forcing the hair to rip from my scalp. "Let me go, you assholes!" I yelled at them between gasping through the pain. Everything hurt. My body was broken in multiple places and each jostle over the ground sent fresh waves of agony surging through me. Soon, the discomfort was too intense and I found myself in and out of consciousness. It was as if my body was trying to protect me. Or maybe I was at death's door.

When they finally released their jaws, I was dumped on the ground, in the dirt. Every inch of my body hurt. My arms and legs felt like they were on fire and my head throbbed. My skin was sticky with blood and sweat and all my open wounds were full of dirt. Even if I survived this, infection would set in if I didn't get medical attention. I knew all this, but I couldn't make myself move. Rolling to my side, I tried to catch my breath. Maybe they were done with me. Maybe they'd leave and hope I'd die. If I could find some strength, I could limp or crawl out of here, right?

I looked around, trying to assess my surroundings. We were out of the cover of the woods now, somewhere different. The full moon was so bright I could see everything clearly. In front of me was a huge rock formation that took up most of my line of sight. Behind me, was the woods. I hadn't been this far before. We were either at the border of pack lands, or we'd ventured beyond.

"Are you dead yet?" Tyler asked.

I turned to see three naked men walking toward me. Tyler

looked smug but his friends didn't look as confident as they had when they started all this.

"What's wrong? Never seen a girl beat to death by her mate before?" I snapped. "You're the ones who did this to me."

"I can't hurt you," Tyler said. "I learned quickly that if I inflict pain on you, it hurts me."

"You're a coward," I said. "You didn't have to do this. What kind of a man hurts someone who can't fight back?"

"You've fought back plenty over the years. Why stop now?" he asked.

"You know I'm no match for any shifter solo, let alone the three of you." Talking exacerbated the pain I was feeling, but as long as I was keeping him talking, he wasn't hurting me.

Tyler knelt next to me. "I can be a generous man."

"You're a monster," I spat.

"I could have them kill you now, if that's easier for you," he said. "Or, we can toss you in the cave. If you get out, you'll survive. Otherwise, you'll perish like the others who were sentenced to their deaths. It's fitting, really. The place you and your whore mother should have been sent years ago. Then none of this would have happened. I'd never even have known you. Think of all the pain you'd have been spared."

I should have known the rock formation was the cave we'd all grown up hearing about. The place reserved for traitors and the worst of the worst. Supposedly, there were exits, but nobody had ever found their way out. It was a death sentence.

"The only reason I had pain was because of you. You made a choice," I said.

"And now I give you a choice. Cave or death?"

"You know what a farse this is? That cave is death," I said.

"So you'd rather face a quick, merciful death?" he mused.

"There was nothing merciful about any of this, you bastard," I said.

"Kyle, kill her," he said.

I looked over to where Kyle and Julian were standing and was surprised that Kyle didn't move. My brow furrowed as I watched his reaction. He was going against Tyler.

"I'll do it, Ty," Julian said.

"I asked Kyle," Tyler said.

"You said we were going to scare her," Kyle said. "You didn't say we were going to do this."

"Are you defying your alpha?" Tyler asked.

"You're not an alpha yet," I said. "Nobody ever saw the mark. You're a fraud. I can't wait until someone comes and knocks you and your father from your pedestal."

Tyler stood then kicked me in the stomach. I groaned, and reached to cover myself, making my broken wrist twist in the process. I screamed as sharp agony shot through my arm.

"That hurt me too, Lola. Why do you make me do that?" Tyler was kneeling next to me again. He brushed a stray strand of hair away from my eyes. "If only you had shifted tonight. Things could be so different for us."

I spat in his face. "I'd never be with you."

He groaned and stood as he wiped my spit from his face. "You bitch. Julian!"

"Stop." I knew Julian would finish the job if given the chance. "Put me in the cave."

"Slow death?" Tyler sounded surprised. "Here I thought you'd take the weaker way out."

"Only you would think death of any kind showed weakness." I glared at him. "I'm going to survive the cave and then I'm going to come back for you."

Tyler kicked me in the stomach over and over until I couldn't breathe. At first, it was nothing but pain, then I couldn't feel anything at all. It was as if my body had given up.

When he finally stopped, I was barely hanging on to consciousness. The copper taste of blood coated the inside of my mouth and I was pretty sure Tyler had damaged some of my internal organs.

"I'd love to see you survive now, crazy bitch," Tyler said. "Get her in the cave."

8

Everything hurt but I wasn't ready to die and I knew the cave was a death sentence. I turned on my side, telling myself that I was fine. I didn't have a broken wrist or a torn up back or bite marks on my arms. I was just imagining it, right? Okay, fine, I still felt like I was nearing death's door, but I had to try.

Kyle and Julian were pushing on a huge boulder that sealed off the entry. Now that I knew it was the cave, it was hard to miss the obviously placed stone that acted as a door.

Turning my attention from Kyle and Julian, I looked over at Tyler. He was watching his friends, oblivious to me. If I was going to attempt to run, this was it. Holding my breath, I braced for the pain.

Wincing, I pushed myself to standing as quietly as I could. Already panting from the strain, I stood on shaky legs. With a quick glance at the distracted shifters, I took off.

The searing pain escalated with each pump of my arms, but I forced it down. I had to get away from these psycho wolves. Under the light of the full moon, I watched for rocks and kept my gaze on the tree line. It was unlikely I'd actually get away from them, but my plan was different this time. Instead of hoping to avoid other shifters, I was hoping I could run into some witnesses. As far as I knew, it was still against pack law to attempt to kill me. Tyler and his thugs had never pushed things quite this far.

And as much as I hated to use the mate card, I knew it was definitely against pack rules to try to kill your mate. You were to protect that bond. Mated pairs resulted in stronger wolves, not only for the bonded pair, but also for their offspring. Even if I couldn't have children who could shift, opening the door to allow a mate to treat their partner the way Tyler treated me was dangerous. Even someone like Ace would have to see that, right?

My foot caught on a root and I went down. Instinct had me cradling my broken wrist so I landed on my right shoulder. More pain surged through me and all the adrenaline that had been keeping the other injuries manageable seemed to wear off at once.

With a whimper, I tried to push myself up. Everything hurt and my body didn't want to cooperate. I lay there in the dirt, breathing heavy, listing to the pounding of my heart. This was it. I guess I didn't need to be trapped in a cave to die. My body was giving up on me. "Fuck me."

"No, I don't think I will," Tyler's voice came from somewhere in the darkness. "If I did that, it would solidify the mating bond, and then where would we be? Instead of breaking the bond, I'd spend my whole life missing you. Who wants that?"

"Just let me go, Tyler," I said. "I'll sever the bond when I'm away from here."

"I can't trust that you'd take care of it on your end," he said.

"Like I want to be bonded to a piece of shit like you," I hissed.

"Pick her up, take her back," Tyler commanded.

Shadowy figures shrouded in darkness moved in the distance. As they drew closer, my heart jackhammered in my chest. I thought of myself as a fighter. Even if I didn't always fight back, I knew when to fight and when to cut my losses to live another day.

I'd played a dangerous game of balance my whole life. I knew when to pull back and I knew when retaliation was worth the risk. Now, I was staring certain death in the face and all the fight was gone. I didn't see a way out of this. My injuries weren't going to allow me the sliver of a chance and Tyler already wanted me dead. Nobody was going to hold back if I fought.

The cave, while a death sentence was my only chance at pulling through. The thought flitted in and out of my mind in a heartbeat. I knew it was futile. I would never survive. I'd starve before I found a way out; and that was if my injuries didn't kill me first.

Julian's face hovered above mine. "Time for you to die, little whore."

"Fuck you." I spat at him. Hey, just because I've accepted that I'm going to die, doesn't mean I have to be happy about it.

Julian wiped the spit off his face, then rose to his full height. He kicked me in the same shoulder that hit the ground, and then kicked me in the back and stomach.

Sometime around the fourth of fifth kick, I must have blacked out. As my eyes fluttered open and I woke, I realized I was moving. Each step jostled me and I winced as fresh pain bloomed with each movement. I was slung over someone's shoulder, being carried like a sack of potatoes.

"I can walk," I said, my voice coming out dry and gravely.

"No, you can't," Kyle said. "You might as well conserve your energy."

"Why? So it takes longer for me to die in the cave?" I asked. "Do you feel good about this? You do realize you're a murderer now."

"I'm not a murderer," he said.

"You're leaving me to die. Just because you're not stabbing the knife in my heart yourself doesn't change anything," I said.

"Shut up or you'll make it worse," he hissed.

"You say that as if I'm not dead already," I replied. "Do you really think I can get out of this?"

My head was spinning and everything felt even more unsteady than it should despite my current predicament.

"I'm sorry, Lola, I don't have a choice, I have to follow my alpha." Kyle sounded a little sad.

I wasn't about to let him feel like he was the victim here. "First of all, Tyler is not the pack alpha. Second, he doesn't have the fucking mark or he'd have shown it to everyone."

"Nobody else has the mark so he'll be alpha by birth," Kyle said. "Look, I know you don't deserve this, but just stop fighting."

"You're a prick, you know that? You act like you're trying to help me but you're just as bad as them," I said through gritted teeth.

"You know that's not the case," he said. "I'm nothing like them."

"Oh yeah? Then why didn't you stand up for me when I was ten and Tyler gave me two black eyes? Where were you when Julian pushed me down the stairs or broke my ribs? Or the time you stood by and watched while Tyler held me under the water in the lake until I passed out?"

"I'm the one who dragged you to shore," he said.

"Doesn't make you a good person," I said. "It makes you a weak follower. You stood by and did nothing. One time of saving me doesn't undo all the hurt you were silent for."

Kyle stopped. "We're here."

"No comment?" I asked.

"I'm putting you down. Don't bother running. Julian is in wolf form." Kyle shifted me so I was brought down from his shoulder.

As soon as my legs hit the ground, they gave way. Kyle caught me, and stabilized me.

"Don't ever touch me again." I pushed his hands away from me. I'd rather fall than be helped by him.

"Stubborn to the last," Tyler said.

"And an utter coward to the last," I spat.

Tyler's nostrils flared and he let out a low growl. "Don't test me."

"Fuck you." It wasn't my best comeback, but who can argue with a classic?

Tyler moved closer to me and I held my ground. Not because I was trying to be overly brave, but because between the throbbing pain and blurred vision, I wasn't sure I would stay standing if I tried to move.

"I'm going to be overjoyed when I feel our bond break. You were living on borrowed time already. I'm just finishing the job my father should have done."

I glared at him. There was no way I was going to let Tyler know how much he'd hurt me. In a final act of defiance, I did the only thing I could think of that might cause him any kind of pain. I grabbed his head and pulled him into a kiss.

I couldn't feel the mating bond, but I knew the physical contact would make it stronger. When I died, he'd feel the pain of losing a mate and he'd hate himself for it.

To my surprise, his hands gripped my hips, pulling my body closer to his. His lips moved with mine, deepening the kiss. Heat rose in my chest, and tingles spread down to my core.

His hand traveled up my back as his tongue slipped into my mouth. Fingers tangled in my hair, he pulled me even closer. The kiss was hungry and angry and it felt like I was releasing all of the pent up aggression I had for him into one far too steamy kiss.

My lips felt bruised as heat grew into the kiss. Tyler's stubble was rough on my cheeks. I hated him with every ounce of my being and I put all my emotions into the movement of my lips.

I was the first to pull away, breaking the connection. Eyes wide, I stared up at him, expecting to see the fire of hatred I'd gotten used to seeing in his gaze. Instead, I saw lust.

And that scared me a whole lot more.

"You think I'll spare you?" he whispered, his voice heavy with passion.

"No, I think now you'll be forced to mourn me, even while you still hate me," I said.

He pushed me, knocking me to the ground. "Get her in there. Make sure she can't leave. Seal it well."

Julian grabbed my arm and pulled. I screamed as my shoulder left the socket. He didn't stop dragging me.

I was somewhere between consciousness as I was dropped

in the cave but I forced myself to my knees. Mustering every last bit of strength I had, I glared at the three wolves. "You do realize I'm coming for all of you when I get out of here."

Tyler and Julian laughed. I noticed Kyle didn't join them. He knew this was wrong, but he wasn't any better. He was the only one with enough of a conscience to speak up but he remained silent.

"Lock her in," Tyler said. "Enjoy death, little wolf."

I tried to stand, but my body wouldn't let me. I was running on pure adrenaline. "You're no alpha and everyone knows it."

"Goodbye, Lola." Tyler was smiling as the rock rolled into place.

I was alone, in the dark. I took a few deep breaths, letting my pulse come back down. As I recovered, the full spectrum of pain surged through me and I collapsed on the ground, letting the tears come.

I was broken, bleeding, and alone. I had two choices, wait for death, or try to find a way out of here.

After giving myself a minute to wallow, I returned to my knees and shuffled forward. There had to be some light somewhere. Even a tiny crack that let in the moonlight. If I had any chance of getting out of here, I needed to see what my injuries were.

Slowly, I made my way through the dirt and rocks, fighting the growing sense of despair. That's when the ground gave way and I was falling. I'd managed to crawl right over a hole in the cave floor.

When I hit the ground, I no longer felt any pain. Then everything went black.

9

Someone was talking and my head was pounding. My mouth felt like sandpaper. What the fuck was going on?

The memories of the cave and Tyler came flooding back like a tidal wave. I should be dead. But I didn't feel dead. I felt like shit. I was pretty sure if I were dead, I'd be feeling nothing, right?

I could feel the ground under me and the breeze moving the air. The smell of campfire and pine filled my nostrils. It was clear I was outside and it seemed dark enough through my eyelids to be nighttime. There was something covering me, a blanket maybe?

I kept my eyes closed and listened for the voices. Had Tyler and his friends come back for me? Were they going to finish me themselves or had they brought me back to save me? Was this all sort of some fucked up head-trip?

A chill went through me when I realized I didn't know these voices. I would recognize Tyler's voice anywhere. I hated that I could, but it was true. And this was not Tyler.

"She's awake," someone said.

Silence fell around me and I slowed my breathing, hoping to fool them. I needed more information.

"We know you're awake, you might as well sit up and open your eyes," a deep, sexy voice said.

With a sigh, I let my eyelids flutter open. It was dark, and it took me a moment to adjust. I glanced around and confirmed I was outside and the only light was coming from a sizzling fire and the moon overhead.

I pushed myself to sitting and quickly realized I was naked. What I thought was a blanket was a men's button up flannel shirt. I quickly pulled it over me to cover myself as best as I could.

"We've already seen you naked," sexy voice said. "You might as well put the shirt on properly."

I looked over at the man sitting by the fire. I only got a quick glance at his handsome face before he turned away from me. He was shirtless and the firelight made all the rippling muscles of his back and shoulders look even more intense than they probably were in real life.

Clearly, he was the one who originally owned the shirt I could use as a dress. Which meant he was huge. He looked big sitting there next to the fire, but the man next to him was equally large, giving the impression that he was a more normal size. Instead, I knew both men were well over six feet. And based on the muscles on him, he was not someone I wanted to piss off.

Next to the two huge men, sat a tiny woman who looked to be about my age. I wasn't sure if she was average sized or she looked smaller next to the two giants.

"Are you decent?" Sexy voice asked, not looking over at me.

I tugged the shirt on and quickly buttoned it. When I stood, the huge shirt fell to cover my hips and ass. It was big enough to act like a dress and I was grateful for the coverage. While nudity wasn't a big deal in the pack, I had no idea who these people were.

The fire crackled and popped, a welcoming warm sound breaking the awkward silence.

I had no idea why I was naked.

Or why I was alive.

"Do you speak?" the woman asked.

Her jet-black hair shimmered in the firelight and her eyes looked kind, her expression resembling pity or concern.

I didn't trust it.

"Yes," I said, testing my voice. "Where am I and why am I naked?"

"You were pretty injured when we found you," she replied.

"But why am I naked?" I pressed.

"You weren't human when we found you," sexy voice said.

"What do you mean?" My brow furrowed and I examined him a little. He was probably in his early twenties. But his expression wasn't nearly as kind or concerned as the woman's.

"Oh shit, did you not know you're a wolf shifter?" The woman looked horrified. "They didn't tell you?"

"No, you're mistaken," I said. "I can't change into a wolf."

"You were a wolf when we found you limping through the woods," Sexy Voice said.

"That's impossible." I felt numb. Like I was having an out of body experience. I couldn't shift. The last thing I remembered was barely clinging to life and then falling to my death.

"It's okay, we're shifters. You don't have to hide that from us," the woman said.

"It's not that." I should have been worried about that, but my mind was too preoccupied with the fact that I was alive when I shouldn't be. Add in that they claimed I had shifted, a literal impossibility, and it was far too much to comprehend.

"You were a wolf when we found you." The woman's voice was gentle.

"I was cursed; I can't shift." Saying the words out loud always hurt. I told myself I'd accepted my path in life, but I'd always wonder what it might have been like if I hadn't inherited the family curse.

"That's terrible, I can't imagine not shifting. You must be in great pain," she said.

"Well, it's a nice story, anyway," Sexy said.

"It's true, but I don't need you to believe me." They'd saved me, which was more than could be said of any of the members of my pack, but they were still strangers.

"What happened to you? Do you remember how you got here?" the woman asked.

"I was in the caves. I fell. It was a long fall." I looked at each of them in turn. There was no way I was going to explain everything. It was embarrassing and made me look weak. "Then I woke up here."

"Your wolf must have saved you. I've heard of that happening, but I've never met anyone who went through it." The woman stood and walked over to me. "I'm Sheila."

"Lola," I said.

Sheila offered her hand and I took it without thinking. None of this made sense. I wasn't supposed to shift. I really should be dead.

As soon as I released Sheila's hand, I rose to my feet and started patting myself down, feeling for injuries. I felt my shoulder, my wrist, my head. My hair was matted with dried blood. My arms and legs were covered in dirt. Some of it stuck there by blood from phantom wounds. There were no signs of the bite marks or broken limbs.

I knew shifters were fast healers, but even my injuries would have taken time. "How long have I been here?"

"We found you last night. You've been sleeping for almost twenty-four hours," Sheila confirmed.

That didn't seem long enough. "How long ago was the full moon?"

"Four days," Sheila said. "Is that when you fell?"

I nodded.

"You were wandering in your wolf form for a while," she said.

"Why are you here?" Sexy Voice asked.

"Can you give her a few minutes before you interrogate her? She's been through a lot." Sheila turned to me. "Ignore Alec, he's an asshole."

"What about me?" The other man asked. I'd almost forgotten he was there.

"That's Malcom, he's also an asshole," Sheila said.

Malcom smiled as if he was pleased to be included.

"Enough," Alec said. "I'm not the one who stumbled into another wolf's territory."

I looked over at the broody male. "It wasn't on purpose, I promise you that. I'm just passing through."

"Let me guess, running from your pack?" Alec asked.

My startled expression gave it all away so I didn't bother trying to hide it. Then I realized we must be close. If I'd shifted and run from there, I couldn't have gotten far. Even with being gone for a few days, it was possible I was still within scenting distance. I wasn't going back. Not for anything. If they knew I was alive, they'd want to take me out.

I stood. "I have to go. Thank you for the shirt and for helping me."

Alec stood and my breath caught. I knew he was huge, but seeing him standing was alarming. He was probably pushing seven feet. The shifters in my pack were all large, most of the males towered over my five-foot-six inches, but Alec was the tallest male I'd seen. "You're not going anywhere."

"Um, yes I am." I turned and started walking.

A strong hand grabbed my wrist. I stopped, knowing that once again, I was outmatched. There were three of them and one of me. And while they were certain I'd shifted, I had no idea if they were telling the truth. If I had, I wasn't sure I could do it again. If I'd shifted to save my life, did that mean the curse was broken or was it a random thing? And had I been granted the extra perks of being a wolf or were they still hidden from me?

I'd been the victim of bullies long enough to know that fighting back wasn't always the best way to survive. I needed a strategy. I turned and looked at the huge male. "Let me go."

"We have some questions for you before you go anywhere," he said.

My heart raced as my eyes traveled from his six pack, up to his rock-solid pecs, to his firm jaw covered in stubble, finally resting on his eyes. My eyes widened for a moment when I realized that each of his irises was a different color. One was a deep brown and the other was bright blue. They were beautiful and unlike anything I'd ever seen.

"Where did you come from?" Alec asked.

"Your eyes are stunning," I blurted out.

Sheila giggled. "I told you they're pretty."

Alec growled. "Tell me where you came from."

"Wolf Creek," I said. "There, happy?"

"Take her back," Alec said as he turned away from me.

"Oh, fuck no. I'm never going back there." I vaguely recalled threatening Tyler and his friends before I was locked in the cave. Someday, I'd like to make good on my threat, but right now wasn't the time.

I pulled my wrist out of his grip easily. I hesitated for a moment when I realized he didn't hold me against my will.

"Unless you give us a very good reason, we have to return you," he said with a growl. "I will not harbor a fugitive. Especially not from Wolf Creek. There are rules in the packs."

"I'm not a fugitive. And I am never going back. If you want to deliver me to them, you'll have to kill me and drop off my corpse." I glared at him and balled my hands into fists. I knew he could take me, but I wasn't going down without a fight.

"Look at her, Alec. Someone beat the shit out of her," Malcom said.

"She said she fell," Alec said.

"You know that's bullshit," Sheila said. "Someone hurt you, didn't they?"

I looked over at her. "I ran because my mate tried to kill me to break the bond."

"She's lying," Alec said. "Don't let her get in your head."

"You don't even know me," I said.

"I know they reserve those caves for criminals in Wolf Creek. You have to fuck up bad to end up in there," I said.

"Unless you're a cursed shifter who can't shift who

happens to form a mating bond with the alpha's son." My eyes widened and I covered my hand with my mouth. I hadn't wanted to share all that with a bunch of strangers. They didn't need to know my past and I didn't want to remember it.

"Let her stay," Sheila said.

"Her mate rejected her, she's got no place to go," Malcom said. "She's definitely an outcast."

His words stung more than I wanted them to and there was a tiny part of me that seemed to be in mourning for the loss of Tyler. I shook the feeling away. I was not going to miss the male who caused me a lifetime of pain.

Alec growled but I ignored him. He was either going to believe me or not.

"Look, I don't need your pity, and I sure as hell am not planning to join another pack, but I'm not going back to Wolf Creek, either," I said.

"You can't go out there alone," Sheila said. "You have no supplies, no clothes, no shoes. How far do you think you'll get?"

I ran a hand through my hair in frustration. Of course my carefully packed bag and all my cash was gone. Tyler had made sure he'd left me with nothing. Not that he thought I'd survive the cave. "I'll figure it out."

"No, you won't," Alec said. "It's a three day walk to the nearest town. And that's for someone who's healthy and has proper supplies."

"I'll be fine but I appreciate your concern," I said.

"If you say so," he said with a shrug.

I shook my head as I turned away. Of course I managed to step on something sharp immediately. "Fuck me."

I grabbed my foot and pulled the stick out of my skin.

Could I possibly go more than twenty-four hours without bleeding?

"Like I said, you're not going to make it on your own," Alec said.

"Thank you for the astute observation." Limping, I carefully stepped forward, not turning back to the group.

"Alec, do the right thing," Sheila pleaded.

"She's practically the poster child for our community," Malcom said.

"Get back here." Alec sighed.

Accepting help from strangers was the last thing I wanted, but I wasn't prepared to go out in the woods alone. I turned and looked at the trio. "You're not going to discuss sending me back again."

"I don't think you're in the position to be making demands," Alec said.

"Then I'll take my chances in the woods," I said. "If you aren't in a position to offer hospitably, I'll be on my way."

"Alec, cut her some slack," Malcom said.

I was surprised to hear the other male advocating for me. "I guess there's only one asshole in the group." I glared at Alec. "Look, if you aren't willing to help me, I get it. None of you know me. That's fine. But either stop judging and let me go, or actually help me."

"I like her," Sheila said.

"If you stay, you're Sheila's problem," Alec said reluctantly.

"Don't worry, sis, I got you," Sheila said.

"I won't stay long. I just want to get cleaned up and see if there's a way I can work to earn some supplies." I wasn't expecting to evoke shifter hospitality, but here we were. It was one of the first safety things we learned when we were young.

If you were ever separated from your pack, you could expect to be taken in and kept safe from harm in any of the official packs.

"You aren't going to try to take me back, are you?" I asked. It was the only thing I had to be concerned about.

"You look to be of age," Alec said.

"I am," I agreed.

"Then it's not our job to enforce another pack's punishment. But if they come into our territory, I won't stop them from claiming you," he warned.

"That's fair." If they did come for me, hopefully it would be long after I'd left this pack behind.

"We'll sleep here tonight and take you to camp in the morning," he said.

I'd learned about other packs growing up. Some were more primal than us, choosing to live in the woods away from humans. I supposed this pack had to be one of them. "This isn't your pack camp?"

"We were scouting when we found you," Sheila explained. "Our camp is about a mile west. Near a lake. Nice place."

The thought of walking a mile on my newly injured bare foot wasn't thrilling, but it beat a three day walk to a town I had no map to get to. Knowing my luck, I'd wander for a week then die of starvation. These wolves were my only shot at survival.

I looked at Alec and realized he was staring at me. My eyes met his and he didn't break his gaze. "Thank you," I said.

His eyes narrowed slightly, as if he was trying to assess if I was being serious. When I didn't follow with anything, he finally nodded, then turned away. "I'll take first watch."

"Great, she can use your sleeping bag," Sheila said.

Alec growled again.

"You sure do that a lot," I commented. "Words might be better. Try this: *No, I don't want the strange girl to use my sleeping bag.*"

Sheila laughed. "She's got your number, Alec."

"She can share my bag," Malcom offered.

"She can use mine," Alec said.

"I'm fine on the ground," I said, sitting back down in the spot I'd woken in.

"You keep talking about how you're *fine* but so far, all I see is a weak little wolf who is lucky to be alive," Alec said.

"Never call me that again," I hissed.

"Lucky?" he asked.

"Little wolf."

"You don't like *little wolf*?" He looked amused.

"What am I supposed to call you, then?" he asked.

"Her name is Lola," Sheila reminded him.

"Lola." The sound of my name on his lips sent a shiver down my spine.

"Over here, Lola," Sheila said, pointing to a sleeping bag.

I walked away from Alec and settled into the offered bag. It smelled like campfire and rain with a hint of musk. It was Alec's scent and *fuck* it was sexy as hell. It was too bad he was such a dick.

Sheila moved her sleeping bag near me. "Don't worry about Alec. His bark is worse than his bite."

"I heard that, and it's a lie," Alec replied.

Sheila chuckled. "You're safe with us. You should get some sleep."

I turned away from her, not in the mood for more conversation, but I wasn't sleepy. I'd just woken from a very long nap and I was surrounded by strange shifters I didn't know.

Soon, I heard the soft, deep breathing coming from Sheila and the snores from Malcom. I turned on my back and stared up at the sky. Stars were visible in the breaks from the trees and the moon was nearly full. If I had shifted, would I be able to do it again?

Crickets chirped and the wind rustled the trees. The sounds of the forest were calming and peaceful, and I almost felt like I could let my guard down. I closed my eyes and tried to feel for my inner wolf. I felt the same as I always had. There was nothing else there. Just the pathetic girl with the smart mouth who always said the wrong thing.

Disappointed, I opened my eyes and looked around. Alec was sitting on a log, staring into the dark woods. There was no way I was going to sleep while he was awake.

I walked over to him and sat down on the log, careful to leave a space between us. "I know you don't believe me but I want to let you know I'll be out of your way as soon as possible."

"You won't be ready for a while. You're stuck with us," he said, without looking at me.

"What is that supposed to mean?" I demanded.

"You're a shifter who doesn't know how to shift and you have one of the most powerful packs out looking for you," he said.

"They're not looking for me. They think I'm dead," I clarified.

He looked over at me. "Did you break the mating bond before they threw you in the cave?"

I blinked a few times, thinking back to those last moments.

I didn't know all the steps necessary to break a bond, but I was pretty certain we hadn't done them. "No."

"Then he'll feel you. He knows you're alive. If he's not looking for you yet, he will."

"Why would he care? He didn't want me," I said.

"Once you connect to your wolf, you'll understand it better."

"Explain it to me," I challenged.

He looked annoyed. "Your wolf and you are two halves of the same whole."

"I know that," I said.

"Despite that, there are still things one half controls more than the other. Your survival instincts, for one, come primarily from your wolf. That's why you're alive."

"So?"

"The bond you share with your mate is also driven by your wolf. The part of us that's more instinct than brain. He'll feel compelled to find you. It might even drive him to start wanting you. Breaking a bond isn't easy, but if it's not done quickly, the bond can get more intense, making the mate hunger for the other." He lifted his chin. "You might find yourself wanting him."

"That is never going to happen," I assured him.

"Your mate will be looking for you soon enough," he said.

"He's not my mate," I said through gritted teeth.

"You might not want to be paired with him, but that doesn't change the fact that the fates put you together. Sometimes, the fates are cruel."

"You sound like you have experience in this matter," I mused.

"I had a mate once," he said.

"And?" I pressed.

"She was killed. Taken from me. It was the worst pain I've ever felt." He looked down at his hands.

Guilt swirled through me. "I'm sorry."

He stood. "If you're not going to sleep, I will. Wake me in four hours."

I watched him as he walked to the sleeping bag. He climbed in and turned on his side. How could he possibly go to sleep while a stranger was taking watch? Either he trusted me or he was so determined to end the conversation that he'd feign sleep. I wasn't sure which it was, but I wasn't about to go poke him and see if he was really sleeping.

I turned my attention back to the woods, breathing in the fresh air and enjoying the peace of the night. I might not have my supplies and I might be stuck in the middle of who-knew-where with strange shifters, but I was alive, and for this moment, I was free.

10

My foot was healed by the time we started for Alec's camp. I tried to swallow back the excitement bubbling inside me. I'd healed from the injuries sustained before and during the cave, but I'd shifted. Until this moment, I wasn't sure I'd retained the magic. I didn't want to allow myself to believe that I could shift on my own, but maybe it was possible.

Sheila, Malcom, and Alec each had a backpack on their backs. Their sleeping bags were rolled and attached to the bottom of the pack. I got the sense they did this often.

"So you three were on patrol?" I asked.

"We had some reports of talismans in the woods," Sheila said.

"She doesn't need to know," Alec said.

"Witches?" I asked.

"Not your business," Alec said.

"I would rather know what I'm getting into. Besides, who am I going to tell? You made it clear that trying to get through the woods to civilization on my own is a death sentence," I reminded him.

"Ignore him, he's just pissed we didn't find anything," Sheila said.

"Another wild-goose chase," Malcom said.

"Is your camp not warded?" I asked.

Malcom laughed.

"What's so funny?" I asked.

"She's from Wolf Creek, you'll have to excuse her witch-loving ways," Alec said.

"I never said I hold any love for witches," I said. "If anything, I'm equally against all magic."

"Strong words for a shifter who had the protection of the Cedar Coven," Alec said.

"I don't know anything about the Cedar Coven but I do know that I have no love for the witch who cursed my family."

"So you really never shifted before?" Sheila asked.

"Well, even if I could have shifted, that was my first full moon," I admitted.

Sheila looked at me as if I'd said something crazy. "You're a late bloomer, then."

"I just turned nineteen two weeks ago. How is that late?" I asked.

"Wolf Creek's barrier has a few other restrictions in place," Alec explained.

"What are you talking about?" I was completely confused.

"Most of us have our first shift around thirteen or so," Malcom said. "It varies from wolf to wolf, but there's no set connection to a specific age. We feel the pull and shift on a full moon when our wolf is ready."

"Are you serious?" I asked.

"It's when we start feeling the bond, too, if we're around our true mate," Sheila added.

I felt like the wind had been knocked out of me. Tyler's abuse had started around that age. Prior to that, I wasn't treated well, but he didn't go out of his way to torment me. Had he been feeling the bond that whole time?

"What is it?" Sheila asked.

"Nothing," I lied. "It's just a lot to learn how much was hidden from me."

"Wolf Creek is the only magically sealed shifter pack in the world," Malcom said. "Y'all are like a cult."

"Not by choice, I assure you," I said. "If I could have left, I would have."

We walked in silence for a bit and I was careful to watch where I stepped. I didn't need another injury even if I did heal faster now. There was so much to think about. Growing up locked away from the rest of society had left me unaware of far more than I realized.

"What's your pack like?" I asked.

"We're more of a group of likeminded individuals than a true pack," Sheila said.

"What the hell does that mean?" I asked.

"We're all feral," Alec said.

It felt like ice was running through my veins and I stopped walking. "Feral?" I should have been more cautious. How had I not seen that coming.

"I don't mean any of you any harm. I'll just be on my way now." I turned and started walking away from them.

"Where are you going?" Sheila called.

"She's from Wolf Creek, remember?" Alec said.

"What is that supposed to mean?" I slowed my pace but didn't turn around.

"Ask her for her definition of a feral wolf," he said.

"Really, please, just leave me alone," I said. "I won't tell anyone I ran into you out here."

"What do you think we're going to do to you?" Shelia asked.

"Let me guess, you think we're going to tear off your head and drink from your skull?" Alec mused.

I stopped walking and turned around slowly. When he put it that way, it sounded ridiculous. "What does feral mean to you?"

"We're rejects or runaways from other packs," Malcom explained. "What did you think feral meant?"

My face and neck felt hot and I knew my cheeks were likely pink. Either these shifters were lying to me, or my pack had lied to me. Honestly, I wasn't sure what was true.

"She thinks we're going to kill her and eat her or skin her alive or some bullshit," Alec said.

"You really think that?" Sheila asked, her tone pained.

"I don't think you'll hurt me." I really didn't. They could have already if that was their plan. "They taught us a lot of things in Wolf Creek that don't seem to be true. I thought all shifters needed a pack. That it was harder being on your own."

Even though that was my plan, I never considered that I counted into that theory since I couldn't actually shift.

"It is harder on your own," Malcom agreed. "That's why we live in a community. We have companionship but we don't have the burden of a pack."

"We prefer to be around others like us. It makes things less complicated," Sheila explained. "But packs have systems, rules, expectations."

"You don't have rules?" I was liking the sound of this. Maybe being feral wasn't so bad.

"We treat each other with respect. If someone crosses the line, they're out," Sheila said.

"Permanently," Alec added. "There are no second chances here."

Okay, so maybe the lack of rules wasn't such a good thing. But then again, I'd done what I was supposed to do and I still ended up in the caves. Living my life was enough to nearly get me killed in my pack. How was being around feral shifters any more risky?

Either way, it was taking a chance. On my own, I had nothing to get me started. No map, no shoes, no food. With the feral shifters, there was a chance at some supplies at the very least. Best case, maybe I could figure this whole shifting thing out.

"Come on," Sheila urged. "You'll see we're not so bad."

Reluctantly, I agreed to follow them. I'd been taught that feral shifters were the enemy, but the members of my own pack had been the ones to try to end me.

Thinking about it too deeply was making my head spin. Exhaustion and hunger were making me feel weak. I hoped I was making the right choice by following my new companions.

I was so lost in my own thoughts that I didn't notice the army green canvas tents parked between the trees. They seemed to appear out of nowhere. Or I was so oblivious to details, that I'd managed to miss them. Either way, I supposed I was going to need more than just a pair of shoes. Not noticing an entire town of tents wasn't a great sign for my ability to survive on my own.

"When you said camp, you really meant it," I said.

"What did you think we meant?" Alec asked. "Too rustic for you?"

"Are you kidding? I grew up in a trailer. It's almost too reminiscent of home." I hesitated about ten feet from the nearest tent. This was the feral pack or group or whatever they called themselves. The place with no rules and no second chances.

"Should I introduce myself to your alpha?" I asked.

"We don't have an alpha. Feral, remember?" Malcom said.

"Who's the closest to a leader?" I felt like I should introduce myself to the shifter most likely to throw down the gauntlet.

"You're with him." Sheila inclined her head toward Alec.

I groaned. Of course he was the leader of a group of misfit, lawless shifters.

"Don't sound so disappointed," Alec said. "I haven't killed you yet."

"So when you said you were sent to look for signs of witches, you mean you decided to go?" I asked.

He shrugged and nodded. "Sounds right."

"So you're paranoid," I said.

"The witches have been trying to eliminate all shifters for the last decade. I wouldn't call it paranoia," he said.

"What do you mean?" I asked. "I thought witches just did their own thing."

"Like I said, you would never make it on your own." He walked forward, leaving me standing there like an idiot.

"Come on, you can bunk with me," Sheila said.

Grateful for her kindness, I followed her into the cluster of tents. As we got closer, I saw that the tents were all on platforms. Well maintained dirt paths connected them, leading around the makeshift village they'd constructed. The tents had lots of space around each other, but they were arranged in a general circular pattern around a larger open space.

Multiple fire pits, a few charcoal grills, and several picnic tables were spread out around a grassy common space. It was early morning but a few of the inhabitants were already up. A small group was brewing coffee over a fire, the scent practically making me drool. My stomach grumbled. It had been a long time since I'd eaten and the scent of coffee reminded me of how hungry I was.

"You need some breakfast," Sheila said.

"That would be nice," I agreed.

A group of children ran past us, nearly colliding into Malcom. He jumped to the side and the kids shouted apologies as they continued on in their game.

Under some of the trees, I caught sight of hammocks, lounge chairs, and more tables. Little groups were gathered all around. They were talking or playing with children or cooking food on grills.

It was the complete opposite of the way Wolf Creek felt. I'd grown up with what could only be explained as forced community. This was different. It felt authentic, peaceful, welcoming.

People waved to Sheila and Malcom and none of them seemed to care that someone new was with them. I wondered if that was due to Alec's presence. Then I realized he wasn't with us anymore. A little weight of disappointment dropped into the pit of my stomach. I should be thrilled that he was gone, but there was something intriguing about him. I told myself it was the safety he could provide, but that wasn't true.

Even my own fight or flight instincts seemed to be taking a nap while we walked through this camp. It felt safer than walking down the halls of school.

We walked past a picnic table lined with fruit. Sheila picked up a banana and handed it to me.

I accepted it gratefully and ate it as we continued to walk. We crossed through the common area, past a little cluster of tents, until we reached a tent that was set back away from the others.

"Here we are. Home sweet home," Sheila said.

We were standing in front of a green canvas tent that looked like it had seen better days. It was the duplicate of the other tents nestled between the trees around the common area.

"Cozy," I said.

"Wait till you see inside." She pulled apart the flap and ducked inside.

I followed her, not really sure what I was getting myself into. Again. That seemed to be the theme of my life lately.

Her tent was more spacious than I expected. Not large by any account, but it easily fit the cot, pair of folding camp chairs, and stacked crates that looked to be her version of a dresser.

She set her backpack at the foot of her cot, then tugged the sleeping bag out. "It's not much, but you're welcome to the sleeping bag and the space on the floor. I'll ask around to see if anyone has a spare cot."

"It's perfect, thanks." I accepted the bag and set it on the floor in front of her folding chairs.

"Now, let's see about getting you some clothes and shoes. She started digging through the crates. She was a few inches shorter than me and much thinner. I didn't think we were close to the same size.

"I appreciate it, but I might be better off keeping Alec's shirt." I tugged on the bottom of the fabric, making sure it was still covering me.

"My ex left some stuff behind," she said. "She was about your size. I should have tossed it months ago, but I guess it's good I kept it."

She emerged from her crates with a pair of jeans and a tee shirt that looked like they might actually fit. "That is very lucky for me. Are you sure you're okay with me wearing it?"

"Yeah, it's a good use for it," she said. "She couldn't hack the feral life. Went back home to her old pack. It happens. I knew better than to get attached to someone with ties to the outside world."

I tugged the jeans on. They were a little tighter than I liked, but they covered me better than the shirt. Then I pulled off Alec's shirt and replaced it with the faded black tee. I wasn't used to going sans bra and panties, but it was nice to have any kind of clothing again.

"We'll have to ask around for some shoes," Sheila said. "I don't think my size five will fit you."

"Nope, not even close," I said.

"Thanks, again," I said. "I will find a way to repay you for all this. I'm just not sure how yet."

"Stay and help us for a while," she said. "I'm sure we can find something for you to do."

"Help with what exactly? I don't think you want me out scouting for witches."

"No, you're not ready for that, but there's other things.

Besides, you could learn a bit. Figure out how to connect with your wolf," she suggested.

I sat down in one of the folding chairs. "What if I can't do it?"

She took the chair next to me. "Every shifter finds a way eventually, even if it takes some of us longer."

I shook my head. "My mom has never shifted. I wasn't supposed to be able to either."

"The curse," Sheila whispered. "Tell me about it."

"I don't know much. I know my grandfather pissed off a witch and *boom* family curse. No shifting for any of us." I sighed.

"But you did it," Sheila pointed out. "You shifted. You broke it."

"My wolf fought to keep me alive but how do I know I can repeat it?" I wanted to believe it, but it seemed so impossible.

"You won't know until you try," she said.

"Not shifting brought me nothing but pain," I said. "If I try here and fail, it's another group of shifters who know."

"You think they'd care? Why do you think we're all here? Some are like you," she said.

"Some can't shift?" I asked.

"No, but they were rejected by their mate. Tossed out of their pack with nowhere to go. Or they didn't agree with the alpha or their family tried to overthrow the alpha and lost. You know how it is, shifters don't just punish the one who did the deed, they punish everyone in the family. It's messed up."

"Why are you here?" I asked.

She rolled up her sleeve and revealed an angry looking circular scar. "I was chosen. Or some shit. But my pack said women can't be chosen. So they burned it off."

"A crescent mark?" I'd never heard of a woman getting a mark from the goddess.

"The mark of a protector," she said. "Ironic, isn't it that I ended up tossed aside after it showed."

"I'm so sorry," I said.

"It's better this way, I didn't need their shit. I'm happy here. I've found a home and a family of sorts. Sure, people come and go, but there's some of us who will never leave. We have each other's backs," she said.

"What about Alec?" I asked. "What's his story?"

Her expression grew solemn. "It's not my story to tell. You'll have to wait until he's ready to share."

"Is it as bad as yours?" I asked.

"Worse," she said. "You wait here. I'll see if I can find you some shoes. Then I'm taking you to Greta. If anyone can figure out what's going on with your wolf, it's her."

I nodded and forced a smile. Sheila's story wasn't so different than mine. She was a victim of things beyond her control. For a culture who prayed to a female deity, they sure were terrible in the way they treated the females in their packs.

I had planned to go to school, to become human and blend in. But that was before my wolf had made an appearance. Now, I was wondering if I could get away with staying here for a while. At least until I could get my wolf sorted out. If I was going to live with humans, I couldn't risk shifting unexpectedly. And it turned out there was a lot I needed to learn about shifter culture.

They had tried to break me in Wolf Creek, but in the end, maybe I was exactly where I needed to be.

11

"HELLO?" A voice I would now recognize anywhere called into the tent.

I stood. "Alec?"

He opened the flap. "I would ask if you're decent, but it's not like I didn't carry you naked for three miles."

"Wait, what?" That was news to me. "You said I was a wolf when you found me."

"You were, as was I, but you shifted back as soon as I growled at you. You gotta work on your wolf's ability to stand up for herself," he said.

"Well, that would have been helpful information when we first met," I said.

"Not really, you couldn't do anything with it. I'm going to wager you still couldn't. Sheila said she wanted to have you work with Greta." He held up a pair of boots. "She also said you needed these."

The black combat boots in his hands were practical, sturdy, and looked like they could do some damage if I ever needed to kick someone while wearing them. Basically, they were my dream shoes. I crossed the tent and took the shoes from him. "Thanks."

A quick glance at the tag let me know they were exactly my size. I wasn't going to question my good luck. There was also a pair of thick socks stuffed into one of the boots.

I sat down on the chair and got to work sliding my freezing feet into the socks and then I started lacing up the boots.

Alec cleared his throat.

I stopped mid-tie and looked up at him. "Would you like to sit?"

"No, I should go. There's lots to do," he said.

"Lots to do at the camp with no alpha and no rules?" I smirked.

He looked like he almost smiled. "Us feral wolves have to get back to work eating babies or whatever else your pack thinks we do."

I rolled my eyes. "First, they're not my pack anymore. Second, I don't know what you do in your free time."

"I'm not going to tell you what I do, but I promise, I don't eat babies." He winked.

"You're something else, you know that?"

"Thank you," he said.

"Anything else you want to share about our first meeting that I might want to know?" I finished tying the first boot. "I usually like to know what happened to me while I was naked."

"Trust me, there was nothing intimate about it," he said.

"Ouch. You know exactly how to make a girl feel special."

"Saving your life wasn't enough?" he asked.

I tied the other boot then stood and grabbed the shirt he'd

lent me. "It is. And once again, thank you for saving me. And for the shirt." I held it out to him.

He moved closer to me and took the flannel. For a moment, he stood a foot away from me, just gazing at me with those gorgeous two-tone eyes. They sucked me right in and I couldn't help but stare back. They really were the most beautiful eyes I'd ever seen.

"I should go," he said.

"Okay, bye," I said, still not dropping my eyes from his. The seconds seemed to drag by as we stood there, locked in each other's gaze. Finally, he broke away and turned and walked out of the tent.

I let out a breath and realized my heart was racing. There was something about Alec that drove me completely crazy. If I was going to stick around here, I was going to have to be careful. He was bad news, that was clear. Plus, he was the leader. Even if they didn't use the term alpha, that was what he was. I could feel a magnetic pull toward him. It had to be the pull to the alpha that other shifters talked about. I never felt it in Wolf Creek but I must be able to sense it now.

The tent flap opened, and for a fraction of a moment, flutters filled my chest with wishful expectation. They fell flat when Sheila walked through the door. My shoulders slumped.

Sheila lifted a brow. "Disappointed that I'm not someone else?"

"No, of course not," I said.

She nodded to the boots. "I see Alec came through."

"Yes, thank you for securing that for me," I said.

"I didn't do anything in that regard, he was already asking around on your behalf," she said.

"Probably ready to be rid of me," I said.

She shrugged. "Could be. But I heard he was trying to find you a cot, too. So, he must not be counting on you leaving too quickly."

"Well, that's very kind of him," I said.

"He's got a nice guy streak. He just doesn't let it out often. Especially not around people he just met. You've made quite the impression on him," she said, her tone playful.

"I'm not sure I like what you're insinuating."

"You do know sex is normal, especially after a shift," she said. "Plus, there's the whole perk of being a shifter and not having to worry about STDs."

"I got sex-ed in school, thanks," I said.

She shrugged. "I'm just saying, nobody would judge if you and Alec…"

"That is not going to happen," I said.

"Suit yourself," she said. "Sometimes I wish I liked dick so I could see what he's like in bed. I'm just not into it."

"Well, you'll have to ask someone who isn't me for a review," I said.

She laughed. "Maybe I will later. Greta is expecting us."

"Now? I haven't even washed the blood off and it's been days since I've eaten a full meal." I would kill for a shower and a hamburger about now.

"Greta first," she insisted. "It's far better to bathe in the evening when there's not a crowd at the lake. Unless you want a crowd."

"No, thanks. I'll wait."

"Good. Then it's settled." She opened the tent flap and stepped outside.

Sheila wasn't going to take no for an answer so I followed her silently out of her tent and back toward the common area. It was full now. Kids were running and screaming, adults were sitting in circles of chairs, others were cooking or playing various games. Things around here looked like they were pretty mellow most of the time.

"Who is this Greta?" I asked.

"She's like the camp grandmother," Sheila said. "She's the oldest shifter here and she knows everything. An afternoon with her is better than years in a classroom. And she's dying to meet you."

I never met my grandmother. Or my grandfather. And from what I'd heard, my grandfather went crazy and killed himself. He didn't seem like he was throwing down knowledge to younger generations. What might it have been like to have elders I could have learned from?

My stomach twisted in nervous expectation. I was excited about meeting Greta, but worried I wasn't going to be good enough. I wasn't exactly a normal shifter. "You sure about this?"

"Absolutely." Sheila paused in front of another green tent. A few boxes of pink flowers in neat rows were set up on either side of the entrance. It created a comfortable, welcoming vibe.

"Go on, she's waiting for you."

I hesitated, staring at the canvas tent flap.

Sheila gave me a gentle push. "It's okay."

Taking a deep breath, I walked forward. "Hello?"

I was greeted by the warm glow of flickering candles sitting on every hard surface. Unlike Sheila's mostly temporary looking furniture, Greta's tent had an actual bed, a solid wood dresser, and a little table with wood chairs. In the center of the floor was a red and gold rug. The whole place felt warm and inviting.

An older woman was sitting on one of the chairs next to the table. She rose when she saw me. "You must be Lola."

"Yes, that's me. You're Greta?" I asked.

She smiled, creating deep creases around her eyes and mouth. Her hair was white and tied up in a bun on top of her head. A few loose wisps framed her lined face.

"Come in, please have a seat," she said.

I followed her to the small table and took the chair next to hers. Without warning, Greta grabbed my face, her paper-thin skin felt cool against my cheeks and my eyes widened in surprise.

"I need to get a good look at you," she said as she held a hand on each of my cheeks.

My eyes darted around the room as I sat there in uncomfortable silence, letting her hold my face. She moved closer to me, her nose inches from mine, her eyes narrowed.

Just as I was about to do or say something very rude, she released me. "Just as I thought."

"What is just as you thought?" I asked.

"Your wolf is ready, but you are not," she said.

"I'm sorry?" None of that made sense. If I could have shifted long ago to escape from my own personal hell, I'd have done it.

"You held off the shift," she said. "It's not good for your wolf."

"It wasn't on purpose," I explained. "I was cursed."

"Yes, yes, I heard. But curses only have power beyond a generation when we let them."

"What does that even mean?" I asked.

"Were you the one who was cursed?" she asked.

"I couldn't shift. I never even felt my wolf."

"But was the curse placed directly on you?" she clarified.

"No," I admitted.

"The shifter who was cursed would likely never break it, but for it to pass onto future generations, the cursed wolves have to buy in, they have to believe they are cursed," she said.

"You're saying this was all in my head?" I asked. "That's insane. Don't you think I'd have shifted if I could?"

"I don't know, you tell me," she said.

"My mom wasn't the one cursed either and she's never shifted. Not once in her whole terrible life," I said.

"That's because she gave up, and she taught you to give up," Greta said.

My mom had given up. But she did that long before I was born, didn't she? I realized I didn't know the exact timeline of the curse. Was it before or after my mom had her first shift? I'd always assumed she'd never shifted but what if she had and then she stopped?

From my earliest memories, I recalled being told I'd never shift. That I was cursed, broken, no good. I'd been told it wasn't even possible before I ever tried. But that wasn't right. You couldn't try to shift. The first shift happened. It wasn't anything done on the part of the shifter.

"If that's the case, why didn't I shift at the full moon like everyone else?" I asked.

"Because you didn't want to," she said.

"Sure I did. If I could shift, I wouldn't have been so weak." I would have given anything to be able to protect myself.

"You had a plan in place, didn't you?" she asked.

"Yeah. I was going to run," I said.

"Your plan was to run. To be human. Not to shift," she said.

She was right, of course. I'd given up on shifting nearly a decade prior. "I don't understand."

"Witch magic has limits. Especially on us. It's why they hate us. We are their creation so we can resist. You must learn to overcome your fear and embrace your true self," she said.

Easier said than done. "How?"

"I will help you, but it's not going to be easy," she said. "The question is. Do you want to be able to shift?"

"Of course I do." It was an easy question to answer. She was right, I had resigned myself to a life without shifting, but given the choice, I'd take it. College could wait a while. I needed this.

The tent flap opened and a kid who looked about ten ran in, breathless. "Greta, please come quick. It's my dad."

"Take me to him," Greta said.

12

GRETA WAS on her feet and out of the tent faster than I expected for someone of her age. I followed, chasing the child and Greta down the pathways, past the clusters of tents, until we reached the woods near where I'd entered when I'd arrived.

A male with sandy-blonde hair was laying on the ground, blood pouring from his nose and mouth. His clothes were torn and his shirt was bloody. He was moaning in pain, his hands gripping for the ground and finding no purchase.

"What happened to him?" Had someone attacked him in the camp?

"Why isn't he healing?" The child asked. "He should be healing. Shift, Daddy. You need to heal."

She ran forward and Greta caught her, then passed her to me. On instinct, I reached for the girl and pulled her into my arms.

"Get the child out of here and keep her away," Greta ordered.

I looked down at the kid. The little girl had the same

blonde hair as the fallen man. She was trying to stay strong but I could almost feel her fear.

"Go, now," Greta barked.

I grabbed the child's hand. "Come on, I need your help."

"What's wrong with my dad?" she asked, her eyes glued to him.

I guided her away, leading her back toward the common area of camp. "I'm new here. Can you give me a tour while Greta helps your dad?"

The child finally looked up at me. "He's dying."

"Greta will help him," I assured her.

"He should be healing," she said.

I tried to hide my concern. Wolves healed fast. Even a major injury didn't linger long but not everything could be healed with wolf strength. Some things were too serious. I couldn't imagine what happened to him here to make him that injured but I needed to stay strong for the girl. "It'll be okay."

She shook her head. "I'm almost eleven. I don't need you to lie to me."

"Alright," I said. "I don't know what happened to your dad but I know Greta will do her best."

"What if they can't fix him?" she asked.

I didn't have an answer for her. "Come on, let's find something we can do while we wait. What's your name?"

"Megan," she said.

"Megan, I'm Lola." I smiled. "Tell me, is there any place we can find something to eat?" Most of the shifters I grew up with would jump at the chance to eat something when they were stressed. I wasn't sure if it would help distract her, but it was worth a try.

"Sure," she said. "I'll show you."

Megan led me back to the common area where several people were out cooking various foods. She introduced me to people and it didn't take long before I had a cup of coffee and a bowl of oatmeal. I ate the food as quickly as possible. I was starving, but my new charge wasn't interested in eating. I knew I needed to find another way to distract her.

"What's your favorite way to cheer up when you're having a bad day?" I asked.

"I guess I like to go for a swim," she said. "But I don't feel like swimming now. I want to see my dad."

"Greta needs to concentrate on helping him. We're going to help him by giving her some time to focus. Do you understand?" I asked.

She nodded. "I'm scared."

"I know. We'll check on him soon, I promise," I said. "Can you show me where you swim? We don't have to get in the water. We'll look and then we can go check in on your dad."

"I can do that," she agreed.

I followed Megan through the trees, deeper into the woods. We left the tents behind and I realized if not for her guidance, I would be totally lost. Alec really had been on to something when he said I wasn't going to make it to town. I had no way of knowing which direction I was headed. It all looked the same.

"What is that?" I stopped walking and pointed to a little cabin. "Are there humans out here?"

"Naw, that's Alec's place," she said.

I stared at the little house and wondered if he was in there right now. What did he do all day as the non-alpha of this feral pack? And why the hell was his home so far away from the others?

"How come he's in a cabin while everyone else lives in tents?" I asked.

"It's the border. Nobody else wanted it," she said. "Don't go beyond the cabin. That's when the bad things happen."

"Wait, you have a border?" I asked. "With magic?"

"No, no magic allowed here. Past the cabin is where the High Key Pack lives. We don't go on their side and they don't go on ours," she said.

"Got it." I understood pack rivalry. At least that was something that seemed to be similar here. "Do you know where Wolf Creek is from here?" I probably should have asked that right away but I think part of me didn't want to know.

"I'm not sure. I think it's a few days walk," she said.

I eased a little knowing there was some distance between us. I still wondered exactly how far I'd traveled in wolf form before the others found me. I might have spent days wandering in circles for all I knew.

"Wait, we're not going into someone else's territory to get to the swimming hole, are we?" I asked.

"No, of course not," she said. "I might be a kid, but I'm not stupid."

"You most definitely are not," I confirmed. I was terrible at this whole distracting the kid thing.

We resumed our walk, away from the cabin. There was a part of me that was a little disappointed. I sort of wanted to go knock on his door. But that was ridiculous.

It didn't take long before I could feel the air getting cooler and damper. The ground was a little softer, and the shrubs around us were greener. We were getting closer to water.

A few cheers and some yelling sent birds flying. I looked up and watched them fleeing the noise and caught a glimpse of the sun through the trees. It was closer to midday than I realized. I wondered how long we'd been walking.

I heard splashes, followed by more playful screams just as the lake came into view. It stopped me in my tracks.

This was not a swimming hole. This was a full on, huge lake. There was a little island in the center of it and it stretched for what had to be a mile across. I'd never seen a lake this size in real life.

"It's beautiful," I said.

"And freezing. Don't let them fool you," Megan said, lifting her chin toward the group of kids on the shore.

They were running around on the sandy beach, their pants rolled up to their knees. Two kids were kicking water on each other in some kind of splashing game and a few quieter kids were skipping rocks. They all looked like they were close in age to Megan.

"You want to go play with them?" I asked.

"Not really," she said. "Can we go back and check on my dad?"

We'd been gone a while. With any luck, it was enough time for Greta to do something to help the poor man. "Sure."

Our walk back to camp was silent and I felt like I'd failed at trying to keep the girl's spirits up. It was tough when I didn't know what was going on or how to comfort her.

When we arrived back to where her dad had been, Alec was waiting but the male and Greta were gone.

"Where is he?" Megan asked. "Is he alive?"

Alec walked toward her then knelt so he was closer to Megan's height. "He's in his bed, and Greta is still attending him. I think he's going to be okay, but he's got a long night of fighting. Do you understand?"

Megan swallowed and nodded.

"You need to be strong, can you do that for him?" Alec asked.

"I can." She lifted her chin and set her jaw in a look of pure determination.

"Good." Alec stood. "Your mother asked that you go to Delilah's. You'll stay with her until your dad is recovered."

Megan nodded. "Thank you."

"Go on, now, they're expecting you."

Megan gave me a weak smile before taking off at a run. I waited until she was out of sight before turning to Alec. He was unexpectedly gentle and sweet with the girl. It was going to be harder than I thought to convince myself that I should avoid him.

"Is he really going to be okay?" I wanted to ask for details about what happened to Megan's dad, but I wasn't sure it was my place.

"I hope so," he said.

"You were very good with her," I said.

"Megan's a good kid."

"She seems sweet," I agreed.

"We need to talk," he said, his tone serious.

"Oh?"

"You're still covered in blood." His eyes swept over me. "Did Sheila not show you where the lake is?"

"Megan did. There were kids playing there, though. Not sure it's the best time to wash up," I said.

"They won't be there now," he said. "It's near lunch."

"What did you want to talk to me about?" I asked, worried he was trying to change the subject.

"Alec, you ready?"

I turned to see a group of shifters walking toward us.

"Going somewhere?" I asked.

"I'll be back soon," he said.

"Um, no. You can't go. You don't just drop the *we need to talk* on someone then take off." My hands were on my hips and I was pissed that he would do that. "Seriously. Not cool."

The group stopped as they approached us and a large shifter with huge sideburns and long dark hair made his way toward Alec. "We're ready when you are."

"We'll talk later," Alec said. "In the meantime, there's a shower that works in my cabin if you want to use it."

He walked away, joining the group of shifters. A few of them glanced at me before turning around and walking away.

What the fuck was going on here? He tells me he needs to talk and then takes off with the guys? I knew Alec didn't owe me anything. In fact, I was the one who owed him. He'd saved my life and I was crazy grateful for the shoes. But I'd just seen a shifter bleeding out and Alec was acting strange.

Something was going on here but I wasn't sure if it was nefarious. Either way, there was no way I was going to Alec's cabin to use his shower. Sure, a shower sounded like pretty much the best thing ever at the moment, but I'd figure out how to find the lake on my own.

I headed back in the direction I'd gone with Megan, but it didn't take me long to realize I wasn't going to find it without help. Fuck. Why was I so bad at navigation? My sense of direction was shit. I wasn't going to find the lake. But I probably could find Sheila's tent. I turned around and managed to find my way back to camp and headed for Sheila's. As I walked there, I couldn't help but wonder what I'd really gotten myself into.

My mind was a tangled mess as I weighed the limited information for pros and cons. There was so much I didn't know about my new friends. I'd been warned my whole life about how dangerous feral shifters were, but I wasn't seeing any signs of them being a threat.

None of them had once hurt me. That was more than most of the people I'd known in my old life. Even those I was related to by blood. While my own mother had never physically harmed me, she didn't lift a finger to help, either. What kind of mother did that?

In the short time I'd been here, this group of feral shifters was more like a pack than my own pack growing up. I saw signs of community, support, kindness, and joy. They shared meals and presented a united front when a problem arose. Shit, another family stepped up to help Megan when her dad was injured. Nobody once even checked on me when my mom nearly died of an overdose when I was twelve.

I knew I shouldn't get too attached and that I should be cautious, but things were looking pretty good from an outsider's perspective. It was all the things I wished I'd had growing up that I never even knew I wanted. I wasn't sure what it meant, but even with Alec's weirdness, this place was better than Wolf Creek.

Surprisingly, I managed to find Sheila's tent. When I stepped inside, it was empty. Instead of risking getting lost forever trying to find Sheila, I decided I'd wait. I plopped down in one of the folding chairs and closed my eyes for a bit.

My mind was too restless to settle so I opened my eyes and looked around the room.

That's when I noticed the little stash of books under her cot. Thrilled to see them, I walked over and sorted through the pile. I had a feeling she'd be okay with me borrowing one to read. It wasn't like I'd take it out of her room.

I settled on a glossy paperback with a woman in a huge, old fashioned dress on the cover. It was well loved and the wear on the spine told me it had been read more than the other books in her little stash. I took that as a good sign and got comfortable on one of the folding chairs.

I was a few chapters in when the tent flap opened, but it wasn't Sheila.

"Doesn't anyone knock around here?" I asked.

"Where exactly am I supposed to knock on the canvas?" Malcom asked.

"Good point," I said as I set the book down.

"Hey, good one. I borrowed that when we had a massive rainstorm and couldn't do anything," he said.

"I didn't expect it to be your style," I admitted.

"There isn't a lot to do around here," he said.

"Wait, why aren't you off doing whatever with Alec?" I hadn't noticed before, but Malcom was absent from the group.

"That's kind of why I'm here," he said.

My brow furrowed. "Oh?"

"You can't stay," he said.

"Excuse me?" I bristled, feeling all the hurt and rejection from Wolf Creek flooding into me.

"It's not safe for you here," he said.

"According to Alec, it's not safe for me out there, either," I said. "Which is it?"

"Alec isn't who you think he is," he said.

The tent opened and Shelia walked in. She seemed surprised to see Malcom. "Hey, Malcom. I didn't expect to find you here."

"Hey, Sheila. I came to check in our foundling," Malcom said.

"She's just fine," Sheila said.

"I see that." He nodded to me. "See you later, Lola."

Sheila narrowed her eyes as she watched him leave, then stared at the doorway for a bit before turning back to me. "Careful with that one. Alec seems to trust him, but I'm not so sure."

"You three seemed so close when I met you." I was going to get whiplash from them.

"I think Alec keeps him close because it's better than leaving him on his own. I don't think he'd do anything to hurt us, but there's something a little off about him." She walked over to the empty folding chair and sat down next to me. "He's never told us his story. Who does that?"

"You won't tell me Alec's," I reminded her.

"That's different. He'll tell you when he's ready. Malcom has never told anyone. Not a single soul."

"Maybe it's painful," I said.

"All our stories are painful or we wouldn't be here," she said. "Look at you. Look at me. We're a pair or rejects. We've got sad stories, just like everyone here. But for some reason, he won't share. Not even when he's drunk. It's weird."

"You know everyone's story?" I was skeptical. Sure, I'd

shared part of mine, but I left out most of the details. "I'm not sure I'd be open to telling everyone."

"When you're here long enough, it comes out eventually," she said.

"How long have you known them? Alec and Malcom?"

"I've known Alec since I got here five years ago. Malcom's only been here about a year." She stood. "But enough with that. We've got shit to do."

"We do?" I asked, surprised. "Would it be possible to add a detour to the lake?"

"Oh, shit, yeah, sorry," she said. "I'll walk you down there and then we can help with the fire."

"We're having a fire?" I asked.

"It's half-moon," she said.

"What is half-moon?"

"Basically, an excuse to get drunk and run around naked or shift. Whatever you're into," she said.

I laughed. "You serious?"

"Yeah. We do it the week after the full moon every month. Full moon, New Moon, Half Moon. We like to celebrate." She grinned. "You're going to love it."

13

As Alec predicted, the lake was empty when we arrived. I was still covered in the grime and dirt and blood from my last night in Wolf Creek. I didn't care how cold the lake was, I just needed to wash the trauma away any way I could.

"I'll see if I can find you some fresh clothes," Sheila said. "You good alone for a bit?"

"Yeah, thanks," I said. "As long as I don't have to try to find my way back solo, I should be good."

"We gotta get you a compass," she teased.

I laughed. "Hopefully, I'll get my bearings soon."

She waved and left me alone on the shore of the huge lake. The water was like glass. A still, silvery gray. Every so often the breeze would send ripples over the surface, making the water seem like it was shivering.

I took a moment to stare out at the island. It was a peaceful sentinel in the center of the water. Covered in thick trees, it seemed a wild place. Like something out of an adventure story. I wondered if anyone ever swam or took a boat out to it.

Unsure of how much time I had, I began to remove my boots and clothes. I was grateful that I could rinse the dirt off in solitude. At least for the first time.

Carefully, I stepped into the shallow water and instantly regretted not taking Alec up on the offer to use his shower. Megan wasn't kidding when she'd warned me that it was freezing. Maybe in a month or two, the cool water would be nice on a hot day, but today it was still a little too cold.

Holding my breath, I ran forward and ducked under as soon as it was deep enough. I emerged with a gasp, then yelled out. "Fuck!"

The cold water was exhilarating and it definitely woke me up fully. I felt more alive than I had in years. Maybe it wasn't so bad to jump in here.

Using my hands, I scrubbed the dirt and blood off my arms and I rinsed my hair as best I could. I wished I had some shampoo to help get all the matted blood out of my hair, but this was better than nothing.

It took a while to scrub everything on my top half clean. I walked to where it was waist deep water and lifted my leg to inspect the place where I'd been bitten. There were tiny pink dots where the teeth had dug into my flesh. Scars that might remain despite the fact that the wounds were healed. There were other marks on me from fights over the years. All reminders of what I'd endured. I frowned at them, wishing I didn't have any visual reminder of my life before.

I continued my inspection of my wounds and rubbed dirt away if I encountered any. There was something stuck on my right hip that hadn't washed off with the initial plunge. I rubbed at it, but it didn't fade. Narrowing my eyes, I took in the strange marking.

No. It was impossible.

I rubbed some more. It had to be dirt.

Dirt that just so happened to be in the shape of a crescent moon with a circle around it.

It can't be real.

I can't have a mark.

I for sure can't have the mark of a mother-fucking-alpha.

My skin was red and raw from all the rubbing. Hands shaking, pulse rising, I stared at my hip. It was a mistake. Some kind of sick joke. Right?

Why the fuck would I - a wolf who had only shifted once as a last resort - receive a mark from the moon goddess? And not just any mark... the alpha mark.

I'd never even heard of a female getting any kind of mark until I met Sheila. Hers had been a single crescent, a protector mark. Mine was obviously the crescent inside a full circle. I'd never seen the mark in real life, but I'd learned about it. We'd all seen it on charts hanging in classrooms. There was no mistaking what kind of mark I had.

The problem was the fact that I had it.

"You all done?" Sheila called from shore.

I hadn't even noticed her approach.

Quickly, I used my arm to cover the mark. It was an awkward unnatural position, but I hoped she didn't notice.

"I found you a towel too," she said. "It's your lucky day!"

I waded through the water and gratefully accepted the towel. Turning away from Sheila, I dried off then got to work trying to dry my hair.

She passed me a pair of jean shorts and a long-sleeved tee. I pulled on the clothes then turned around to face her. "Thanks."

"No problem," she said. "If you stick around here, we'll have to make a trip to town to get you a few more things."

I wasn't really sure how to respond to that. The whole staying thing wasn't finalized in my mind. There was also the lack of funds. "I'm probably going to have to find a job in order to afford anything. My mate made sure my bag with my life savings didn't make it in the cave when he tossed me in."

"We have some connections. Ways we can trade skills for supplies. Don't worry about it." She shrugged.

"What kind of skills?" I asked, my mind going right to how my mom had made a living.

"It's not important," she said. "No need to worry about it now. Your first priority should be to figure out your wolf situation. But not tonight. Tonight is for fun."

"I don't think I even remember what fun is," I admitted.

"You're going to love this." She grinned. "Come on, you can help me gather some wood on our walk back."

We both had a handful of kindling by the time we reached camp. But the pile of dry sticks in my arms was nothing compared to what we found. "You weren't kidding when you said bonfire."

A massive pile of wood was artfully arranged in a towering stack in the center of the common area. All the tables and seating had been moved out of the way, leaving the grassy space open with the future bonfire as the centerpiece.

Sheila tossed her kindling in a small pile next to the wood. "I told you. It's kind of a big thing. Any excuse for a party, right?"

"The only thing my pack did was a ceremony on the full moon for the kids who had just turned nineteen. But even that was a drag," I said. "Though, I'm sure there were parties I wasn't invited to."

"Not anymore." Sheila threw her arm over my shoulders. "You're one of us now."

Warmth filled my chest. It was nice to feel like I was wanted somewhere. Like I had an actual chance at belonging.

"Now, I'm going to give you the secret to having the best half-moon party ever. You ready?" She looked like she was about to explode if she didn't finish talking.

"I'm ready," I said.

"You take a nap." She laughed. "For real. We're up till the sun rises and you don't want to miss a second."

I hadn't slept last night after waking to find myself with strangers and the initial excitement was wearing off. I probably should sleep. "Alright. I'm in."

We walked back to her tent. When we went inside, we discovered that someone had set up a cot in the place where I'd set the sleeping bag. The bag was on top of the cot and a pillow was sitting on top of that.

"I knew Alec had a thing for you," Sheila teased.

"It's just a cot," I said.

"Deny all you want but when the two of you are making out by the light of the bonfire, I'll know I was right," she said.

"That's not going to happen," I assured her.

As I snuggled into the sleeping bag, I thought about what it would be like to kiss Alec. To feel his strong body against mine. Tingles built low in my belly and I had to fight the thoughts. There were good things about him, but I wasn't sure how long I'd be here or what he was really like. I couldn't afford to get attached to someone only to have my heart ripped to pieces.

For the first time in my life, there was a possibility of friendship and belonging. I couldn't risk that for anything.

14

"Lola? Lola, it's time to wake up," a gentle voice called.

My eyes fluttered open and I saw Sheila sitting on her cot. She stretched, lifting her arms above her head. "You were out."

Surprisingly, I slept like the dead. I didn't even remember falling asleep and I'd had no dreams. I rubbed my eyes, then sat up and stretched before standing up. "How long were we asleep?"

"Few hours," she said.

My stomach growled and I covered it with my hand.

Sheila laughed. "Let's find some dinner."

I pulled on my combat boots, which looked amazing with the shorts Sheila procured for me, and then the two of us emerged from her tent. The sky was purple and I couldn't even see the sun anymore. It was that magical time of evening right before it changed from day to night.

There had been people around the common area every time I'd passed through, but as we got closer, I realized I'd only seen a fraction of the shifters who lived here.

There were easily a hundred or more shifters gathered

around the massive pile of wood. It wasn't lit yet, but as the sky darkened, I had a feeling we were close.

A group of children ran by. They were carefree and joyous as they weaved around adults. The older people just moved aside for them, unconcerned. Some of them even smiled or laughed when the kids passed by. That kind of interaction didn't happen where I grew up. Kids played, but always away from the adults.

Sheila dragged me to a table lined with food and we piled up plates. It was the first real meal I'd had in days and I enjoyed every bite of grilled meat and fresh vegetables and even a slice of cake. I had no idea where the food came from, but I wasn't about to argue.

There was movement near the bonfire and the chatter of conversation quieted. My heart raced and I tensed. "What's going on?"

Sheila grabbed my hand. "You gotta see this." She led me through the crowd, taking us closer to the fire.

Greta and an older male I didn't recognize were next to the pile of kindling Sheila and I had added to earlier today. It had been pushed up under the larger pieces of wood. Newspaper and other flammable items were also mixed in with the sticks.

"They're going to light it," Shelia whispered. "The tradition is that the oldest male and female of the group light the fire. Then we get to party."

Greta lit a match, and held it to a torch of some type the older male was holding. Once it caught, she stepped back and shook out her match. The male lowered the torch until the newspaper and kindling caught. Then he stepped back.

The fire ate through the sticks and newspaper, moving and

dancing and growing as it climbed up the larger pieces of wood. A cheer rose up through the crowd. Sheila joined in, yelling with the others. I was swept up in the excitement, joining in with whoops of my own.

The fire crackled and wood shifted as the bonfire took form. It was on its way to being a massive fire and it had enough fuel to burn all night. No wonder Sheila had recommended the nap. It was going to be a late night and giddy anticipation rolled through me. This was already more fun than any gathering I'd been to in my old life.

The shifters around me backed away from the fire and the yelling gave way to howls. The energy around us felt electric, like there was a collective sense of joy and elation. It was exhilarating and I was loving every second of it.

Then the clothes started to come off. Shirts thrown aside, pants tossed to the ground, underwear and bras flew through the air. There wasn't a speech or any announcement. They were just naked. Though, that didn't last long, because as soon as their clothes were piled off to the side, they ran toward the woods, shifting while in motion.

I stared, open-mouthed, as they flawlessly changed. None of them seemed to convulse or struggle. It was fluid. Beautiful and seamless transitions from human to wolf.

Something deep within me felt like it was waking. An energy that wanted desperately to get out.

For the first time in my life, I knew with absolute certainty that I was feeling my inner wolf.

Soon.

At that moment, I knew I was going to be joining them in the shift. It would be my turn soon enough. I wanted it. For real wanted it. Not just a passive longing. I was determined to make it happen.

"I'm going to run with them for a bit. Will you be okay here?" Sheila asked.

"Yeah, go, have fun," I said, making sure I hid the disappointment in my tone. I wasn't upset that she was leaving, I was discouraged by my lack of ability to shift.

"I'll be back soon." She already had her shirt off and quickly removed her clothes before running after the rest of the shifters.

I watched them leave, longing to join them.

"You can feel it, can't you?"

I turned to see Alec, shirt off, walking toward me. His gorgeous eyes pulled me in right away and I had to fight to break eye contact. Fortunately, there was plenty to look at. All those muscles. Holy hell, he was easy on the eyes. My gaze drifted down to his rounded shoulders and his biceps, then I moved lower, checking out his six pack which took me right to his happy trail. Finally, I was staring at the bulge in his pants.

And let me tell you, it was an impressive bulge.

"My eyes are up here," he said.

Fuck. What was wrong with me? I looked back up at him. "I see you're making a habit of not wearing a shirt."

"Shifting with clothes on isn't a great idea. I'd ruin too many shirts if I did that," he said. "Don't worry, you'll get used to it."

"I grew up in a pack of shifters, naked people don't bother me," I said.

"No?" He raised a brow. "Good."

Alec didn't waste any time unbuttoning and dropping his

jeans. Turns out, the man didn't bother with underwear. Not that he needed to be concerned about what he was packing. I might be a virgin, but I'd seen my share of dicks. Alec's was right up there with the largest I'd seen.

"You can close your mouth now," he said.

I knew my face had to be as red as my hair. I'd seen almost everyone I knew naked at some point. But Alec was different. Seeing him naked awakened things inside me I thought were dormant.

All this time, I thought I wasn't big on sex. Turned out, I wasn't around the right kind of male.

There were attractive members of my old pack. Tyler was gorgeous and I knew it, but the whole regularly trying to kill me thing eliminated the attraction.

I didn't have that issue with Alec. If anything, he was even more alluring because he'd technically helped save my life. That had to be it. The whole Prince Charming, damsel in distress thing.

"I suppose it was only fair that I return the favor," he said. "You look pretty good naked, too."

"Uh, thanks." Internally, I was wondering if the two of us could be naked together.

He turned but I called out to him. "Wait! You owe me an explanation from earlier."

"Later," he said.

"You gotta give me something," I demanded. "Where were you all day?"

"Trying to figure out if your life is in danger," he said.

"You're messing with me," I said.

"Just trust me a little bit, okay?" he said.

"I don't know you well enough to trust you," I replied.

"Forget I said anything earlier today. It wasn't a big deal," he said.

"You're lying," I said.

"Look, I don't want to concern you if there's nothing to worry about. You said it yourself, I get paranoid. I'm sure it's nothing," he said.

"Then tell me," I said.

"I already warned you that your pack would come looking for you," he reminded me. "I thought they might be close. But now I'm not sure."

My heart felt like it fell into my stomach. "Are you going to send me away?"

"You don't stand a chance out there if you can't shift," he said. "I can at least buy you that much time."

So much for fitting in and finding a place I belonged. My time here was a ticking clock but that was all I'd ever been promised. I nodded. "Thanks."

Alec nodded in return, then took off at a sprint, following the others. His long legs moved quickly over the earth and after a few strides, his body started to change. Just like the rest of the shifters, he seemed to melt into his wolf form with ease.

Whatever they were teaching here, it looked far more comfortable than the shifting I'd seen in the past.

I watched until I lost sight of him and then I realized how quiet it was. The sound of the bonfire was deafening in the silence of the night.

My inner wolf felt like she was whimpering and scratching at my bones. She wanted out, but she didn't know how to make it happen. *I'm sorry.* I wished I could follow them into the woods, run free and then transform back at will.

Why don't you?

I wasn't sure if the question was coming from me or from my wolf. Though, I suppose it didn't matter which part of me it was. We were supposed to be the same; two halves of a whole. But I didn't feel that connection yet, which is why I hesitated.

I could try to shift. I might even succeed. But then what? I didn't know what I had to do to become human again. Last time I'd been a wolf, I had no memory of it. What if the wolf part of me gained full control and ran back to Wolf Creek?

I couldn't risk it. I had to learn how to do this properly or not at all. Learning how to shift was the only help I'd get while I was here so I had to do it right. Once I mastered it, I was on my own.

My inner wolf seemed to whimper again, defeated. Then I didn't feel her at all.

15

By the time the wolves started returning to human form, I had to make a choice. I could either enjoy the limited time I had here, or I could mope and make myself miserable.

I'd spent too many years being unhappy. I wasn't going to do it anymore. I knew I wouldn't go back to Wolf Creek for anyone or anything. It wasn't worth it. Even if I did want to make Tyler, Julian, and Kyle feel the kind of pain they'd inflicted on me. I wasn't like them. I didn't get off on causing harm. It was better for all of us if I vanished. Besides, Tyler would have to deal with the bond between us his entire life. That was probably a greater punishment than killing him.

Sheila was back in her clothes, her face flushed and her eyes wild. "That was a great run."

"You looked like you were having fun," I said.

"I can't wait till you get to join us," she said.

My chest tightened but I managed a smile. I knew that once I could shift, I was out of here but I didn't need to think about that tonight.

"Drinks?" Sheila asked.

"Hell, yes." I followed her toward a keg and we grabbed a couple of red plastic cups full of beer. It tasted terrible but I didn't think we were drinking it for the flavor. While I'd had a drink on occasion in the past, I'd seen too many examples of what happened when you got drunk to let myself go all in.

We wandered around the bonfire and I met a lot of shifters. Some of them still naked, drinking beer and chatting without any concern. I found myself hoping I'd run into Alec in that state. *Stop it, Lola.* I had to get him out of my head.

As the night wore on, my cup was never empty. I was a little unsteady on my feet, but I had nowhere to be and I'd talked myself into to having some fun. I'd been the responsible one my whole life, why not let go a little?

We were chatting with a group of shifters around our age and Sheila was practically eye fucking one of the females in the group. I wasn't even sure how it happened, but suddenly, they were making out and started to distance themselves from the group.

"You know, I keep asking her out but she just won't bend," a male said.

"She's not into dick," I said, matter-of-factly.

"What about you?" he asked.

I narrowed my eyes, forcing myself to concentrate through the booze induced haze. He was handsome. Tall, like all the male wolf shifters I knew. He was broad shouldered and strong with olive skin and jet-black hair.

"You're checking me out," he said.

"Yes, I am," I agreed.

"I think that means you like dick," he said.

I nodded. "I think that means I do."

He laughed. I vaguely registered that I was giggling. Which

I never did. Was I flirting? Maybe. Maybe I even wanted to make out with this handsome shifter. Didn't I deserve to enjoy myself too?

For a moment, I wondered if it was a good idea. I didn't know him. But I'd honestly never made out with anyone. I was nineteen fucking years old. I should be enjoying myself.

I winced, my brain was rebelling against the conflicting thoughts in my head. It was too difficult to concentrate right now. Besides, giggling was fun. Drinking was fun. This random wolf shifter in front of me was fun.

And he was hot. Yep. I liked dick. "You're hot."

He moved closer to me and set his hand on my back, pulling me up against him. He ran his other hand through my hair. "You are fucking gorgeous. I'm going to do all sorts of things to you."

"You are?" I asked, my mind was foggy but my body was reacting to his touch. His hand was on my ass, squeezing and rubbing. Little ripples of pleasure came from his touch. I wanted it. I needed it.

He lifted my chin and lowered his lips to mine. He tasted like cheap beer and tobacco but I ignored it, too drunk to resist. The kiss was sloppy and wet, but I went along with it. Somewhere in the back of my head, I wasn't sure I should continue, but the thought didn't last long.

His tongue was in my mouth now, and my body felt like it was on fire. There was a part of me that needed the sexual release, but it didn't feel quite right.

When his hand went down the front of my shorts, warning bells rang in my head. I tried to pull away from the kiss, but he pressed his mouth harder against mine. His fingers rubbed against my clit and I panted into the kiss. The touch felt good, but also wrong. Why couldn't I make myself stop this?

As his fingers neared my entrance, I regained some clarity. I didn't want this. He tasted like cigarettes and he wasn't who I wanted to be with. I pushed away, managing to move my mouth away from his enough to get a word out. "Stop."

He pulled his hand out of my pants, then gripped me closer, pushing his lips on to mine again. The pressure was intense, and it was hurting me. I shoved him again, but he held me closer, forcing the kiss on me.

I pulled away again. "Stop!"

"Just give in, baby," he said. "I'm going to make you feel so good."

"I said stop." My mind wasn't fuzzy anymore. I knew I didn't want this.

Growling came from behind me and the man holding me suddenly released his grip.

"The lady said *no.*" Alec looked like he was ready to attack.

I scrambled away, giving distance between me and the male I'd been making out with.

"I didn't know she was yours," he said. "I wouldn't have kissed her if I knew."

"You pack your things and leave now. She said *no.*" Alec growled.

"We were drunk, she was enjoying herself," he said.

"You leave or I will make you leave," Alec said.

The man growled and his hands balled into fists. My chest rose and fell as my breathing quickened. He looked like he was ready to attack.

"This place gives feral wolves a bad name," he hissed. "You might as well be a pack."

"Out," Alec said.

The man growled again but he turned and walked away. I watched until he was out of sight. Only then, did I start to catch my breath. How had I let that happen? What the fuck was wrong with me?

"Are you okay?" Alec asked, his tone gentle.

"I'm sorry," I said. "I shouldn't have."

"This isn't on you," he said. "You told him to stop. This is on him. You are not responsible for that asshole's behavior."

"Is that how feral wolves act?" I asked. "It's what I was told, I'm not going to lie. But it didn't seem like that here. I thought you were different."

"I am different. I mean, we're different. It's not like that here," he said. "I don't allow that kind of behavior."

"How are you not the alpha?" I said. "You run the show here. They listen to you and respect you. You lead better than the alpha I grew up with."

"It's just not how things are done," he said.

"I don't know how to do this," I admitted.

"Do what?" he asked.

"All of it. I don't know how to be normal."

"Never try to be normal. That's what we all ran away from. Where I came from, it was assholes like Lucas who ran the show. Brute strength, preying on the weaker shifters… If that's normal, I don't want any part of it."

"Where are you from?" I asked. "Sheila wouldn't tell me your story."

"Which is why Sheila is one of my best friends. She's fiercely loyal. Though I'm not sure why she left you alone." He frowned.

"She got busy with a brunette," I said.

He hummed.

"Listen, thank you for coming to my rescue. Again. One of these days, I'll be able to actually defend myself." I shook my head. I was so tired of being weak.

"You'll feel better when you learn to shift," he assured me.

"Then what? Then I take my chances again?" I shook my head. "Never mind. It's not your problem. You've done more than enough for me already."

"You're going to be okay," he said. "There's a fighter in there. You just need to give yourself permission to let it out."

"Maybe. But I think I had enough excitement for tonight. If you see Sheila, can you let her know I headed in?" I asked.

"You're going to miss the rest of the fun," he said.

"I think I had enough fun for one night. Sleep well." I didn't wait for a response before walking away from him. I couldn't trust myself not to make any more foolish mistakes.

I dodged party-goers on my walk back, trying to make myself small and less obvious. It was the same tactic I'd used to survive in Wolf Creek. Blend in, follow the rules, play the game.

As I walked into Sheila's tent, I wiped the tears from my cheeks. I wanted things to be different for me. I was so sure I could handle things once I left but nothing turned out the way I expected.

Tomorrow, I was going to see Greta again. I didn't want to be weak anymore. I wanted to connect with my wolf, to gain the power I needed to fight back.

Then, if I ever did have to revisit my past, I'd be ready.

16

SHEILA WASN'T in her bed when I woke the next morning. I figured that meant things went well with her hookup. At least one of us was getting some action.

I cringed at the thought. I could have had some if I wanted it, but I wasn't interested in the pushy male who had his tongue down my throat. Lucas, I think Alec called him.

Tossing the sleeping bag aside, I climbed off the cot and stretched. I was still in the same outfit from yesterday and since I didn't have a change of clothes, this was as good as it was going to get.

My temples throbbed and my tongue was like cotton. The forth cup of beer was probably a mistake. Since I didn't drink often, I wasn't great at holding my liquor.

I ran my fingers through my hair to work out some of the tangles, then slipped on my boots. Hopefully, there was coffee to be found. Then I needed to find Alec before I went to Greta. It felt a little weird with how we'd left things last night and I wanted to assure him that I would respect his decision to send me away. Though, honestly, I was sort of hoping that in the light of day, the news was better and maybe I wouldn't have to rush out of here.

The common area was nearly empty but it was still early. Most of the shifters were probably sleeping off last night's festivities. An elderly couple sat on a bench, a few others were gathered around a fire cooking something that smelled amazing, and some kids were playing tag. It wasn't nearly the bustling chaos of last night but it was nice to see I wasn't the only one awake.

"Lola, right?" A woman who looked to be in her late thirties signaled for me to walk over to her.

She had an espresso pot on a grate over a fire pit so as long as she was willing to share, I wasn't sure I cared how she knew my name.

"Hi, I don't think we've met formally," I said.

"I'm Penny, Megan's mom." She smiled. "Thank you for what you did to help distract my girl. They told me that you got her away so she didn't have to see Justin in that state."

"Megan's a great kid. I'm glad I could help. How is Justin?" I asked.

"He's going to pull through."

I set my hand on my chest, relieved to hear it. "Thank the gods."

"I've never seen anything so scary my whole life," she admitted. "The toxin is scary shit."

My brow furrowed. "Toxin?"

"I thought you were from Wolf Creek?" she looked confused.

"I am, but I don't know what you're talking about," I said.

"I thought everyone in Wolf Creek knew about their tactics."

"I wasn't really part of the crowd, if you know what I mean," I said.

"Well, count your lucky stars you're out of there," she said.

"I do, every day," I said.

The espresso maker started to spit and gurgle. She removed it from the rack and set it on a stone next to the fire pit. "Espresso?"

"I'd love some," I said.

She poured us each a cup and then sat down on a bench. I took the space next to her and breathed in the aroma of fresh brewed espresso. "It smells amazing."

"Nectar of the gods, for certain." She took a sip.

"Can you tell me more about the toxin that was in your partner?" I asked.

"I can't believe you didn't know. But maybe it's just the alpha and his favorites that use it." She shook her head. "Fucking misogynistic assholes." She glanced over at me. "Sorry. I know they were your pack."

"Don't apologize to me. You hit the nail on the head. Fuck the lot of them."

She chuckled. "Alright, then. No love for Wolf Creek."

"None. They never treated me like pack," I admitted.

"You're in the right place, then," she said.

A lump rose in my throat. I thought maybe I was in the right place, but my time was limited. I took a sip of the espresso and reveled in the bitter sweetness as it coated my tongue. It was delicious. "This is perfection."

"It really is," she agreed. "You're a good fit here. Nobody would know you're from Wolf Creek."

"Thanks," I said, not really sure what else to say.

"You should know that of all the packs, Wolf Creek is seen

as the worst. They're violent, controlling, and carry a big stick. A really big stick."

"They were that way with those of us who lived there too," I said. "Is the toxin the stick?"

She nodded. "It's one of a kind. Nobody else has the recipe, though gods-know nobody else would want to use such a terrible weapon."

"What does it do?" I asked.

"It takes our ability to shift, and with it, our ability to heal. While it's in our bloodstream, we're essentially human. We have all of their weaknesses and none of our usual shifter strength," she said.

My lips parted and I stared at her in disbelief for a moment. That was my life. Everything I'd ever known was the pain of being human. But as far as I knew, nobody else in my pack experienced that aside from my mom. How could they have had something like this and never told us?

"How is it applied?" I asked.

"They use a dart, shoot it at their victim," she said. "Most of the time the shifter doesn't survive."

"That's awful." I wouldn't wish that on anyone. Okay, that's not true. Something like that would be very fitting for certain people I'd left behind in Wolf Creek.

"How do you cure it?" I asked.

"You don't," she said. "You have to wait for it to leave your system and hope that you can heal from the wounds they give you before you die. That's the part that makes it so terrible. They use it first, then they attack and leave you to bleed to death."

"Only Wolf Creek has this?" I asked.

She nodded. "When it was invented, the high councils all

tried to get the recipe and destroy it but the inventor fled. Wolf Creek welcomed him with open arms."

"Sounds like something Wolf Creek would do." My throat felt tight. How could such a horrible thing exist? Of course Ace would use it against other wolves.

I tensed. "What happened to Justin? Why did they use that on him?"

She shrugged. "That's the part I can't figure out. He was just going to trade for supplies with the High Key Pack. They knew he was coming, and they claimed they had nothing to do with it. I don't know why he was attacked."

I swallowed hard. If someone from Wolf Creek had attacked a feral shifter, did that mean they knew I was here? Were they waiting for me or were they right outside town, waiting to attack us all? This had to be what Alec was talking about.

"Thank you for the coffee," I said, setting the unfinished cup down. I had to find Alec and figure out what was going on.

I walked away from the common area, toward the woods, hoping I was following the correct route. Squirrels darted in front of me, running when they heard me approach. Birds called warnings to each other, but other than that, the woods were silent.

It was still early enough that a chill hung in the air and dewdrops clung to the pine needles. I rubbed my arms with my hands to get some warmth. The deeper I walked into the woods, the cooler and darker it got. I wasn't sure I was going in the right direction, but I had to find Alec. This couldn't wait. There were far too many questions circling my mind.

Growing up, we'd been taught that the Wolf Creek Pack

was powerful. A favorite pack of the wolf shifter king, a model pack, blah blah blah. It got old fast. All the crowing about how excellent we were while keeping strangers out and never allowing us to explore the rest of the world.

I'd grown up so isolated in my pack, that I no longer knew what was true and what had been hidden from me. Why didn't I know about a toxin that could prevent a wolf from shifting? Was that something the others knew about? Or was it only Ace and his crew?

It was odd that there was a toxin that existed that could cause the exact problem I had. If not for the fact that you had to be shot with it, I might have worried it was used against me. But why bother with me? I wasn't important enough for them to care about. Plus, there was that whole mated to the alpha's son thing.

I stopped walking as a strange sensation washed over me. Longing, desire... there was a tiny part of me thinking about Tyler.

Fuck no.

I pushed the thought aside and continued on my quest to find Alec's cabin. Tyler definitely would have known about that toxin and he never did anything to try to leave Wolf Creek or stand up to his dad. He likely enjoyed using it against others. Nobody with the sadistic streak like Tyler's should have access to a weapon of that kind.

After a while, I realized I'd likely gone the wrong way. I should have found the cabin by now. Or at least the lake. *Shit.* I abandoned a perfectly good cup of coffee for nothing.

Carefully, I turned around and tried to follow my tracks back to camp. After what was probably thirty minutes of walking, I realized I was totally lost.

Now what? I had no landmarks to go by and there was no path out here. Knowing my luck, I'd probably wandered on to the High Key Pack's land. I wasn't sure if shouting for help would benefit me or get me killed.

This was totally on brand for me. Why couldn't I be good at something I could actually apply to real life experiences? Calculus wasn't going to help me out here.

I had to be the worst wolf shifter in the history of the world. Sure, I couldn't reach my wolf, but you'd think I'd have some sense of direction or at least self-preservation.

Discouraged, I sat down on a fallen log to collect myself. "Well, Lola, you really did it this time. Great work."

"You know, they say you're only crazy when you talk to yourself, if someone answers back," Alec said as he emerged through the trees.

I jumped from my seat. "Where did you come from?"

"My house." He pointed behind him.

I groaned and slapped myself in the forehead. I could just make out the outline of his home through the trees. I was right there, circling his fucking house and missing it.

"We can not leave you alone, can we?" he asked.

"I would have found it eventually," I said.

"What is this now, three times I've saved your ass?" He tapped thoughtfully on his chin.

I rolled my eyes. "You didn't save me. I was fine."

"I've heard that from you before," he said.

"Look, I came to find you because I heard about Justin and the toxin," I said. "Is that what you were going to tell me about yesterday?"

"Yes, but I wasn't certain it was related to you. I'm still not sure if it was bad luck, or if they know you're here," he said.

"If I stay here, I'm putting your whole pack at risk," I said.

"Community, but yes," he said.

"You're a pack and you know it," I said.

He shrugged. "I'm not an alpha."

"Whatever. None of that matters. What does matter is that I don't want anything bad to happen to the people here. None of them deserve that."

"I agree," he said.

"I have to leave," I said, the realization falling on me like a ton of bricks. It had been one wonderful day of pretending I might have found a place I belonged. But that was all it was, pretend.

"You need to learn how to shift or you don't stand a chance," he said.

"I can't put these people in danger." I'd only been here a short time, but even I could tell the shifters who lived here didn't deserve to be attacked by my old pack.

"Leave that to me," he said. "You find Greta. Figure your shit out."

"You have a good thing going on here," I said. "I don't want anyone to get hurt because of me."

"You like it here, don't you?"

"Sure," I replied. "Nobody is slamming my head against a wall or breaking my ribs."

"They really did that to you?" he asked.

"It doesn't matter. Like you said, I need to learn how to shift." I stood. "I'm going to talk to Greta."

"There might be another way out of this," he said.

"What do you mean?" I asked.

"We could break that bond you have with your mate," he suggested.

"You mean I could kill him?" I clarified.

"You can't, he's your mate. But I could," he said.

I shook my head. "I can't ask you to do that for me."

"Can't or won't?" He narrowed his eyes. "Have you forgotten what he did? Or is the bond taking hold?"

"No!" I recoiled, taking a step away from Alec. I had a lingering memory of wishing Tyler dead, but now I couldn't make myself want that for him. "Is there another way to break the bond?"

"Yes. But you'd have to go back to Wolf Creek." His eyes were locked on mine. He was deadly serious.

"You know that's a death sentence for me," I said.

"Not if we're smart. You need to get close to him, but not that close," he said.

"I don't want to go near him. What if..." I couldn't finish the thought.

"What if you start to feel things for him?" Alec asked. "That's going to happen no matter what. The longer you fight the bond, the more it will build. I wager you weren't keen on keeping him alive when he left you for dead. Now, you're a simpering mess."

"I am not a simpering mess," I said through gritted teeth.

He smirked. "Maybe not yet, but you will be."

We stood there for a moment as I considered his words. The more time passed, the more I would want Tyler. It didn't seem possible, but mating bonds were magic we couldn't fight. The thought of having actual desires for Tyler made me feel nauseous. At least I still had some control.

"What would I have to do to break it?" I asked.

"Well, I could kill him for you," he offered.

"No," I said, far too quickly. "What's the other way?"

"It won't come cheap," he said.

"What do you mean?" I asked.

"If you want my help, it's going to cost you," he said.

"I don't have anything," I said. "You know that."

"Your mother does," he said.

"What?" How would he know my mother and what could she possibly have that he would want. "My mom has nothing. She lives in a trailer and is probably starving to death since I'm no longer there to bring her groceries."

"Your family hasn't always lived in Wolf Creek," he said.

"When did you become the expert on my family?"

"The wolf who fled with the toxin was cursed by witches. They wanted to teach him a lesson, hoped he would learn how terrible it felt to be a shifter who was stripped of his ability to shift."

It felt like the wind was knocked from my lungs as the meaning of his words hit me. "It's not possible."

"Everyone outside Wolf Creek knows the story of your family's betrayal." He shook his head. "I wasn't sure if it was true until I met you. It all lines up. You're from Wolf Creek, your family was cursed. If there's any record of your grandfather's work, it's probably with your mother."

I glared at him. "You knew all this the first night we met and you said nothing."

"I had to be sure I could trust you. What if you were sent here to spy on us?"

I felt foolish for letting him in, but his comment about trust made up for it. Alec wasn't one to trust easily so the statement meant a lot. But that didn't mean it made what he was asking any better.

"You want the toxin," I said.

He nodded. "I think there might be some notes or information with your mother. If you can get me that, I'll help you break the mating bond."

"What do you need it for?" I didn't want to see more of that weapon out in the world. It was bad enough that Wolf Creek had access to it.

"That's my business. This is the deal, take it or leave it," he said.

I thought about my last night in Wolf Creek. My mom stayed in her room while Julian threatened me. She never told me about my family history or why we couldn't shift. The whole town treated me like shit despite the fact that they were profiting off my grandfather's invention.

Then images of Tyler flooded my mind. The disappointment on his face at the full moon ceremony, the flash of hatred in his eyes when he looked at me, his hands around my throat in the bathroom. All those images flashed through me in a heartbeat, then the memory of our kiss forced its way to the surface. My cheeks felt hot and I found myself longing to feel his touch.

It took far too much willpower to send the vision away and recall why I hated Tyler. Alec was right. The longer I waited, the worse it was going to get. I had to end the bond between us.

"It's a deal," I said. "I'll get what I can. You help me break the bond. And if we can't break it fast enough, I want you to kill him."

My heart was racing, elated at the thought of breaking my ties to Wolf Creek. There was nothing for me there once Tyler was gone. My mom had left me years ago. The mating bond was the only thing standing in my way.

Alec lifted a brow and the corner of his lips turned up in a vicious grin. "There's that killer instinct I knew was in there somewhere. I think this means you're officially feral. I'll make the arrangements. We'll leave by the next full moon. You have two weeks."

17

My head was pounding by the time Alec left me at Greta's tent. I think I mumbled a thank you before he left, but with the hangover in full force, it was difficult to remember.

"Is it bright out there or did you have too much to drink last night?" Greta said by way of greeting as she opened her tent flap.

"Both," I admitted.

She chuckled. "Come on in, I have something to fix that."

I followed her into her tent and sat down in a chair next to her little table. She busied herself pouring something into a cup, then walked over to me.

"It tastes like death, but it'll knock the hangover out." She set a glass of brown liquid down in front of me.

I picked up the cup. "Cheers." After a hesitant sip, I nearly spit the liquid across the room. "You were not kidding."

She sat in the chair across from me. "It's easier if you do it all at once."

After a steadying breath, I knocked the drink back,

fighting my gag reflex as I swallowed it all. Wincing, I set the glass on the table. "What was that?"

"You really don't want to know," she said.

I smacked my lips, trying to get rid of the taste. "Gross."

"It works, though," she said.

Already, the headache was easing. "Wow."

She grabbed the glass and stood, then walked over to the corner of her tent. When she returned, she had a bottle of water and a box of cookies.

"You've got your own little stash in here, don't you?" I asked.

"There's perks to being the oldest and wisest shifter here. People bring you things." She slid the box of cookies closer to me. "Have some carbs and some water. You'll be right as rain in a few minutes."

I followed her instructions, eager to wash the taste of the hangover concoction out of my mouth. She sat quietly watching me eat for a few minutes. Three cookies later, the taste was finally gone. I took a long drink of the water, then set the bottle down. "Thank you."

"I was young once," she said. "I could hold my liquor, though. You're going to have to work on that."

I laughed. "Aren't you supposed to tell me to not drink?"

"Where's the fun in that?" she said with a grin.

"I can see why people bring you cookies," I said.

"I also really love strawberries if you ever feel the need to suck up to me."

"I'll keep that in mind." I made a mental note to try to send her some once I left. Was that even possible? Could you mail things here? Maybe I could come visit.

"I imagine you didn't just come for a hangover cure," she said.

"I'm here about my wolf," I said.

She hummed. "Yes, it is time for you to connect. You've felt the stir?"

I nodded.

"Then my work here is done," she said. "If you can feel the wolf, there's little I can do."

"You're kidding, right?" I stared at her, my eyes wide.

"Your wolf wants out and you need to let her out. You have to get in touch with yourself and what you want. She's not going to emerge unless you allow her to," she said.

"But how do I do that? I want to learn how to shift. I want to connect with my wolf." It was more important than ever now to learn how to shift. I needed to be able to tap into the strength the wolf could give me. Along with my wolf came the ability to see in the dark, healing, increased ability to sense danger, even feel other's emotions. It would give me a major advantage to being able to keep myself alive.

"You need to stop holding back and fighting against the things you want," she said. "Discipline is important, but when you deny yourself everything you want, your wolf feels that. There has to be balance. Time to work, time to play. It can't all be focus all the time. When you shut down your intuition and desires, you also close off your wolf."

"I don't do that. I let myself have fun. How do you think I ended up with a hangover?" I asked.

"A few drinks and early to bed isn't fun," she said.

I pressed my lips together. I was being judged by a grandmother for not staying out all night to party. "I had an incident with a shifter that made me reconsider."

"I heard," she said. "You're big news around here. Lots of folks were waiting for a reason to send Lucas away. They're grateful to you for standing up to him and showing his true colors."

I didn't feel like I'd really stood up to him. Alec had been the one who dealt the final blow. "So I was supposed to stay out after that?"

"You can do whatever you feel compelled to do, but you have to ask yourself, what is it that you want? What drove you to that situation last night?"

"I don't know. I thought you were supposed to make out with random people to have fun." Even as I said it, it sounded stupid.

She gave me a dubious look. "You did not."

"Fine. I wanted to make out with someone. He was a poor choice."

"We're getting warmer," she said. "You wanted something but you didn't go after your heart's desire. You went for a backup. That's never good. We shouldn't constantly deny ourselves what we truly want. I get the sense that your whole life has been denial."

I wasn't enjoying where this conversation was going. I had spent my whole life doing what I needed to blend in, to survive. My plan was to leave Wolf Creek, go to college, and get a job. All my choices were based on being able to take care of myself. I planned to blend in and pretend to be human forever. In all my thoughts about the future, I never considered what I'd want if I had choices. I just assumed I didn't. "I'm not even sure I know what I want."

"You have some thinking to do, then," she said.

"Yeah, I guess I do," I said.

Greta stood. "I'd suggest finding somewhere quiet to think. What is it that you want? How can you show your wolf that you're not going to hold everything back?"

I looked up at her. "I don't know where to begin."

"Try having some hard conversations with yourself. You might need to discover who you are outside of Wolf Creek. Who is Lola? What do you love to do? Where do you want to go? How do you want to live? We might get a longer life than humans, but our time here is limited. We shouldn't waste it."

Realizing that I'd never once made a decision based on what I wanted was a tough pill to swallow. Greta was right, I didn't even know who I was. I'd chosen to find a city to run to so there was more crowd to blend in with, but I didn't even know if I wanted to live a life like that. I was good at math, but I pushed myself to get away from Tyler, who spent his time in art classes. Every choice I made was based on what would keep me safe.

Shit. Who was I?

I stood, feeling numb. "I think I'll go for a walk."

"Come see me tomorrow, tell me what you've learned," Greta said.

"Okay." I wasn't really paying attention to her as I left the tent. When I'd decided to get help with releasing my wolf, I thought for sure there would be some exercises, guidance, maybe even some magic or something. I didn't think it would be all up to me.

The common area was packed now, folks sticking to the seating in the shady areas near the trees. The sun was blinding and it was warm enough that I needed to roll up my sleeves.

The thought of simply spending my time trying to connect with myself was terrifying. There wasn't an itinerary for that. No rules, no schedule, no plans. How was I going to manage that?

Learning about Wolf Creek through the eyes of the feral shifters taught me there was so much I didn't know. What else was I missing about the world? When I was preparing to leave, I figured I had the skills I needed. Instead, I found out most of what I learned was a lie.

I spent the next hour walking around the makeshift town, taking in the sights of shifters at work or play. One shifter was working on fixing up a car. I stopped to watch him working with the tools under the hood. He was sweating and covered in grease, but he looked determined and seemed to be enjoying the work. I moved on and paid close attention to the tasks all the shifters were completing. Someone was working on a painting, another shifter was knitting while watching a couple of kids play.

All of them looked at ease and comfortable. They had hobbies and seemed content. The problem was that every time I tried to picture myself doing the things they were doing, I cringed internally. I had no interest in knitting or painting or even fixing a car. Though, I did like the idea of having a car so I could come and go as I pleased.

A familiar laugh grabbed my attention and I turned to see Sheila walking hand in hand with the female from last night. She noticed me and waved, then changed direction to walk over to where I was.

I headed over to meet her. "Looks like you two had a good night."

"It was a great night, wasn't it, Anja?" Sheila pulled Anja

closer to her and I noticed a crimson tint on both their cheeks.

"Okay, so you two are adorable and don't make me jealous at all," I said.

"So she didn't hook up with Alec," Anja said.

I scoffed. "Sheila! I told you that was not going to happen."

Sheila shrugged. "You just keep fighting it."

Nope. No way. I was not going to let Sheila's taunting get to me after everything Greta just told me. Figuring out my shit had nothing to do with Alec. Was he hot as fuck? Yes. Was I attracted to him? Yes. But I wasn't interested in a one-night-stand with him or anyone else.

"Did you see Greta yet?" Sheila asked.

"Yes. I have to figure out what I want out of life, I guess." My shoulders slumped. "Does anyone know what they want out of life when they're nineteen?"

"I do," Anja said.

"You do?" I lifted my eyebrows.

"I'm not going to stay here forever," she said. "I needed a place to recover and get my head together. In the fall, I'll head to the city and I'm going to audition for the Ballet Company."

Anja did have the tall, slender build of a ballerina. "Were you a dancer before you came here?"

"I was, but it wasn't my choice. I got burned out and thought it was dancing I hated. Turns out, I hated having controlling parents who forced me into it while never allowing a break," she said. "Did you know the first time I ever had a cupcake was when I arrived here? Even my diet was monitored to the very last crumb."

"That sounds awful," I said.

"I know dancing professionally won't be easy. I have the discipline and the drive, but it needs to be mine," she said.

"I get that." It was as if Greta had freaking planned this conversation. Good for Anja, she had a plan. What the fuck was mine?

"If you ever get the opportunity to hook up with a dancer…" Sheila said.

Anja elbowed her in the side. "Hey."

Sheila laughed. "I'm sorry but it's true."

"What about you?" I asked.

"I'm good here," Sheila said. "I get to help protect people like me who have nowhere else to go. But I'm twenty, so maybe that's why I have my shit together."

I smiled. "I thought I had my shit together."

"You know what helped me the most?" Anja asked.

"What?"

"Living. Not obsessing or thinking or worrying. Just living. Maybe you need to do something fun, take your mind off things," she suggested. "When I arrived here, it was the first time in my life I didn't have every minute of my day planned. I did whatever I felt compelled to do. The rest seemed to work itself out in the background while I was busy enjoying my life."

"I'm not great at doing nothing," I admitted.

"So find something to fix or help with," Sheila offered.

"Alright, I will." I turned and headed toward the male who was fixing the car.

"Good luck," Sheila called after me.

"Can I help you with that?" I asked.

An older male with gray hair and a lined face looked up

from the hood of the car. "You want to help me fix my car? You a mechanic or something?"

"Not at all. I want to learn. And I need a distraction, if I'm being honest," I said.

He narrowed his eyes and stared at me for a moment. Then he handed me a wrench. "Alright. Might as well put you to work."

18

WORD GOT out fast that I was looking to find ways to keep busy. I found myself helping weed garden beds and chase kids around. I read books to a blind shifter, learned how to cook chili in a huge pot, and told ghost stories around a campfire.

Best of all, I finally found my sense of direction. I could make it to the lake and back by myself and managed to keep my bearings all over camp. A few times, I found myself at Alec's door, but he was never home. Nobody seemed to know where he was, but any time I asked, he was simply, *away*. It was probably better that way. While I wanted to ask him for more details about his plan to help break my mating bond, it wasn't going to solve my wolf problem.

The days bled into night and I'd collapse on my cot, exhausted. My mind didn't race, I didn't worry, I didn't overthink anything. I was too tired to wonder.

It made the time fly, but it didn't help me get any closer to figuring out what I wanted or drive any connection with my wolf.

"Knock, knock," I said as I pulled the tent flap open.

Greta greeted me with a warm smile. “Any updates for me today?”

“I haven’t shifted if that’s what you’re asking,” I said. “It’s been a week, Greta. Nothing is changing.”

“I’m going to tell you the same thing I told you yesterday, you have to give it time. Your wolf doesn’t trust you yet.”

“I don’t have time.” I hadn’t told Greta the specifics of my conversation with Alec, but I got the sense that she understood. I still wasn’t sure of it myself. First, I thought I was going to have to leave. Then, I found out we might be able to break the bond, but I didn’t know what that meant for me. Either way, I knew my best chance at survival was to have the ability to shift. At the very least, I needed enough control over my wolf to know she wouldn’t break free while I was around humans.

The wolf shifter council didn’t do much to govern the packs. There was a king, and a whole system that I never cared to learn about. The only thing that stuck was that if you shift in front of humans, you’re going to draw attention. And not the good kind.

“There has to be something I’m missing,” I said.

“You’re still not letting go,” she said.

“Sure I am. For the last week, I’ve had no schedule and no plans. I’ve helped people and spent time wandering and I’ve swam in the lake and I’ve stayed up late drinking and having fun. I’m doing whatever I feel like doing and it’s not changing anything,” I said.

“There’s got to be something you’re missing,” she said. “Your wolf knows you’re holding back.”

“Without leaving here, I can’t do much else,” I said.

“What about your mate?” Greta asked.

"What about him?" I snapped. She'd never brought up Tyler before and I'd never asked her about him. Aside from Sheila, Alec, and Malcom, nobody knew that I had fled a mating bond. At least I didn't think so. I'd told people I'd left due to being mistreated and the reputation of Wolf Creek was bad enough that they didn't question me.

"Have you let yourself consider what it means to walk away from a bond like that?" she asked.

"No. And I'm not going to waste any time thinking about Tyler," I said. "He's dead to me."

Something stirred inside me. A sensation I hadn't felt in a while. I couldn't explain it, but I knew my wolf was reacting. *You have got to be fucking kidding me.*

Greta lifted a curious brow. It was as if she knew exactly what I was feeling.

"Before you say anything, please don't," I said. "If it comes down to me staying human forever or me having to be with that asshole, I'm choosing myself."

My wolf seemed to whimper. *So now you want to come out and play.*

"He tried to kill me. Multiple times, I might add. Sure, he usually stopped short of full-on murder, but what kind of sick fuck throws around their mate like that?" I asked. "Not to mention the fact that he literally left me to die. So while he might not have dealt the final blow, he set it up for me to end up dead while he celebrated my demise. He's a sick fuck."

"I'm not saying you need to be with him or that you should want him at all. I'm saying you need to process the trauma you've been through." She stood and walked over to me, then took my hand in hers. "Maybe you can't move on with what you want because you haven't let yourself heal. Your wolf is the primal part of you that thrives on instinct. You have to give your wolf time to adjust to losing a mate, even if you know it was for the best."

"I can't think about my past," I said. "I can't."

"You might have to," she said.

Feeling defeated, I left Greta's tent. I wasn't ready to unpack years of trauma, yet when I thought about Tyler, I'd felt my wolf for the first time in a week. *You know why I hate him*. I found myself talking to her as if she was someone else. It felt a little crazy, but it also made me feel better.

We deserve better. I could sense her inside me, vibrating. The energy almost felt like she was pacing. As if she was waking and restless after being shut indoors for too long. *Welcome back. Are you ready to try working with me?*

She didn't respond, of course, because I was the one who controlled her. Or at least I would eventually. *I need you to work with me. We're in this together, you know.*

"You look deep in thought," Malcom said, breaking me from my musings.

"Do you ever talk to your wolf?" I asked without preamble.

"Well, hello to you too," he said with a grin.

"Sorry. Hi." I had seen Malcom a few times in passing during the last week, but he was gone nearly as much as Alec. "Were you out with Alec?"

"Yes, I was," he said. "And to answer your previous question, yes, I do talk to my wolf. Sometimes I swear he talks back."

"Well, I feel less crazy, now," I said.

"That's got to be good, right?" Malcom said. "If your wolf is responding to you, I bet you're closer."

"Shhh." I pulled Malcom aside. "I don't want everyone to know."

His brow furrowed. "You really think they don't know?"

"Have you been telling people about my problem?" I asked.

"No, it's not my story to tell," he said. "But if you think they haven't noticed that you haven't shifted in front of anyone, you're mistaken."

"There hasn't been a full moon yet. Lots of shifters go a month between shifts," I said.

"Yeah, when they're thirteen," he said. "This isn't Wolf Creek. We shift as nature intended out here."

"I've only been here a week," I pointed out.

"Listen, even if they've figured it out, have you noticed that nobody cares?" he said. "Why do you think they would? We're all here for a reason."

"Because of my family." The truth of what my grandfather did had weighed heavily on me for the last week. It was painful to realize I was related to someone who created something so terrible.

"Look around you, Lola. Most of us are here because we don't fit in with our families. We left them and chose new families. We aren't our parents or our grandparents. We make our own choices," he said.

"Why are you here?" I asked.

His jaw tightened and his nostrils flared. "I'm not in the mood to talk about myself."

"Okay, I can respect that," I said. "Is Alec back, too?"

Malcom nodded. "He is."

"Where were you guys? He's been gone all week," I said.

"Do you remember what I said to you in Sheila's tent?" Malcom asked.

I nodded. "Sure, but Alec's been nothing but nice to me." He did want me to steal information about a dangerous shifter toxin from my own family, but nobody's perfect, right?

"I know he's working on something with you, but please, reconsider before you go anywhere alone with him."

"Why?" I asked.

Malcom's expression was difficult to read. It was as if he was struggling to get the information out. "I'm not sure, but I've got a bad feeling. Something's going on and I'm not sure I'd want to be there when it goes down."

Alec probably hadn't told Malcom that we were planning to break my mating bond. I wondered if he was being sneaky about it to keep anyone from finding out the real reason I was here. Breaking a bond wasn't seen as a good thing where I came from. It was viewed as a violation of the sacred goddess's will. It rarely happened. "I think I'll be okay. But thank you for the warning."

Malcom grabbed my hand and gave it a squeeze. I was a little surprised at his touch. We weren't close, and it didn't feel intimate, but there was compassion and concern in the gesture.

"Be careful, okay?" He released my hand.

"I will, thanks." I excused myself and headed back to my tent. Between my wolf making an appearance and Malcom's warnings, I could use a few minutes alone to clear my head.

19

When I stepped into my tent, I discovered I wasn't alone. Alec stood when I entered. "How's the soul searching going?"

"I wasn't under the impression that Greta was sharing the process with you," I said.

"There's not a whole lot that happens here that I don't know about," he said.

"Then you already know the answer to your question."

"True. Which is why I thought I'd see if I could help," he offered.

"Where have you been all week?" I asked. "I could have used the help."

"I'm afraid I had to deal with some things away from camp," he said.

"Any of it having to do with me?"

"Yes," he said. "Your pack is out hunting you. We can't wait until the full moon. We'll have to go while they're weaker."

"When?" I asked.

"We'll go tomorrow."

My heart raced. I wasn't ready. I couldn't shift and I wasn't mentally prepared to face them. "I can't."

"You have no choice," he said. "If we play this right, you won't even have to see him if that's what you're worried about."

"How do we do it?" I asked. "Break the bond, I mean."

"I have a plan, you're going to have to trust me," he said.

It wasn't the first time he'd asked me to trust him. He still hadn't earned my trust. Not fully, anyway. Though, he had saved my life and he was trying to help me. "You still want me to look for that information?"

He nodded.

"What if I can't find anything?" I asked.

"You will." He sounded totally confident.

"You aren't going to tell me what you're doing with it, are you?" I asked.

"I can't," he said "It's too risky. Nobody knows about this. I'm already involving you more than I should. I'm trusting that you won't tell anyone about this."

Flutters filled my chest. Did it really matter what he was doing with the information? Wolf Creek already had the toxin in their possession. How much worse could I make things? The rage I felt when I left was creeping back in and to my surprise, my wolf wasn't fighting me.

Tyler's face flashed in my memory and I felt my wolf stir. But this time, she wasn't bringing a sense of guilt with her. I swore I could feel her anger magnifying my own.

Yes. Now you understand why we have to do this. I had to break free of Tyler's grip and of my past. I couldn't hold on to Wolf Creek. I needed to let it all go.

That's when I realized I'd been asking the wrong questions.

"I have to be honest, I don't want that toxin being used against innocent people. It shouldn't exist. You and I both know that."

He took a step toward me. "I want to tell you, I do. But if you know, you're going to be in far too deep."

"I don't want to know everything. But I want you to answer one question for me."

"Go ahead," he said.

"Will you be moving against Wolf Creek?" I balled my hands into fists, all the hatred I'd been harboring when I was tossed in the cave came flooding into me. It was familiar and comforting. Where had that all gone? Had it all been my wolf keeping it away? Or was I fighting it? Taking the easy way out again.

I had a score to settle and I was tired of running from my past. My wolf felt like she was running circles inside me. We were finally on the same page.

Greta was right, I had to let myself go there. I had blocked out the anger and rage. I'd told myself it was better to never return but that wasn't what was going to drive me forward.

Alec smirked. "When I have that recipe, I intend to make all of them pay."

It was exactly what I wanted to hear. Something snapped inside me and I leaned into it, letting instinct take over.

I wanted to make Wolf Creek pay for what they did to me. I also wanted Alec. And I was done playing it safe. Done staying hidden and following the path of least resistance. I wanted to feel alive and enjoy life.

Before I could let myself overthink things, I moved

toward Alec and threw my arms over his shoulders, moving one of my hands to the back of his head. I rose to my toes. He lowered his face to mine and our lips met like an explosion.

Our kiss was all passion and hunger. All this time, I'd needed this release. I'd felt the attraction linking us since we met. It had been there the whole time, simmering between us. His lips moved in perfect time with mine, the pressure intense. I needed this. I needed him. My body knew how to respond, urging me forward. Our tongues met and I matched him stroke for stroke.

When he pulled away for a moment, disappointment flared, only to be quelled by his teeth on my lower lip. I moaned as he sucked and nibbled, sending shivers all the way to my core.

Suddenly, he stopped and set his hands on my face, his gorgeous eyes locked on mine. "If we keep going, I'm not going to want to stop."

"I don't want you to stop," I said.

"Are you sure?" His eyes were heavy with lust, his breathing rapid. I could almost feel how desperately he wanted this. It matched my own desires.

"I want you," I said. "All of you."

His mouth claimed mine again and I pressed into him, our bodies glued together, closer than I'd ever been to another person. I couldn't get enough of him. I needed more.

Large hands slipped under my tee, sliding around to my bare back, up to my neck. He tangled his fingers into my hair, urging me even closer to him, deepening the kiss.

My whole body felt like it was on fire. My skin tingled and everywhere his fingers touched I felt a heightened sensation.

I'd never felt pleasure like this. Not even from my own fingers on my clit.

The thought drove me wild. I'd explored my own body but never had a partner to help. I didn't want this to end as a make-out session. I was ready to feel a man inside me. I wanted all of him.

Not taking my lips from Alec's, I found the button of his jeans and worked them open. He growled and pulled away from the kiss.

Surprised, I jumped back, panting as desire still coursed through me. "What's wrong?"

"I can't be the only one naked," he said. "If my clothes are coming off, so are yours."

I bit down on my lower lip, my eyes dropping to watch as he stepped out of his jeans. I'd seen him naked before, but that was when he was about to shift. It was different when he was getting naked just for me.

He was fully erect and I swallowed hard when I took in the sight of his length. For a moment, I wondered if I'd made a mistake in my choice for my first time. It might have been easier to go with someone smaller. Or at least average sized. Alec was neither of those things.

"My eyes are up here," he teased.

I looked back up and realized he'd already removed his shirt. A fully naked, gorgeous wolf shifter was standing in front of me and I wanted to soak him all in. "You know exactly how hot you are, don't you?"

"I've been told before," he said.

"I'm sure you have."

"But I've never been told by someone as beautiful as you,"

he said. "How long are you going to keep me waiting? It seems wrong that I'm the only one who's naked."

"Give me a second. I'm enjoying the view," I said.

He charged me and scooped me up, throwing me over his shoulder. When he moved forward, he kicked over the lantern on the floor and the room went dark. Neither of us seemed to care. It was just light enough for me to make out his shape, but I couldn't see details. Not that the details were needed for what we had planned next. I squealed and laughed as he dropped me onto my cot. It bounced and groaned at the impact.

"Is this thing going to hold us?" I asked.

"Why don't we find out?" He unbuttoned my shorts. I lifted my hips so he could pull them down. Then I sat up and pulled my tee over my head.

"Fuck, you're gorgeous." His eyes traveled up and down my body and to my surprise, I didn't feel self-conscious. It wasn't light enough for him to see everything, but he was getting an eyeful.

Where I grew up, I always worried about how I looked or what I was wearing. Mostly, because I didn't want to draw attention to myself. I rarely did anything to make myself look pretty. I didn't wear clothes that showed off my body and kept my hair simple. My whole life, I had the sense that I was meant to hide so if anyone noticed me, I would shut down, find a way to flee.

With Alec, I didn't need to do that. He made me feel like it was safe to be who I was. And I had to admit, it was nice to have someone tell you that you're beautiful.

"Are you going to kiss me or are you just going to stare at me?" I demanded playfully.

Alec growled again as he pounced on top of me. The cot shuddered and collapsed, sending us both tumbling to the ground. We rolled over and I was now on top of him.

"Guess it won't hold both of us," he mused.

I laughed. "You owe me a new cot."

"I have a real bed in my place and I could probably make some room for one more," he said.

"Was that a sleepover invitation?" I asked.

"Maybe," he said.

"You don't even know if the sex is good yet," I warned.

"The company is," he said.

My heart fucking melted right there. I was so in trouble with this one. Alec was all the things I thought I never wanted. I'd spent my whole life avoiding the alpha-types. In a million years, I never would have guessed I'd lose my virginity to one of them.

I leaned down and kissed him, gently this time. He returned the motion with soft, tender kisses. Then he grabbed hold of me and turned so I was under him.

Breaking the kiss, he began to move his lips lower. He kissed my jaw and my neck before moving to my breasts.

When his tongue found my sensitive nipples, I gasped in surprise. He knew exactly how to make my body respond. Just as I was appreciating the feel of his lips and tongue, his hand moved to my inner thigh. Gently pressing on my leg, he parted them, and his finger began to work my clit.

My eyes rolled into the back of my head as the sensations came together in unison. Breathing faster, my hips lifted and lowered as he increased speed and pressure, driving me closer to orgasm. It didn't take long before a wave of pleasure rolled through me and I cried out as climax crashed around me.

But he didn't stop there. Slowly, he inserted a finger inside me and I tensed, my eyes widening. I knew this was where we were going, this was what I wanted, but this was new.

He stopped, removing the finger. "You okay?"

"Don't stop," I said.

With a grin, he slid the finger back inside me, and he moved his head lower, until he was positioned between my legs. I knew what he was doing, of course, I'd heard lots of conversations about sex, but I had no idea what to expect.

Then his tongue flicked over my clit and I suddenly understood all the hype. "Holy shit."

He added another finger inside me as he continued to suck and lick my clit. I winced as he stretched me, but I adjusted surprisingly quickly and the moment of discomfort gave way to increased pleasure.

"Oh my gods," I gasped.

I gripped the sleeping bag on the floor under me, squeezing the fabric between my hands as the pressure built. I'd never felt anything like this. My hips were moving in time to his motions, my back arched, I was panting, struggling to get a full breath as the pleasure built. Finally, I couldn't take it anymore and an explosion of sensation coursed through me. "Fuck!"

Alec stopped what he was doing and looked up at me with a self-satisfied expression.

Sweaty and shaky, I smiled. "You have a gift."

"That was just the appetizer," he said.

"I don't know how you'll top that," I challenged.

He climbed on top of me, settling his hips between my thighs. Nervous flutters swirled in the pit of my stomach.

I gripped his muscular back and stared into his eyes. He

looked different somehow. He wasn't the same in here with me as he was when we were around the rest of the pack. It was as if I was seeing another side of him. Or all of him.

Alec brushed some hair off my forehead. "You are so fucking beautiful. That asshole made the biggest mistake of his life when he sent you away."

My stomach tightened. "I really don't want to talk about him right now."

He leaned down and pressed his lips to mine. I welcomed the distraction, Alec's kiss sending away all thoughts of anyone else. He grounded me, kept me here, in the present, making me feel more alive than I had in my whole life.

I could feel his cock at my entrance, he moved slowly, pressing little by little. I dug my fingernails into his back and deepened the kiss to distract myself.

Suddenly, he was inside me. I gasped, and winced through the discomfort, breaking the kiss. I closed my eyes, taking steadying breaths.

Alec caressed my face. "Why didn't you tell me?"

I opened my eyes. "I didn't want you to stop."

He was looking at me as if I was fragile.

"And I didn't want you to look at me like that."

"Is this okay?" he asked.

I smiled and nodded, then moved my hand to his cheek. "I'm glad it's you."

He kissed me softly and began to move slowly inside me. For the first few thrusts, I started to question what the big deal was. The foreplay had been better than this. It was slightly uncomfortable, but with each thrust it was getting easier. While the pain subsided, there wasn't any pleasure. A little disappointed, I wondered why anyone went this far.

Oral sex might be the best thing ever. Or maybe I was doing it wrong.

Alec adjusted and lifted my legs, making my hips turn upward and I gasped in surprise. "Oh my god."

He grinned. "That's better, isn't it?" He thrust again, slowly.

My breath hitched. *So this is what I was missing*. "That feels amazing."

He picked up the pace and I started to moan, my body taking over, each thrust sending me closer to climax. *Holy shit*, I was wrong. This was better than foreplay.

"Lola, come for me," he said.

The words sent a shiver through me and I found myself reacting. The building orgasm exploded and I cried out. He continued thrusting and wave after wave rolled through me, one climax rolling into the next like ripples on water.

Alec grunted as he came, his body shaking for a moment before he stilled. I hadn't realized my eyes were closed. I opened them and looked up at him. He wore a lazy smile on his lips. "What did I tell you? It got better, right?"

"I might need to try it again before I can make a decision," I teased.

He chuckled, then leaned down and kissed my forehead. "We better get dressed before Sheila finds us."

That's when Sheila walked in. She turned on a lantern next to her cot before turning to face us. I let out a little yelp of surprise and quickly covered myself with the shirt I was holding.

20

SHEILA LOOKED AT ME, then over at Alec. Then her eyes found the broken cot.

"I knew it!" Sheila said.

"Fine, yes, you were right. Can we get a couple of minutes?" I asked.

"This is my tent," she teased.

"Please," I said.

"Fine, I'll wait outside," she said dramatically. "Next time put a sock on the door or something."

"Is that even possible on a tent flap?" I asked.

"Alec does live alone, just saying," she said on her way out.

I looked over at Alec and the two of us burst into laughter. "I guess we weren't fast enough."

"What did she mean by that?" Alec asked. "When she said she knew it?"

I rolled my eyes. "She's been saying the two of us should hook up for a while."

"She's smart," he said.

I pulled my shirt over my head. “She’s pretty great.” When I poked my head out of my shirt, Alec was glaring at me.

I looked around. There was nobody else in the tent. That look was aimed at me. “What’s wrong?”

His eyes moved down to my still naked hips. “Were you going to tell me?”

I looked down and caught sight of the mark. “Fuck. I forgot about that.”

“This is why they’re after you, isn’t it?” he asked. “You’re marked as an alpha. How could you not tell us? You put all of us at risk.”

“No,” I said. “It’s not like that. I didn’t even know this mark was here until after I arrived.”

“I can’t believe how foolish I was,” he said. “You can probably shift, too, can’t you.”

“Are you kidding me right now? You think I’ve been lying to you?” I couldn’t believe what he was saying. How could he think I’d do that to him? “Why would I do that? How would that benefit me?”

“If you show up in Wolf Creek with that mark, they have to hand the pack over to you. Is that why they wanted you dead? To keep you from taking over?”

“You’re not listening to me. I didn’t even know until I got here,” I said “And I can’t shift. No pack would have me as their alpha even if that’s what I wanted, which I don’t. You believe me, don’t you?”

He leaned down and grabbed his jeans, then pulled them on.

“Alec, talk to me. You have to tell me you believe me,” I said.

“Okay,” he said, his voice tense. “I believe you.”

He said the words, but it was clear he wasn't being honest.

"Don't do this to me," I said.

He turned and grabbed his shirt from off the floor. In the dim light of the lantern, I could make out a familiar mark above his right shoulder blade. The same crescent moon surrounded by a circle. The mark I wore on my hip. The mark of an alpha.

"Are you fucking kidding me?"

He stood up and turned to face me.

I walked over to him and shoved him. "You have the mark of the alpha. You, who refuses to claim the title and lead these people. How can you judge me?"

"I might have the mark, but I have no pack to lead. Your pack is still alive. You don't know me. You don't know anything about me." His expression was dark, his tone angry.

I stepped back, my chest tightening as anger and fear mixed. "I don't know anything about you because you won't tell me. I've been nothing but honest with you since we met."

He pulled his shirt over his head. "I was the last of my pack. The only survivor of a massacre. When the mark showed up, it was the fates way of reminding me of all I lost. My family, my mate, my home… It was all taken from me by your pack."

"They're not my pack," I said through gritted teeth.

"They are and you are supposed to be a leader and you walked away," he said. "If you gave a damn, you'd step up and be the leader you were marked to be."

"I'm sure that would go over well. The cursed girl who can't shift wants to step up and take over as leader of the people who spent years abusing her. You have no idea what I've been through."

"You can change that," he said. "You don't have to give up."

"Don't you dare lecture me," I said. "You have a pack right here that you refuse to step up and protect."

"I do everything for these shifters. I lead them," he said.

"You deny them and yourself of true family by refusing to form a pack," I said. "You know what you're risking by keeping them feral."

I knew that not everything I learned was accurate, but I had been taught the importance of pack. It strengthened shifters to have that bond with others. It also gave them legitimacy in the eyes of our king. Packs could ask for resources, they could find allies in other packs, and they could grow and thrive. Staying feral kept Alec's community weaker. If they were a pack, they'd probably have the funds for homes and schools and infrastructure. Instead, they live in tents.

"Don't lecture me on pack," he said.

"Get out of my tent," I said.

To my surprise, he didn't argue. When he walked out the door, I thought I'd be happy to see him leave. Instead, I fell to the ground, my whole body shaking. I took deep breaths, trying to calm myself.

How had everything gone so impossibly wrong so quickly?

"Hey, you okay?" Sheila asked.

I looked up to see her standing in the doorway. "You heard all that, didn't you?"

"Do you really have the mark?" she asked.

I nodded.

"Look, try not to take it personally. Alec lost everything. He struggles with the idea of pack because he thinks he's cursed or some shit. I think he feels like if he was in a pack, he'd lose it all again," she said.

"Then why give a shit about what I do with my pack?" I asked.

"You have a pack. They suck ass and they should probably all die a fiery, explosive death, but they're alive." She sat down on the ground next to me. "Give him a little time. I think he was surprised."

"He was surprised? Imagine how I feel." I shook my head. "I didn't ask for this."

"I know what you mean." She touched her scar.

"I'm sorry," I said. "I didn't mean to be insensitive."

"You weren't. You're fine." She stood. "I know what we need."

"About a gallon of tequila?" I asked.

She laughed. "Come on. I have just the thing to help us clear our minds."

Curious, I followed her out of the tent. We hurried past the common area and ducked into the woods. My heart beat faster as we approached Alec's house but thankfully, we didn't slow down.

When we reached the lake, Sheila started to take off her shoes. "The kids will be gone any minute and we'll have the whole place to ourselves."

She sat down on the sand and leaned her head back, her eyes closed. "Isn't the sun marvelous today?"

I didn't see how this was going to make me feel better, but I joined her. Closing my eyes, I leaned my head back. The warmth of the sun did feel amazing on my skin.

"You know, Alec is my best friend. But he can be a real dick sometimes," she said. "But he'll stick to his word. Whatever you two have planned, he'll follow through. Even if things don't work out romantically."

I wasn't sure how to respond to that. I still wanted that bond broken, but I wasn't sure I was ready to face Alec.

The sky was streaked with pink and the heat of the day made the cold lake water feel blissful. I'd let Sheila talk me into a swim and we'd spent the last ten minutes floating in the water. It was dinner time for most people and the kids playing at shore had run off shortly after we arrived.

It was peaceful and calm. I was starting to understand why Sheila was so happy here. It was a good place to at least figure out where you wanted to go next as Anja had mentioned. I wasn't sure what my next steps would be. Especially after the way Alec and I left things.

I didn't want to talk to him, but I had to know what was going on. The unknown about our next steps with the plan were getting to me. Would we still be going to remove my mating bond? Or had he decided he no longer wanted to help me at all?

I turned so my legs touched the bottom of the lake. We were in chest deep water, my head barely above the surface. "We should probably head back now. I need to find Alec and figure out if I still have plans for tomorrow."

The last thing I wanted to do was talk to him again, but the need to break the bond and get even the slightest revenge on Wolf Creek was pulsing through me. I had to follow through with this. Returning home and facing my past, instead of running, was important. I was starting to wonder if it was exactly the step I needed to finally connect with my inner wolf.

"Your return to Wolf Creek?" she asked.

I opened and closed my mouth a few times, not sure how to respond. Alec had made it clear he didn't want me to tell anyone about me looking for information about the toxin, but I wasn't sure what he'd told people.

"I know what's going on," she said. "Alec doesn't keep much from me."

"You were here all week while he was out doing who knows what," I said.

"Someone has to stick around here sometimes when he's out. Especially if we've got trackers from Wolf Creek on the prowl," she said.

I scrunched up my face, guilt making me feel like shit for bringing threats anywhere near this blissful community. While I was confident my old pack knew nothing about the mark, Tyler and I had that bond intact. I winced at the memory of kissing him before I was tossed in the cave. I'd wanted him to miss me, but I hadn't wanted him to come looking for me. Why didn't I think of that possibility?

"Don't worry," she said. "Alec has a plan to take care of it. It's all going to be fine."

"You really trust him, don't you?" I asked.

"He takes care of his friends," she said. "Come on, let's head back."

A weight settled in the pit of my stomach. I wasn't sure where I stood with him in that regard. We were friends? After what just went down, I had no idea. The part that bothered me the most was that I wasn't quite sure what I was hoping for. I wasn't great with relationships. I'd never had an actual friend before let alone a lover. While I was pissed at how he'd reacted, I had no idea where to go from here.

We swam to shore and shook off the water as best as we could before slipping back into our clothes. My shorts and tee were soaked, making my shirt completely transparent. I guess a perk of going back to my mom's trailer was that I could pack a bag of clothes. I'd lost my best clothes wherever I'd dropped my bag, but I would give just about anything for some clean underwear.

Our walk back took us past Alec's place. I paused, wondering if he was there right now. All the windows were dark and I figured there was a good chance he wasn't there so I continued on. Sheila either didn't notice my distraction, or she kept quiet.

I was shivering by the time we reached the common area. "Any chance you have another shirt that might fit me?"

"I got you," she said.

Sheila turned on a lantern when we reached her tent. My heart sank when I saw that the cot was back to normal. Alec had either had it fixed or found a replacement. Was that his attempt at an apology or was he simply fulfilling his role as the leader of the feral shifters?

"You'll want to get some sleep tonight," Sheila said. "I don't know all the details, but I think tomorrow will be a big day for you."

"If it's still happening," I said.

"You had a fight. It happens. But we never let disagreements take us away from our plans. We have to be careful out here to survive," she said.

I swallowed down the guilt again. I shouldn't be here. I'd put them all at risk. Alec knew it from the beginning, yet he let me stay. I should have taken my chances walking to town and found a job. Stuck to my plan. Moved on with my life as a human. My wolf seemed to growl at the notion.

I sighed. *I'm not going to go back to the old plan.* I couldn't now that I'd started to wake my wolf. I had to break the bond with Tyler and learn to shift. Once I passed off the information about the toxin, I could rest easier knowing that Wolf Creek would get the punishment it deserved.

I finished buttoning up the plaid shirt I'd borrowed. It was nice to have something with long sleeves again as the evening grew colder. "What exactly do you know about my return to Wolf Creek? Because Alec has been minimal on the details with me."

"That sounds right. He never really tells me the plan until it's time to go. I do know he got a car so you don't have to hike back there," she offered.

"That's good news." I hadn't even considered that part of it. A days-long walk with Alec might have been something I'd enjoyed not long ago. Sleeping under the stars, cooking over an open fire, sharing a single sleeping bag…

I shook the thoughts away. That wasn't going to happen and this trip wasn't a romantic tryst. Driving meant a few hours there and back and then hopefully, I could put this all behind me. Once it was finished, I'd either stay here and avoid Alec, or I'd move on to somewhere new.

My wolf felt restless. *Same, girl.* I hated the lack of information. Was it possible that Alec was out in the common area? Most evenings, it was the place to be. The shifters here shared meals and stayed up until the fires died. Sometimes they'd shift and run in the woods. Sometimes they played cards or sat and talked. Whatever was going on tonight, there was a good chance Alec would be there. If we were heading out tomorrow, he wasn't going to leave camp tonight. I wasn't sure how to handle talking to him, but I knew the longer I waited, the worse I was going to feel. "You think there's some food left from dinner?"

"Good call," Sheila said as she finished getting dressed. "I'm starving."

We headed out into the dark. In the distance, I saw a few tiki torches and some solar lights that were used in front of various shifter tents. It was an eclectic place with a variety of different styles all coming together.

The common area was still hopping and I could smell burgers cooking on a grill. "Follow the smoke."

Sheila laughed. "That smells amazing."

Mario, my new friend who had been fixing up the car, was grilling burgers on his camp sized propane grill. He waved when he saw me. "Hungry?"

"You always have the best food." It was true. He was by far one of the best cooks in the camp. Possibly one of the best cooks I'd ever known.

His wife, Paula, beckoned us to the picnic table near their tent. We sat down and joined the couple for burgers and tomato salad and watermelon slices. It was like summer on a plate.

Now that I wasn't soaking wet, and I had food in my stomach, I was handling my emotions a little better. I should have expected something like that from Alec. He could deny it all he wanted, but he was an alpha through and through. His outburst was exactly why I wanted to shield myself from males like him. I didn't need him. Sure, the sex had been amazing, but I had nothing to compare it to. For all I knew all sex was that great. I could find someone else. It wasn't like the two of us were heading to relationship status anyway.

So why did my stomach do somersaults when I noticed him walking toward us?

As he got closer, I realized the expression on his face was grim. Something was wrong. He stopped at our table.

"Hey, pull up a chair. There's plenty of food," Mario said.

"Thanks, but I'm not hungry." He looked down at me. "We need to talk."

21

"I'M EATING," I said.

The mood at the table around me shifted. It was like I could feel the tension in the air and I was pretty sure my companions were holding their breath.

"This can't wait," he said.

"It's going to have to wait," I countered.

He growled.

"Lola..." Sheila elbowed me.

"Unless someone is dying, I am going to finish my dinner." I wanted to speak to Alec, but his actions weren't giving me confidence that he was going to react any better to me than he had earlier.

I took a bite of my hamburger. After my last experience leaving Wolf Creek and going without food for several days, I wasn't about to waste a good meal.

To my surprise, Alec sat down on the bench next to Sheila. Tension hung thick in the air but I went back to my dinner, pretending I wasn't bothered by him.

"I'm sorry," Alec said.

All heads turned to him, then I felt their eyes on me. My cheeks burned. "You're sorry?"

"I had no right," he said.

I wasn't expecting an apology. Sure, I sort of hoped he'd see how much of a dick he'd been, but I didn't think he'd admit to it. Let alone do it in front of other people.

"Thank you," I said.

"Are we okay?" he asked.

"Yeah." I wasn't sure that was true, but I wasn't in a place to work through my emotions right now.

He nodded, then rose from the table. "I'll come by tomorrow morning. You should get some sleep tonight."

"Alright," I said.

Without another word, Alec left us sitting there in silence. I looked down at my food but my appetite was long gone. *Dammit, Alec*. He ruined a perfectly good hamburger.

"Who wants pie?" Mario asked, breaking the long silence.

"I definitely want pie and if she's not having any, I'll take hers," Sheila said.

"Pie sounds great." I forced myself to eat the rest of my food, knowing it was going to be a long day tomorrow. I wasn't sure if breakfast was part of our preparation for breaking into my old home and eliminating a mating bond.

I managed to participate in casual conversation, but my head and heart weren't in it. As soon as it was socially acceptable to say goodnight, I excused myself from the group.

Tomorrow I was going to return home. It felt surreal to consider voluntarily going back to Wolf Creek. Greta had been clear, though. I had to face my past and figure out what I really wanted. I think going back was the only way I could move forward.

The worst part of the whole thing was that I had to trust Alec. I had no clue as to how we were going to get in and out undetected. He'd mentioned that I needed to be close to Tyler, but I didn't know what that meant. At least he'd be there with me.

Despite everything with Alec, he had stood up and helped me every time I needed it. Things were different between us now, and while I wasn't sure what was coming next, I supposed I did trust that he would help keep me safe.

If only I had managed to figure out how to shift before going back. I'd feel a little better if I could be more on par with the strength of the others. Alec was going to have to be enough.

I knew I needed to sleep, but I was still awake when Sheila crept into the tent. I kept my eyes closed and pretended I was asleep. Soon, I heard her slow breathing.

Crickets chirped and a breeze rustled the canvas sides of the tent. The calming sounds of the night should have lulled me to sleep, but I was far too restless.

Finally giving up on sleep, I sat up and pulled my boots on. Maybe a short walk and some fresh air would help.

The common area was empty and the moon was a sliver giving very little light. I'd never seen darkness like this. Wolf Creek wasn't a large town, but there were always lights on somewhere. Streetlights, signs on shops, even windows in people's homes. Someone was always awake whenever I went out, no matter the hour. Crossing my arms over my chest against the cold, I kept walking.

I was pretty sure I was the only one awake right now. My heart ached and my throat felt a little tight. I'd been lonely my whole life. When I was younger, I was desperate to belong. I wanted friends just like anyone else. As I got older, I convinced myself I was better off without them. Spending a week here might have made everything worse. I had a brief shining moment of feeling like I fit in. I was welcomed here. Nobody treated me like I was contagious or pushed me around just for existing.

My feet had carried me to the woods and I hesitated as I stared into the darkness of the trees. Without the sun, it was pitch black in there. While my sense of direction had improved, it probably wasn't a great idea to try to navigate in the dark.

I turned and took a few steps before I heard a twig snap. Heart racing, I turned around, half expecting to see a bear or some other bloodthirsty creature.

"It's just me," Alec said.

"What are you doing out here?" My eyes widened when I realized he was naked. "Without clothes?"

"I went for a run," he said. "Couldn't sleep."

"Naked?"

"I shifted," he said.

"Of course you did." I felt like an idiot.

"Can't sleep?" he asked.

"It's hard when I have no idea what to expect tomorrow," I said harshly.

"I was going to talk to you about that earlier tonight, but I got the sense you didn't want to see my face," he said.

"I didn't. I did. I mean, I don't know what I wanted," I said.

"Look, about the mark, I didn't expect to see it."

"The part that bothers me is the fact that you think I'd lie to you about it," I admitted. "You and your friends saved my life. I know the risk you took bringing me here. I wouldn't disrespect you that way. I don't want anyone getting hurt because of me."

"I know," he said.

"You have to know that I'd rather take my chances in the woods alone than bring harm to anyone here. If I knew they were after me, if I knew about the toxin…" I sighed. There wasn't much I could change now.

"Tomorrow, we'll drive to the edge of Wolf Creek and hike in. You said your mom lives in the trailer park, right?"

"Yeah," I agreed.

"While you go there to retrieve whatever you can find, I'll prepare what we need to break the bond. Is there a place we can meet that has strong community ties but isn't too crowded?" he asked.

"There's an old barn on the south end of town. They have most of the ceremonies there, but it's not used during the day," I said.

"Good, we'll meet there once you find what you need," he said.

"How do we do it?" I asked. "Break the bond, I mean."

"Greta gave me some tips, things we can try while you're closer to him." He moved closer to me and I held my breath. I could see him better out of the shadows of the trees. Even in the darkness, seeing him naked sent a wave of lust through me. I still wanted him.

"Okay," I said. "I'm trusting you with this."

"I know," he said.

"After the bond is broken, do you think they'll stop coming after me?" I asked.

"Yes," he said.

"Good." I was too afraid to ask about what would come

next. Would I be welcome back here? Would Alec and I ever get beyond this awkwardness between us? Part of me was still confused while the rest of me was ready to jump on him right here.

"I should go." I couldn't trust myself to stay any longer. There was too much at stake tomorrow. Once we did what needed done, I would figure out what was going on with Alec.

"Try to get some sleep, Lola," he said.

"You too." I turned and walked back to Sheila's tent without looking back.

22

"LOLA, IT'S TIME TO GO."

My eyes fluttered open to see Alec standing over me. My heart started racing and I was excited to see him. Then I remembered why he was here and all of yesterday came crashing in around me.

"Shh, Sheila's still sleeping," he warned.

I wasn't sure how long I'd slept or what time it was, but this trip down memory lane wasn't going to be any easier no matter when I went or how rested I was.

Tossing the sleeping bag aside, I sat and tugged on my boots. Then I followed Alec to the front of the tent. I paused at the door, glancing behind me at Sheila. My stomach tightened and I suddenly wished I'd said goodbye last night, just in case.

For some reason, I had a sinking feeling I might not be returning here. I wasn't as set on running anymore, but I knew I couldn't put Sheila, Mario, Megan, and all the others I'd met at risk. If it was too dangerous for me to return, I'd find somewhere else to go.

With lingering sadness, I exited the tent. Hopefully, we'd cross paths again if I wasn't able to return. I tried not to focus on the what-ifs, or even the aftermath of my actions. To do this, I needed a clear head and focus. As Greta pointed out, I had to try to live in the present and follow my feelings and intentions.

The wolf part of me was pure instinct. She'd saved me when I was on death's door. I was going to need her today more than ever.

"You ready?" Alec asked.

He was wearing jeans, a black tee, and black combat boots. He'd fit right in with the Wolf Creek crowd.

"I thought you might want this." He held out a baseball cap. "Your hair is pretty distinctive."

"Thanks." I accepted the hat and pulled it on. It didn't cover the long hair that hung down my back, but I could tuck it into the cap when we arrived.

"Mario is lending us his car," he said. "I think you made quite the impression on him. He never lets anyone borrow it."

"Well, not to brag, I did help rebuild the transmission."

"If we break down, you're going to have to fix it. You definitely know more about cars than I do," he said.

"How about we plan not to break down?" I suggested.

"Even better." He started walking toward Mario's tent and I followed him.

Mario and Paula weren't around. In fact, we were the only people walking around the camp. It was a little after sunrise, early, but not early enough that I thought we'd be alone. It didn't matter. It was probably easier this way. Saying goodbye would make it harder for me to stay away if things went south.

Soon, we were on a dirt road, driving through the trees. "I didn't know this was here."

"The road isn't on any maps," Alec said. "It's also the only way in or out of our camp."

"So, is this officially feral land? Or are you all a bunch of squatters?" I asked.

"Greta actually owns it all. Five-hundred acres. We're bordered by the High Key Pack and the National Forest. Then, it's the Wolf Creek Pack on the other side."

"Wait, so this is Greta's land but she gave you the cabin?" I was surprised she wouldn't take it for herself.

"She likes her tent. I tried to object, but it sat empty for a few years so I finally caved and moved in."

"Where exactly are we?" I felt foolish asking. Especially because I should have been more concerned sooner. "Geographically, I mean."

"We're on the border between Washington and Oregon. Where our tents are set up is technically Oregon, I think. But I've never cared much about human borders. The shifter borders are more relevant to us."

"So this whole time, Wolf Creek has been a short drive away." I knew I couldn't have gotten far after I fled, but it made my skin crawl thinking about how close they'd been this whole time.

"About a hundred miles. Easy enough by car, not as easy by foot, wolf or human," he said.

"Lots of pack members in Wolf Creek have cars. They came and went as they pleased. But not me. Not anyone under nineteen. We were trapped." As I said the words, I realized there was already a major flaw in our plan.

"You can't get in," I said. "The border keeps outsiders out. You're not pack. You can't cross."

"I can with you," he said.

"You sure?" I asked.

"You'll have to hold my hand as we pass through, but your connection will get me in fine."

I'd never thought about returning here, let alone bringing a visitor so I honestly never asked. It made sense that there was a work around.

We drove in silence for a while and Alec turned from the dirt road onto a narrow, paved road. It was a beautiful day. The sun was shining, the trees around us were bright green and the sky was a brilliant blue. Under different circumstances, this would be a fun way to pass the time. If only we were headed somewhere else. Fuck. Anywhere else would be better.

I watched out the window as Alec took us onto larger roads, and through a few smaller twisty roads. I had no idea where we were going and I stopped trying to pay attention to the route. With my terrible sense of direction, I'd need to take this exact trip several times before it sunk in.

When we stopped, panic gripped me. How could we already be at Wolf Creek's border?

"You know what to do, right?" Alec asked as he killed the engine.

It seemed impossible now that I was facing it. "What if I really can't find anything for you?"

"I trust you," he said. "If there's nothing there, I'll still help you."

I narrowed my eyes. "Is this because we had sex?"

"It's because you're my friend," he said.

My breath hitched. An actual friend wasn't a big deal to most people, but I'd never had anyone who would claim to be my friend. Not one person my entire life. "I'll do my best."

He opened his door and took a final deep breath before exiting the car. I walked around to where he was standing at the edge of the road. I could feel something in the air. It was unnatural, like a current. I wasn't sure if it was my imagination or if the air in front of me was shimmering.

"The border," I said, without thinking.

"That's it." He held out his hand. "Should we test this theory out, then?"

I reached for him and he clasped his hand around mine, making me feel small. It was warm and comforting. "You'll be there when I'm done, waiting for me?"

"I'll find the barn, and then I'm not going anywhere until you're with me," he said.

"Let's do this." I took a step forward and he walked with me. My shoes crunched over pinecones and I dodged branches as we went deeper into the woods that surrounded my old home.

A rush of something cold seeped through me, all the way to my bones. It made me gasp, then it was gone as quickly as it came.

"We're through." Alec released my hand.

"Can you find your way around or do you get lost at home too?" he asked with a grin.

"Once I see something familiar, I'll be fine. Right now, I have no idea where we are."

We continued forward and I caught glimpses of grass through the trees. We were nearing the end of the woods and emerged right into the field by the barn. "Well, well. Looks like step one for you is easy," I said.

"I take it this is the barn?" Alec asked. "It's not much. I expected a structure that was still in one piece."

The barn had never been in great shape, but in the short time I'd been away, it had fallen into more disrepair. The entire roof had collapsed and only two of the four walls were standing. "Something must have happened."

"Or it was built poorly," Alec offered.

"Maybe," I said.

My hands were shaking. I forced myself to calm down. There was nothing to be concerned about. I could get through town like a ghost. Nobody expected I'd return here and nobody was looking for me.

I shoved my long red hair under the ball cap, then turned to Alec. "You can wait near the barn. If anyone comes by, you could always duck inside."

"Oh, I see, you're hoping I die while you're away," he teased.

"You'll be fine," I said. "I doubt that cabin of yours is a whole lot more stable."

"Don't tell Greta that. She helped build that place," he said.

Somehow, that didn't surprise me.

"How long do you think you need?" he asked. "So I know when to come looking for you."

"Don't come looking for me. I'll be fine. Give me two hours. Three tops," I said.

"Good luck," he said.

23

The trailer park was about two miles from the barn. The route was familiar, something I'd done a hundred times or more. A life spent avoiding others had taught me all the less traveled paths and given me an edge at staying invisible.

I kept my head down and walked past homes and stores. I knew enough to act like I belonged without making eye contact. My fifth-grade teacher walked past me on the street. My pulse raced, worried she'd stop me and say hello. She didn't even acknowledge me.

Soon, I was out of the shopping area and cutting through neighborhoods and parks. In the distance, I could make out the trailer park that had been my home my whole life.

Some of the residents were outside this morning. Ethan McIntyre, a regular of my mom's, was sitting in a blue plastic kiddie pool with a can of beer in hand. I wrinkled my nose. How my mom was willing to even let him in her bedroom, let alone between her legs was a mystery to me.

A dog barked and ran toward me, only to be pulled back by a chain. *Fuck*. My heart was racing and I felt like a criminal.

Sure, I was after something that didn't belong to me. That was if it even existed. But I was sneaking into my own house. It wasn't like my mom would give a shit if I took anything. She'd likely not even notice that I stopped in.

Finally, I arrived at the shitty trailer I'd grown up in. Rust covered the exterior and the places that still had paint were chipped and peeling. Everything about it was even worse than I remembered. What was with this place? How was it that it all got even more run down in the week I was away?

Deciding it didn't matter how I entered, I went for the front door. It was less noisy and my mom would probably think it was a visitor. I figured I could be down the hall and in my old bedroom before she got to the living room to check.

Carefully, I turned the door handle and pushed the aluminum door open. It creaked a little, but nothing like the back door had last time I'd used it.

I stepped inside and froze. I wasn't alone.

"I told you never to come back." My mom was sitting in a chair in the living room. She blew a cloud of smoke from her lips.

"I'm not staying."

"I don't have any money if that's what you're after," she said.

My jaw tensed. "Real nice, Ma. Like I don't know that you don't have any money."

"What do you want from me?" she asked.

"What happened to you?" I couldn't help it, I had to say something. "You were a good mom once. You cared for me. Unless I imagined all of that."

"I did the best I could," she said.

"No, you didn't. You gave up. You had a child to take care

of and you quit. You quit on yourself and you quit on me." I was louder than I meant to be, but I was furious. All these years, I'd held back my resentment. Living with her might have been worse than living on my own. Yet, I couldn't run from Wolf Creek. I'd been a prisoner here with a mom who didn't give a damn about me.

"You have no idea the hell I've been through. You're alive and you were out of here. That's all I wanted for you. I wanted you to have a better life than I did. A chance at starting over. I told you to leave. You can't even do that right." She took a drag on her cigarette.

"You want to help me?" I demanded. "Fine. Here's your chance. I need whatever was left behind by my grandfather."

She coughed, choking on the smoke she'd just inhaled. After catching her breath, she smothered her cigarette in the ash tray. "What are you talking about?'

"I know, Mom," I said. "I know what he did and why he was cursed. All the things you hid from me. I also know his curse was his alone. Not yours, not mine. I could shift if I didn't have it in my head that I couldn't."

She pursed her lips and didn't deny a damn thing.

"You knew?" I'd never felt so betrayed in my life. "How could you?"

"It was better this way," she said. "If you shifted, you'd draw attention to yourself."

"I drew attention to myself by not shifting. Did you not notice my black eyes? The broken ribs? The bruises I came home with every day from school? How was that better? What the fuck were you protecting me from?" I demanded.

"You think you know pain but you don't know what I spared you from."

"Then tell me," I said.

"If you shifted, it was a matter of time before your father found out about you," she said.

"So what?" I cried.

"He can't know about you," she said.

"You said he didn't know you were pregnant. How would he even find me?" I asked.

"He'd find you," she said.

Rage bubbled inside me. I clenched my fists in frustration. We were getting nowhere with this and I was wasting my time. "Are you going to give me any actual information I can use?"

"About your father? No."

"Then we're done here. If you care about me at all, I need whatever you have about the toxin. Then I'm gone for good," I said.

She reached for her box of cigarettes and pulled one out. Her hands were shaking as she lit it.

I wanted to feel sorry for her, and there was a tiny part that did. She was my mother after all, but she hadn't protected me the way a mother should.

She took a long drag, then blew out the smoke slowly. I winced and turned away from the cloud. She knew I hated it but I wasn't going to give her the satisfaction of knowing she was getting to me.

"You sure you know what you're doing?" she asked. "That information is worth millions."

"Then why didn't you sell it?" I asked.

"I know you think little of me, but even I have standards," she said. "That toxin is the most dangerous thing ever created for wolf shifters. In the wrong hands, it's been used to wipe out entire packs."

"Funny how you worry about other shifters when you couldn't give a damn about the one shifter you gave birth to," I snapped.

She stood. "It's okay if you hate me. I made my choice and I can live with it. Now, it's time for you to decide if you can live with yours."

She walked over to the ratty couch that nobody ever sat on and started pulling cushions up and tossed them on the floor. There was a bed inside, folded up. She tugged on the handle and opened up the mattress.

I expected to see something on the bed, but other than a mattress covered in questionable stains it was empty. This was just a wild goose chase. "Are you stalling for some reason?"

"You think I'd turn you in to those assholes who call themselves leaders? I'm not a traitor, Lola," she said.

I wasn't so sure about that. She'd kept the fact that I could shift from me my whole life.

She held the cigarette between her lips and walked to the kitchen, returning back to the couch with a large knife.

"Do you need help?" I asked.

She glared at me, then shoved the knife into the side of the mattress. Dragging the knife through the fabric, she tore a huge hole in the side.

After tossing the knife on the ground, she shoved her hand inside the destroyed bed. A moment later, she emerged with a leather-bound journal.

She took another drag on her cigarette as she walked over to me, the book held out.

"This is it?" I asked as I took the book from her.

"That's all I got. Whatever you're doing with it, I hope it's worth it," she said. "You should go. Whole town's been warned to keep an eye out for you. Something about you being a traitor to the pack." She looked down at the book. "They catch you with that, they'll have all the evidence they need to kill you on sight."

I slid the journal in the waistband of my shorts, then covered it with the back of my shirt. "Thank you."

"Good luck, Lola," she said.

There were a million things I wanted to say to my mom, but none of them would come out right. I ended up nodding, then made my way to the door. I wasn't willing to spend another second here. The sooner I broke that mating bond, the sooner I could get on with my life.

24

My mind was racing as I took the long way back to the barn to avoid running into anyone. I was wanted in my hometown, despite the fact that I wasn't the one who tried to kill anyone.

Fucking figured.

The book I was carrying might be worth millions, but at this point, I didn't care about anything other than Wolf Creek getting what was coming to them. They already had the recipe for the toxin, but they were the only pack with that knowledge. I knew it was an awful drug, but maybe it wouldn't be such a bad thing if the playing field was leveled.

I arrived at the clearing much faster than I expected. Grateful for no run-ins with locals on my walk, I crept around, searching for Alec. He wasn't outside where I'd left him, but at least I didn't see any signs of anyone else. He must have taken his chances inside the broken down barn. I wondered if someone had come by here.

For a moment, I worried that he'd been caught and I picked up the pace, jogging over to the barn. I walked around the dilapidated building, peeking into the holes in the walls. “Alec?” I whispered as loud as I dared.

After a full circle around the barn, I didn’t see any signs of people. “Alec?” I called his name a little louder.

Where was he?

“Over here,” he called.

I let out a relived breath when I saw him walking toward me. He was coming from the direction of the woods. It probably was a safer place to hide than the crumbling building.

“Did you get it?” he asked.

I pulled the journal out of my waistband. “She warned me a few times about how dangerous this is.”

“Your mom saw you?” he asked.

“I didn’t tell her anything,” I assured him. “I just asked for the book.”

“And she handed it over, just like that?” He sounded surprised.

“Look, do you want this or not? It wasn’t a pleasant meeting with my mom and I’d rather not relive it right now when we have more important things to do.”

“You’re right.” He took the book from me. “Thank you for doing this.”

He slid the book into his own waistband and covered it with his shirt.

“What’s next? How do we break the bond?” I asked.

I noticed movement and looked toward the woods. Four figures were walking toward us. “Oh, shit. They know we’re here.”

I grabbed Alec’s hand and pulled, trying to run in the opposite direction but Alec held me fast.

“What are you doing? We have to run,” I said.

Alec tightened his grip, holding me in place.

"Alec?"

I looked behind him and could make out Ace, Tyler, Kyle, and Julian. They were nearly on us and if I had any shot at getting away, I had to go now.

I pulled, trying to break Alec's grip, but he was far stronger than me. "Let me go, Alec."

"I'm sorry, Lola." He pulled me toward him and wrapped both his arms around my chest. I was facing away from him, pinned against him.

"Alec, what are you doing? Let me go, now!" I fought against him, trying to break his hold on me. He didn't budge. I tried kicking, but I wasn't at the right angle to hit anything.

Desperate to get free, I dug my fingernails into his arms. He grunted, but didn't release his grip.

Ace, Tyler, Julian, and Kyle stopped in front of us. Each of them wearing matching victorious smiles.

"Alec, let me fucking go." I stomped on his foot as hard as I could.

"Fuck, that hurts!" Alec squeezed me into him tighter. "Stop moving. You're going to make things worse."

"Please, Alec," I pleaded. None of my usual tricks to get away were working with him. Alec was much stronger than any of my old bullies.

Ace threw a paper sack at Alec's feet and it tipped to the ground, revealing stacks of hundred dollar bills. "I think you'll find it's all accounted for."

"What are you going to do with her?" Alec asked.

"That's not your concern," Ace said.

"Alec?" I looked over at the man I'd thought was my friend. "How could you?"

"It's nothing personal," Alec said. "I did what I had to."

"How can you possibly say this isn't personal?" I growled, the sound coming from somewhere beyond my control.

"Hand her over," Tyler said. "We gave you your money."

"I am not going anywhere with you," I hissed.

"You don't have a choice," he said.

"Be grateful for him, darling," Ace said. "I could have killed you in that tent where you were sleeping, but Tyler wanted you back alive."

"You were there?" I looked at Alec. "They were there and you didn't tell me?"

My heart felt like it shattered into a million pieces. How long had he been planning this? "You are such an asshole."

How does someone have sex with the person they're preparing to betray? At least Tyler was always up front about his hatred of me. Alec made me feel safe, earned my trust, then took it all away.

Tyler walked closer to us and I lashed out, trying like hell to break Alec's hold on me. "Let me go, you piece of shit!"

"Hold her still," Tyler said.

"What are you doing?" Alec asked.

"Your job was to deliver the merchandise, not ask questions," Tyler said.

Something sharp bit into my arm and I hissed in pain, then everything went fuzzy. I swayed and my knees gave way.

"What did you do to her?" Alec asked.

"She's not your problem anymore," Tyler said.

I fought to keep my eyes open but my body was giving way to whatever Tyler had injected in me. My head lolled to the side and my jaw went slack. Eyelids heavy, I finally gave in and let them close.

* * *

My tongue felt like sandpaper and my head throbbed. I opened my eyes and tried to sit up, but my legs and arms were bound. The floor below me was soft and as my eyes adjusted, I realized I was laying on a bed. My limbs tied to the headboard and footboard.

There was minimal light coming in through what looked like thick curtains. It was likely day, but I had no idea if it was morning or afternoon. Memories came flooding back and my chest tightened as I recalled Alec's betrayal. How could he do that to me? He knew how my pack treated me and he knew I didn't want to be with Tyler, but he brought me back. He never had any intention of breaking the bond. He used me to get the information about the toxin, then sold me to my vicious mate.

I fought against tears, knowing that whenever my captors walked in, they'd think I was emotional over getting caught. I probably should care that I was tied up but my stupid broken heart was causing more discomfort than the familiar threat of Tyler's violence.

Until this moment, I hadn't realized how much I gave to Alec. It wasn't even about my virginity. That wasn't all that special growing up in a pack like I had. Sex was fun and partners changed often unless a mating bond formed. I'd held off, though. Not that I had offers, but I wanted to be with someone who cared for me. At least cared for me at the time we had sex.

But it was all a lie. He'd used me and turned me over to the people who nearly killed me. Had he even cared about me at all?

I trusted him.

I never trusted anyone.

And now I was back where I started.

I thought I'd felt pain before, but it was nothing like how I felt now. The heaviness in my chest was crushing. I felt more broken than ever. How could he do this to me?

The door opened and light flooded the room.

"You awake?" Tyler asked.

"Let me go, Tyler," I demanded.

He sat in a chair next to the bed, a bottle of water in his hands. "Thirsty?"

I glared at him.

"It's just water," he said. "You need to drink."

"You had your friends beat the shit out of me and left me for dead. Then you shot me with something that knocked me out. You think I'm going to trust you?" I was never going to trust anyone again after what I'd been through.

"If I wanted you dead, I'd have let my father kill you. That's what he wants, you know." He lifted the bottle toward me.

"Why am I here, Tyler?" I asked.

"Drink some damn water, Lola," he said.

I was desperate to feel moisture in my mouth again and what was the worst that could happen? I was pretty sure I was dead either way. I opened my mouth and let him pour some water in. It dribbled down my chin and Tyler wiped it away with his fingers.

After a few more swallows, I looked back at Tyler, trying to read his expression. "Talk."

"I haven't been able to shift since you left," Tyler admitted. "My wolf is protesting or something. The bond is strong between us."

"So?" I didn't give a shit about Tyler not being able to shift. "It sucks not being able to do the one thing shifters are supposed to do, doesn't it?"

"That's the thing, Lola," he said. "If you could shift, I would have gladly taken you as mine. You're beautiful."

"I'm not docile, and I never will be," I warned. "And I will fight back no matter what. You can't throw me around, Tyler."

"I heard you shifted," he said.

I closed my mouth. So that was what this was about.

"I want to complete the bond with you. The fates want us together. I will work to be more respectful," he said, though it sounded like it pained him.

"You can't be serious." I tugged at my restraints. "You drugged me and tied me up. How the fuck is that respectful?"

"I'm working on it," he said. "And I needed you not to run."

"No," I said. "I'm not completing the bond with you."

Tyler sighed and stood. "You don't have much of a choice. You complete the bond with me, or my dad puts a bullet through you. Maybe being with me and learning how to be a real wolf would be better than dying."

"What would you do if you were me? How would you respond to being asked to bond with the person who spent the last decade beating the shit out of you?" I asked.

"Here's the thing, Lola," Tyler leaned closer to me. "If you're not my mate, there's nothing stopping me from throwing your mom in the caves for being a traitor."

My lower lip quivered and I bit down on it to steady myself. My mom was awful but she was still my mother. "You wouldn't."

"I'll be the alpha of this pack in a matter of years. You're either rising with me, or your whole family is going down.

You have a week to decide. I want to announce our bond before the next full moon. You will complete the bond with me. I'd rather do it with your cooperation but I am not opposed to force."

Tyler left the room, closing the door behind him.

I sucked in deep breaths, my heart pounding hard. Tyler was insane. He wasn't used to not getting his way and this time, I might finally be in a situation I couldn't get myself out of.

I tugged on my restraints again, pulling hard. There had to be a way out, but how? *This would be a really great time to shift.*

My wolf wasn't responding. Even the little glimmer of a connection we'd had seemed to be gone.

Tyler gave me a timeline. I had a few days, unless he changed his mind. There had to be something I could do. I had to figure out a way out of here. I refused to bond with Tyler and I refused to die. It wouldn't hurt if I could make Tyler suffer on my way out. Besides, I had a score to settle with a feral shifter.

WOLF UNTAMED

MOON CURSED BOOK TWO

1

My wrists were rubbed raw from the ropes. No matter how much I turned and moved, it only made the restraints cut into my flesh more. Grunting with frustration, I tried again. Wincing against the pain, I blew out a breath to keep myself from crying out.

Time didn't matter in this dark room. I'd been in and out of consciousness several times. Whatever they'd given me took a while to leave my bloodstream. Or my body was making me sleep to avoid the discomfort.

This waking was a little different. My mind was less foggy and I was more aware of my surroundings. Squinting into the dim room, I looked for anything that might help me identify where I was or how I could get out. Aside from the bed I was tied to, there was a dresser and a window. Little flutters of hope filled my chest and I tugged on the restraints again. If I could break these, that window was my ticket to freedom. Unfortunately, they held fast. Whoever had tied me up had done a good job. *Fuck.* I had to get out of here.

As far as I knew, Tyler had only visited me once but I

remembered his threats clearly. A chill rippled through me at the thought that he could have been in here while I was asleep. Anyone could have been. How much of the drug had they given me and what exactly was it?

It was likely I'd been dosed with the anti-shifting drug. The very thing I'd given the recipe for to Alec. The thought of him made me grit my teeth. I was never going to forgive him. I wasn't going to forgive any of them. Alec, Tyler, Ace, Kyle, Julian… their names circled my mind on repeat. A list of people I needed to punish. I was done being the victim.

Another thought struck me as I considered the others at the feral camp. Had anyone else known what Alec was planning? Malcom had tried to warn me and I ignored him. Then there was Sheila. She was Alec's right hand woman, but she'd been at the camp with me while he was out brokering deals for my return to hell.

Sheila was probably in on this too. Which meant I couldn't trust anyone. I should have fled from the camp right away and stuck to my initial plan. Trying to find a place to belong was a distraction. Friends weren't real. They were just people waiting to betray me. I was fully and truly alone. I always had been. Maybe that was my true curse in life.

The door creaked and I turned toward the sound. "What do you want?" My voice came out gravely and dry.

"Is that any way to greet your alpha?" Ace asked.

My whole body tensed. Tyler was bad, but all the damage he'd done to me over the years was a product of his upbringing. Where had he learned to be so savage? Aside from that, there was the fact that Tyler had made it clear that his dad's intentions were to end my life.

"What do you want?" I repeated. I was done being afraid.

Done worrying about the consequences of my actions. They were going to kill me or not. Whatever I said or did wasn't going to change a fucking thing.

"That's an intriguing question." He sat on the chair next to the bed.

I resisted the urge to pull on the restraints. He'd get pleasure from seeing me struggle and I knew damn well they weren't going anywhere. They'd done it right when they'd tied me up. Made you wonder how much practice they had at this. The thought sent a shiver down my spine.

"What I want seems to be irrelevant at the moment," Ace said.

"Just spit it out," I said.

"You are a firecracker, you know that?" he asked.

"I want to live my life in peace," I replied.

"And you can, if you submit to your mate as is your place," he hissed.

"I will never be with Tyler, and you don't want me to be with him. Why not let us break the bond?"

"Because his wolf has chosen you. It's the only reason you're alive. I would have killed you while you slept in that tent." He leaned closer. "If you were my mate, I'd have killed you myself and dealt with the pain of the loss. You might be an attractive woman, but you ruined yourself when you fucked that feral shifter."

I tensed. How did he know that? Were they watching me the whole time I was there or was Alec going around bragging about it? And why the hell would he tell people he hooked up with me and then turn me over to them? My head was spinning and my heart ached all over again. Just when I thought I'd gotten over the pain of losing Alec and focused on the anger, it all came flooding back. I hated myself for having any desire for him. I hated that I missed him despite what he'd done. It wasn't fair. My stupid heart needed to get her alliance straight. Alec was an asshole and I hated him. I just couldn't get all of me on board with it yet.

"You're lucky I kept that information from Tyler," Ace added.

"That's all I have to say to get him to stop this bonding nonsense?" I asked. "Bring him in, I'll tell him now."

Ace stood and lifted his hand. I barely had time to tense before his open palm hit my cheek. I gritted my teeth and my eyes watered as the sting on my face lingered.

"You keep your whore mouth shut. Once that bond is in place, you'll be faithful and if you're not, I will kill you myself," he said.

"Why go through all this trouble?" I asked. "You have no interest in having me in your pack. I know you don't want me with Tyler."

Ace growled.

"He really can't shift, can he?" Tyler had told me as much, but it hadn't sunk in before. "You think us bonding is the only way?"

"You will complete the mating bond."

I grinned. "If you kill me, your son could be like me. Never shifting again. Then how will you parade him around as the false alpha?"

Ace stood so fast that he knocked the chair to the ground. "You don't deserve the kindness Tyler is showing you."

Laughter bubbled up in my chest and it came out unbidden. Crazed, insane laughter. "That's what this is? Kindness?"

"I told him to take you in the field while you were unconscious. He is determined to have you submit on your own." Ace grinned. "Keep laughing. Tomorrow he'll be claiming you weather you like it or not."

That stopped my laughter. I glared at Ace. "Break the bond, asshole. He'll get his shifting back and I'll be out of your life forever."

"It's too late for that," he said. "Submit or not. I don't care how the bond is formed."

I was left alone in the dark and my chest felt like I had a hundred-pound weight sitting on my ribs. Breathing was hard as dread gripped me. I must have been more out of it than I realized. Tyler had given me a few days, but my time was up. How had time gone so quickly?

The door opened again and a smaller figure stepped into the room. "Lola?"

It was a female voice but I didn't recognize it. Squinting into the dark, I tried to make out the newcomer. "Who's there?"

"They sent me to talk to you," she said, the figure moving closer to the bed.

In the dim light, I recognized Viki, Tyler's mom. She was a timid woman who always took a back seat to her husband. I rarely saw her, but when I did, she nearly faded into the background. It was common knowledge that Ace wasn't faithful, but I'd honestly never heard anyone speak badly about Viki. She was everything I wasn't. Quiet, demure, subservient. I felt bad for her. What had Ace done to break her like this?

"I'm not going to change my mind." There had to be a way out of here that I wasn't seeing yet. I was determined not to be forced in a bond I didn't want.

"They're not going to let you go," she said. "And they're not going to allow death as an alternative."

My brow furrowed.

"They will force the bond on you. I've heard them talking. It's the only plan. Tyler will claim you and you can either participate or remain tied up."

"What the fuck is wrong with all of you?" I demanded.

"Tyler isn't all bad," she said. "You might come to love him in time. In your own way."

"The way you are with Ace? No, thank you," I said.

"It's different with me and Ace," she said. "We're not true mates."

This surprised me. Not that I knew much about the personal lives of the members of the pack, but I assumed if Ace bothered to settle down, he'd only do it with a true mate.

"I can see you didn't know." She righted the tipped chair and sat down. "My father was alpha. No alphas had stepped up to take his place and when he died, Ace was the strongest and I knew he'd protect me. I know it doesn't seem like it, but there were far worse options than him. I took the lesser of the evils."

"I don't want that life," I said.

"I know. But true mates are different. They're rare and precious. You probably already feel something for Tyler, even if you're fighting it. You will be true partners in time. He will treat you well, I believe that," she said.

"You're kidding, right?" I stared at her wide-eyed. "How closed off do they keep you? Do you have any idea what he's done to me over the years?"

She nodded. "I do. And I know why."

"I'm listening, but I'm not going to change my mind," I told her.

"He's felt the bond to you most of his life. Fighting the bond manifests in strange ways. For him, it was to be aggressive toward you to keep the emotions from surfacing."

"That's not an excuse and doesn't make any of it okay," I said.

"No, it doesn't. But notice that he hasn't hurt you since you returned. He's been in here checking on you night and day. He won't allow anyone in to hurt you. Ace and I only got in just now because he finally agreed to go to sleep. He's allowed the bond to form and he has prevented his father from killing you," she said. "You should have seen him when Ace said he was going to take you out. I've never seen Tyler move so fast. He would kill his own father rather than see you harmed. The bond is strong between you."

"I don't feel a thing," I lied. I didn't feel affection for Tyler, but there was something there and it made me feel uncomfortable and nauseous. Stupid mating bond. I hated it and I hated everything about him and this whole stupid pack.

"They're going to allow you to use the bathroom so you can clean up. If you choose to allow the bond, they'll untie you," she said.

My heart raced. That was the best news I'd heard since arriving. Without the restraints, I had a chance at escape. I knew I had to be careful about how I approached this. Did I pretend to go along with it so I could be free? If I jumped too quickly, they'd know.

"And if I don't?" I asked.

"Then he'll complete the bond against your will. None of us want that," she said.

"Why can't they just break the bond and let me go?" I asked.

"Ace says it's because Tyler can't shift, but that's not the truth."

"What is the truth?" I pressed.

"Tyler is forcing himself not to shift," she said. "A mother knows these things."

"Why would he do that?" I asked.

"Because for him, the bond is already complete. For him, you are his true mate and he will stop at nothing to have you."

I swallowed hard. That was not the answer I wanted. "I don't have a choice?"

"I'm afraid not," she said.

This was my chance. I knew I was only going to get one shot at getting out of here. "Okay. Let me get myself cleaned up so I can be ready."

I could almost feel Viki's relief. "I'll let them know."

I knew it wasn't real. I knew I was planning to escape, but my emotions were a wreck. My mind raced with a million possibilities. What if I couldn't get away? What if Tyler had his way with me? What if I started to desire him the way he wanted me? What if this was my life and I was stuck here forever?

I couldn't let that happen. One step at a time. First, out of these ties, then find a way out of this house. If I could do that, I could flee to the forest and then I'd at least have a chance. It was all I could hope for.

2

When the door opened again, I steeled myself for what was to come. If I was going to get out of here alive, and untouched by Tyler, I was going to have to give the performance of my life. Viki had been easier to fool, but I wasn't sure anyone else would have accepted that I'd taken this path so quickly.

"They don't trust you yet." I recognized Kyle's voice before I realized the silhouette approaching was him.

"How appropriate. I don't trust them, either," I said.

"You're really going to go through with it?" He sounded surprised.

My brow furrowed and I peered into the darkness, trying to make out his expression. "Why do you sound so surprised? Isn't this what you all wanted? You won. I lost."

Even saying the words made my stomach lurch uncomfortably. I wasn't planning to go through with it but the thought of giving in was almost too much for my mind to process.

"Sure, I suppose," he said. "You know, when I heard you'd

survived the cave, I really thought you had a chance at escaping."

"Quit talking to me like we're friends," I snapped.

"You go through with this and you're going to have to play nicer," he said.

I forced my jaw closed and didn't respond. Keeping up this rouse was harder than I anticipated.

"They sent me to get you to the bathroom. I was told to beat you into submission if you try to flee." His tone was warning but fell a little flat.

"You don't sound like you enjoy your position as much as you used to," I said.

"You know nothing about me," he said.

"I know a lot more than you think." Kyle was weak. He followed whoever would give him the best chance at survival. Like me, he'd grown up in the trailer park, but after he'd gained Tyler's favor, his family mysteriously inherited a home away from the trash I grew up with. "Tell me, Kyle, just what is the going rate for your loyalty these days?"

He growled and I could feel the tension filling the room. For a moment, it almost felt like my wolf was stirring. I hoped she was waking and ready to help me get the fuck out of here.

"When I untie you, you will not run. They have every exit blocked and they will take you to the brink of death so Tyler can complete the bond." Kyle walked closer to me. "Do you understand?"

"Yeah, yeah. Don't run or the mate who supposedly cares about me will force himself on me." I shook my head. "Am I the only one who sees the absolute insanity in this whole situation?"

"Believe it or not, Lola, you're not the only one who had to make difficult choices," he said.

"Yeah, your life seems real hard," I said.

"Just stop talking." His fingers worked the knots around my right ankle.

"You think you're one of the good guys, don't you?" I asked.

"I told you to stop talking."

I scoffed. "Truth hurts, doesn't it?"

He didn't respond and I got the sense that our conversation was over. He freed my right ankle and moved to the left. It didn't take long before all my restraints were off.

I swayed when I sat up, my head spinning as I got used to sitting again. Rubbing my wrists, I gave myself a moment to take a few breaths. I was grateful to be free and needed a shower more than I ever had in my life.

I could see Kyle better now that he was closer and I realized he had a new scar on his jaw and visible signs of a nearly healed black eye. That had to be very recent since shifters usually healed in a day. What had he gotten himself into while I'd been away?

"Here." Kyle handed me a granola bar. "It was all I could grab."

Since it was wrapped, I accepted it and tore it open. I hadn't eaten since they tossed me in here. My stomach growled in response to the thought of food. I moaned when I took the first bite. My face heated. I hadn't meant to do that but when you're that hungry, anything tastes amazing.

Quickly, I finished the bar, then reached for the bottle of water Tyler had left on the nightstand by the bed. I washed down the food. "Thank you."

"Come on. They're waiting for you," he said.

"They?" I bristled. "Great. Can't wait."

He walked toward the door and waited for me to follow. With a heavy sigh, I followed. My footsteps felt uneasy but I wasn't about to let on how weak I felt. Between not wanting them to have the satisfaction, I also needed to fake it for myself. If I was going to get out of here, I had to have enough strength to follow through.

We walked down a well-lit hallway lined with photos of the Grant family. Tyler and his parents, baby pictures, first day of school, fishing, camping. All the photos you'd expect to see from a happy family. It was unsettling seeing it here. I knew how dysfunctional it all was, but they sure did put on a good show.

I couldn't help but feel a little bad for Viki. She'd settled to keep herself safe. I wasn't going to make the same mistake. I didn't live through hell my whole life to give up now.

We reached a closed door at the end of the hall and I vaguely remembered that it was the bathroom. Faded memories of being dragged here, my arms bound, flooded into my head. So they'd brought me here a few times to pee but I hardly remembered it through the drug induced fog. At least that explained why I wasn't wearing urine-soaked shorts.

You'd think that knowing I'd been using the restroom would bring me comfort. Instead, it made my chest tighten in fear. If the drugs they gave me had made me so out of it, I was able to walk to the restroom and not remember, what else had they done to me? I was alert enough to walk, but until we went down this hall, I forgot it even happened.

"Go ahead," Kyle said. "I'll wait here. There's no windows in there."

"What did they give me earlier?" I asked.

Kyle looked confused.

"The drug they shot me with," I explained. I knew the answer, but I wanted confirmation. "What was it?"

"You know what it was," he said. "Go. Before they come looking for you."

Frustrated, I turned the doorknob and entered the bathroom. At least it was empty and I was alone. The problem was, as Kyle had mentioned, there were no windows. With Kyle blocking the exit at the door, there was no way I was going to get out unless I was ready to blow past him and take my chances.

I was still weak from my ordeal. It would be nearly impossible to get past him in my current state. Still, I knew I was going to have to try. It was my best chance.

Hoping the shower might help stimulate my aching and drowsy body, I went ahead and pulled my clothes off and stepped into the tub, pulling the curtain closed behind me.

The hot water was a balm on my aching body. I scrubbed everything, being gentle on the red marks where the bounds had cut into my wrists and ankles.

I hadn't had a shower since the day I left Wolf Creek. Washing my hair with actual shampoo rather than just rinsing in a lake was a luxury I hadn't realized I'd missed so much.

The water felt amazing and my body did feel stronger and more alert when I turned off the shower. I took a few deep breaths, going over the plan in my mind one more time.

I was going to dry off, put my clothes back on and then I was going to run. No stopping for anything. I had to get out of the nearest exit.

Now would be an excellent time to connect with me and shift, I told my wolf.

She didn't respond.

Of course not.

As usual, I was on my own.

I pulled back the shower curtain and grabbed a towel from the wall. Quickly, I dried off, then hung the towel back up. Then my whole plan fell apart.

You have got to be fucking kidding me.

Where did my clothes go?

My pulse raced. They'd grabbed my clothes while I was in the shower and left me with nothing. Fuck me.

Did this mean they were intending on going right to the whole completing the bond thing? This was not my plan.

I had two choices. Run naked or run with a towel around myself.

I looked down at the mark on my hip. I'd nearly forgotten it was there, but I knew it wasn't going to be overlooked by Tyler. Covering my mark with my palm, I recalled how Alec reacted when he saw it. Everything changed between us in that moment. Had he been planning to betray me the whole time or just after he saw the mark?

Had he been so threatened by a woman with the mark of the alpha that he'd turned me over? The hypocrite had a mark of his own that he did nothing with. He refused to rise up and take control and be the alpha he was born to be.

Was I doing the same thing?

No. We weren't the same. I didn't want anything to do with Wolf Creek. The Moon Goddess was wrong to give me this mark. It was some kind of cruel joke. Just like the fates when they'd placed me with Tyler. It was another way of punishing me for something I didn't do. Maybe my family line really was cursed. Sure, I'd been able to shift once. But maybe that wasn't the only piece of the curse. Maybe we were given the things we wanted least. For any other shifter, a true mate was a blessing. Shit, even the mark of the alpha would be welcomed by anyone. Sure, it didn't happen for women, but a stronger woman would embrace it.

For me, this mark was a death sentence.

Ace would kill me on sight if he saw it. I was a threat, and I knew it.

So I'd run with the towel.

Wrapping it around me as best I could, I took a deep breath and set my hand on the doorknob. I was either headed to escape or things were about to get a whole lot worse for me.

3

My whole body tensed like a spring as I threw the door open. Without thinking, I exploded forward, expecting to have to run through Kyle. I only got a few steps before I slammed right into Tyler's broad chest and fell to the ground.

"I thought you'd try something like this," Tyler said. "Told you taking her clothes wasn't enough to stop her. Though I have to admit, I thought you'd be streaking naked down the hall."

I clutched the towel tighter around me and tried to regain some of my dignity. "You know I don't want this. Why keep pushing me? Just let me go."

"We've been through this, Lola. And you're out of time. I will claim you as mine tonight. I'd much rather you agree to it. I think you might even enjoy yourself." He offered his hand and I turned away from him.

Pushing myself from the ground, I held the towel tight and glared at him as best I could. "I will never stop fighting you. Even if you managed to complete the bond, you'll never have my heart or my submission."

"Tyler, can't you give her a little more time? The bond will draw her to you if you just..."

"Enough, Kyle," Tyler said, cutting him off. "I'm done being patient."

"This is you being patient?" I scoffed.

"Back to your room. You can wait there for me," Tyler said.

I looked past him and noticed there wasn't anyone else in the hall. I had to try one more time. Quickly, I stepped to the side then started running.

Tyler growled and managed to grab hold of the towel, pulling me back. I let go of the towel, risking being naked for a chance at escape. Arms pumping, I raced down the hall and flew down the steps, taking them as fast as possible.

My eyes widened when I emerged into the living room. Ace and six other adult shifter males rose from their places on the couch and chairs. I froze and assessed the room. The front door was through the living room, beyond this gathering of shifters. To my right, I could see the kitchen and the back door. It looked like the safer shot.

I moved forward, heart racing as my bare feet pounded against the wood floor. My fingers brushed the doorknob just as a pair of strong arms pulled me down.

Fighting tears, I hit the ground hard, my chin making contact with the floor. Shooting pain spread up my jaw and I took a sharp breath in to prevent from screaming. Tears streamed down my face but I ignored them. I would deal with the pain later. Instantly, I started kicking and fighting, clawing my way toward the exit. I was so close.

Ace had a hold of me, he grunted and growled as he pinned me down. "Stop fighting, you little bitch."

"Hold her down, Ace," one of the others called.

"Girl's got a wild streak," another said.

"Let her go, Dad!" Tyler's voice cut over the grunts and shouts.

Ace stopped squeezing me for a moment, then resumed his full hold.

Tyler growled. A strange sensation snaked its way through my body and every part of me felt alert. I tensed, reacting to his tone. It wasn't fear exactly, but that one sound had grabbed my full attention.

"Let. Her. Go." Tyler's words were powerful. Even his father had to feel it because he eased his grip.

I stayed on the floor, face down, my mind racing. I was outnumbered and the chances of me making my way through the door were pretty much non-existent. Before I could decide what my next move should be, the pressure of Ace's grip released and I heard the distinct sound of a fist against someone.

Startled, I managed to scramble away. Two large men were blocking the door, but my attention went right to the fight going on in front of me.

Tyler and Ace were at each other's throats. Tyler got a blow in his dad's jaw, but Ace hardly seemed to feel it. Without hesitation, Ace shoved Tyler into a bookcase. The whole shelf rattled and books came crashing down around him. My heart hammered against my ribs and icy fear squeezed my chest. "Tyler!"

Instinct took over and I ran toward him, pushing him away from the bookshelf before it crushed him. We landed on the ground, me on top of him, panting and naked.

Ace grabbed my arm and hauled me off Tyler, pulling me up against him. I twisted, trying to break his grip. He held me fast but I wasn't going to go easy. Pulling back my fist, I landed a punch on the older man's cheek. My knuckles felt like they'd been broken and I hissed in pain. *Fuck.* Punching someone was a lot more painful than I thought it would be.

He growled, then landed an uppercut under my chin. My head lolled back and my vision went blurry. I could vaguely hear screaming and chaos but everything sounded like it was coming from very far away. As if I was at the end of a long tunnel.

When he threw me to the ground, I wasn't prepared, but I managed to land on my hands and knees. My mouth was full of blood and I spit it out on the floor under me, doing my best not to swallow it all. My stomach lurched at the sight of all the red on the floor. Between the aching pain and the taste of blood, I knew that punch had done some serious damage.

"Enough!" Tyler dropped to his knees next to me. His fingertips gently touched my cheek. "Are you okay?"

His touch made me feel calmer. For a moment, I considered crawling into his embrace and letting him hold me. I'd be protected and safe in his arms. Part of me ached for it. Holding myself back was harder than I thought it would be. The mating bond was growing. Alec had been right. Even Viki was right. I was feeling something for Tyler.

"I am not okay." I wasn't even referring to my injuries. The thought of having feelings in any way for this piece of shit was not okay. None of this was okay.

Ace leaned down and spoke quietly. "Show him the mark," Ace whispered. "How long have you been lying to us, you little bitch?"

He had kept his tone low enough that nobody aside from

me could hear him. I didn't know how to respond. He wasn't outing me in front of everyone, but he knew.

"This ends now, Dad. She's my mate. I will not have her disrespected like this." Tyler stood and grabbed a blanket off a chair. He walked over to me and draped it over my shoulders.

Grateful, I pulled it around me. I was fighting against the warm feelings toward Tyler but I wasn't going to turn down something to cover myself with. Especially now that Ace brought up the mark. I had to change the subject. Tyler couldn't know about that. I needed to get myself out of here but this chance was over. Time for a change of plans.

"Can you take me back to my room?" I asked Tyler in my most pathetic tone.

He helped me to my feet. "Of course."

"She's playing you," Ace said.

"I've heard enough from you," Tyler said. "Come on, Lola. You can get some rest and we'll complete the bond tomorrow. I'm not going to make you do it now."

I nodded and walked along with Tyler. My mind was at war with my heart. For some reason, there was a small part of me that was terrified about leaving Tyler. I'd reacted when I saw him threatened and I'd saved him. Stupid instincts. If I'd let that bookcase fall on him, he might be dead. The bond would be broken and I'd be free. Well, Ace would probably have killed me, but it was possible I could have fled in the aftermath.

I didn't want anything to do with Tyler. Why had I saved him?

Mating bonds should be outlawed.

On our walk back to my prison cell, well, the room they kept me in, I reminded myself of all the terrible things Tyler had done to me. But that kiss in front of the caves kept forcing its way into my memories. I wasn't going to let the bond win. I was going to choose my own path. Tyler wasn't it.

"Sit," Tyler said as he stopped in front of the bed.

I obliged, hoping that if I played the docile, injured damsel in distress, he'd leave me sans bindings. There was a window in this room and that was my ticket out of here.

"I'm sorry for my father," he said.

"It's not much different than how you treated me," I said, unable to help myself.

"I told you, I'm working on it," he said.

A knock sounded on the door and then it opened. Viki stood in the threshold. "Why don't you let me help her get cleaned up."

"Sure," Tyler said. "I'll come check on you soon."

I forced a smile but internally, I was fighting the urge to vomit. Thank the gods. The sick feeling Tyler gave me was back. The moment of strange attachment to him seemed to have passed. I had to get the fuck out of here before something like that happened again.

Viki walked into the room, then closed the door behind her. "Before you try it, there's three guards outside your window. I know why you ran, and I'm glad you had your chance, but it's over now. You're not going to be able to get away from this. Your best bet is to let the bond connect you so you can enjoy yourself a little."

I glared at her.

"I saw how you rushed to Tyler. The bond is there. If you stop fighting it, you might find happiness." She opened a drawer and pulled out a washcloth, then walked over to the bottle of water on the table. After pouring a little water on the cloth, she started to wipe my face.

Her words had rendered me too numb to react. Defeat began to sink in, making me feel like I'd lost everything. How was I going to do this? I couldn't be with Tyler and I wasn't sure I could get away.

Silent tears rolled down my cheeks but I didn't even bother to wipe them away. After all I'd faced, and all I'd fought for, how was it possible it would end like this?

"Ace saw the mark. He's going to kill you tonight while everyone is sleeping unless you complete the bond before he gets his chance," Viki said.

My eyes moved to hers and panic sent my heart racing. "You're sure?"

She nodded. "Like I said, you're out of time."

I swallowed hard, returning my gaze to my hands so I didn't have to look her in the eye anymore. This couldn't be the end for me. There had to be more to my story.

Soft footsteps sounded on the floor but I didn't look up. The door opened and closed. My mind raced, my heart beat so quickly I thought I might be having a panic attack. How badly did I want to live? I'd flirted with thoughts of death in the past. Some days, I'd even wished for death to find me. But I'd had a taste of freedom. Even if Alec had violated my trust in the worst possible way, being with his pack had shown me what was possible. I had to believe that not everyone there was in on his betrayal. Happiness or at least some kind of life beyond this was possible.

I had to fight.

I stood and dropped the blanket to the ground. It didn't take long to find the light switch so I could see better. Then, I walked to the dresser and was rewarded with drawers stuffed of random old clothes, towels, and sheets. It was a hodge-podge of fabric. After a few minutes of digging, I found clothes that would work.

Dressed in actual underwear, a pair of gym shorts, and a faded old tee, I started to feel hopeful again. I had clothes on, that was a good first step. Now, I just needed to figure out the way out of here.

4

Six grown shifter males seemed like overkill. Or maybe it was a compliment. Either way, with that many outside my window, I wasn't taking that exit. With an irritated sigh, I backed away from the window. There had to be another option.

I walked to the door and crouched on the ground to look under the crack. Details weren't clear, but there was obvious movement and shadows indicating people guarding the door.

They weren't taking any chances of me getting lucky enough to get by them. I knew I had two choices: accept my fate and yield, or find a way to fight.

Giving up was easier and I would be lying if I said I hadn't contemplated it. Thankfully, the pity party hadn't lasted long. Thinking of the look on Alec's face when he saw me alive was enough to push me. I needed him to know that he wasn't successful at getting rid of me. I was going to get out of this. Without a mating bond.

I dumped everything from the drawers, I checked in the closet, I even crawled under the bed. The room was free of anything I could use as a weapon. With a huff of frustration, I sat on the bed to think. Worst case, I made a suicide run to get out of here. Or I guess I could play the willing mate and see if I could convince Tyler to move our intimate time elsewhere. If we were alone, could I fight just him off? That didn't seem likely, and I hated the idea of being alone with him anywhere. Realistically, he was stronger than me. There was too much chance of him getting what he wanted.

Rage roared inside me. How dare he even consider forcing himself on me. This whole pack was fucked up and I wanted all of them to pay. Nobody should be treated the way I was growing up, but this was beyond what I ever imagined.

The door creaked and I jumped to my feet, fists clenched. I wasn't ready. I needed more time to figure this out.

Kyle lifted his hands in mock surrender. "I'm not here to hurt you."

"What the fuck do you want?" I demanded.

He closed the door then took a few tentative steps closer to me.

"That's enough," I said, holding my hand up in front of me. "Back the fuck off, Kyle."

He kept his hands in front of him and took another step. "I need you to listen to me."

I took a step back. "I don't want to hear anything you have to say."

"Even if it's about Alec?" he said the name so quietly, I wasn't sure I heard him correctly.

"What did you say?"

This time, when he moved closer, I didn't flinch.

"They'll kill me if they hear what I say," he whispered.

My brow furrowed, I was confused but intrigued. It was

probably some kind of ploy, but what else did I have to lose at this point. I moved closer to him. "If you touch me, I'll kill you."

"I know you will," he said. "Give me a second..." He backed up and raised his voice. "Tyler is the best thing that ever happened to you. I know you've been through a lot, but this is the right choice. You two have a bond."

I winced but caught on that he was feeding the people behind the door some words to keep them happy.

Kyle quickly walked toward me and I tensed, but held my ground. "Talk fast," I said quietly.

"I overheard Ace. I know about the mark." He looked down as if he'd see it glowing through my clothes, then he returned his eyes to mine. "I need to know if it's true."

"Why do you care?" I asked.

He lifted his shirt and pulled his jeans down enough to reveal a mark on his hip bone. The double crescent mark of a protector.

"You never said anything." I was completely surprised. Most of the wolves who got marks didn't shut up about them.

"You know why," he said. "Tyler doesn't have one. When mine showed up, he took me into his inner circle. It changed everything for my family. I didn't have a choice. I thought he was my alpha. I thought I was doing my duty."

I rolled my eyes. "You were a blind follower."

"They promised treatment for Blaire," he said.

"Your sister?" I'd seen his younger sister only a few times when we were kids. She wasn't even old enough to be in school yet.

"She needed surgeries. Medicines not available in pack lands. She'd have died," he said. "If I stopped..."

"Is this supposed to make up for how you treated me?" I asked.

He shook his head. "No, but I'm going to start working on that now."

I scoffed.

"Your friend is in the basement. Locked in a cell."

"I don't have any friends." The words stung, but it was the truth.

"He got himself captured to try to get to you," he said. "The feral shifter. Alec."

My chest tightened. He'd come back for me? How was I supposed to react to that? He was the reason I was here in the first place. He sold me out for the toxin and cash. I was nothing to him. For all he knew, they'd kill me the moment he walked away. He'd sold me out. Him coming back changed nothing. "So what?"

"Don't you get it? He tried to play both sides. Or he grew a conscious. I don't know what feral wolves do. Either way, they caught him at your window. You were still unconscious."

"How is any of this helpful to me?" I demanded. "Are you trying to threaten him in hopes that I'll fuck your friend?"

"Seriously, Lola. Get over yourself. I'm trying to help you. Can't you see that?"

"Nobody helps me," I said.

He lifted his shirt again. "I am a protector. *You* are my alpha. Not Tyler. You."

I felt like the air had been knocked from my lungs and I stared at him in horror. "I am not an alpha. The mark is a mistake."

"The moon goddess doesn't make mistakes," he said.

"Then how do you explain the mating bond with Tyler?" I asked.

"I don't know. But our pack has been under the rule of a tyrant for too long. You either step up and do your job or you don't. That's not my call. That's yours. Just know that whatever you choose, I'm with you," he said.

"No." I shook my head. "You're no better than them. Besides, your sister."

"She got what she needed. She's going to be okay. My mom can protect her from here. And you were right. I'm not better than them. But I do want to start trying to make amends."

The door opened and we both turned toward it. Ace was standing in the threshold. Behind him, I could see several other shifters. There was a clear message. I wasn't going anywhere.

"She's ready for Tyler," Kyle said. "She knows her place."

"Nobody asked you to interfere." Ace's expression was murderous.

"I overheard," Kyle said. "She's agreed to get a tattoo. Something to commemorate her bond. On her hip."

I swallowed and forced myself to maintain a defiant glare at Ace. Internally, I felt sick at the thought of having to be with Tyler. If Kyle was going to help me get out of this, playing along might be my only hope.

Ace's expression relaxed and he lifted a brow. "Oh?"

"Do you want to send the tattoo artist tonight?" I asked, surprising myself with how even my tone was. "I was thinking I'd get a dark gray wolf. Same color as Tyler's."

Ace narrowed his eyes. "What brought this change?"

"When I realized I might lose him, I felt the bond," I said. It was true, I had acted on instinct to save Tyler. It didn't mean I wanted to be with him.

"I'll see what I can do," Ace said. He turned to Kyle. "Good work, Sinclair."

Kyle nodded.

Ace closed the door behind him, leaving me alone with Kyle.

"Are you serious about what you said?" I whispered. It was impossible to trust him, but I wasn't sure I had another choice. "If this is some sick joke, I will find a way to take you out with me."

He smirked. "I know you would. But you've got the mark. You're my alpha even if you're not ready to accept it yourself."

I sighed. Telling him I didn't want the job wasn't going to get through to him right now. "If you're serious, how do I get out of here?"

"Don't you want to rescue your friend?" he asked.

Fuck. I did want to help Alec despite what he did to me. What was wrong with me? On the other hand, I was not going to risk my freedom. "I need out of here. He made his bed. I will not risk my life for his."

"Cutthroat."

"You know what he did," I said.

"He tried to have it all," Kyle said. "Tried to play both sides. That never works."

"Good thing you know that. Because if you're playing me…"

"I'm not. You're going to have to trust me. Eventually," Kyle said. "I won't ask for it yet. I'm going to earn it."

"Does all this mean you have a plan to get me out of here?" I asked.

"You're not going to like it," he said.

"I don't care what it is as long as I get out," I said.

"With or without the feral shifter?" Kyle let the words hang between us. He didn't look like he was judging me or expecting me to answer a certain way. Was he really going to go along with whatever I chose? Was this happening?

"I can't risk my freedom. You're the one with the plan. Can I do both?" I asked.

"If you're willing to give my plan a chance, I think we can," he said.

I knew I wasn't going to get out of here without some help. "Fine."

"Give me five minutes," he said. "Be ready."

5

THE SECONDS DRAGGED BY, turning into the longest minutes of my life. I didn't have a clock in here, but I was pretty sure it had been nearly a half hour already. *Shit.*

I'd totally been played.

I shouldn't have believed Kyle. What was wrong with me? Why was I constantly seeking allies when I knew everyone was just going to let me down in the end?

The door opened and I spun on my heels to face the newcomer. Kyle's hair was a mess, his eyes were wide, his cheeks flush.

"What happened?" I had planned on asking more questions, but it was clear by his disheveled appearance that something was going on.

He pressed his finger to his lips, then bolted for the bed, sliding under it and pulling the comforter down over the edge to hide him. Before I could figure out what was happening, the door opened again and a huge, bald shifter male peered in. His nose looked like it had been broken a few times and his bushy eyebrows made his eyes look like tiny specks on his squishy, pink face.

Baldie stomped into the room with a grunt. "Where is he?"

"Where is who?" My heart pounded and my stomach twisted into knots. Whatever was going on, I hoped it was the plan to get me out of here. And I really hoped it was going as anticipated.

He walked to the closet and slid the door open, then stuck his head inside. I kept my gaze on him, afraid to turn to look toward the bed where I knew Kyle was hiding.

After looking in the empty closet, the huge shifter scanned my room, glaring at the pile of clothes on the floor.

"What? They tossed me in here naked. I had to find something to wear." I shrugged. My nose caught a strange scent. Like smoke. "Is something burning?"

With a growl, he turned and left the room. I let out a relieved breath but remained in place, my eyes fixed on the door. A few long moments passed, and it didn't open. There was a more obvious scent of smoke in the air now, but I figured grunting bald shifter had it under control. I turned toward the bed in time to see Kyle crawling out from under it.

"What the hell?" I whispered.

Kyle held up one finger as if to tell me to wait. I glared at him. Trusting him might have been a huge mistake.

Suddenly, an alarm blared and I covered my ears. "What the fuck?"

My eyes widened. The smoke might not be under control. "What did you do?"

"Time to go!" He grabbed my hand and pulled me toward the window. Instead of the six shifters that had previously been standing outside, only one remained. He looked up and us and waved. While he was a little rough around the edges, I was pretty sure I'd be able to recognize the familiar form of Alec for the rest of my life.

"You saved him first?" I yelled at Kyle.

"I told you that you wouldn't like it," he said as he pulled the window open. He pushed out the screen, giving us a clear exit. "Now, jump."

We were on the second story and while I'd considered this as a way out, it didn't seem as great of an idea as it had when I first contemplated it.

I heard the distinct sound of cracking bones and when I looked back over at Kyle, he was in his wolf form. He growled at me, then he leaped through the open window, landing ungracefully, but seemingly unharmed.

He was back in human form so swiftly, it made my head spin. Quickly, he moved alongside Alec and the males stretched their arms out. Alec and Kyle were going to catch me.

"You have got to be kidding me," I shouted.

"Just fucking jump, Lola," Alec said. "Now."

Dammit. This was my best chance. Taking a deep breath, I climbed onto the window so my legs were dangling out. Then I pushed off, hoping I wasn't going to end up with a broken leg and remain trapped here.

I landed hard, but I was in strong arms rather than the ground. The two males set me down and I was pleasantly surprised that I was in one piece. So far, Kyle's plan wasn't so bad.

"Time to run," Kyle said. He shifted into wolf form quickly.

Alec reached for my hand. "We gotta go."

I pulled my hand away. "I can run by myself."

He nodded. "After you."

I coughed, the air was full of smoke now. Kyle had literally set the house on fire. For a moment, I had a fleeting worry for Tyler, but it passed quickly. The dark part of me hoped that both Tyler and Ace were trapped inside.

With all my attention focused on getting away from pack lands, I took off at a sprint. Kyle's wolf ran alongside me, with Alec in his human form on the other. It was almost too much to process. I couldn't forgive Alec, but I also couldn't even let myself go there right now. I had to get away from here. Then I could start to figure out what the fuck was going on in my far too complicated life.

My body protested the running, cramps biting into my sides. Wincing, I slowed down, pushing through the pain, unwilling to stop. I might not be sprinting anymore, but I wasn't about to ease up until I was in the clear. I'd gone days without enough food or water. I was exhausted and not at my usual fitness levels.

As soon as we got to the cover of the trees in the woods, I stopped to catch my breath. I glanced back at Tyler's house. Flames were coming from the window of the room I'd just left and smoke rose in large clouds. In the distance, I heard the sirens racing to put out the fire. They'd be distracted for a while.

"This way to the barrier," Alec said. "We can't stop yet."

"No. You don't get to lead the way." I turned to Kyle's wolf. "How do we get out of here?"

The wolf started walking and I followed without looking over at Alec. For all I knew, Kyle was leading me into a trap. I didn't give a damn where we were going if it meant I could walk away from Alec and not listen to him.

To my great relief, Alec moved alongside me, unspeaking. We crossed a narrow creek, and walked through bushes. I ducked under tree branches and sidestepped a few places of thick underbrush. Finally, I felt the icy sensation of passing through the magic of the ward.

I let out a long breath of relief. It wasn't like I was any more protected here. Tyler or any of his cronies could walk right through that barrier and grab me. But there was something amazing about being outside the border. The ability to leave was still a novelty that I wasn't going to take for granted.

Kyle's wolf stopped walking. His body shuddered and I turned away so I wouldn't have to watch him break and re-form into a human. Once the sounds of cracking eased, I looked back to where he was standing.

Alec tossed him a pair of jeans and a shirt that I didn't even know he'd been carrying. I supposed that made sense I didn't notice. I'd done everything I could to avoid looking at him.

"You said your car is near?" Kyle asked.

"Wait, your plan is trusting him?" I glanced over at Alec, then turned back to Kyle. "We're better off on our own."

"Lola, now isn't the time," Alec said. "The car is this way." He started walking.

"You expect us to follow you? After everything you did to me?" I demanded.

Alec stopped and turned. "I'm trying to save you. For once in your life, accept some help."

"I did that when I followed you to Wolf Creek. I asked for your help breaking the bond. I stole from my own mother. I risked my life. You betrayed me." I could feel the anger rising alongside something else. A little hint of what I swore was my wolf. She had my back on this. It gave me the confidence I needed to press forward.

"If you have a car nearby, where are the keys?" I asked.

"Under the floor mat on the back passenger side," he said. "You didn't think I'd bring them to Wolf Creek with me?"

I looked over at Kyle. "You trust this asshole?"

"Asshole?" Alec set his hand on his chest. "You wound me. I thought we had something special."

I growled. Low and guttural. The growl of a wolf.

"Well, nice to see you again, too," Alec said. "I think your wolf likes me."

"Don't even think about it. You mean nothing to either of us," I snarled. "Kyle, tell me there's another way out of here that doesn't involve going with this man."

"He has a car, Lola. We could use the help getting away faster. The fire won't occupy them for long," Kyle said.

"It's not just the car you need," Alec said. "I have information."

"I don't want any of your information," I said. "You are a liar."

"I know who your father is," he said.

That got my attention. I tried to hide the surprised look, but I knew I wasn't fast enough. "Why would I care?"

"Because you aren't meant to be feral. You need community, family, love. You were never going to be happy at camp," he said. "And not to be dramatic, but you're in danger because of who your dad is."

"You know nothing about me," I said. "And I don't believe you about any danger. Why would you suddenly care about that? You sent me to a den of vipers without a second thought."

"I know you better than you think and I hate myself for what I did, but I did what I had to," he said.

"I trusted you and you used me," I hissed.

"I didn't have a choice. We both played our roles," he said.

"Don't you dare tell me you did all this to help me or some shit," I accused.

"Then I won't say that. I can't change the past," he said.

"You sound really broken up over it," I said.

"You two can fuck and make up later," Kyle said. "If we're going to have any chance at getting away alive, we need to go now."

"That is never going to happen," I assured them. "There is nothing going on between us."

"I thought you enjoyed our night together," Alec said.

"You need to stop talking," I warned.

"Fine, no fucking. Ripping each other's throats out it is. But later. Not now," Kyle said.

I knew he was right. Wolf Creek would send shifters after us. And if Tyler was fit enough to shift, he'd scent me without much effort.

"If you screw us over, I will ruin your life." I glared at Alec. Just seeing him sent all kinds of emotions tumbling through me. I hated what he did to me. But I knew the two of us would be connected for the rest of our lives. It wasn't something that sat well with me right now. I needed to get away from him and get him out of my head.

"I really am sorry for what I did to you, Lola," Alec said. "I wish there had been another way."

"Just show me where your car is." I didn't want his apologies. The hurt was too deep to heal.

6

"WHERE EXACTLY ARE WE HEADED?" I asked from the back seat. I'd happily declined the front. It was too close to Alec for my comfort.

"Camp," Alec replied.

"You can't be serious. That's the first place they'll go looking for me," I said.

"I don't think so," Alec said.

"They know you came back for me. Why wouldn't they try looking at your camp? Even if not to find me, to ask for information."

"I'm glad you finally acknowledged that I came back for you," he said.

"That's what you got out of that?" I scoffed.

"I got myself caught," Alec said.

"He made them think he had a recipe for the toxin so they went after him," Kyle said, his tone giving away his disbelief. "Somehow, they think you gave it to him."

"Wonder why they'd think that?" I said, my tone dripping with sarcasm.

"What am I missing?" Kyle asked.

"My grandfather, the one who was cursed, is the same asshole who invented the toxin. Turns out the thing that Wolf Creek uses to maintain its dominance is the same thing that cost me a chance at a normal life."

"Wait, what?" Kyle sounded stunned.

"Fucked up, right?" I couldn't keep the disdain out of my tone.

"I knew things were bad in Wolf Creek, but I didn't know they were that bad," Kyle said.

"You do realize that nothing about growing up in Wolf Creek is normal. I'm sure they fucked both of you up. Bad," Alec said.

"Says the guy who denies all the basic shifter protocol," I accused.

"Speak for yourself, alpha girl," he said.

"Alright, I know I have a lot of catching up to do, but right now, I need you two to focus. Whether you like it or not, my plan for getting Lola to safety involves both of you." Kyle turned in his seat and fixed his gaze on me. "My job is to protect you. It was determined by the gods. So, please, Lola, let me do my damn job."

I still didn't believe he was being genuine despite how serious he sounded. It was going to give me whiplash. "You do know that you can't go back to them now. They'll know you helped me."

"One of these days, you'll see that I'm on your side. I'm going to help you," he insisted.

"You're going to get us all killed by listening to him." I lifted my chin toward Alec.

"We had a spy in the camp," Alec said. "It didn't take much

for me to let slip that I had the recipe in front of him. They came for me that night. I didn't fight them. It got me back in for a chance to rescue you. While I was away, a friend planted the car for us."

"Your rescue plan was to get thrown into a cell in the same building as me?" I rolled my eyes. "Excellent plan."

"I got you out, didn't I?" He growled.

"Don't get pissy with me. You didn't get me out. Kyle did," I said.

"Who do you think got through to him?" Alec asked.

"Enough!" Kyle shouted.

I snapped my mouth closed. I'd never heard Kyle take command like that.

"You two are like children. This is literally life or death. I am going to keep you alive despite the fact that you seem to have a fucking death wish." He took a deep breath and blew it out, his frustration clear. "They think Alec is dead. I started the fire in his holding cell. They'll find a body. Please don't ask me for details."

I blinked a few times, letting the words sink in. "What did you do?"

"What I had to. I told you, I will protect my alpha," Kyle said.

My chest felt tight. I wasn't sure how to process this. Kyle had never been as aggressive toward me as the others, but he was still part of the trauma of my past. But he got me out. And he killed a member of the pack to do it. He was in even deeper shit than I thought. They could come after his family if they made that connection.

Kyle was all in with me. Even if I didn't trust him, I was all he had now. His family would have to disown him to have any chance of maintaining their lives. They were likely going to be ostracized and that was a best-case scenario. If Ace knew the extremes of Kyle's actions, his whole family could end up in the caves. Including his sister.

I wanted to believe him. I wanted to trust him. But I'd been too hurt for too long. I wasn't sure I could ever move on enough to form a friendship with him.

"I don't know if I can ever forgive you." I looked from Kyle to Alec. "Either of you."

"You don't have to," Kyle said. "I told you, I'll earn your trust eventually. I don't expect absolution."

Somehow, his words were exactly what I needed to hear. How the fuck had I ended up in a car with a former enemy and the man who broke my heart and betrayed me? I covered my face with my hands for a moment, taking a breath before dropping my hands. "What's your plan?"

"Thank you," Kyle said. "Alec said you have friends at his camp. The spy returned to Wolf Creek, so we should be relatively safe, but we can't stay long. What we need is time for you to finally get a handle on your shifting. Then, we have to deal with your father before you can challenge Ace to claim the pack."

"Wait, what?" My pulse raced. "I didn't agree to that. What if I don't want to go back to Wolf Creek or have anything to do with my father? And I have to point out how there's nothing in your plan about breaking my mating bond with Tyler."

Both males were silent and they turned away from me. I got the distinct impression they were avoiding the subject on purpose.

"Don't you dare," I threatened. "There is no option besides severing that bond. I will not live with that forever."

"I heard how you saved him," Alec said.

"So? That doesn't mean I want to be with him. It means I'm a good person. I don't let others die, even if I don't like them," I said.

"The bond between the two of you is strong," Kyle said. "Tyler was already changing his mind about forcing the bond. He wanted you to get there on your own. It was Ace who pushed."

"I don't care. There will never be anything between Tyler and myself. Ever. Do you understand?" I was pissed. How dare they even suggest such a thing.

"Well, once you re-claim the pack, you can do whatever you want with him. Send him to the caves, banish him. The choice will be yours," Kyle said.

"I want the bond broken." I wasn't even about to go into detail about the whole *claiming my pack* thing.

"And what is all this about my father?" There was far too much going on right now. "How does everyone else but me know this information? Does everyone in Wolf Creek know?"

"He told me," Kyle said. "And trust me, nobody else in Wolf Creek knew or your life would have been very different."

"But you know now?" I asked. "Who my supposed father is?"

Kyle nodded.

"My mom said I should stay away from him. She said the reason she never told me I could shift was because if I did, he'd find me." Not that my mother had a great record as a parent. For all I knew, she was lying to me. Or maybe she didn't even know who my father really was.

"He knows about you," Alec said.

My breath hitched. My father knew about me and who I was? A little part of me was furious that he never came to look for me. I was also a little disappointed. He probably didn't want me. Anger surged. I didn't need him, anyway. "What if I don't want to know who he is? It's not like he tried to help me."

"You might not have a choice," he said.

"How do you know?" I asked, my tone accusatory. "Another thing about me that you knew before we even met?"

"Yeah, sort of," he admitted. "I've been trying to find the recipe for the toxin for years. My research led me to your father."

"So you've been obsessed with my family for years? And then you seduced me? What the actual fuck is wrong with you?"

"Dude, that is super messed up," Kyle agreed.

"Okay, you and me, that was real. I liked you, Lola. I never planned what happened between us. And I certainly didn't want you to get hurt," he said.

"Funny way of showing it when you turned me over to my abusers," I said under my breath. I didn't want to go around in circles about this again. We all knew it wasn't going anywhere.

Deep down, I knew I wasn't going to get out of this on my own. Kyle might mean well, but he wasn't much help. Like me, he'd been isolated in Wolf Creek. We needed someone who was more educated on the outside world. Unfortunately, Alec was that someone. I had to accept help from him for the moment, but as soon as I got back on my feet, I had to go it alone again. Maybe I'd let Kyle tag along. I wasn't certain yet.

The one thing I did know, was that nobody had asked what I wanted. Before I pressed the issue, I needed to work through it for myself. I had no idea how I wanted to move forward. Did I want to return to Wolf Creek? Did I want to be an alpha? I'd never even imagined myself in that role before. Add in the information about Alec maybe knowing who my dad is, and I was in way over my head.

"Lola?" Alec's tone was gentle and familiar.

It sent a little shiver through me. *Dammit.* I wanted to stay fully mad at him at all times. He couldn't go around using that tone with me. "What?"

"Are you alright? This was a lot," he said.

"No, I'm not alright," I admitted. "Nothing about my life is *alright*."

"I wish I could take everything I ever did to you back," Kyle said.

"That's not what I'm talking about." I wasn't sure what I wanted from either of them. First, I thought I wanted nothing more than to be alone and figure this out on my own. Now, I wasn't sure what I wanted. I hadn't ever let myself think about a future as a shifter. I'd only ever thought about survival as a fake human.

"I don't know how to do any of this," I said. "My wolf doesn't respond to me, I've never felt welcome in a pack, my own mother stopped trying. And I'm not even sure I want to know who my dad is."

I looked at the back of Alec's head. He was focused on the road in front of him, but I knew he was listening. "Let me guess, my dad isn't just some random guy my mom got busy with. There's more to this. He's going to be awful. What if I don't want anything to do with him? Fuck, what if my mom was right and him knowing I'm alive makes my life even worse? If that's even possible."

"One step at a time," Kyle said. "Figure out your wolf, then we go from there."

"I tried that before. I was close. Then, I had to leave it all behind to go make Alec some money." The pain surged in, as raw and fresh as when he'd turned me over. I guess I did need to think about it. "I hope you got enough for selling me out."

"I didn't have a choice," Alec said. He didn't even turn to look at me. I should be grateful he was so focused on driving, but I knew it was out of avoidance rather than safety.

"I don't think I can do this," I said.

"Do what?" Kyle asked.

"Any of it. Go to the camp. Be around all those people who think I'm a total sucker." I liked the feral shifters. I'd made friends there and it was embarrassing to walk back there after making a fool of myself. "Wait, is this how you pay for things at the camp?"

"No, of course not," Alec said. "Sure, we might get involved in things that are a little shady, but we'd never turn over another shifter for money."

"So I was just an exception," I said.

"None of them know what happened," Alec said. "They weren't involved and they aren't to blame. This was all on me."

"Sheila?" I asked.

"Not even Sheila," he said.

"So what do they think happened?" I asked.

"They think you were captured," he said.

"Wonderful, so you get to go back as the hero and I'm the victim. Again." I shook my head. "No. I'm done being the victim."

"If it will help, I'll tell them Kyle got us both out. Let him be the hero," Alec said.

"Tell her why you did it," Kyle said.

"I don't want to know. His reasons don't change his actions. There was nothing that would justify what he did to me," I said.

"That's fair," Alec said. "And for what it's worth, everyone at camp was sorry when you left. I think all they'll care about is that you're back safe."

I swallowed against a lump in my throat. As much as I hated to admit it, I missed the camp and its residents. "Kyle, what do you think? About going to the feral camp?"

"I think it's our best shot. It's almost like hiding in the open. I don't think they'll expect you to return to your last location. Besides, we could use the help," he said.

I hated the whole thing. People didn't help me. Ever. I was always on my own. Any plan that revolved around others was too risky. On the flip side, I was a broken shifter with a murderous mate and would-be father-in-law. *Fuck my life.*

"I don't want to talk to you when we get there," I said to Alec.

"Fine by me," Alec replied.

"I'll need a tent for me and Kyle," I said.

That made Alec turn to look at me. "*Him?*"

I raised a brow. Was that jealousy in his voice? Maybe he should have thought of that before he betrayed me. "So far, he's the only one who seems to be looking out for me."

"Isn't he one of the guys who used to beat you up?" Alec asked.

"He is, but he never sold me to my enemies," I said.

"I saved your life," Alec said.

"That doesn't mean you own it," I snapped.

"He gets a second chance, but not me?" Alec sounded pissed.

"He didn't take my virginity and then turn around and hand me over to a mate who spent the last decade beating the shit out of me," I said.

"It's going to be okay," Kyle said. "We'll get through this. I swear."

His words were surprisingly comforting, but the tension was thick between me and a very silent Alec. I was done talking to him. I said what I needed to say and I was pretty sure there was nothing he could do to change things between us. Like Kyle, I supposed I could view him as an ally if he demonstrated his ability to help, but we couldn't go back to the way things were.

Alec slowed the car down and I realized we were already back at the camp. I saw the green tents dotting the outskirts of the common area. It was probably around dinner time since there were so many shifters gathered around outside. As Alec pulled the car into the space by Mario's tent, I noticed the huge stack of wood in the center of the common area. "Bonfire?"

"Tomorrow's the full moon," Alec said. "We'll light it then."

My stomach twisted. It had already been a month since I'd shifted to keep myself alive. In that time, I'd tasted freedom, and had it yanked away.

"I need to see Greta," I said.

"I'm sure she's already waiting for you," Alec assured me.

When the car was stopped, I didn't bother with goodbyes. I opened the door and walked out, headed toward Geta's tent.

7

WHISPERS AND STARES followed me as I made my way to Greta's tent. I wasn't about to stop and chat. How was I supposed to explain what happened? For them to have thought I was captured, it meant that Alec told them that right away. Then, he went and got himself captured. What did the residents think when they saw Alec hauled off? Or had he managed to get captured away from them?

I shook my head, trying to make myself stop worrying about the logistics of the strangest failed rescue attempt. And yes, he failed. If he went into captivity with the intention of trying to turn one of my assailants, he was doomed from the start. The fact that Kyle turned was pure luck. Without him hearing about my mark, it never would have happened.

I avoided eye contact when I saw Mario walking toward me. I felt awful. We had borrowed his car, but I wasn't in the mood to talk.

"Hey, Lola, I've got a new car arriving next week. Want to help me build the engine?" Mario asked.

I looked up at him, surprised that he picked up right where we left off. "That sounds fun."

"I'll make sure I save some of the challenging stuff for you to help with," he said with a grin.

I smiled back. It was unlikely I'd be around to help him with this project, but I didn't have the heart to disappoint him. Especially since he sounded so genuine.

"Lola, I've been waiting for you." Greta had just walked out of her tent. A rush of relief washed over me.

"You better run. She doesn't like to wait," Mario said.

"When you get as old as me, you don't have time to wait," Greta called.

"I better go." I waved to Mario before hurrying over to Greta. I was confused about my place here and wasn't sure who was friend or foe. Alec hadn't even mentioned who the spy was. But I couldn't deny that the shifters here had been kind to me. They'd taken me in and let me be part of their community without asking for anything in return. Well, aside from the obvious. But were they all like Alec? Waiting for the right moment to use their friendship with me to their advantage? Or were there actual nice shifters here?

"Took you long enough to get out of there," Greta said.

From anyone else, the comment might have sent me into a rage. From Greta, it was playful. "I had to cause some damage on my way out first."

"Well done." She held open her tent flap for me.

I ducked into her tent, my response playing in my mind. Kyle had caused some serious damage on our way out and I had yet to get any of the revenge I'd promised. Shame settled into my gut. I wanted to be strong and stand up for myself, but here I was, getting rescued again. That had to stop happening. First step, freeing my wolf.

A restless, fluttering sensation swirled in my chest. I froze in the center of Geta's tent, trying to decipher what the feeling was. I'd thought about my wolf, then I had felt something. The feeling swept through me again. I smiled despite the fact I had no idea where to go from here. All I knew was that my wolf was responding.

"They used the toxin on you, didn't they?" Greta asked as she settled into one of the chairs.

I walked over to the table and took the chair opposite her. "Yes. But I think it's worn off."

Greta smiled. "You're feeling your wolf."

"I think I've felt her a few times in the last day or so. I definitely felt her just now." I looked at the older woman. Her eyes were bright, her smile infections. I couldn't help but smile back at her. "Do you think it means I'm ready?"

"Do you know what you want now?" She asked.

The question took me by surprise, though it shouldn't have based on my previous conversations with Greta. On the drive here, I thought the whole situation would require days of reflection and wresting with my own demons. But as soon as Greta posed the question, I knew the answer.

"Yeah, I do," I said.

She nodded. "Then I imagine you are ready. The first shift is always easiest on a full moon. Tomorrow is your night."

My stomach twisted into knots. Anticipation made my chest feel tight. The stirring of my wolf rose to meet it. *So, you're ready now.* I found myself falling back into the habit of speaking to my wolf as if she was someone else. At least this time I managed to do it in my head.

Of course she didn't respond, but I got the sense that she approved of my decisions. The funny thing was that all the crap I gave Alec about not stepping up to embrace his role as alpha was exactly what made me realize what I needed to embrace mine.

The mark on my hip wasn't a curse. It was a gift. I wanted Ace and Tyler and everyone else who hurt me gone. I wanted to make them suffer for what they did to me. If I managed to prevent anyone else from going what I went through, I should take the chance.

My life hadn't been easy, and I knew that it was a miracle I was alive at all. It almost felt like I needed to do something bigger to celebrate the fact that I survived. Challenging for the title of alpha at Wolf Creek would be fucking huge. Besides, it would cause immense pain to the people who hurt me.

There was only one thing they wanted. Power. They wanted to keep Wolf Creek prisoner and stay at the top of the food chain.

The only way I'd truly hurt them would be to take the power from them and put myself in charge. I couldn't deny that seeing them meet a bloody end wouldn't be a nice addition, but I knew what I had to do. I was going to fight for the pack that refused to fight for me. There was always going to be someone weak they'd try to break and I couldn't let it keep happening. I had to stop them. And I had to make sure they couldn't ever hurt anyone else again.

I stood. "Thank you."

"Don't thank me. You're the one who's doing all the work," she said.

I smiled and gave her a nod before making my way out of the tent. Kyle was standing outside, waiting for me. He tensed like a soldier standing at attention. Having him around was going to take a lot of getting used to.

Trusting Kyle was going to be damn near impossible, but I was going to need help. I needed to know if he really had my back. There had to be a way to test him, at least a little. Kyle was still a mystery to me. He'd been a fixture of my childhood, but he was quieter than others. I didn't even know of any skeletons in his closet. Everyone in Wolf Creek had skeletons.

Then I remembered, he'd been short on details about how he'd gotten us out of Wolf Creek. He'd also hinted at some rather unsavory things. Was he hiding something? I had to know. If nothing more than to make sure I knew what I was getting into with our alliance.

"I need to know what you did when you got Alec out."

"You don't want to know," he said. "If you don't know, they can't punish you if we get caught."

I shook my head. "We're so far beyond that and you know it. If we're going to do this, we have two options: succeed and free our pack from the tyrant that is Ace Grant; or we get caught trying and we're both killed."

"So you've decided to go for it?" He lifted a surprised brow.

"Someone has to. Might as well be me," I said with a shrug.

"Loving the confidence," he deadpanned.

"I'll work on it. But seriously, Kyle, tell me what happened," I said.

He took a deep breath and looked down for a moment before looking back up. "I wasn't on guard duty. Nobody was, honestly. They had him so drugged and bound, there wasn't any risk of him getting out."

I winced, hating the visuals in my mind. Imagining Alec

dosed with toxin and tied up made my heart ache. I forgot how bad it must have been for him. Despite all he'd been through, all I did was worry about myself. I never even asked him if he was alright. Now I knew why only Kyle shifted on our way out of there.

"So what did you do?" I asked.

"I told someone I had intel on a break out. Convinced him that if he was the one to catch it, he'd get a boost in the inner circle." Kyle cleared his throat. I could tell he didn't want to talk about this.

"So when that person went to check, you made the switch?" I offered.

He nodded. "I killed him. Fast. As painless as I could. Then I got Alec out and dragged his body in."

"Who?" I asked.

He swallowed. "I need you to know something."

"What's that?" I asked.

"That I will not betray you. You are the rightful alpha," he said.

My heart raced and I sucked in a little breath as fear clawed at my chest. With the comments in the car, I didn't think it was possible, but my mind went right to the one person I shouldn't give a shit about.

"Tyler?" The word came out breathy and small and I hated how much I cared. The bond had to be driving me. There was no other explanation but knowing that didn't make my concern any less.

"Julian," Kyle said.

My shoulders dropped in relief and I turned away from Kyle, hoping to hide some of the emotion in my expression. I ran a hand through my hair. *Get a hold of yourself.* I knew that mating bonds got stronger over time, and faded if a mate died, which meant Tyler wasn't dead. He'd simply been the one person my mind decided to worry about in that moment. *Stupid bond.*

The momentary connection to Tyler passed and Kyle's words sunk in. I turned around slowly. "Julian is dead."

"He was a threat," Kyle said. "You should have heard the things he said about you. And that was after Tyler told us he wanted to honor his claim on you. He had no respect for the bond. If he ever got you alone..."

All the terrible things Julian did to me over the years crashed in around me. I saw myself pinned on the floor in my mom's trailer. I remembered when he pushed me down a flight of stairs at school. All the comments and snide remarks flooded in. Julian was a sadist. He enjoyed every second of being Tyler's henchman. While Tyler had the mating bond as a reason - not an excuse, mind you - but a reason for being drawn to me, Julian's reason was nothing more than enjoying causing pain.

"I didn't have a choice," Kyle said.

I looked up at him, our eyes meeting. I got the sense that he was concerned that I didn't approve. He seemed to want to please me. There was something between us that felt different. I felt a connection. Not romantic, not even friendship. It was something else I couldn't pinpoint.

My wolf seemed to be pacing inside me. She was impatient, but she wasn't upset. I didn't know how I knew, but my wolf wanted me to accept Kyle. To trust him even. It felt too soon. There was so much bad blood. But Julian's death was a peace offering of sorts. Even if Kyle didn't realize it.

"Julian didn't deserve the kindness you showed him in

quick death," I said. "I'm glad he's gone. You made the right choice."

Kyle lifted his chin a little. It was a nearly imperceptible visual that he was proud. My words had an impact on him. We all knew there was a pull to an alpha when you were a member of that pack. Was Kyle already feeling that pull toward me? I got the impression he was.

Even stranger, I could feel a little connection to him. The marks we received from the goddess were sacred and intentional. We all knew that. I never studied them in depth since I never intended to stay. I wondered if his mark and his role connected us more than a typical pack relationship. Was that how it worked for an alpha with the protectors? If I did pull this off and become alpha, I had some studying to do.

"I'm going to trust you, Kyle. I don't know if I'm making the right choice, but I know we won't pull this off if we don't trust each other," I said.

"You won't regret it," he said.

"I think there's going to be a lot of things I regret as we go down this path, but I get the sense that trusting you won't be one of them." I'd never been great at following my instincts, but I needed to start. Going against what I wanted and what I knew was right was what locked me away from my wolf.

"Tomorrow I'm going to shift," I said. "Will you run with me?"

He smiled. "Definitely."

8

"You need some rest," Kyle said as he started walking. "First shift takes a lot out of you. I'll show you where they set us up."

"Technically, it won't be my first shift," I admitted.

Kyle's brow furrowed. "Alec mentioned that the curse wasn't an issue anymore but I didn't know you'd shifted."

"Well, since I've decided to trust you and all, I guess you should know." I matched his pace and walked alongside him, hoping his sense of direction was better than mine. "After you and your friends threw me in that cave to die, I fell through a hole and thought I did die."

"Not my friends," he cut in.

"Fine. Your former alpha." It sounded both strange and comforting to say those words. The unsaid was that I was his current alpha. It was a bizarre feeling. Especially since our pack was currently at two members.

"What happened?" he pressed.

"I honestly don't remember, but my wolf forced the shift and got me out of there. Alec found me and brought me here."

I winced when I said that part. Another reminder of the fact that Alec had saved my life.

"I had no idea that was how you got out. Or how you met Alec." Kyle was quiet for a moment as he continued forward, toward the woods and the lake. I wasn't sure we were going the right direction, but there was a little part of me hoping he would get lost. Then it wouldn't just me be who sucked at keeping my bearings here.

"He said I was in my wolf form when he found me," I added. "I do owe him for that."

"At least you know you *can* shift," he said.

"I haven't since but it's good to know the curse was a sham. For a while, I wasn't sure I could repeat it. Now, I think I'm finally ready," I said.

"So you were never cursed?" he asked.

"Nope. Neither was my mom if you can believe it," I said.

"That makes sense," he said.

I stopped walking. "What do you mean?"

He stood next to me. "My mom used to talk about your mom from time to time. They were friends when they were younger. I thought maybe she was mixing people up, but I know I heard her talking about your mom shifting."

"Maybe it was before my grandfather was cursed?" I offered.

"Maybe," he said. "I don't know the timeline. But why would a shifter who knew how to shift and had been shifting suddenly stop unless they were forced?"

"I don't know. Why would she return to Wolf Creek and keep me from my dad?" I asked. "Why did she quit parenting me and decide to earn her money on her back?" I shook my head. "I had to stop asking so many questions about my mom."

"Do you want to know who he is?" Kyle asked.

"I can't believe Alec told you. Or that he's known pretty much since he met me and didn't bother to say a word." I shook my head. "He just keeps showing me how much worse he can get, doesn't he?"

"I don't think he meant to hurt you," Kyle said.

"Are you kidding me? I told him everything. He knew how bad my life was and he still handed me over to them," I said.

"You know how silver-tongued Ace can be," Kyle said.

"You're seriously defending him?" My jaw dropped open. "You know, if you're going to be on my team, it's not going to work well if you're taking the side of the man I can't stand."

"And you and I aren't going to work well if you don't take my advice seriously. You don't have to accept it, but my job is to protect you. If you can't trust my judgement enough to consider my suggestions, I can't keep you safe. We have to listen to each other. For now, it's just the two of us. We're going to have to do our best to navigate the limited resources we have. And Alec is a resource."

I scowled. "Fine. I will take your comments into consideration."

"That's all I'm asking," he said.

"Did he tell you how he made me fall for him?" I asked.

"I got a few details. He also told me how sorry he was and how much he still wanted you. It was kind of pathetic actually." He elbowed me playfully. "You can do better."

"Not helping," I said.

"I tried," he said with a smirk.

"Okay, where is this tent you're taking us to?" We were in the woods, away from the others. "We're lost, aren't we?"

"Not a tent," he said. "They're letting us use this little cabin out here."

"The cabin?" I had to make sure I'd heard correctly.

"Yeah, it's supposed to have a shower. And not to be rude, but you could use one."

I had to smile at that. "Right back at you."

"I'll let you go first, then I'm definitely taking a turn," he said.

"The cabin is Alec's house. Did he tell you that?" I asked.

"No, but he told me you might refuse to stay there." Kyle led us down the little path in the woods and I could already see the cabin. We were nearly there.

"The thought crossed my mind," I admitted. "But as long as he's not there, I'll accept the space. And the shower."

I knew we weren't in a position to be picky. Plus, the cabin had the added benefit of being rather secluded. I wasn't in the mood to interact with the rest of the camp. Especially since I had no idea what I was going to do when I saw Sheila or Malcom. Sheila had been my first real friend ever. So I thought. And Malcom had tried to warn me about Alec. What else did he know that he hadn't shared? I wondered if he'd be someone I could add as an ally.

I followed Kyle up the steps that led to the front door. He opened it and we walked into a cozy, bright, welcoming space. A worn couch covered in blankets sat on one side of the room, on the other was a double bed with a patchwork quilt. A lamp on the bedside table was on, giving the space a warm glow. On the right was a little alcove with a window. It held a small table with three wood chairs around it. To the left was a single door. My guess was that it was the bathroom.

No kitchen or other rooms, but it was enough space for the two of us. The cabin was homey and peaceful. Despite the fact it had been Alec's home, I felt at ease here. It didn't look like it had even the slightest bit of Alec's personality. I knew the cabin had once been Greta's and it looked exactly as I'd imagine a space she'd decorated should look.

I walked to the door and opened it to reveal a tiny bathroom complete with sink, toilet, and shower. It sure beat peeing in the woods. "Not bad."

"You sure Alec lived here? It looks like it belongs to a grandmother," Kyle said.

"It did," I said. "I guess Alec never updated it."

"Well, guess it's ours for a few days while we figure out our next steps," he said. "Why don't you shower. I'll see about some food."

"Thanks." I stepped into the bathroom. Fast shower, then food. It was exactly what I needed. Well, and some sleep. But at this point, I might as well wait till evening and just sleep all night.

The water pressure was non-existent, but I managed to get washed up with the surprisingly nice smelling soap. After drying off, I put back on the same weird borrowed clothes. I frowned down at the ill-fitting, dirty garments. One of these days, I'd have my own clothes again. And more than one pair so I could wear things that were clean.

My hair was a soaking wet tangled mess hanging down my back. I looked around the bathroom in the hopes of finding a hair tie. Under the sink was a pack of toilet paper but nothing else. Not a single sign of a woman ever staying over. Somehow, that surprised me. Had he cleaned the space out or was Alec not having women over? When we hooked up, it had been in my tent. Maybe he was a no sleepovers kind of guy.

The sound of a door closing made me jump. Then I remembered that Kyle was bringing food and I quickly left the bathroom.

Kyle was in the room, and he did have food, but he wasn't alone. I crossed my arms over my chest and waited for Alec to say something.

"Might as well give him five minutes, Lola," Kyle said. "That's all."

After our earlier conversation, I felt like I owed it to him to be supportive. Kyle and I hadn't said it, but it felt like we'd started over. Clean slate and all that shit. Besides, as much as I hated to admit it, Alec was helping us. It was probably out of guilt, but we could use the assistance for now.

"Five minutes," I said.

"Can we go for a walk?" Alec asked.

I glanced at Kyle. He held up a sandwich. "It's portable."

"I hate you right now," I said.

He handed me the sandwich. "I know."

Annoyed, I walked to the door, knowing that Alec would follow me out. I wasn't in the mood to deal with him, but the sooner I got his over with, the better. I quickly moved down the steps and started walking.

"Slow down," Alec called.

I stopped and turned, prepared to say something snarky. Instead, I noticed his limp. My shoulders dropped and my brow creased in concern. How could I forget? If they gave him the toxin, he couldn't rapid heal. If it wasn't out of his system yet, he was basically human.

"Are you okay?" I asked, not masking my concern.

"You were right about that pack of yours," he said. "They like to hurt people who can't fight back."

He had dark circles under his eyes, but none of the usual visual damage on his face that I would typically carry. They hadn't hurt him the same way they usually hurt me. "What did they do to you?"

"Did you know your mate is into whips? Like old school torture shit." He turned and lifted his shirt, revealing the marks crisscrossing his back.

I dropped the sandwich and walked over to him. Alec lowered his shirt, and turned to face me. We were the closest we'd been since he'd prevented me from running from my old pack. It felt too intimate, but I let myself linger there, inches from him.

My heart raced, my breathing quickened. All my senses felt like they were on overdrive. I could feel Alec's body heat, I could smell his scent. I wanted to help him, to comfort him, but I held back, unable to let myself follow through on the desires. Once, he was comfort and support. Now, he was a reminder that I had to protect my heart.

I took a step back. "Did he see your mark?"

"I don't think so. He enjoyed ripping my clothes to shreds with his whip. Fucking sadist. Kyle brought things for me to wear when he got me out," he said.

"Does Kyle know about your mark?" I was suddenly nervous that I'd lose my only ally to Alec. Surely, Kyle would offer to follow him instead. As much as he'd been begging me to hear Alec out, I started to wonder if that was the plan.

"He doesn't know. And I'm not going to tell him." Alec

studied my face, his gorgeous, two-tone eyes felt like they might penetrate my soul.

I tore my gaze away. Everything about this felt too personal.

"You're the only one who knows about it," he said.

I looked back at him. "That's impossible. Sheila?"

He shook his head. "I've never told her. After what she went through, I couldn't face her knowing I had a mark that I never acted on. And yes, I know I'm a hypocrite."

"I wasn't going to say it, but I was thinking it," I admitted.

He smirked. "I know."

"What about the other girls you've been with?" There was obvious jealously in my tone. "There's no way I was the only one." I tried to cover my slip up by pretending I wasn't hurt. I got the sense he saw right through me.

"I told you, I had a mate once. There was her. Then there was nobody until you," he said.

My heart felt like it was shattering into a million pieces. Desire coursed through my veins. I still wanted him, even after all he'd done to me. I was broken. Something was seriously wrong with me. I deserved to be with someone who had my back, no matter what. Someone who wouldn't turn on me when it got difficult. I would rather be alone than worry that I couldn't trust my partner.

"I can't," I broke eye contact and looked down at my hands, "I can't do this with you."

"Do what, exactly?" Alec asked.

"Pretend to be something we're not." I forced myself to meet his gaze. My wolf was reacting, clawing and restless. She was just as stressed and confused as I was. Alec hurt me. I couldn't let anyone hurt me again.

He ran a hand through his hair. "Fine. We keep it all business."

"Fine," I agreed, but my heart was protesting. I hated this. Why did he still have a piece of my heart? And why had he ruined everything between us? We were just getting to know each other. What if we could have had something amazing?

I swallowed hard, trying to push all the *what ifs* from my mind. It was too late for any of that.

"Are you going to try to shift tomorrow?" he asked.

"Greta can't keep anything to herself, can she?" I asked.

"I didn't hear it from her. It's a full moon. It makes sense. As long as the toxin is out of your system," he said.

"I felt my wolf today."

"That's good, you should be ready. You're going to love running in the woods. It'll change everything once you connect with your wolf."

Flutters of anticipation swirled in my gut. I was excited for the shift, and nervous about what would come next. "What about you? Is the toxin gone? Can you feel your wolf?"

"Not yet, but I'm hoping the full moon helps him fight back against the toxin."

"They must have given you a lot," I said.

"Maybe," he said. "I wasn't fully conscious for most of it. Or I blocked it out."

"I get that," I said.

We stood in awkward silence for a few moments. Things used to be easy between us. I hadn't known him long, but we'd had something special. Now, it was long gone.

"Now what?" I finally caved, the silence was too much. "Is there anything else you want to say?"

"It can wait," he said. "After you shift, we can talk. Then you can decide about your next steps."

I didn't want to press today. Exhaustion was kicking in and the sun was dipping low in the horizon. "Alright."

He turned and walked away, leaving me standing outside his cabin feeling uncomfortable and anxious. There was a part of me that wanted to chase after him and beg him to let us go back to where things were before we went to Wolf Creek. I cursed myself under my breath and turned back to the cabin. There was no changing the past.

All I could do now was try to make the best of my future.

9

KYLE WAS HOLDING out another sandwich as soon as I walked in the door.

"You were watching?" I grabbed the sandwich and took a bite. This time, I was going to make myself actually eat it.

"I didn't listen, but I kept an eye on you," he said.

I probably should have been upset, but it was oddly comforting knowing someone had my back. Sure, things with Kyle were weird, but if he wanted to cause me harm, he'd have done it already.

"You okay?" he asked.

I wasn't sure how to answer that. Kyle knew more than he'd shared and largely because I'd asked him to keep it that way. If he was being honest about not listening, he didn't know what our conversation had been about. For all Kyle knew, it was a lover's quarrel.

My stomach tightened and the food in my mouth tasted like ash. Was it ever going to get easier to sort out my feelings about Alec? Did it matter if I was just going to return to Wolf Creek, anyway?

"Do you think I have what it takes to be alpha?" I asked.

"You can't be any worse than the alpha we were raised with," he said.

That was probably true, but it wasn't reassuring. Almost anyone would be better than Ace. Or Tyler. Knots formed in my stomach as I contemplated what I was going to have to do.

"It's not going to be easy. Once I show my mark, they're not just going to hand over control," I said.

"I doubt it. That's why I think we need some help. Probably more than just Alec, too," he said. "You're probably going to have to challenge Ace. Or Tyler, if Ace stepped down and let him take over." Kyle sighed. "Be realistic, Lola. Could you hurt Tyler?"

I wanted nothing more than to see Tyler pay for what he'd done to me all these years. I tried to imagine the two of us facing off in an alpha challenge. Every time I pictured myself going in for an attack, I stopped short. Frustrated, I visualized myself as a wolf, going after Tyler's wolf. I met the same resistance.

"Fuck." Even in my head, I couldn't hurt Tyler. I looked over at Kyle. "We have to break that bond."

"I know. And we will. But I don't think we can do it alone," Kyle said. "What about the shifters here? Would they rally for you? Could you convince some of them to follow you?"

"There's one I wonder about, but I don't know about the others. They live here for a reason. They want to be without a pack. I can't ask them to risk their lives to help me gain power over a pack I don't even like," I said. "Am I doing the right thing? If I'm being honest, I hold no love for Wolf Creek."

"You weren't the only shifter being terrorized in Wolf Creek," Kyle said. "Other students were threatened, bullied, and pushed around. Even adults were told what to do, where to work, who they could be with… It's broken."

"I'm broken. Because of that place," I said.

"You were chosen for this. Probably because of what you experienced. They need someone like you who knows what it's like to be on the outs," Kyle said.

"If I do this, I'm tearing down that barrier," I said.

"Good." Kyle's jaw was set and he looked more deadly than I'd ever seen him. "That barrier almost cost my sister her life. We couldn't take her anywhere to get help. She was trapped inside because of that stupid age rule. We had to rely on the charity of Ace Grant. I don't have to tell you what that costs someone."

"So, we need help," I relented. "What about my father? How does that play into all this? Alec said I was in danger. Was he being dramatic? Do you really know who he is?"

"I do," Kyle agreed.

"Do I need to know? Can I just pretend nobody knows and move on with all the other complications in my life? It's a lot already to deal with a mating bond I don't want and an alpha to take down." Did everything in my life have to be difficult? It felt like I should get to take the easy way out once in a while.

"You probably need to know before you move on since you've decided to challenge for alpha," he said.

"What does my dad have to do with that? Is he from Wolf Creek? Or is an alpha? I don't know why he'd care," I said. "He's never bothered to show up and if you believe my mom, he didn't even know I existed before Alec got involved."

"It's complicated," Kyle said. "I won't tell you until you're ready, but I think you aren't going to have a choice."

"That makes no sense," I said.

"It's hard to explain without telling you his name," Kyle said.

"I still don't know if I want to know," I said.

"I get that." Kyle took a deep breath. "Alright, let me see if I can explain without telling you. So, shifter politics 101: The alphas are linked with the higher alphas, right?"

I thought back to my high school Shifter Politics class and tried to recall the structure. "Shit. I'm going to need a crash course in all this. I don't remember this stuff and if I do it, I'm going to do it right."

"That's not why I'm telling you this. You think Ace is doing anything by the book?" Kyle looked skeptical.

"Probably not," I agreed. "But I'm not Ace. I will do it correctly."

"I know you will but here's the thing, Lola. If you are alpha, you'll be connected to the higher alphas."

"You mean the king."

He nodded.

"So?" I wasn't following why any of this would matter. "It's not like I'm the one who made the toxin or was cursed. They can't punish me for what my grandfather did, can they?"

Kyle blew out a frustrated breath. "Lola, you have to hear this eventually. Sooner rather than later. I wish I could shield you from it until you were ready, but you dad knows you're alive. And I have a feeling even if you don't go looking for him, soon enough, he'll come for you," Kyle said.

"Well, that's fucking ominous," I deadpanned.

"Please don't make me keep this from you anymore. You need to know this."

"How bad is it?" I asked.

Kyle whistled.

"Wonderful." I took another bite of my sandwich. I wasn't feeling hungry anymore and the sandwich might as well be made of sawdust. But it gave me something to do.

Still chewing, I wandered over to the little table and sat down. Kyle joined me, taking a seat on one of the empty chairs. I continued to eat, sure that Kyle was going to blurt out the name of my father. Would I even know who he was? I was so isolated in Wolf Creek that I didn't know of many shifters outside the barrier.

Oddly, that gave me a little bit of hope. It was likely I wouldn't know who he was or why he was so terrible. Maybe he was alpha of another pack and had a bad reputation. If I'd never heard of him, it wouldn't matter. I'd know so when alphas gathered, I wouldn't be caught off guard. If we were both alphas, we'd have to meet eventually. Or maybe he was wanted and I'd be responsible for reporting him if he crossed into our territory. Sure, that would be awkward, but it wasn't like I actually knew the guy.

As I chewed the last bite of food, I wiped the crumbs off my fingers. Then I looked at Kyle. "Okay, lay it on me. Who is this big, bad dude who is so awful that I had to avoid him at all costs?"

"You sure?" Kyle asked.

"Two minutes ago you were begging for me to let you tell me," I blurted out.

"You can't un-know this," he warned.

"Kyle, how bad can it be? What is he a gangster? A murderer?"

Kyle looked a little green.

"What could be worse than that?" I asked.

"Well, let's just say that if you try to overthrow Ace, you'll be following in the family tradition of challenging an alpha," he said.

"Enough, Kyle. Spit it out, already," I snapped.

"Your dad is Spencer Lupton," Kyle said.

I blinked a few times as the name rolled around in my mind. *Spencer Lupton.* Even I knew that name. Shortly before I was born, the wolf shifter king's brother, Spencer, tried to take the throne. He was detained and as far as I knew, he spent the rest of his life in exile or jail or something. The details were fuzzy because I never gave a shit about the royal family. They never did a thing for me. Why would I care if some rich asshole's brother wanted some shiny crown for himself?

"I'm sorry, it sounds like my dad has the same name as the traitor who tried to take the throne. But that's not possible." I waited for Kyle to explain that he just shared the name with the famous traitor.

"He was barred from having offspring by the king," Kyle said. "Any child of his would be killed."

"So you're saying that if the shifter king finds out about me, I'm dead?" It didn't seem possible. I was nothing. Nobody. At least I was right now. If I moved forward with the plan to take on Ace, I would be an alpha and then I'd be connected to the king himself. If I didn't end up dead in the process. "This whole thing is insane, you do realize that, right?"

"It sure seems a lot like fate, if you ask me," he said. "Maybe you're supposed to help right his wrong of something by making your own pack better."

"Fate is making a lot of mistakes lately. Giving me an alpha mark and a bond with Tyler come to mind." I ran a hand through my hair.

"What am I supposed to do with this information?" I asked.

"Well, now you know why Alec said he was dangerous," Kyle said. "And you know that we have to be careful."

My brow furrowed as I thought about all the new information and what it meant for me. "I can't be alpha, can I?" It surprised me how much that hurt. Until that moment, I wasn't aware of how badly I wanted to help the people of Wolf Creek. Even if they never did anything to help me.

I looked up at Kyle. "If I won the challenge, the king would feel me. He'd know, wouldn't he? He'd know we were blood. I'm guessing that's what all this is about."

"There's a way to fix this," Kyle said. "Your father is willing to help."

"Why would he help when he could turn me in to get on the king's good side? Or kill me himself, even? I remember my history classes well enough to know how murderous and dangerous Spencer was. You think a man like that cares about his kid?" I tensed. "Holy shit, you said he already knows about me. Alec told him about me. I'm already screwed, aren't I?"

"Calm down, Lola. Alec's already fixed this," he assured me.

I wasn't listening, though. My mind was overwhelmed with far too much information. I stood, knocking the chair to the ground in the process. I ignored it and walked to the center of the room. This was far worse than I expected. My mom had said she wouldn't let me shift to keep my father from finding me and now it made more sense.

Aside from alphas connecting with the king, parents were connected to their children. The only thing that broke that connection was a completed mating bond. Which I was not going to do. Some stupid protection kind of thing. If I was in wolf form, and my father was in wolf form, he'd be able to feel me well enough to know where I was. Without a completed mating bond, my dad could track me down the second I shifted. All he'd have to do was be in his wolf form himself. Which, he was very likely to be tomorrow night since it was a full moon.

"I can't shift tomorrow." I turned to Kyle. "If I do, he'll know where I am."

"He already knows," Kyle said.

"So what, that's it? I shift tomorrow, and the king's guard comes and takes me out?" I blew out a frustrated breath. "How is he going to help us if I'm dead?"

"First of all, the king doesn't know about you and he won't know about you since you're not yet an alpha," he said.

I knew the mark wasn't enough to take the title, but it still made me nervous. "What about my father? How can Alec be so confident that he won't turn me in or harm me?"

"He's agreed to break his claim on you," Kyle said.

"Can that be done?" I asked.

"With enough money, you can pay a witch to do anything," Kyle said.

"And he's willing to finance that?" I asked. "And don't get me started about how I feel about getting a witch involved."

"Alec took care of that part. That's what he used the money from Ace for," Kyle said. "The witch is already paid and your father already contributed his blood for the spell. It's done. As soon as you're ready, you can break the claim."

I stared at Kyle in stunned silence.

"Don't be so hard on Alec. He didn't think he had a choice and Ace told him you'd be safe. Alec thought he'd have you out of there by the next day. The spell isn't cheap and Ace paid well," Kyle added.

"He knew all this and he didn't tell me?" I asked.

It was Kyle's turn to be silent.

"I don't understand. This is crazy. Why would my father agree to this? He's never even met me. And everything we've ever heard about Spencer Lupton paints him as a scary mother fucker." I wasn't going to lie, I was a little worried about what might happen if I ever met him.

"You'll have to ask Alec that. I guess he wants to help you but I don't know the details," Kyle said. "You know what I know."

I felt shaky and unsteady. Slowly, I righted the upended chair and sat down. This changed things but I couldn't wrap my head around what it all meant. Alec was trying to help me. My father was an outlaw. I was supposed to be dead.

How the fuck was I supposed to overcome all of this and somehow take the alpha title from my old pack?

"If it helps, I think everything is happening as it should," Kyle said.

"Easy for you to say," I snapped. "My life has been a living hell. And now I find out that if I had shifted so I could fit in, I'd have been killed. How am I even supposed to process that?"

"The choice is yours now, though. You and me, neither of us had options or freedom to decide while we were in Wolf Creek. We can change the path, we're not stuck doing the wrong thing in order to survive."

"What if we're still doing the wrong thing?" I asked. "What if the king finds out I exist even with the broken claim?"

"Then we figure it out together," Kyle said.

“Who knew the outside world would make Wolf Creek look like the easier bet,” I said with a laugh.

“The right choice is rarely the easy one,” Kyle said.

“When did you get so wise?” I teased.

He smiled. “When I got a new alpha who was willing to let me be myself.”

10

WHEN KYLE INSISTED I take the bed, I was too tired to put up a fight. I climbed in and snuggled under the sheets. The blankets smelled like Alec. And why wouldn't it? It was his bed.

My throat tightened as I thought about everything I'd learned. Aside from my pack hunting me, there was a chance my father's family would kill me if they ever found out I was alive. Then there was this new news about Alec. I didn't know if it was the truth, but if Alec sold me out to earn the cash to help me, where did that leave us?

Asshole could have explained it to you. I realized that if he'd told me, I'd have refused to comply. I would have taken my chances with the royal family rather than return to captivity in Wolf Creek. Alec would have known that. But he should have given me a choice.

Why would the shifter king even care about me? I was nobody and I had no interest in getting involved in royal politics. Shit, if not for the mark on my hip, I wouldn't even be going back to Wolf Creek. It was possible the royal family would leave me be. Nobody knew my relation and it wouldn't look great for them to take out a nineteen-year-old shifter just for being alive.

I could hear Kyle snoring on the couch. He offered to stay up and keep watch, but I insisted we both sleep. While I wasn't convinced we were safe here, at least Alec's cabin was outside the main camp. That was probably why we were stashed here. Kyle had resisted, but when I pointed out that tonight was our best chance at a good night's sleep, he relented.

It was true, with the damage caused by the fire and the full moon tomorrow, we likely had one more night before they'd come after us. Ace didn't miss Full Moon Ceremonies. He could send some of his henchmen after us, but I had to hope Alec's theory that they'd avoid the camp was good. Hiding in the place I was most likely to go seemed counterintuitive, but it could save me if they figured I'd avoid it.

My thoughts were jumbled, leapfrogging between reflections about Alec, my mom, Tyler, Wolf Creek, and a million other directions. It felt like I'd never get myself calm enough to sleep.

Somehow, I settled enough to let sleep find me. I woke to the sound of running water and turned to see Kyle was missing from the couch. The bathroom door was closed, the sound of the shower carried through the tiny cabin. Sunlight poured in through the windows. It was warm and bright and far too cheerful compared to my mood.

I sat up and tossed the blankets aside. My mouth was dry and I had a headache, but it wasn't as bad as it had been when I was in Wolf Creek. If anything, I was probably dehydrated.

To my surprise, I noticed there was a whole spread on the

little table. A pitcher of juice, a few bottles of water, a box of pastries, and a bowl of fruit. Where had that come from?

The sound of the water stopped. I stood and stretched, then wandered over to the table and poured myself a glass of juice. Grateful for the food, I decided I should eat before I get any more bad news that ruined my appetite.

I was halfway through my second pastry when Kyle joined me at the table. His hair was still wet and like me, he was in the same clothes he'd been wearing. "You found breakfast."

"Yeah, thanks," I said.

"Someone named Sheila brought it by," he said.

A flicker of guilt passed through me. I'd been here all night and I hadn't stopped by to say hello to her. If Alec was right, and he'd left her out of his plans, it was possible Sheila really was my friend. I had serious trust issues. What if she was honestly just a nice person and I couldn't let go of my own misconceptions?

"That was nice of her," I said.

"She asked me to let you know her tent is open anytime," he said as he took a bite of a muffin.

"I'll go see her after we eat." I did miss her and I wanted to see how she was doing. Hopefully, everything here had been boring and safe while I'd been away.

"Fill up, you'll need your energy tonight," he said, his mouth full.

"Do you think it's a good idea for me to do it?" I asked. "Shift, I mean."

"You need to learn," he said. "It's not healthy for a shifter to stay in human form forever. They say it makes you go mad."

"I've heard that but how many of those shifters had a

homicidal family after them?" I asked. "It still seems dangerous."

"Pretty sure you already blew your cover when you shifted before, right?"

"But can't they only connect while you're in wolf form?" I asked. "It's been a month. He doesn't know if I'm still here. Unless Alec gave him all the details."

"He's helping you break the claim. He's not going to come after you and the king won't know about you until you're an official alpha." He reached for a banana. "Breaking that family tie with him will keep you safe. Once that's done, nobody will know he's your father. Besides, I'm pretty sure he's locked up somewhere."

"Which makes me wonder how Alec got to him in the first place," I said.

"Probably better we don't focus on all the details. I have a feeling we might be better off not knowing everything," Kyle suggested.

"Why do I have to have so many connections to people I don't want to be connected to?" I asked.

"The Tyler thing still baffles me," he said. "Fate is a bitch."

"Yeah, putting us together was beyond cruel," I agreed.

"We'll break your mating bond as soon as we can," Kyle said.

"So, I guess I shift. Then we find the witch and break the claim so I can get back to all the other drama I was already involved in." It sounded crazy when I said it out loud.

"It's the right choice," he assured me.

I finished my last bite then stood. "I'm going to find Sheila."

He shoved almost an entire banana in his mouth at once. I wrinkled my nose. "Do you chew when you eat?"

He took a few very full chews, then swallowed. "Let's go."

"You don't have to follow me everywhere," I said.

He lifted his brows in silent comment.

I scowled. "Is this how it's going to be? You follow me everywhere for the rest of my life?"

"Just till I know you're safe," he confirmed. "I'll feel better when the claim is broken and you're officially alpha. Till then, I have to keep you alive to make those things happen."

"Fine. You might as well tag along." I walked to the door with Kyle at my heels.

It was strange knowing that tonight I was going to try to shift. I'd wished for it for so long, then I accepted the fact that I'd never complete a shift. Standing at the precipice of gaining a connection with my wolf was unreal. I still had a hard time allowing myself to think it could happen.

Go figure, me actually getting to shift would make my life even worse instead of better. As I walked toward camp, I thought about my mom's warning last time I'd seen her. She didn't want me to shift no matter what. She'd stopped shifting herself, I was more sure of that now. Had she done it to keep me from getting curious and trying to shift? Had her lack of shifting turned her into what she was?

When I was young, I remembered her as a caring and loving mom. We finger painted with pudding, we played in the creek. She braided my hair and sang songs to me before I went to sleep.

She wasn't always the way she was.

My heart ached as the pieces fell into place. She'd sacrificed everything for me. A wolf who doesn't shift goes insane.

We'd all heard that growing up. My mom changed over the years. She was a shell of the person she used to be. All because she stopped shifting.

My throat felt tight and my eyes were burning as I held back tears. Could that be fixed? Could a wolf who stopped shifting be healed? Or was she going to be stuck in this prison in her mind forever?

When I saved my pack, I was also going to save her. I'd shift, then I'd make her shift. Tonight was more important than I realized. It was my first step toward being the person I had to be. I was going to embrace the mark and be the leader my pack deserved.

"You'll help me tonight?" I asked Kyle.

"Of course," he said.

"At moonrise, I'm going to do this," I said, more for myself than anyone else.

My wolf seemed to leap for joy inside me. I couldn't help but smile. It was time.

11

Sheila was sitting in a lawn chair outside her tent. Next to her was a little folding table and another chair. Two mugs sat on the table. "Did I interrupt?"

She grinned and jumped from her seat. I was swept up into a bone-crushing hug. "I was so worried about you. I can't believe they caught you." She released me from the hug but kept her hands on my shoulders. "Are you alright? Did they hurt you? And please for the love of the moon goddess, take me to Wolf Creek with you next time so I can beat the shit of those assholes."

"I missed you too," I said.

"Tell me you're not going back there," she said. "Cause I heard a rumor that I'm not fond of."

"Where did you hear this rumor?" I asked.

"I guess it was more of a heads-up than a rumor. Alec says you're going to go back," she said. "But he's mum on the fucking details. Since when does he leave me out of shit?"

She sounded hurt and it made me think Alec probably had been honest when he told me that he'd acted alone. "Sit, sit. I hoped you'd come. Coffee is likely cold by now, but it's still coffee."

"I'll let you two catch up," Kyle said. "I'm going to check out the camp. Think you can keep out of trouble while I'm away?"

"I'll do my best," I said.

"We'll be here," Sheila said. "I promise she'll be safe with me."

Kyle didn't look like he fully trusted her, but he nodded. "Holler if you need me."

"I'll be fine," I said. "Thank you."

"First of all, your new bodyguard is super cute. Seems pretty dedicated to you," she said.

"We've been through a lot already," I said.

"You trust him?" she asked.

"Well enough," I said.

"Tell me everything," Sheila said. "What the fuck happened after you left? I thought you and Alec were going to break that bond to your mate. Then he comes back and says you're captured and then he vanishes. Malcom said he was captured too. I'm totally lost."

I settled into the chair and picked up the surprisingly still warm coffee. After a few glorious sips, I set the mug back on the table. "You want me to start from the beginning?"

"Please. I thought I was in the loop, but I guess I wasn't. Honestly, I knew Alec was up to something but I figured he'd tell me in his own time." She set her cup down. "Lola, what the fuck happened?"

So many people were after me at this point, I figured it didn't matter if I let Sheila in on it. There were countless ways for all of this to go south, I might as well have a friend who cared on my side.

"How much do you want to know?" I asked. "Cause I'm not sure I understand it all, and honestly, I don't think I can ever look at Alec the same way again. I know he's your best friend."

"Spill."

I took a deep breath and explained the whole thing. I told her about the recipe for the toxin and Alec selling me out. I glossed over the most gruesome details about my week of captivity, but gave her the gist. When I explained how Kyle helped me get out, her jaw dropped fully open.

"Wait. Alec sold you out to your old pack?" Her eyes narrowed and her expression looked murderous. "I'm going to kill him."

"Wait," I said. "Kyle told me he used the money to help me with something even more complicated, if you can believe it."

"What the fuck could be more complicated?" she asked.

"I'm not sure I'm ready to share that part," I admitted.

"He had no right," Sheila said. "He never should have done that to you."

"I know," I agreed.

"I wanted to be the cool aunt to your kids," she said with a pout.

I nearly spit out my coffee. "We hooked up one time. We weren't even an official couple and you were planning on us having kids?"

She shrugged. "I was pretty sure it was one of those soulmate forever things."

"I have a mate, remember. He tried to kill me. I'm not sure I'm in the market for one ever again." Maybe it was good that

Alec and I didn't go further. I wasn't sure I'd ever be in the place to give my heart to someone.

"That's why it was perfect. Alec lost his mate tragically. Yours deserves a torturous, fiery death. Oh, please tell me he went down when Kyle started the fire." Sheila jumped a little in her seat, a bit too excited about the thought of someone dying horribly. But then again, this was Tyler.

"I don't think so. I'm pretty sure I still feel the bond and if he was dead, I don't think I would," I said.

Her shoulders slumped. "That sucks."

"Tell me about it," I said.

"You up for the party tonight?" She lifted her cup in the direction of the pile of wood ready for the bonfire.

"I'll be there."

She quirked a brow. "Tell me that means what I think it means."

I grinned. "I'm going to shift."

She squealed and nearly dumped the remains of her cup on me as she leaped from her chair to give me another hug. "You are going to have the best time."

My stomach twisted into nervous knots, but I knew I had to complete the shift before I could attempt any of the other things I needed to do. Connecting with my wolf would bring additional perks. Aside from being faster in wolf form, I should have added strength and healing. Plus, I could connect better with those in my pack.

I frowned, a little sad about that. Would I feel the emotions of shifters in Wolf Creek or would that be barred from me since I wasn't there? I had no idea how this was going to play out. There wasn't much choice other than taking it one day at a time.

"Tell me what I missed while I was away," I prompted. A subject change was very much needed. I was tired of the constant worry and speculation.

She told me about her dates with Anja and how they'd decided they were going to try a long-term thing for a while. It was adorable how her whole face lit up when she talked about her.

"Mind if I cut in?"

I'd been so engrossed in Sheila's conversation, I hadn't noticed that we had a visitor. Malcom was standing in front of us, a camp chair in his arms.

He set the chair down in front of us, forming a little circle. "Welcome back, Lola."

"Thanks." I wasn't sure how to engage with Malcom. He'd been the one to warn me about Alec. Did that mean he'd known the plan the whole time or was he just wary of the camp's leader?

"I'm glad to see you're okay," he said. "I'm sorry for what he put you through."

I narrowed my eyes. "You knew."

He nodded. "I'm sorry."

"Wait, you were in on this but nobody told me?" Sheila gasped. "Since when are you inner circle and I'm on the outs? What the fuck?"

"I was the backup plan. I didn't find out until Alec came back to camp," he said. "If they didn't make it out by the full moon, I was on deck."

"Why the full moon?" I asked.

"Cause there was a chance you could both shift your way out on the full moon if you were trapped."

All my anger returned. "You do realize my mate was

threatening to complete the bond without my consent? His father was encouraging him to do so. If he'd gotten his wish, I'd be trapped in a bond with him. What were you two thinking?"

Malcom's expression darkened. "He did what?"

"You heard me," I snapped. I wasn't eager to repeat it.

"I'm going to kill that bastard," he said with a growl.

"Get in line," Sheila said.

"Great, you all want to kill Tyler, but it doesn't fix what I just went through or what he could have done to me. Why did you go along with that? You were the one warning me to keep my distance," I pointed out.

"That was before I knew the details about your history," he said.

"What the fuck are you talking about?" I asked.

"It seems you and me have something in common," Malcom said.

"We do?" I lifted a skeptical brow. "Do you have a mate who wanted you dead too?"

"No, I've never formed a bond," he said.

"What could possibly justify you going along with that plan?" I demanded.

"First of all, I didn't know what Alec had in mind until after he already handed you over. Second, I agreed to help get you out," Malcom said.

"Okay, fine. But why? Why did Alec get you involved and why did you agree to help?" I asked.

"I'm not an asshole. I wasn't going to let you die there. Of course I'd help."

"Why wait, then?" I asked.

"Alec had a plan," he said. "And he told me why he did it."

"The money thing?" I wasn't buying it.

"We share the same blood," he said. "You're not the only one with daddy issues."

My lips parted in surprise. Was he saying what I think he was saying? "It can't be..."

"Welcome to the fucked-up family tree," he said. "I don't agree with Alec's actions, but you need that spell."

"What is he talking about? What spell?" Sheila asked. "What am I missing?"

"That's why you've never shared your story," I said. "You were hiding."

"Bingo," Malcom said.

"How?" I couldn't finish the thought but Malcom seemed to read what I was asking.

"What is going on here?" Sheila repeated. "Please help. I'm lost."

I couldn't focus on her right now, I was far too engrossed in what Malcom had to say. "Explain yourself."

"I found out about seven years ago. My mom told me the truth about my dad when I had my first shift. I was a late bloomer at fifteen." He shrugged. "She told me I should run so he wouldn't find me. I had a few run-ins with the law, if you know what I mean, and I made friends with a witch. Worked for her for two years in exchange for a masking spell. Figured if I was off-grid for two years, they'd count me as dead. Then I came here. I didn't know we shared this until after you left. When Alec came back, he told me what he did and about your dad. So, I finally shared my story and I offered to help."

"Holy shit." I stared at him, open mouthed. *I have a brother.* Things kept getting weirder and weirder.

"Is this supposed to make sense?" Sheila asked. "Who are you hiding from?"

I looked at Malcom. This wasn't just my secret to tell anymore, it was his, too. I stared at him, still dumbfounded by this new information. "When you're ready to share, I'll share."

"Please, someone, tell me what is going on here," Sheila said, exasperated.

"We have the same father," Malcom said.

"I was sort of guessing that. It's weird, but not that weird. Lots of shifters can't keep their dicks in their pants." She looked from me to Malcom a few times. "But explain the rest. I know there's more."

"Our dad is Spencer Lupton," Malcom said.

"Oh, fuck. I thought I had it bad. Neither of you are supposed to exist." Her brow furrowed. "Wait, isn't he in jail?"

"I was born before he took the throne. Lola's mom was pregnant with her when Spencer tried to take the throne. And it turns out, both our moms kept us from him so he didn't know about us." Malcom turned to me. "Unless your mom told him. But Alec said Spencer didn't know."

"She told me she fled when she found out she was pregnant," I said. "Do you think she knew what he had planned?"

"It doesn't really matter," Malcom said. "I guess my mom got lucky. She says they broke up a week before she found out she was pregnant. She never bothered to tell him cause she said she didn't want to deal with the drama of raising me as the bastard of a royal. A few years later, he got busted. Turns out, she made the right call."

"Does he know about you now?" I asked. "I guess he knows about me."

"I don't think so. And I'm good keeping it that way," he added.

"Kyle said he's already given some blood to do the spell. You're going with me, right? You should have your claim broken too. Just in case."

He shook his head. "I'm not worried about me. The masking spells seemed to have done the trick. Besides, I was clearly born before the edict about him not procreating. I'm probably safe. It's you who is far more at risk."

"Your mom kicked you out," I said. "You're clearly not safe."

"If they were going to come for me, they would have already," he said.

"No way." I shook my head. "I'm not doing it solo. If the king could come after me, what's to stop him from coming after you? And what kind of monster wants to kill children, anyway? The king sounds awful."

"I've never seen him do anything to help shifters in our community. The alphas run everything and there's nothing to keep them in check. I don't even know why he still has that title," Sheila said.

"Maybe he shouldn't," Malcom said. "Who knows, maybe our dad had the right idea."

"I doubt we'll ever know," I said. "It's not like we can ask him, right?"

"Alec talked to him," Malcom said.

There was a piece of me that wanted to meet my father and ask him to explain himself. Everyone who was supposed to protect me as a child let me down. What would make him any different? "It doesn't matter. We have what we need from him. We don't need to go down that path."

I caught sight of Kyle walking toward us and I waved him over. He glared at Malcom as he approached. Kyle was taking this protector thing pretty seriously.

I jumped from my chair and met him before he reached the rest of the group. "Have fun exploring?" I asked.

"It's nice here," he said.

"Did you hear about Malcom in all the other secrets you learned about me before I learned about them?" I asked.

"Name didn't come up," he replied.

"Well, it turns out I have a brother from a different mother," I said, trying to keep my tone light.

"For real?" His brow furrowed.

"I guess so," I said.

"Well, I suppose we recruit him," he said. "The rest of the camp seems happy to stay here, unaffiliated."

"You were asking people to join us on our possible suicidal crusade?" I hissed. "Why would you do that?"

"I didn't ask them directly," he assured me. "I just asked them how they liked being here and if they'd ever go back to a pack."

"Oh, that's not suspicious at all." I rolled my eyes.

Malcom was approaching so I gave Kyle a little nudge. "Meet Malcom, my brother." It sounded weird saying the words but I had no doubts he was honest with me. I somehow knew.

Kyle extended his hand and Malcom accepted. After an awkward handshake, the two males stared each other down for a moment.

"Well, this is awkward." Sheila had joined us in the little circle we formed near her tent.

"Kyle, Malcom; Malcom, Kyle," I said. "Now we all know each other."

"You're telling the truth?" Kyle asked. "About your father?"

"It's my deepest, darkest secret, so maybe not say it so loudly," Malcom said.

"Alright. So you're going help us, right?" Kyle said, cutting to the chase.

"Um, sure, but I usually like to know what I'm getting into," he replied.

"Alec didn't tell either of you why I might return to Wolf Creek after all this, did he?" I asked.

"I imagine it's to break that bond," Sheila said.

"There's more," I admitted.

"Lola, I don't think you should…" Kyle didn't get to finish his warning before I lifted my shirt and pulled my waistband down just enough to show my mark.

"…show them," he finished with a sigh.

"Holy shit, is that?" Sheila leaned in and then looked up at me. "You're an alpha."

"That's impossible," Malcom said.

"Hey, you've heard my story. I doubt it's as rare as the packs want us to think. The males just want to keep the power," Sheila said.

"You're going to challenge the alpha," Malcom said.

"I'm going to challenge the alpha," I agreed.

"You're insane," Malcom replied. "But I'm in."

"Same," Sheila said. "I might not have my mark anymore, but for you, I'd step up and fulfill my role as a protector."

I hadn't expected so much support. For a kid who grew up with no friends, I sure had come a long way.

12

The day went by far too quickly. I was welcomed by the members of the camp. None of them asked about my time away, but I got the sense they were concerned. It didn't feel like they were ignoring it, but rather they were afraid to upset me. I wasn't used to others being worried about me. It honestly made me a little uncomfortable.

My cheeks hurt from smiling, but I was able to sneak off alone for a few minutes as everyone prepared for the bonfire. Even Kyle was distracted by the ordeal. Like me, he wasn't used to such spectacle, and I could see the excitement in his eyes.

As the day faded into twilight, I could feel my wolf growing more restless. She knew it was time for us to make this thing official. I hoped we connected quickly and that I'd gain control of when I shifted without too much practice. After finding out that wolves shifted as early as thirteen outside Wolf Creek, it made me feel like I was already behind.

From the little bench I was sitting on, I watched as the members of the camp threw on more logs and started laying food out on long picnic tables. It was going to be a hell of a party.

Alec appeared in the crowd, smiling and chatting with the shifters he walked by. I hadn't seen him all day and my stomach did an annoying flip at the sight of him. After learning about what he'd done, I still wasn't sure how I felt about him. I supposed I was less angry. It came from a good place, but it resulted in me having another week of trauma. I didn't deserve that. Nobody did.

From across the way, his eyes found mine. I tensed and considered my next steps. Part of me wanted to dart off, continue avoiding him. But I realized that was a bit childish. I was going to have to deal with him, and eventually, I'd have to figure out what my heart really wanted.

He strolled over to me, moving at a pace so slow, I thought maybe he wanted me to flee. I held my ground. "How are you feeling?" I half-shouted as he approached. I wanted to get the first word in. Okay, so I'm sort of childish. What was it about this man that made me feel so unhinged?

"Better," he said. "I'll probably be good as new by tomorrow." He stopped in front of me, and the air between us felt heavy with tension. I missed our easy connection and conversation. I even missed when we used to snap at each other.

"I wish I could run with you tonight," he said.

"Your wolf isn't ready yet?" I was a little surprised.

"I'm starting to feel him, but I'm not optimistic," he said.

"I'm sorry," I said.

"I'll watch from the sidelines. Maybe I'll get a run with you another time," he said.

"Sure," I agreed.

"Kyle said he talked to you," he said.

“When did you and Kyle become so chummy?” I asked.

“Since he saved my life.”

“Ouch.” His comment was clearly a dig about how he’d saved my life. He’d also handed me over to my pack to be tortured. “You’re never going to let me live that down, are you?”

“Remember how I asked you to trust me?” he asked. “

“Yeah,” I affirmed.

“I always had your best interest in mind. Even if I didn’t go about it the best way,” he said.

“That almost sounded like an apology,” I pointed out.

He opened his mouth to say something, then closed it, as if second guessing himself.

“You and I can’t fix what’s broken between us if you’re keeping things from me,” I warned.

“Can it be fixed?”

“I don’t know,” I said.

“You know why you need to do the spell,” he said. “You’ll do it, right? You can’t move forward with that claim in tact. Your father is going to get you killed.”

“I know.” I knew he was right, but I wasn’t sure I wanted to agree to it so quickly. It made sense, but I’d never been thrilled with the idea of magic or witches. Magic kept me locked up in Wolf Creek and I thought it had prevented me from shifting. Turned out, that was all the bad luck of having a criminal for a father.

A horn blared and we both turned toward the sound.

“Bonfire time,” Alec said as he extended his hand toward me.

I hesitated, then accepted his help up. That was a mistake. His touch was like a sizzling fire, spreading right to my chest, then down to my center. I quickly pulled my hand away. I couldn't do that with him now. I needed to figure out what was going on in my own head before I complicated things more.

We walked silently toward the bonfire just as Greta passed off the torch to an older shifter male. The male lowered the torch to the kindling, setting it ablaze.

It didn't take long for the fire to eat through the smaller fuel and start licking its way up the logs. Cheers erupted and clothes started flying. It was time to shift.

My heart hammered in my chest and my stomach was a ball of nerves. I wasn't sure if I was going to vomit or pass out. Maybe both. I wanted this for so long, and now it was time.

"You got this," Alec said.

Kyle jogged toward me, Sheila, and Malcom at his sides. "You ready?" Kyle's eyes sparkled in the firelight. He looked happier than I'd ever seen him. Shit, I wasn't sure I'd ever actually seen him happy.

"Just toss the clothes aside and call to my wolf?" It seemed too easy.

"Or call to her now and destroy those awful clothes," Sheila said. "You might be better off naked after this."

"One of these days, I'm going to have a closet of my very own with more clothes than I could ever wear," I said, "but right now, this is all I've got." I pulled the shirt over my head and tossed it aside. Kyle, Malcom, and Sheila started taking their clothes off too.

Out of the corner of my eye, I noticed Alec had moved back a little. He was fully clothed, but I could see that he was watching me. It wasn't like he'd never seen me naked before.

And I suppose he would be curious to know if I could pull off a shift.

Ignoring his attention on me, I finished undressing, then without waiting for my friends, I took off at a run. It felt like my wolf was running with me, the two of us working in unison to take long strides toward the trees ahead. I could feel her, and I didn't fight it. *It's time.*

A howl bubbled inside me, building and fighting to make its way out. My body felt different, and for a moment, it was as if I was experiencing something from outside myself. As if I wasn't physically present. My wolf took over, leading us in a graceful dance as my bones reformed into something new.

It didn't hurt like I expected, I felt stretched and some of my joints popped, but sooner than I realized, I was seeing the world differently.

The howl that had started as I began my change exploded from my lungs, a long, intense sound that echoed through the cold, night air. Three howls returned the greeting and my wolf stopped and turned. She was leading the charge, but I could feel the connection. We were one and the same. Two halves of the same soul. I felt it now. I knew what they meant. We were one.

I caught Kyle's scent first as his wolf bounded up to me. I didn't even realize he had a scent I recognized until then. Behind him, Malcom and Sheila joined. I knew them by smell and I could feel them. We weren't pack, but I could feel their elation. Pure joy seemed to radiate from all of them. It was contagious and my heart felt as if it might burst.

I'd never felt so free in my life. I needed this. My wolf pawed at the ground, reminding me that we were meant to run, not stand here. I howled again, my friends once again answering the call. Then all four of us sprinted into the woods.

I ran for hours, chasing my friends, winding between trees, splashing through a creek, and leaping over fallen logs. I'd never felt so free and alive. How had I gone my whole life without this sensation?

Finally, I had to slow down. My wolf was panting, her exhaustion was my exhaustion. We'd both had enough.

My friends didn't seem as tired as me, but they were more experienced. When I turned and headed back to camp, they all followed. So this was what it was like to be in a pack. This was why they said wolves needed each other. Running alone would have sated some of my wolf's urges, but I knew she was enjoying the companionship. We needed each other.

Gratitude made my heart swell and I emerged from the tree line satisfied, tired, and happy. There were a few others around the bonfire, but many wolves were still running. Nearby, Shelia shifted back to her human form. Malcom and Kyle followed.

"You were a natural, Lola," Sheila said. "Now, let your wolf know you're done for today. Remind her you'll do this again soon."

I followed her instructions, letting myself relax a little, easing some of the adrenaline that came from the shift and the running. My body tensed and rippled, I could feel myself changing. It was a little more uncomfortable than the shift to a wolf, but it didn't last long.

Panting, exhausted, but exhilarated, I grinned at my friends. "So that's what I've been missing."

"Not anymore," Sheila said. "You're a full wolf now."

I forgot about that. We were considered full wolf shifters

once we had our first shift. Since my first wasn't of my own accord, I'd never counted it. This one had been all me. No more curse, no more playing human. No more settling for less.

Alec walked over to us and my breath hitched. Goosebumps trailed down my arms and my nipples tightened. I shook the sensation away. Of course I reacted, it was cold out here. It had nothing to do with Alec.

As he got closer, I caught his scent and I had to force myself to not moan aloud. *What the actual fuck?* Something was very, very wrong with me.

"You did great," he said.

I bit down on my lower lip and looked up at him through my lashes. "Thanks."

Catching myself, I gasped, and blinked. Why had I just turned on sexy, flirting Lola? I cleared my throat. "Thanks."

He smirked and his eyes dropped, scanning my body. A delicious shiver ran down my spine and I could feel the wetness spreading between my legs.

"I need my clothes," I managed before walking away.

Quickly, I found my clothes and pulled them on. I could smell Alec behind me before I even turned. His scent was driving me wild. It was taking every ounce of my willpower not to rip his clothes off him right here.

I spun around to face him. "Did you need something from me?"

"I know what you're feeling," he said. "I can smell it on you, I can feel your responses to me."

"Excuse me?" I blurted out.

"It's normal, don't worry, give it about a half hour and it'll fade," he said.

"What are you talking about?" I asked.

"The desire to fuck my brains out." He shrugged. "It's pretty clear you're struggling with that. I would offer my services, but I don't think I'd be welcomed right now. Just know, it's normal after a shift to want to succumb to other physical urges."

My core was practically pulsing with desire and I had to fight against my body. It wanted him, he was absolutely right about that. But he was also right that I wasn't interested in following those primal instincts right now.

"Why you?" I asked.

"Maybe because you saw me first. Maybe because we have a history. Maybe you simply want me," he said. "It doesn't matter the reason."

"Well, I don't," I said.

"Don't what?" he asked.

"I don't want you." The words were harder to get out than I thought they'd be.

"Well, I guess I misread the situation. I'll see you later, Lola," he said.

I held my breath, biting back a moan at the sound of my name on his lips. Holy shit, that was an uncomfortable side effect of a shift. I hoped it got easier with practice.

That's when I noticed a few pairings around me. Other shifters had returned, and there were several who were engaged in very heavy make out sessions at the least, and a few who weren't shy about taking things further. I guess I missed that last time since I'd been distracted.

"Lola, you want some food?" Sheila called.

I jogged over to where she and Kyle were standing next to a table of desserts. There were at least eight different kinds of pie and more cookies than I'd ever seen. Where did they make all these? I wasn't going to bother asking, I was starving after the time in the woods.

We filled our plates with too much sugar, then found some burgers at another table. I sat down on a bench and Kyle and Sheila squeezed in on either side of me.

After a few bites, I turned to Sheila. "How do you overcome the whole post shift thing?"

"You mean sex?" she asked, her mouth full of food.

"Oh, that's tough," Kyle said. "Worst part of shifting if you ask me."

"I think if you give in every so often, it makes it easier when you don't," Sheila said. "Why? You thinking of taking a tumble with anyone in particular?"

"No," I said, way too quickly.

She took another bite of her burger. "Shame. I do hope I still get to be an auntie one day."

I elbowed her, then we both laughed. I hadn't realized how much I missed her until today. When this was over, would I move to Wolf Creek forever? If I did, I was taking down the barrier, so it wasn't like we'd be too far to visit. I would miss seeing her daily, though. She was the best part of this place.

She was loyal and kind. What kind of person agrees to have your back when you've got to try to take over an entire shifter pack? Concern rolled through my stomach like a wave. What if something happened to her while she was helping me? What about Kyle and Malcom? Even Alec crossed my mind. I didn't want anything to happen to any of them.

I promised myself I wasn't going to allow it. Now that I knew what it was like to have friends, I would do anything in my power to keep them safe.

13

When I fell into bed, I was more tired than I'd ever been in my life. It was a different kind of tired, though. My inner wolf was satisfied, a feeling I wasn't familiar with.

"You're going to sleep like the dead tonight," Kyle said. "Sleep after a shift is better than sex."

I laughed. "Good. Cause sleep is all I've got."

He sat on the edge of his bed. "I get that. There wasn't exactly anyone I was interested in back home."

"Maybe you'll find your mate once we break that barrier. New people will be able to come in and everyone will be free to go explore the world." I yawned. It was getting difficult to keep my eyes open.

"Maybe." He stood and walked over to me. "Go on, under the covers."

"I can tuck myself in," I said.

"Sure. You look like you're ready to pass out on top of your blankets and you never bothered to take off your clothes," he pointed out.

With a groan, I rolled off the bed so he could toss back the covers. Then I climbed back in, still dressed. I was far too tired to worry about what I was sleeping in. Kyle pulled the blankets over me. "Sleep well."

I don't think I responded. My eyes were already closed. I didn't even recall hearing Kyle walk to his bed.

* * *

I WAS BACK in Wolf Creek, walking through deserted streets. Everything looked ancient and abandoned. Paint was peeling from the buildings, doors hanging by hinges.

Ahead, I noticed the grocery store where I'd worked. The windows were boarded up and the closed sign was duct taped to the window. *What the fuck was going on?*

I jogged over to the store and peered in the windows. The shelves that I'd stocked for years were mostly empty and there wasn't a soul in sight. Concerned, I moved the door and tried the handle. To my surprise, it opened. I stepped inside and a cloud of dust floated up around my feet. The floors I'd spent all that time sweeping were covered in a thick layer of grime. The registers were open, the drawers balancing precariously. Some of them were missing buttons and had cracked screens. None of it made sense. Even if they closed, Jud wouldn't leave all this stuff behind. And it would take years to look this beat down.

"Hello?" I called out, half expecting Jud to answer me. All I got was eerie silence.

A mouse scuttled by, making me jump. What happened here? Jud kept the place meticulous. If he knew there was a mouse in here, he'd personally hunt the creature down.

I walked toward the shelves. A single can of beets, covered

in dust, sat on a shelf. Spider webs had claimed the empty spaces. Everything looked like it had been abandoned for a decade.

This couldn't be real, could it? I had to be dreaming. Wolf Creek didn't look like this. *Wake up, Lola.*

A door slammed, sending my heart into frantic pounding. "Who's there?"

Cautiously, I walked toward the back of the store, and crept slowly into the back room. It was dark and dingy back here. Nothing like it should be.

The back door leading to the ally was open, it wavered in the wind, nearly blowing closed before blowing open again. I took a deep breath. There wasn't anyone here. It was just the wind.

Despite my confidence that I was alone, I found myself tiptoeing toward the door. My pulse raced, and I tried to remind myself that this couldn't be real. There had to be something about this dream, though. If I wasn't waking, there had to be a message for me. Something I was missing.

I stepped through the door into the familiar alley. This looked exactly as I remembered it. It was dark outside, a canopy of diamond dusted stars overhead. No moon. Crickets chirped somewhere nearby, but there were no human sounds. No cars, no people walking by. Just me and nature.

In the inky darkness, I narrowed my eyes to investigate the alley. The dumpsters were still in place, as was the chain-link fence. Other than that, I couldn't see much.

A loud slam made me jump and scream. I turned to see the back door had closed. Panic surged through me, sending a rush of adrenaline. I ran back, grabbed the door and pulled. It didn't budge. "Fuck."

"You are even sexier when you use language like that," a voice cut through the silence of the night.

My whole body tensed. I knew that voice. I would know it anywhere. Why was *he* here? I turned slowly to face Tyler. "What do you want?"

As soon as I saw him, the tension melted away. Almost like I wanted to see him. Like I was relieved. That couldn't be right. I didn't want to see Tyler. I wanted him gone, away from me. Didn't I?

He took a few steps closer and my breath hitched in anticipation. There was no fear, no hatred, no anger. I tried to pull those emotions to the forefront, but they refused to come to the surface.

My inner wolf seemed to leap inside my chest, rejoicing at being reunited with Tyler. *With our mate.*

"No," I said. "I don't want to be with you." Even as I said the words, I couldn't make myself believe them. It was as if my mind was being overridden by the mating bond. I was reacting on instinct rather than logic.

Tyler brought his hand to his chest and groaned as if wounded. "You always know exactly what to say to hurt me. But I'll never give up on you. We're connected, two halves of the same soul."

That can't be right, could it?

Suddenly, the whole ally was spinning around me. It was like being sucked down a drain, only I wasn't moving. The world was spinning. Faster and faster and faster. I closed my eyes. *Time to wake up. Wake the fuck up.*

When it stopped, I was standing out by the old, broken-down barn. There was a full moon and my wolf stirred, ready to run. Now, this was an improvement. I wouldn't mind a dream where I got to run as my wolf. I embraced the pull of my wolf, and shifted without pause.

Soon, I was running through the woods, away from Wolf Creek. The air smelled sweet, and the earth was cool under my paws. I howled and another howl responded.

A dark gray wolf appeared next to me and my heart nearly exploded with joy at the sight of him. Tyler's wolf and my wolf ran as one, side by side, our paces matching step for step. It felt natural to run with him. My wolf was totally at ease. Everything about it felt right.

Tyler's wolf fell back and nipped at me playfully, my wolf jumped in delight, then gave chase, running through the woods at breakneck speed. Tyler's wolf took a while to catch me, but eventually, he caught up and lunged on top of me, pinning me to the ground.

My wolf panted, exhausted from the chase, but I wasn't ready to be done yet. I rolled, knocking him from me and ran again. This time, he stayed alongside me until we reached a meadow.

In the light of the moon, the tall grass took on a silver glow. White flowers dotted the landscape and the trees surrounding the clearing gave the sense of privacy. It was like a secret world, hidden in the woods.

Exhausted and elated, I relaxed, sitting back. My wolf was tired and happy. She was ready to shift back. With a shudder, I began to change into my human form.

Suddenly, Tyler stood in front of me in his human form, naked in the moonlight. I stared at him, taking in his broad shoulders and the curve of his impressive muscles. He growled and I looked up at him, our eyes locking.

My heart raced, excited flutters filling my chest. My body

was already responding, like a woman in heat. I wanted him. No, I needed him.

Tyler closed the distance between us and I gasped as he swept me up into his embrace. My breasts pressed against his firm chest, his erection was hard against my stomach.

I was already wet between my legs. There was a tiny part of me crying out against this, but I silenced it quickly. My mind was too fuzzy to concentrate on anything other than having Tyler.

He tangled his large hand into my hair, grabbing a handful of it and pulling forcefully to guide my face closer to his. When his lips touched mine, it felt like something exploded inside me.

The kiss was hungry, his lips forceful. He slipped his tongue into my mouth and I moaned as he deepened the kiss. My hands moved up his back, feeling the rippling muscles under my fingers. He was solid and smooth. I felt safe in his arms, like I was exactly where I belonged.

Suddenly, he pulled away. With a smirk on his lips, his eyes moved over my body, taking all of me in. A shudder traveled through me. I stepped back, taking the chance to explore his body. My fingers trailed over his pecs, down his sculpted abs. I lingered for a moment before taking his cock in my hand. He groaned as I stroked him.

With a growl, he grabbed a fistful of my hair and claimed my mouth again. The pain of him pulling my hair mixed with the intense pressure of his kiss nearly sent me over the edge.

Tyler's hands moved down my back until they gripped my ass. With little effort, he lifted me and I threw my legs around his waist. He didn't take his time before thrusting his cock inside me. It was aggressive and fast, the entire length filling me in one motion.

I gasped, then winced as he filled me completely. He lifted me by my ass, up and down, helping me ride his rock-hard length. I gripped his shoulders to brace myself, then moved my arms around his neck.

Our kisses were violent and angry, but full of desire. I never wanted to part from him. As pleasure began to build, I had to pull away from his lips. Gasping for air, I moaned as each thrust got me closer to climax.

Tyler's lips moved to my neck and I tossed my head back, enjoying the dual sensation of him inside me and his lips on my sensitive skin.

Pressure built, and I screamed as a cascade of pleasure surged through me. My whole body shook as I orgasmed, but Tyler didn't stop. He continued on, sending me over the edge again and again.

Then, I felt his teeth on my shoulder and he bit down. I cried out as pain mingled with the pleasure of yet another orgasm.

My eyes snapped open and I woke tangled in the sheets, covered in sweat.

What the fuck was that?

I stared at the ceiling. My skin felt tingly and I was panting. It had all been a dream, but it felt so real. After taking a few deep breaths, I got my heart rate and breathing back to normal. What was wrong with me? Why had I dreamed about Tyler? *Fucking mating bond.*

The room was still dark and I could hear the sound of Kyle breathing heavily. He was sound asleep. I wasn't sure what time it was, but there was no way I was going to risk going back to sleep now.

I stayed awake until I caught the first signs of the sunrise through the window. Then, I got up and headed to the shower. After that dream, all I wanted to do was wash myself.

It had to be the shift last night. The whole increased sex drive thing was more serious than I thought.

Instead of being excited about my next shift, I was dreading it. If it came with dreams about Tyler, I wasn't sure shifting was worth it. Until I broke the bond with him, I might hold off. I could almost feel my wolf pouting, but she wasn't putting up a fight. I couldn't handle having dreams like that about Tyler.

I closed my eyes and let the warm water wash over me. It was bad enough that I wasn't feeling disgusted by the dream itself. The worst part was the concern over what it all meant. The bond was getting stronger. What if I got to the point where I couldn't resist him? What if the bond overruled my mind and I let him claim me?

Where anger used to be, I only felt fear. I couldn't put off breaking that bond. It had to happen. Fast.

14

I BARGED into Shelia's tent, startling her awake. She sat upright and her eyes widened immediately alert. "What's wrong?"

"I have to find Alec. Where's he staying?" I asked.

She raised her brows. "Oh? You have to, huh?"

I rolled my eyes. "Give up on us getting together and help me, please."

Her brow furrowed. "Hey, tell me what's going on?"

I probably looked a bit insane. I sure felt like I was. My hair was in a messy, wet bun and I was in the same clothes I'd been wearing for days. My head was spinning a million miles an hour, trying desperately to force the thoughts of Tyler from my mind. Every time I let down my guard, I pictured his lean muscles, his dark hair, those hungry eyes.... *Fuck*. I had to get him out of my head. I had to break that bond.

"I had a terrible dream," I admitted. "I'm worried I'm putting everyone here in danger and I want to move on with our plans. Breaking the mating bond, breaking my dad's claim, all of it."

Okay, so it was a little bit of a fib, but I wasn't ready to admit to anyone, including myself, that I'd let a sex dream about my mate get to me.

"Must have been some dream," she said, sympathetically. "Want to talk about it?"

"Nope. Hard pass." I shook my head.

"Okay, well, he's been staying here." She gestured to the unmade cot that I'd slept in for a while. "But I don't know if he even came back last night. It has to be hard watching everyone else shift while he waits for that toxin to get out of his system."

My chest tightened. I felt both guilty and sorry for him. I knew that pain well and while I could think of a few shifters I'd like to shove that toxin into, I wouldn't wish it on anyone lightly. Especially not Alec.

The tent flap ruffled and we both turned. Alec stepped in and froze as the fabric door closed behind him. "I didn't expect to walk into this. Why do I suddenly feel like I'm in trouble?"

"We can't wait," I blurted out. "I need the mating bond broken. Now. How do we do that?"

"She had a nightmare," Sheila offered.

Alec's upper lip twitched and he scowled. "The bond is getting stronger."

"It needs to stop," I said. "I can't keep doing this."

He took a deep breath and his expression softened. "I know what you're going through, but we can't risk returning there yet. Especially after you shifted last night. The witch is ready to do the spell. We can leave today."

"We can't break the bond somehow first? There has to be a way to do it without returning to Wolf Creek. Please, I can't keep letting this bond get stronger." I felt so out of control and confused. It was getting harder to remind myself the reasons why I shouldn't be with Tyler. It was like living in someone else's memories. Most of me could recall his strikes against me, but there was this other part of me that was acting as if none of that ever happened.

I didn't want to wait, but I also didn't need the shifter king coming after me. "Has anyone seen any of the Wolf Creek shifters around nearby? We have that to worry about too."

"Scouts have them nearing the city. Another reason to act now. They're heading in the opposite direction we need to go," he said. "Plus, you could use a few more shifts to help you prepare. Once you go back to Wolf Creek, you have to be ready for all of it. Breaking the bond isn't the only thing on your to-do list there."

My stomach tightened. I was going to have to challenge Ace as soon as the bond was broken. They'd surely detect my presence in town once I arrived. We'd have a small window to get the bond broken. I realized I didn't even know the steps we'd have to complete. "You can really do it, can't you? Or was all that a lie to get me to go back?"

"Oh, for fuck's sake, Alec, please tell me you know how to break her mating bond," Sheila said.

"I know how to break it," he said. "It's not going to be easy, and we'll have to capture your mate, but I doubt you care if he gets banged up a little in the process."

I gasped, then covered my mouth to stop myself from blurting out something stupid. Why should I care if Tyler got hurt? I groaned. "You see what I mean? I went from wanting to kill him with my bare hands to worrying about his safety. That's not right. It's messing with my head."

"You know, I can just kill him for you. Then it would be over and done," Alec offered.

"I like that plan," Sheila said.

"I'm not stooping to his level," I said, though the part of me that wanted him gone was strong enough to revel in the idea of never having to see Tyler again. He'd put me though so much pain, he deserved to be punished. But I had promised I would be the one to inflict the pain. And to do that, I had to break the bond first. "Besides, if anyone kills him, it's going to be me."

"Welcome back, Lola. I was worried I'd lost you to him for a minute there," Alec said.

"You don't have me, either," I reminded him.

"It was a general statement, not a marriage proposal," he snapped.

"Alright, play nice, kids," Sheila said. "Do I need to send you to your designated corners?"

"Knock, knock," Kyle's voice called into the room as he pulled back the tent flap. He didn't look surprised to see all of us gathered. "I guess I'm going to have to stop going to sleep."

"I didn't want to wake you," I said.

"Well, the gang's all here," Sheila said.

"We're missing Malcom," I pointed out. "I want him to go with me. He should get to use the spell, too."

"We don't have enough to cover two," Alec said.

"Well, I'll ask the witch for an IOU," I said.

"That's not how it works," Alec said. "Malcom gets a touch up on his masking spells every few months. He's safe."

I didn't like the idea of getting my claim broken while Malcom remained vulnerable. I figured I could press the issue once I met the witch and saw what the spell entailed. "He's coming with us, though, right?"

"If he wants," Alec said.

"I can go wake him," Sheila offered.

Alec nodded. "Might as well get this started. Pack light. We've got a three-day hike."

"We can't borrow the car?" I asked.

"There's no roads where we're going," he said.

"Wonderful. Why do I feel like this is going to end badly?" I asked.

"We're voluntarily going to see a witch who is willing to do blood magic on a member of the wolf shifter royal family. There's pretty much nothing that sounds good about that," Sheila said.

"You're sure this is necessary?" Kyle asked.

"I'm sure," Alec said.

"I don't know why I'm trusting you with this," I said to Alec. "But somehow, you managed to convince Kyle that all this wasn't some sick joke. So, I'm going along."

"I get that," he said. "I really don't care what you think of me because when this is over, you'll still be alive."

I didn't have a good response for that, so I looked over at Sheila. She seemed like she believed him. I hoped we were making the right choice.

"Come with me, Kyle. You can help me grab the supplies," Alec said.

"I'll get Malcom," Sheila offered.

"I'll come with you." I followed her out and we walked to Malcom's tent.

He was already outside, lacing up his boots. He lifted his head when he saw us. "I take it, it's time to go?"

"You ready for this?" Sheila asked.

"Would it matter if I wasn't?" he replied.

"Not even a little," she teased.

Going to see a witch in the middle of nowhere sounded like suicide. But then again, what in my life wasn't going to get me killed lately?

15

THE FIRST DAY of walking had been awkward and quiet. Thankfully, the rough terrain gave us all an excuse to stay quiet. From what I could tell, our group was in decent shape, but our route was all uphill, over rough and unstable ground. By the nightfall, we were all exhausted.

A fire crackled in the center of our makeshift camp. I dug through my pack and found a blanket I could use to protect myself against the cold, night air. When I pulled it out, a package of cookies came along with it. I grinned and held them up for the others to see. "I take it Greta knows what we're up to?"

"I never told her, which means, she knows everything," Alec said.

I opened the package and offered them around the group. Everyone took a few and chewed them quietly. We'd already eaten some of the food from Alec's bag, but jerky and canned fruit left something to be desired. The cookies were a nice treat.

"We should get some rest," Alec said. "I can take first watch."

"We should have a pair on watch," Kyle said.

"I'll take first watch with him," I offered. There was no way I was going to be able to sleep anytime soon. My body ached from the hiking we'd done all day, but my mind hadn't settled. Plus, I was honestly terrified I would have another dream about Tyler. That was the last thing I wanted.

"You three sleep," Alec said. "I'll wake the next group in four hours."

"You sure you don't want to sleep first?" Sheila asked as she stifled a yawn.

"We'll be fine," I said. "Sleep."

"I'm here if you need me," Kyle said. "But promise you'll actually wake me."

"I will," I assured him.

The fire crackled and the wind rustled the trees. It was a beautiful night. The moon was nearly full, casting a silvery light over the forest. If not for the fact that we were making our way to a witch, I might have enjoyed the beauty of the secluded campsite.

Alec was sitting on a large rock, out of the way from the flatter area where the others had set up their sleeping bags. I walked over to him and sat down on the space next to him. We were only a few inches apart, but it was the best seat if I was going to stay awake and watch the woods for a few hours.

Aside from the occasional stoking of the fire, neither of us moved or spoke. It was probably a good hour before I got too restless to sit in silence anymore. I stood and stretched, then walked in a quiet circle around our camp before returning to the rock.

"I was thirteen when I had my first shift," Alec said.

I looked over at him, surprised that he was the one to break the silence. "That's young, right?"

He shrugged. "Most of us shift between thirteen and fifteen. In packs outside Wolf Creek, we start to worry if you haven't shifted by sixteen."

"It must have been nice to grow up somewhere where it wasn't so restricted," I offered.

"It wasn't a glamorous life, but I had a decent childhood. My parents were kind and loving, I had friends and family nearby. Everything was simpler then," he said.

"Sounds wonderful." I knew he had tragedy in his past, I'd heard some mentions of it, but I didn't know the whole story. Keeping my responses short was safer. I didn't want to bring up any bad memories or ask questions that might cause him pain. I might not be happy with him right now, but I wasn't an asshole.

He stood and added a few pieces of wood to the fire, then returned to the rock. I wanted to ask questions, especially about why he was helping me. Why did he care about a random shifter who passed through his camp?

Instead, I could only come up with small talk. "At least the weather is nice."

He chuckled. "Yeah. We're lucky it's not raining. This whole forest would be a mud pit we'd have to trek through."

"How did you meet this witch?" I asked.

"We've been working on something together," he said.

"Oh," I said softly. "So, we're back to the secrets?"

He glanced over at me. "I'm not trying to keep things from you. I'm not sure how much you want to know. You've been through a lot."

"So have you," I pointed out. "I can handle it. Just tell me what you're so afraid of sharing. Let me in, just a little."

"Like how you let me in?" he accused.

"That's not fair. I told you everything. You know about my mate and how I was treated. You know all my pain. And you still sent me back. I know nothing about your past," I said.

"You're right." He stood and walked to his pack, then pulled out a flask. After a long drag, he walked back to the rock and sat before offing the flask to me. "You told me about your mate and about your life in Wolf Creek. It's only fair if I do the same."

I took a swig, the liquor burning my throat on the way down. It made my eyes water a little. "What was that?"

"Bourbon," he said. "Takes some getting used to."

He took another swing, then closed the flask. "My mate and I grew up together. We'd been friends our whole life. So when the mating bond appeared, it was natural to fall into each other. We were happy."

I knew she'd died, but he'd never talked about her other than that. "I'm sorry for your loss."

"She'd have liked you," he said, glancing up at me. "She was feisty, and strong, and never quit anything."

"What was her name?" I asked.

"Sofia," he said.

"Beautiful name," I said.

He hummed and nodded.

We sat without speaking for a long while, the sound of the fire and the wind the only noise. For the first time since my return, I didn't feel the need to fill the silence or escape from him. I was content to just be. He'd opened up and shared something, and I appreciated how difficult that must have been for him. I never knew his mate, but I knew how strong the bond could be. And what I was experiencing was for someone I didn't want to be with. I couldn't imagine how crushing it would be to lose someone you wanted to be with.

"My pack was small. Right on the border of Wolf Creek. There weren't many of us left, but we had been there a long time. It was our home for generations. Wolf Creek wanted the land. We turned them down." He took another sip from the flask and offered it to me.

I declined. "I'm not sure I like where this story is going."

He nodded, knowingly. "They attacked while I was away at my first year of college. Used the toxin to weaken everyone and prevent shifting. Then, they killed anyone who resisted, which meant, they killed every member of my pack. I never even got to bury her. They burned all the bodies. There were no survivors. Not even the children."

My lips parted and my eyes widened. I tried to process the utter horror of his story. How could anyone do such a thing? I recalled a ceremony years ago for new land acquired by the pack. I didn't know the details because I hadn't been welcome to attend, but the posters were all over the school. I was young, and it didn't cross my mind to question why any of it was happening.

"I'm so sorry." My words sounded hollow, empty. How could I express exactly how terrible I felt for him? "Nobody should have to endure what you went through. And nobody should kill innocents. I knew my pack was made up of monsters, but I didn't know how hateful and truly monstrous they were."

"I know." He turned to me. "Now you know why I needed the recipe."

"No, I don't," I replied. "Honestly, it makes me regret giving it to you. We don't need more of that out in the world."

"I'm not trying to make it," he said. "I was a chemistry major before the attacks. I have friends in the field working on an antidote from a scientific perspective. And that witch we're seeing, she's been working on potions and spells to see if we can fix it with magic."

"Wait, what?" It seemed too good to be true. "How would that work?"

"I'm not sure yet. A pill, maybe, or a potion or some kind of herbal mix. If my pack had something, anything, they might have stood a chance. They couldn't shift, and they couldn't heal. Instead, they were slaughtered."

I wiped a tear from my cheek. The more I learned about the pack I'd grown up in, the worse it got. I wasn't sure if my mom was originally from Wolf Creek, but I didn't know if where she was from was better or worse. Add in the fact that my father's family would kill me on sight, and I wasn't sure there were any good packs out there. Maybe feral shifters were the ones with the right idea.

"I don't think I can do it," I said.

"Do what?" Alec asked.

"Take over Wolf Creek." I shook my head. "I can't lead a place like that. I don't want anything to do with them."

"Their history is exactly why you should be going after this," he said. "You got that mark for a reason."

"What about you?" I asked. "What if you challenge Ace?"

"My pack is gone," he said.

"If you won't claim Wolf Creek, you need to look around at what you've built," I said. "Your community is more pack than anything I grew up with."

"Packs complicate things," he said.

"Yet, you want me to go run one?" I asked, skeptical.

"It's different for you. Your pack is still there and it needs to be run by someone with compassion and intelligence."

I lifted my brows. "That is high praise for someone you hardly know."

"It doesn't take much time with you to know your heart is in the right place," he said.

I took a deep breath and blew it out slowly. None of this was what I expected. I wanted so badly to be angry with him. He wasn't making it easy.

"We should wake the others," he said.

"Okay." It hadn't felt like four hours, but I honestly wasn't keeping track. Either way, after everything I just heard, I could use some time to process and I probably wasn't the only one. That had to be near impossible for him to share with me. No wonder Sheila insisted that it was his story to tell.

"Thanks for telling me all of that," I said.

He gave me a weak smile. "You deserved to know after everything I put you through."

My heart felt like it was going to explode. I was so overcome with sympathy for Alec, and at the same time, I was wondering if there was anything between us I could still salvage.

With everything I had on the horizon, I wasn't in the right place to assess my heart. Quietly, I stood and walked toward my sleeping bag.

Out of the corner of my eye, I caught sight of the others waking. Kyle stretched and turned toward me. "You good?"

I nodded.

"Five more minutes," Sheila moaned.

"You got this, protector," Malcom said, using the title she'd have if she was in a pack where her mark had been honored.

"Way to use my words against me," she teased.

"Stop your chatter, the others need some sleep," Kyle said.

Alec was already in his sleeping bag, his body turned away from me. I hoped he would be able to get some sleep after reliving his past.

I settled into my sleeping bag, lulled to sleep by the quiet, muffled conversation of my friends but my slumber didn't last long.

16

I WOKE to screaming and chaos. Snarls, growls, teeth, and fur. All around me was a battle that I was somehow in the middle of without warning.

A huge gray wolf bounded toward me and I rolled to the side, just as another wolf tackled my attacker.

Heart racing, mind spinning, I crawled away from the mess so I could figure out what was going on. This was not what anyone expected to wake up to. Wolves were attacking each other and honestly, I couldn't tell which were my friends and which were foe. I had to shift. I should be able to feel my friends better in wolf form. It was the only option.

I called to my inner wolf, begging her to come to me. She rose up, but fell flat. *I thought we worked through this. I need you.* She didn't respond. Of course she didn't, but I didn't even get an emotional response. This was not the time I needed her to fail me. *Come on.* I closed my eyes tight and tried to urge her to the forefront. It was futile, she wasn't responding. *Fuck.* My eyes snapped open. If my wolf was having performance anxiety, I needed to figure something else out.

The fight seemed to be moving them away from our campsite, pushing into the woods. I wanted to follow, but in human form, I'd be a liability. Shit, who was I kidding, in wolf form I was a liability. Alec was right, I didn't know how to fight yet.

Frantic, I stood and moved behind a tree, observing the violence. If there was a way to pinpoint which wolves were friends, maybe I could do something to help.

Someone grabbed me and I screamed just as a hand moved to cover my mouth. "Shhh, it's me."

I caught Alec's scent and relaxed a little. He lowered his hand.

"What the fuck is going on?" I hissed.

"They ambushed us. We gotta get out of here." He grabbed my hand and pulled me away from the fight. "Can you shift?"

My wolf responded to that and I felt her snapping to attention. She clawed at my insides as if she'd been desperate to get out. *Oh, so you want to run away. I get it.* Pissed that my inner wolf was a coward, I pulled on his hand, stopping in my tracks. "We need to help them."

"You aren't ready. You need to shift," he said as he released my hand. "Now."

He was in his wolf form quickly and my wolf reacted. The shift was uncomfortable this time, my body breaking and reforming in a stressed hurry. My wolf and I weren't on the same page and I was resisting her desires. I wanted to fight, and she wanted to flee. I glanced toward the action, wanting nothing more than to charge in and help, but my wolf held her ground, forcing me in place. Why wouldn't she let me go to them?

I could sense that Alec's wolf was impatient, he lifted his

chin and took a few steps. It seemed like this was my only option. Human me was useless in a wolf fight, and wolf me wanted to run.

I felt like a failure, like I was abandoning my friends but I was new to this and if they had to protect me, they probably couldn't fight as well. Running might be better for all of us. I hated myself for it, but I needed to get out of here.

Alec's wolf growled and my wolf responded, instinctively trusting him to lead us away from the fight. I ran ahead, Alec at my heels. Someone had attacked us, that was clear. And my other friends had stayed behind to give me time to escape.

It was either Wolf Creek, or somehow, the shifter king's guards had heard about me and were making good on their punishment for my father. Either way, I was the cause. I stopped running and turned around. I should go back, I should help. This was my fault, not theirs. If anything happened to them because of me, I'd never forgive myself. My wolf tried to urge me forward, but I resisted. It felt wrong to leave them.

Alec's wolf was by my side, his teeth bared in a threatening manner. He didn't want me to stop. He gave a sharp, gruff sound like a command. I whined, lifting my chin in the direction we'd just come. My wolf was pulling me toward Alec, but I couldn't shake the feeling that I was abandoning my friends. His wolf nodded the other way, insisting I follow him. I could feel his urgency. It was an almost desperate fear radiating from him. He was worried about me. I could sense how badly he wanted us to flee.

What if the attackers left to chase us? It was possible they'd leave my friends if they didn't find what they wanted. I had to hope that was the case, and if it was, I had to create more distance between us. We could be leading them away.

Reluctantly, I turned away from the camp, and took a few hesitant steps. I didn't know where I was or where I should go, and even as a wolf, I wasn't confident in my sense of direction. Alec bounded in front of me and started moving forward. He must have remembered how often I got lost when I first arrived at his camp. He picked up the pace quickly, and I matched it, following him through the woods.

We'd lost our friends, our supplies, everything. And it was all my fault. If it weren't for me, we wouldn't be in this situation in the first place. What had I been thinking allowing my friends to risk their lives for me? I should have done this on my own. Or maybe with Alec, since he apparently had a death wish. That was the only reason I could think of that he'd risk getting caught by my pack after everything they'd done to his. He was probably the only other shifter outside Wolf Creek who knew just how brutal they really were.

I wasn't sure how long we ran, but I was struggling to keep up. Alec's wolf seemed like he could run forever. My wolf wasn't used to this. I was struggling to get over the rocks and tree roots. A few times, I got caught in bushes or scratched by branches. My body wasn't the same size it used to be and when I slipped into taking full control over my wolf self, I made mistakes.

It was a challenge to find a balance between my wolf self and my human self. I wasn't trusting enough to let her take the lead for long, but I wasn't great at navigating life as a wolf. We'd run together so beautifully on my first shift, but under pressure, we weren't finding our stride. There had to be a better way to work together but I had a feeling the key was going to be practice. I wasn't sure I had time for that. I had to figure this out quickly.

Finally, Alec's wolf stopped and turned to face me before sitting back on his rear legs. He was panting and I was glad to know I wasn't the only one who was exhausted.

My body shuddered and my muscles felt like they were stretching and bending in ways they shouldn't. I'd never started a shift without another wolf going first, but I think my wolf was too tired to stay in this form. A few more uncomfortable twists and a couple of snapping bones later, I was sitting naked in the dirt. Everything hurt.

It took all my willpower to stay seated. All I wanted to do was curl up and lay on the earth.

Then I saw Alec naked and the exhaustion was replaced by my sex drive. My heart raced and warmth spread to my core. *Oh, fuck, not this again.* In this moment, there had never been a more desirable male in my presence.

I knew Alec was hot. I'd been attracted to him since we first met, but he was off limits. There was too much history and too much at risk if I jumped on top of him.

But those muscles, those gorgeous eyes, his full lips.

Send help.

"You okay?" he asked.

"Sure," I said, ignoring my inner-slut who was currently telling me to jump him. "What happened back there?"

"I don't know. Malcom woke me, then he shifted."

"You think it was Wolf Creek?" I asked.

"Probably," he said. "I doubt the king's guard is even looking for you yet. You're not a direct threat."

"Then why are we going through all this to break my dad's claim?" I asked.

"Because once you become an alpha, you're inner circle to the king. He'll have no choice but to make an example of you," he said.

"Why did you have to go hunting down my father in the first place? He never even knew I was born. What were the chances we'd shift at the same time and he'd even know what he was feeling was a connection to me?" I asked.

"I didn't know you when I first found him. I hunted down information about your mom and found out she'd had a child that could, in theory, be his. I wish I could take it back. I was chasing the toxin recipe and I thought if I gave him information, he might help me," he confessed.

"Did he?" I asked.

"No, he didn't know anything about the toxin," Alec admitted.

"So it was all for nothing," I mumbled.

"I'm sorry. After we met, I went back to see him and asked if there was a way to keep you safe. He offered some blood. Said he needed to atone or something," he said.

"I just wish his atonement wasn't because my life was at risk," I said, bitterly.

"I'm sorry for all the hurt I've caused you," Alec said.

I looked up at him, our eyes meeting. He seemed sincere. Alec had a way of getting to me when nobody else could. *Dammit.* I wanted to stay mad at him. I wasn't ready to work through my feelings with him. Not with everything else I was dealing with.

"Where is he?" I asked.

"Exile," he said.

"Where?" I asked.

"Chicago," he said.

“What’s so bad about Chicago?” I asked. “Can’t he just leave?”

“I forget how much they didn’t teach you,” he said.

“Well, tell me now,” I replied.

“Chicago is vampire territory. Your uncle, the king, worked a deal with the vampire king. Your dad steps a toe out of line, the vamps get to take him down.”

“Fuck,” I said.

“Yeah,” Alec agreed.

“Now what? Do we try to find the others?” I asked.

“No, we keep going,” he said. “That was always the plan. If we were attacked, they were to provide the distraction.”

I jumped to my feet. “When were you going to tell me this? I didn’t sign up for my friends to be sacrificial lambs.”

Alec stood. “We knew you’d react like this.”

My breath hitched. He towered over me and my chest filled with flutters. I couldn’t help but let my eyes trail down his chest to his hips. I let out a little gasp when I noticed his cock was fully erect. He was just as turned on post-shift as I was.

“Lola?” Alec’s tone was playful.

Busted. I looked up at him, grateful that the silvery glow of the moon probably didn’t show how red my face was. “I’m mad at you.”

“What’s new?” he teased.

“Why can’t you just be honest with me?” I asked.

“Because things are complicated with you,” he said.

“No, they’re not,” I insisted.

“You want honesty?” There was a touch of a growl to his tone.

My toes curled and a shiver ran down my spine. Every

second I stood there facing him was a second closer to my willpower breaking down.

"All I can think about when I'm around you is that night in the tent and how I fucked up the best thing that's ever happened to me," he said. "I think about how stupid I was to turn you over to Wolf Creek. I wish I'd killed your mate that night and made all of the shifters who hurt you pay."

How was I supposed to react to that? It wasn't fair. He was saying all the right things. Shit, I'd want to ride his cock without him saying a word. Post shift sex drive was no joke.

"You made a choice," I said, trying to turn things around. I had to remain in control. I couldn't have sex with Alec, could I?

"I'm willing to keep working on making it up to until you forgive me," he said.

"I don't know if that's possible," I admitted. He sent me back to the one place he knew I'd be harmed. It wasn't right.

He took a step closer to me and I froze in place. I wanted him, but I wasn't ready to let him off the hook for what he did to me. As if sensing my hesitation, he took a step back. "We should see if we can find somewhere to sleep."

"Like a tree?" I asked. "Cause there's pretty much nothing around here."

"There's some caves nearby, we'll try those," he said.

I tensed. "Not a cave. Please. Anywhere else but that."

"We need some cover," he said.

"Last time I went in a cave, I nearly died," I reminded him.

"If it's too much, we won't go inside," he said.

I didn't like the idea of any cave, but I nodded. It would provide more cover than the elements. We were naked and had no fire or supplies. Maybe I could make it work for one night.

The cold night air on my bare skin was painful. Goosebumps spread on my arms and legs. I covered my chest with my arms, trying to maintain some warmth. Every so often, I stepped on something sharp and hissed in pain. What I wouldn't give to come across some human campers we could borrow clothes and shoes from. Okay, steal them, but it was an emergency, maybe they'd give them to us. Unfortunately, there was no sign of life. We were isolated here.

We didn't speak as we walked, but I was grateful for the silence. When we were talking, I was closer than I wanted to admit to giving in to him and I wasn't ready to forgive him. I needed more time to work through everything. There was too much between Tyler and Wolf Creek and my father to add other complications.

My mind wandered and I thought about Sheila, Kyle, and Malcom. Were they safe? Were they hurt? Did they have to walk through the woods naked? Visions of my friends suddenly turned into thoughts of Tyler. I shook my head at the unwelcome intrusion.

I squeezed my eyes closed, and forced the pictures of him away. That stupid mating bond was messing with me. I focused on other things. The wind blowing through the trees, the sound of my feet walking over the dirt, the feel of my hair whipping around my face. Anything and everything to get him off my mind. The harder I tried to make it stop, the more I tried to think of other things, of anything, the more intense my thoughts about Tyler got.

Unbidden, the memory of the kiss in front of the caves crashed into my mind I recalled the way my body responded to him. I should have felt the urge to throw up, but it wasn't there, instead there was a sense of longing. I was losing control of my own emotions. Pushing the thoughts away, the memory of the dream came rushing in. It had felt so real. His skin, his hot breath, my beating heart … holy shit, he bit me.

I never let myself think too hard about the dream, but in my dream, he'd completed the bond. And I'd let him.

My chest tightened as terror gripped me. Was I losing myself to the bond? What would happen when I saw him again?

"There they are," Alec said.

His words broke my dark thoughts and my vision seemed to re-focus on the world around me. Ahead, I saw the opening for a cave. Though, it was almost too shallow to be called a cave. A stone archway extended from a rock, providing a covered space only about ten feet deep. Unlike the cave I'd been trapped in, it didn't extend into deeper tunnels or connect to other caves. Most importantly, there was no rock to roll in front of it.

"I'll make sure it's not occupied," Alec said. "Wait here."

"Gladly," I said.

A moment later, he emerged. "It's not too deep and it doesn't look like anything has made it into a home. It's not much, but at least we'll have some protection from the elements. Think you'll be okay to come in?"

"Yeah, thanks," I said. "Tomorrow, we need to find some clothes."

"Agree." He walked in and I might have checked out his bare ass as he ducked down a little to dip into the entrance.

Damn, he was sexy. And he knew it.

I moved toward the cave, trying to push the naughty

thoughts of Alec away. They were quickly replaced by images of Tyler.

Was this how it was going to be? Post shift, I was doomed to have sexy thoughts about my mate? I tensed. What if I had another one of those dreams? What if it pushed me closer to completing the bond with Tyler? There had to be something I could do to stop this.

Fighting the urges post-shift had caused the dream, and seemed to make the bond deeper. I wasn't going to chance that happening anymore. Sex was part of life. Especially for a shifter. I was tired of fighting it. We were freezing, alone, and naked in a cave. For all we knew, we'd be hunted down by my old pack tonight. Life was too short to turn down all the things that made it worth living.

Alec sat on the dirt and looked up at me. "It's not the Four Seasons, but it'll do."

I marched over to him and dropped to my knees. Things were complicated with Alec, but he wasn't Tyler. Before I could change my mind, I reached for the back of his head and pulled him into a kiss.

17

Alec gently pushed me away. "What are you doing?"

"Kissing you," I said, leaning in to do it again.

"This is the shift."

"So?" I licked his lower lip.

He groaned. "Lola, I want you. You have no idea how badly I want you. But I won't take advantage."

"What happened to the cocky asshole who said he'd offer his services the other night?" I asked.

"Oh, he's still here. He still wants all of you. But it has to be because you want me, too."

"We shifted hours ago," I reminded him. "Don't you think I'm clear-headed enough to make my own decisions now?"

"Are you?" he asked.

"Stop talking, Alec. I want you. It doesn't have to be a thing. It can just be two people having fun together. Besides, we'll be warmer this way."

"You don't seem like the casual sex type," he said with a frown.

"Don't judge me," I snapped.

"I'm not judging." He leaned forward and placed a soft, tender kiss on my lips. "I'm wondering why I'm getting so lucky."

I claimed his mouth, kissing him hard and fast. "Stop thinking. Just kiss me."

His lips moved against mine as he pulled me into him. I was on his lap now, my legs hanging over one side. Alec's hardness was against my thigh and I was desperate to feel him inside me.

"I thought I'd never get to touch you again." Alec's words were breathy, coming out between kisses.

I pulled away and locked eyes with him. "This doesn't mean everything is fixed between us."

"I'll take what I can get." His hand skimmed up my side until it reached my breast. He caressed each breast before moving to play with my nipples. I bit down on my lower lip, enjoying the sensation of his hands on my body. He moved to my back, caressed my breasts, and slid his hands down my thighs. He was exploring every inch of me and it was driving me crazy.

"You sure about this?" he asked, his hand paused on my inner thigh, dangerously close to finding my center.

My breathing quickened. "There are worse ways to pass the time while on the run."

"I'll try not to disappoint you," he said.

"You aren't so far," I teased.

Alec's hand dipped between my legs. I parted my thighs, and his fingers immediately began to stroke my clit.

"I'm just getting started," he promised.

"I like where it's going so far." I was already a little breathless as he continued to work my clit.

As the pleasure grew, I arched my back and widened the space between my legs. Alec slipped a finger in, his other hand taking over the stimulation on my clit.

The added sensation of his finger inside me, quickly sent me over the edge. I cried out as I orgasmed, coupled with a huge feeling of relief. Was that the post-shift desire sated?

I didn't have much time to think about what happened because my attention didn't linger on inner thoughts. My mind and body wanted more.

"Your turn," I said, taking Alec's cock in my hand.

He shivered a little as I closed my fingers around him. After a few strokes, he was groaning in pleasure. His eyes closed for a moment, then when he looked back at me, I saw a different side of him. His gaze was more animal than man. It activated something in me. My whole body felt like it was on fire and the only thing that could quench me was Alec.

I adjusted so I was straddling him, my hips inches from his length. He wrapped his arms around me, pulling me in to him. I lifted my hips and he slipped easily inside my already soaked pussy. With a thrust, he was fully inside me and I gasped as he hit a spot that sent a shiver down my spine.

Alec's hands were on my hips, helping to guide my moments. I was still learning what I liked and how to enjoy the feel of a man. After a few adjustments, I found my rhythm. Each thrust sent him deeper and I moaned over and over as I got closer to climax.

My back arched and I tossed my head back. Alec's hand supported my head, his fingers tangled in my hair. His other hand caressed my back, helping me continue to move without having to think. I felt relaxed and free.

It was absolute trust, pure instinct. I was driven only by

pleasure. Just as an orgasm built, Alec pressed his lips to mine. I had to pull away to take a breath, then quickly went back to the kiss. Gripping his shoulders, I continued to move my hips while his hands explored my back and ass.

We kept our lips locked together, his tongue darting in and out of my mouth, and mine meeting his stroke for stroke. A few times, he nipped at my lower lip, sending a shockwave through me each time. It was like a miniature orgasm with each little nibble. Something about the tiny bit of pain sent me right over the edge. It didn't hurt exactly, but the pressure was just right. It was as if he knew what to do to send me into climax after climax. Finally, he tensed and groaned as he came.

Panting and sweaty, our foreheads met and we stared into each other's eyes. I could see little flecks of gold in both his irises. Up close, his stunning dual-colored eyes were even more beautiful than I remembered. My breathing slowed, getting more relaxed. Alec's breathing slowed to match mine.

We stayed that way a long while, looking deep into each other's eyes. I'd never felt more connection to another person or more alive in my life. I was pretty sure I could feel his emotions. There was mixture of elation and satisfaction with a touch of sorrow. The realization sent a rush of panic through me.

We were too close. I was falling and I couldn't afford to. I had to break the moment. I blinked and pulled away from him. This couldn't be anything more than it was. We were trapped alone, naked, post-shift. Any pair of shifters would have done the same.

"That was great," I said.

"Yeah, it was," he agreed.

"Thanks for that, I needed the distraction," I admitted.

"Should I feel dirty right now? Was I just used for sex?" he teased.

"We both needed that, and you know it," I said.

"I hope we can do it again another time," he said.

"Maybe." I wasn't feeling quite as opposed to working on things with him as I had been.

Sex with Alec was simple. Effortless. Amazing. It was everything I wanted. Our relationship wasn't. Outside the bedroom, or in this case, the cave floor, things were confusing and messy.

I slowly pulled myself off him and we managed to find the softest, least rocky part of the cave floor to lay on. Alec lay down first, and stretched out his arm. "Come on."

I stretched out on the ground next to him and he pulled me in so my head was resting on his chest. He wrapped me in his strong arms, our bodies touching as much as possible.

Curled up together, we'd stay warmer. Somehow, laying with him on the floor felt more intimate than what we'd just done. I had some serious issues. It wasn't just my thoughts about Alec I needed to work through, it was also my own shit I had to figure out.

"What are we going to do about the whole naked in the middle of the woods thing tomorrow?" I asked.

"We could cover ourselves in mud and pretend to be Bigfoot if we come across any hikers," he suggested.

I laughed. "I'd rather avoid the mud, but I have a feeling hikers would be just as terrified about two naked people, too."

"Maybe," he said.

"How far off course are we? Do you know where we are?" I asked.

"Well, I know I can't count on your sense of direction," he teased.

"If we had to do that, we'd be better off making this cave our home and hoping someone found us before we died," I said.

"I can get us out of here," he said. "We have a rendezvous location with the others. If my guess as to our location is accurate, we'll be there by lunchtime tomorrow."

At the mention of food, my stomach rumbled. "Well, hopefully they salvaged our packs."

"Why don't you get some sleep." He stroked my hair gently, the motion making my eyes heavy. I wanted to argue with him, volunteer to take watch, but his touch was soothing and my body couldn't resist.

When I opened my eyes, sunlight was pouring into the cave and Alec was gone.

18

"You have got to be fucking kidding me." I stood and dusted the dirt and pebbles from me as best I could. I was covered in dirt, freezing cold, and completely embarrassed.

Sure, my slumber had been blissfully devoid of Tyler, and I hadn't expected anything from Alec, but where the fuck was he?

I crept to the front of the cave and peered outside. The sun made the woods look almost cheerful this morning. Birds flitted from tree to tree and somewhere nearby I could hear a woodpecker pounding away. A light breeze rustled the trees and carried the fresh, clean scent of pine.

I covered my chest, aware that it wasn't doing much to hide me from anyone who might have stumbled upon our sleeping spot. It did make me feel better as I ventured into the openness of the woods.

Hoping I'd find Alec nearby, I started walking away from the cave. *Fuck*. I hopped on one foot, grabbing my other foot. Of course I'd managed to step on something sharp. Carefully,

I pulled out the pointy stick and tossed it aside. My foot was still a little tender when I set it back on the ground.

What was I supposed to do now? There was no sign of Alec and I had no idea where we were. He'd mentioned that there was a place to meet our friends but even if I knew the location, I wasn't sure I'd be able to navigate there. Where was he? I wondered if he'd gone off to check our location or find something to eat. What were our chances that there was a home nearby with coffee and pastries?

I considered shifting. If I was in wolf form, at least I wouldn't be naked. Plus, it was possible my wolf was better at directions than I was. Or maybe she could scent something.

The sound of a branch snapping made me tiptoe back to the cave. I peeked out, hoping it was a small animal and not a predator or human. My shoulders relaxed when I caught sight of Alec.

He was wearing what appeared to be a blanket around his chest and waist like a toga. In his arms he had a bundle of fabric. I didn't care what it was. Blanket, nightgown, whatever. Anything to act as some warmth would be very helpful.

I stepped out from my hiding place. "So you went out to find clothes?"

"Went for a run this morning at sunrise to scout ahead a bit. Happened upon some trash left behind by humans." He held up a beach towel. "It's not much, but it'll get us where we need to go."

I grabbed it from him and wrapped it around myself. It was caked in mud in places as if it had been outside for a while. I wasn't in any position to be picky. My body was covered in dirt and grime as it was. A little more dirt wasn't going to make much of a difference. "Thanks."

"They didn't leave any shoes behind," he said, glancing at my feet.

"I'll live," I said. "Did you see anything on your route?"

"Other than the empty beer bottles and stuff I grabbed for us, we appear to be in the clear."

"Should we head to meet our friends?" I asked.

"Let's go," he said.

We started walking side by side. I spent most of the time with my eyes on the ground to make sure I wasn't ending up with too much damage on my poor feet.

"About last night…" Alec said.

My eyes widened and I wondered where he was going to go with this. I kept my eyes on the ground, not looking up at him on purpose. What if I melted into a puddle of affection when I met his eyes? I wasn't ready to be emotionally involved. "What about it?"

"I know it was a post-shift, keep-warm thing," he said.

"Yeah. It was fun," I added.

"It was fun," he agreed.

An awkward silence fell between us. This was why I probably shouldn't have had sex with him last night. It was going to change things between us. Though, things weren't great between us before the sex, either.

"So, how far away is this rendezvous location?" I had to say something. Anything.

"Another mile or two," he said.

"You seem to know this area well," I pointed out. "No map or anything."

"I told you, I've been working on the antidote. I come here pretty often. Sheila comes with me sometimes so she picked the meeting place."

"Sheila knew you wanted to create an antidote?" I asked.

"She's the only one at camp who knew. Now, you and Malcom know, too," he said.

"And Kyle," I added.

"Right, I forgot about him." He grunted.

"What's with that?" I asked. "You don't like Kyle? He thinks you're his best friend or something. Believes everything you've told him."

"I like Kyle fine. I don't like how close he is with you," he said. "But that's not my place."

I lifted my brow. Was he jealous? That was interesting. "You're right, it's not your place."

I glanced over at him and caught a momentary scowl on his expression. If he was jealous, it was cruel of me to let him think Kyle and I were anything more than what we were. There was zero romance or chance of romance between us. I just didn't feel anything for him. He was handsome, but that spark had never existed and I was confident it never would.

"But, since you brought it up, there's nothing there between us. He's a friend. A new friend at that," I said. "He risked everything when he helped me. He's just as dead as I am if we ever return. I owe him."

"He saved my ass, too," Alec said. "I owe him for that and for getting you out."

"You realize that could have been prevented," I reminded him.

"You're never going to let me forget that, are you?" he asked.

"It's a hard thing to let go," I replied. "They could have killed me. Or Tyler could have…"

"Ace told me he was going to make his son break the

bond." Alec glanced over at me. "Since it was what you wanted, I figured it was the best way to do it. They'd get him close enough to make it happen."

"How did you know he wouldn't kill me to break it? That was an awful big risk if you actually cared about me," I snapped.

"He promised me he'd release you once it was done, but I didn't believe that. It's why I got myself caught. Though, I honestly thought he'd force the bond to break. I was blinded by what I wanted," he admitted.

"What do you mean, *blinded by what you wanted*? The money? If you got rid of me, there was no need to pay your witch friend to do the spell," I pointed out.

Fear rolled through me and I wondered if I'd been played again. Why would he need so much money to have a witch do a spell for me if they were friends anyway? "You're keeping things from me again. The money doesn't make sense. None of this makes sense. Why would a friend who has been helping you charge for a spell?"

Alec stopped walking. "Supplies and alliances cost money. She's not doing anything for me out of the goodness of her heart. She might be working on the antidote with me, but I keep her in supplies so she doesn't have to leave her house. It's a good arrangement, but I'm not foolish enough to think she wouldn't hand me over if there was a better offer."

"So why do you trust her?" It seemed like a huge risk.

"Because she never leaves and nobody know she's here. It would be a challenge for anyone else to buy her loyalty," he said.

"She's working on the antidote but charged an obscene amount for a spell?" I still wasn't convinced.

"It's blood magic. If her coven catches her, she's at risk of having her magic siphoned. The payment had to be worth it," he said.

"Fuck. This is bad, Alec. It doesn't seem like it's worth the risk. What if the coven finds out and comes after you?" I asked.

"It's possible," he said with a shrug.

"I'm not worth all this," I said. "I could have gone into hiding, or found a witch who could do a spell like Malcom has. There were other ways. Pissing off a coven of witches is fucking suicide. If they find out, they're not just going to kill you; they'll make your life hell."

"It's going to be fine," he assured me. "She's not going to talk."

"We could still skip the spell. It hasn't been done yet," I offered. "I can't be responsible for bad things happening because of me. It's not right."

"Stop it, right now," he said. "You need to start having some sense of self perseveration. Can't you see that you're worth all this risk?"

"What? Because I have some alpha mark? You have the same mark," I reminded him.

"Because you matter," he said. "Since we met, I haven't been able to get you out of my head. I haven't felt this way about anyone since..." he shook his head, "never mind. It's insane. Just trust me on this, you're worth it."

"What about you?" I demanded. "How will any of this be worth it if you end up dead?"

"I can't lose you," he said. "When my pack was slaughtered, I wasn't there to help. I am not going to sit by and do nothing to prevent the death of someone I care about."

“We’re risking too much. They could come after your camp, your home,” I said.

He shook his head. “I’m not alpha. They are not connected to my actions in any way. It’s shifter law. I’m not responsible for them and they are not responsible for me. They’re all instructed to turn me in to save themselves. And they would. We’re feral, Lola. Not pack.”

“You’re wrong. You don’t use the title, but they’re your pack. I promise you, not a single one of them would turn you over.”

“I hope you’re wrong about that,” he said.

“I hope the witches don’t catch us,” I said.

“I can’t change anything I’ve done. But I can make it so you’ll be safe. You don’t deserve the life you had. It’s time to change that,” he said.

“I could say the same thing about you.” How could he risk so much to help someone he barely knew? “What if I don’t do it? What if I don’t agree to the spell?”

“Listen, I’ve told you everything. It’s already in motion. The damage is done. If you don’t follow through and break the claim, it’ll have been for nothing.” He was so close to me now that we were nearly touching. “Once we break this, we’ll have options. And you’ll get your life back.”

Part of me wanted to reach for him. I wanted comfort, support. But I was confused. Nobody had ever cared for me and he’d risked everything to help me. “No more lies. No more masking the truth.”

“Promise,” he said.

I took a deep breath and started walking. “We better find our friends.”

19

As we walked, I tried to send away any thoughts that entered my mind. There was too much to consider and too much at stake. *One thing at a time.* That was the only way I was going to get through this. We stopped at a stream and drank some of the best water I'd ever tasted. Other than that, there were no breaks. I was eager to find my friends and make sure they were safe.

"If Wolf Creek tracked us here, you think they'll find us again?" I asked.

"The others can take care of themselves. I would guess our immediate threat is gone," he said.

I hated that my friends had to cause harm to others on my behalf. Granted, the assholes from Wolf Creek deserved it, but I didn't like that my friends had to take on the burden of protecting me. I wanted to be strong enough to fight my own battles and I was willing to put in the work to make myself and my wolf stronger.

Ahead, I noticed a strange looking tower. It was bright

blue and might have once been a tree. It wasn't much thicker than the tree stumps around it, and it was only a little taller. "What the hell is that?"

"That's our meeting place," Alec said.

"Subtle," I deadpanned.

"Nobody knows it's there. Random hikers find it from time to time, but it's not on any shifter radar," he assured me.

"What is it, exactly?" I asked.

"I heard it was created by some artist. Not sure why or what the meaning is."

"Is it a tree stump?" I asked.

"It's a big ass pole. They shoved it way down in the earth. It's not even made of wood," Alec said.

"That's the oddest thing," I said.

"It makes for a good meeting place, though. It's fairly easy to find and if anyone does see us waiting there, they assume we're hikers passing through," he said.

"Unless it draws the attention from shifters we don't want around," I replied.

"True, but we're not going to stay there," he reminded me.

The strange blue pole looked like it wasn't too far away, but it was hard to tell how close we were. The path took us straight uphill for a while, then it leveled out and we emerged into a clearing. The blue pole stood proudly in the center. It looked even more out of place up close. The bottom of the pole was covered in spray paint and parts of it were rusting. Beer cans, red plastic cups, and other trash scattered across the clearing. Most of it looked like it had been there for a while, untouched. That made me feel a little better.

"Doesn't look like this place is too secret anymore," I said.

"Humans use it in the summer sometimes," he said as he kicked some of the trash out of his way.

I frowned at the cigarette butts and other debris. It was awful that they'd left it all here. I didn't have time to clean up other people's messes right now, though. At this moment, I needed to find my friends and put out the fires already burning in my life.

"Where are they?" I asked quietly. The clearing felt too open and exposed. I didn't like standing next to such an obvious landmark without anywhere to hide.

"They should be here," he said.

I looked over at him. "What if something awful happened to them?"

"I'm sure they're fine. If they aren't here soon, they must have gone to the next stage of the plan."

"Truth, remember?" I asked.

"I swear I wasn't hiding anything. We had this as our meeting place, but if they couldn't get rid of the attackers, they were to lead them away from our destination," he said. "They might have had to do that."

I hated the idea of my friends on the run, being chased by shifters from Wolf Creek. "That's not a comforting thought."

"I know. But they wanted to help you. We all do," he said. "We'll meet them after. We can't stay any longer."

"You're not going anywhere," a loud, clear male voice called.

My whole body tensed and I turned in the direction of the sound of my mate's voice.

Tyler stood near a tree on the outskirts of the clearing. "You shouldn't have run."

"What are you doing here?" I demanded.

"My friends chased the others, but I've been following your scent the whole time. It was nice of you to split up. Makes this easier for me," Tyler said.

"I told you, I don't want to be with you," I said. "Stop trying."

"I was being nice. I was willing to wait for you. You are my mate. You are the one who is supposed to comply," Tyler growled.

"No. You are the one who should," I snapped. I was done being afraid. Done backing down and running.

Hands balled into fists, I took a step toward him. "You have two choices. You can break the bond and accept your place as a member of my pack, or I will kill you myself."

Tyler laughed. "*Your* pack? It's *my* pack. You are mine. Same as a pair of shoes or an obedient dog. You're my property."

I lifted my shirt enough to show the mark. "I am your alpha."

Tyler's laughter died. "I thought they were lying. My dad said he saw the mark, but I thought it was his excuse to kill you."

"You will allow me to break the bond," I insisted. "That is your only option."

Alec growled. He'd been silent this whole time, letting me handle Tyler, but I could sense his rising anger. "She's giving you a choice you don't deserve."

"She's my mate, not yours. What do you know about pack or mating bonds, feral trash," Tyler spat.

Alec growled again.

I moved in front of him, preventing him from lunging right for Tyler's throat. Tyler deserved to die for what he'd done to me. But whenever I tried to allow those thoughts into my mind, the bond pushed back. It was as if my only option was to let him make amends and go on his merry way.

The tiny part of me that was resisting the mating bond wanted to rip his throat out, but the bond had gotten too strong. It was keeping me from acting. I wasn't sure if I was going to be able to fight him or if I'd run to him.

My pulse raced and my mind felt like it was at war with itself. Fighting the bond was getting more difficult. I stared at Tyler, determined. "If you care about me at all, you will break this bond. I can't be with you. After everything you've done to me, I deserve this one act of kindness."

"I challenge you," Alec said.

"What?" I turned to him, my eyes wide. "No, Alec. Please, don't do this."

His jaw was tense, his expression determined. I could tell I wasn't going to be able to talk him out of this. Challenging for alpha wasn't the only kind of challenge the packs upheld. You could challenge for a mate. It was archaic and disgusting. Men fighting over the rights of another human being. I'd never seen it done, but I'd heard stories growing up. It was supposed to be romantic or some bullshit. What they didn't mention was how the woman had no choice but to go with the winner. How was that romance?

"You'd risk your life for her?" Tyler sounded amused and a little disgusted.

I perked up at that a little. There was a part of him that didn't want to be with me, either. "Tyler, you don't have to do this. Just let me go."

"Are you afraid to fight me? Did they even teach you how to fight in that pack of yours or is beating innocent girls all you know how to do?" Alec challenged.

Tyler growled and his body was already tensing unnaturally. He had a wild look in his eyes. "When I win, I'm going to make you watch me claim her."

"Never going to happen," I said though gritted teeth. "I'll kill you myself before I surrender to you."

"The bond won't let you," Tyler said. "I've tried to cut you out, but every time I fight it, I just want you more. I know I'm not alone. I see you in my dreams. We're connected. The bond keeps getting stronger."

I swallowed hard and tried not to let him know how much his words got to me. It was all my nightmares and fears. I glanced over at Alec.

He nodded and I felt a silent exchange between us. He knew I was afraid and he wasn't going to let me down. I wasn't sure how I knew that, but I was certain those were his thoughts as he tossed the blanket aside.

Tyler stripped and suddenly, there were two huge wolves growling at each other.

I grabbed Alec's blanket and got out of the way, positioning myself behind a tree so I could have something to block me if they came my way. You did not want to be in the middle of two wolves fighting. It wasn't pretty and I knew if I got too close, I was in danger of becoming collateral damage.

The two wolves circled each other, growling and snapping their jaws. Hackles up, they both looked as tense as springs as they eyed their opponents.

I hated that I was in the background, waiting as two males fought for my honor or some shit. It was everything I said I would work against. I'd been determined to protect myself and stand up for myself since leaving Wolf Creek. I made baby steps by connecting with my wolf, but she was still new at this. We weren't ready to get in the middle of a fight like this.

Tyler's dark gray wolf jumped forward, testing the reflexes of Alec's lighter gray wolf. Alec dodged with ease, moving with the grace I'd come to associate with the feral shifters. Tyler repeated the same thing several times, Alec dodging each attempted attack with ease.

The frustration of Tyler's wolf was evident. He was impatient, with big movements that Alec saw coming a mile away. At first, I wasn't sure why Alec was toying with him. I hadn't seen the feral shifter fight, but he was strong and fast and had been united with his wolf for a long time. He had the mark of an alpha, which in theory, made him stronger and faster.

Then, I realized with each attempted attack, Tyler was getting a little slower and Alec was correcting a little less. Alec's wolf was wearing him out and studying the other wolf's moves.

Tyler lunged again, and this time, Alec rose up on his back legs, claws out, striking down the incoming wolf. Tyler's wolf was knocked to the ground, his paws struggling to right himself before Alec charged him again.

Teeth and claws came for Tyler before he was even on his feet. Alec was merciless in his attack, pinning the other wolf until he let out a pathetic yelp. A moment later, Tyler freed himself from Alec and leaped onto him, slicing him in the stomach. Alec growled and quickly struck back, knocking the other wolf down again. Tyler righted himself and attacked Alec, snapping his jaws around his leg.

Alec yowled and jerked his leg away, but Tyler held fast. My heart pounded and just as I was going to leave my space by the tree, Alec broke the hold. He snapped back at Tyler but he dodged.

I was holding my breath and my brow was creased with worry. Each time one of them got the upper hand, I felt a pull toward the injured male. My mind wanted Alec to win, but my instincts forced a reaction every time Tyler was injured. It was torture.

The wolves continued to fight, their attacks taking them farther from my spot until I couldn't see what was happening. Carefully, I moved, walking toward the sound of the growls and falls and thrashing.

When I found them, Tyler was on the ground, and Alec was holding him down. Both wolves were bleeding and their fur was matted. I could see Alec's wolf breathing heavy, his sides moving in and out. He let out a low growl, his gaze fixed on the wolf under him.

Surrender, Tyler. I wasn't sure if the thought came from me or my inner wolf, but it sent a surge of joy through me. I was able to take a side. I wasn't feeling the pull to Tyler. *Surrender.*

Alec released the other wolf and took a step back. He was still tense and ready, but he was giving Tyler space to get back to his feet. Tyler's wolf stumbled, nearly collapsing as he stood. *Good.*

The anger and hate I felt toward Tyler wasn't clouded by my mating bond. I wasn't going to concern myself with why I was getting lucky, but for now, at least, I was granted a moment of clarity.

Tyler's wolf shuddered, then his body began to break and

bend. I turned away, wincing at the cracking of bones as his human form returned.

When I looked back both Tyler and Alec were fully transitioned. They faced each other, both males breathing heavy. Their bare skin was covered in claw marks and bruises. I knew they'd both heal in a matter of hours, but for now, the fight was over.

"You lost," Alec said. "Release her from the bond and never speak to her again."

Tyler turned from Alec and walked back toward the space they'd started the fight. He grabbed his clothes and slowly stepped into his jeans.

Alec followed and I walked over to him, handing him the blanket he'd been using in place of our missing clothing. We stopped in front of Tyler.

"You won," Tyler said.

"Break the bond," I said.

"The problem is, I don't know how to break the bond," Tyler said.

I turned to Alec. "How does he break it?"

"You two need to be touching," Alec said. "Then when both your inner wolves agree to break the bond at the same time, it'll be done."

"It's time, Tyler," I said.

Tyler shrugged. "Fine."

Alec nodded encouragement.

I walked closer to my mate, ready to break the bond that had kept the two of us connected through a cruel twist of fate. We were so close to escaping the punishment of being forced together.

"Ready?" I asked.

He offered a hand and I accepted. The mating bond roared back to life inside me like a wave, crashing over my senses and sending a shockwave of longing through me. I sucked in a breath and fought against the sensation. *You don't want this.* I reminded myself of the awful things he'd done to me, trying to force back the connection I felt between us.

"She feels it," Tyler said. "She won't be strong enough to break it."

"Fight it," Alec said.

"I don't want you, Tyler," I forced the words out, but they were hollow, empty. How could this happen? I glanced over at Alec, his expression was hopeful and encouraging.

Tyler leaned closer to me, his lips brushing against my ear as he whispered. "Complete the bond."

My breath hitched and I pulled away from him. The bond was there, taunting me, tempting me, connecting me to the male standing in front of me. It would be so easy to let fate win, to surrender. Fighting back was harder. My mind felt fuzzy and for a moment, I wondered why I was pushing back. A mating bond was a gift, wasn't it? I deserved to be happy. That's what a mate was supposed to bring: happiness.

That isn't what Tyler will bring.

My inner wolf was the one who brought me back to my senses. If she was fighting the bond, I knew we could do it.

I closed my eyes, forcing myself to remember the hurt Tyler had caused me. My wolf stirred within me. *Is this what you want?* She seemed to want to make sure I was ready to break the bond. To live with the consequences of my actions. It was rare to find a true mate. It could bring power and strength and happiness. But that wasn't what Tyler would bring me. He'd bring me nothing but pain. *He has to go.*

I opened my eyes. "Tyler, I reject you."

He snarled, his upper lip curled. "I thought you might say that."

Suddenly, Alec pushed me aside, and I landed on the ground, no longer holding Tyler's hand.

Confused, I looked up just in time to see Tyler stabbing Alec with a syringe. Alec's eyes widened, then he collapsed.

"That was supposed to be for you, but now your feral boyfriend will pay the price." Tyler's eyes flashed with hateful malice.

I scrambled to my feet and ran to Alec. I could see his chest rising and falling slowly, but he wasn't moving. "What did you do?"

"Just some toxin," Tyler said. "I've never given anyone that much. Wonder if he'll ever wake up."

"I don't care if you're my mate," I said. "This ends now."

I sidestepped Alec's fallen body and punched Tyler as hard as I could in the jaw. Searing pain spread over my knuckles and I winced, shaking my hand out for a moment before throwing another punch.

Tyler stopped me this time, catching my fist. "You are no match for me."

"Maybe not, but if I die trying, at least I know you'll never find peace," I spat.

Tyler pushed me hard and I stumbled, but managed to stay on my feet. He walked away from Alec and charged forward. I put my fists up, ready to defend myself as best I could.

"Lola? Alec? Anyone out there?" A voice called from the distance and I turned slightly, half worried I was hearing things.

"Alec?" Another voice called.

My heart raced. Our friends had found us. "Over here!"

"Enjoy your last minutes with the feral shifter. By the time he's dead, you'll be coming for me. You're never going to break this bond. The harder we fight it, the stronger it gets. So keep fighting it. Then I won't even have to come to you because you'll be like a bitch in heat, drawn to me," he said.

"Fuck you." I took a step forward and punched him with my other fist.

Searing pain screamed through my left hand, matching the pain I was still feeling on the right. I didn't care. "You will never win."

He reached up and touched his eye, which was already blooming with a purple bruise. Too bad it would heal before he returned home.

His eyes went to something behind me, then back to me. "See you soon, Lola."

Tyler raced off, in the opposite direction from the sound of the footsteps of my incoming friends.

I raced to Alec and fell to the ground next to him. "Please be okay." I pressed my fingers to his neck, feeling for a pulse. My shoulders relaxed a little once I found it.

"Lola! Thank the moon goddess we found you," Sheila said.

I turned to catch her eye and watched as the smile faded from her expression. "What happened?"

Sheila, Malcom, and Kyle looked exhausted and dirty, but they appeared unharmed.

"We had a run in with my mate," I said.

Sheila was next to me now, her hand on his chest. "He's breathing but not healing."

She was right. His wounds from the fight were bleeding heavily, and none of them appeared to be slowing. *Shit.* How had I missed that? I was so worried about the toxin, I didn't even consider the other side effects.

"What did they do to him?" Kyle asked.

"Toxin. A lot of it. We're going to need some help," I said.

Sheila turned to Kyle and Malcom. "Can you two carry him? We have to get him to the witch."

20

SHELIA NAVIGATED for us while Malcom and Kyle took turns carrying Alec. I kept constant, obsessive lookout for Tyler. We couldn't risk anyone knowing where the witch lived or what she was doing. But we couldn't afford to wait to go to her for help, either.

Every hour, when the males switched who was carrying Alec, I checked his breathing and heartbeat. I wasn't sure if it was in my head or not, but it felt like it was getting harder to find his pulse.

Furious at myself for causing so much harm, I focused on the anger I felt toward Tyler. It drove me. As long as I felt mad, I wasn't feeling the pull toward the bond.

"I should have let the bookcase slam into him," I muttered under my breath.

Sheila slowed down and matched her pace with mine. "How you doing?"

"This is all my fault," I said. "The whole mess. How did I end up as a damsel in distress always waiting for someone else to save my ass? It's not right. I swore that I'd be stronger when I got free of Wolf Creek."

"You're no damsel," she said. "You're our friend, and you needed help. That's what friends do. They help each other. Even when it's not easy."

"I could get you all killed. That's beyond just a little help," I pointed out.

"That's part of being a friend. Especially when you're in a feral group. All of us have people who want us dead. You gotta stop thinking you're special," she teased.

I smirked and glanced over at her.

"You'd do it for me," she said. "Tell me I'm wrong."

"I'd do it for you," I agreed. If her old pack was after her, I wouldn't think twice about running toward danger to protect her. So this was what it was like to have friends. Friendship was fucking dangerous. But it was so much better than being alone. It was worth it.

"How far are we?" I asked. "Didn't Alec say three days?"

"Yeah," she said. "We'll have to break for the night. Especially since those two are going to need a rest from carrying Alec."

I looked back and saw Kyle carrying Alec on his back. It wasn't easy to carry someone who was unresponsive, but the two large males were doing a great job of sharing the burden and continuing forward. Good thing they had that extra shifter strength. They almost made it look easy but I knew they had to be feeling worn down.

"Tell me about this witch," I said. "What should I know?"

"Well, she's different, but she's a witch, so maybe that's normal." Sheila didn't sound convinced.

"What do you mean *different*?" I asked.

"She's quirky, I guess," she clarified.

"Is she dangerous?"

Sheila chuckled. "No way. Her coven is a different story."

"We've got a long walk ahead of us, I could go for a story," I said.

"Well, she's kind of like us, from what I've gathered. She was kicked out of her coven. She's different, so they treated her differently despite the fact she's crazy powerful. Assholes."

"She's an outcast like us?" It made sense why she lived alone and stayed away from her coven. It also helped explain why Sheila and Alec trusted her.

"If she were a wolf, she'd live in camp," Sheila said. "She's got a lot in common with us. Her coven thinks she's dead and that's the way she wants to keep things. Our arrangement with her helps keep her off the grid. She gets to stay in her house all the time, and we get help when we need it."

"For a price," I said.

"Yeah, we pay her. Money or sometimes other things, but it's worked out to our advantage to have a witch on our payroll," Sheila said with a shrug.

"Alec said you bring her supplies," I said.

"We do. Every few weeks, Alec drops off groceries and whatever random shit is on her list," Sheila confirmed. "Sometimes I go with him."

"So she's friendly?" I was hopeful that I didn't need to fear this witch the way I'd been taught to fear them.

"Sure, for a witch," Sheila said. "She seems like she means well, but sometimes she freaks me out, if I'm being honest. But please don't tell her that."

"I definitely won't," I promised.

We walked in silence for a while, then I started asking

questions about the people at camp to pass the time. It seemed like a good distraction for Sheila.

She'd been at camp for years and knew everyone. She told me about Mario and how he'd won his first classic car in a poker game with a goblin. He'd been a chef in a major city and while she didn't know exactly why he'd gone feral, she was pretty sure the goblin mafia was involved.

"I didn't even know there was a goblin mafia," I admitted.

"There's a seedy underworld for every species," she said. "But out of all of them, the vampires are by far the worst. Nobody crosses them."

"I always thought the witches were the worst," I said.

"They're awful, but they are a bit more straightforward. Vampires will spend decades waiting for the perfect revenge. That whole immortal thing works in their favor, I suppose," she said.

I'd never met a vampire. Or a goblin. Or even a human, to be honest. I'd been so sheltered where I grew up that all I knew about the outside world was from books and lectures in school. I'd ignored more than I should have because I didn't think I'd need to use it since I was hoping to blend in with humans and ignore the supernatural world. Now, I wished I'd listened better.

"Where do witches fall into all this?" I asked.

"Well, they hate us," she said. "There's been escalating violence between witches and wolf shifters for years but neither of the governing bodies seem to care. It's like it doesn't exist. It feels like we're nearing war, but nobody wants to officially acknowledge that. I think the packs are going to be fucked if the witches decide to strike. The king doesn't seem to have any kind of plan."

I frowned. I'd been taught that you didn't cross witches, but I never learned that it was still a problem between them and us until I met the feral shifters. I hoped things didn't escalate to the point of war. Especially since the king didn't seem to do much to actually help anyone. "What about Wolf Creek? What do you know about my pack?"

"Well, your pack is notorious for sure. Definitely the one pack you don't fuck with because they'll hit you with the toxin and destroy you."

"How did I not know about that?" I asked, feeling stupid for being so blind.

"I doubt they were teaching you about it in school. I mean, your family invented the damn toxin and you didn't even know. They went to pretty great lengths to keep it secret," Sheila said. "To the rest of us, Wolf Creek looks like a cult. But it seems like you weren't part of the inner circle."

"That's true," I agreed. "What else don't I know?"

"Well, most packs have to worry about witches. Expect for Wolf Creek. I'm not sure of the full extent, but I heard your pack does things to appease them."

"Like what?" I couldn't imagine what the pack gave in exchange for being on the witches' good side.

"I've heard all kinds of stories. Crazy things like sacrificing babies, or creating wolf-witch hybrids, to simpler things like growing herbs for them." Shelia shrugged. "Who knows what the truth is."

I caught the sounds of Kyle and Malcom mumbling and figured they were moving Alec again. I turned to them and offered my help to get him onto Malcom's back, then felt for Alec's breathing and pulse.

"How is it?" Shelia asked.

"He's still breathing, but it does feel weaker," I said. "Maybe we should stop and see if rest would help him?"

Sheila turned and looked toward the sky. The sun was low in the horizon and it would be dark in about an hour. "We might as well find a good place to camp."

We walked a little longer until we found a grove of trees that might help shield us from view. Not that it protected us if my mate was tracking my scent. I had to hope his cocky threats about me coming to him were enough to send him back to Wolf Creek with his tail between his legs.

The group had managed to salvage two of our packs, so we set out a sleeping bag for Alec. My heart felt like it was shattering when I looked down at his face. Alec's eyes were closed, he had deep scratches on his right cheek, and cuts and bruises all over his body.

I untied one of the bandages we'd made from a blanket before we started walking. The bleeding has stopped, but the cut was still deep. Around the edges of the wound, it was red and angry. I reapplied the bandage and quickly checked the rest of his wounds. Thankfully, all the bleeding had stopped but none of them looked clean. "He's still not healing."

"What I wouldn't give for a fucking first aid kit," Sheila said.

"We had one, just in case. But the fuckers destroyed that pack when they attacked us," Malcom said.

"Should I rinse it at least?" I asked.

"We only have one bottle of water left." Sheila handed it to me. "Might be better to see if you can get him to drink. Hopefully, the witch can help speed the healing."

I hated feeling so helpless. I pulled down Alec's jaw and poured a tiny bit of water in his mouth, then I lifted his head, cradling it in my arms. He swallowed on reflex, which had to be a good sign, right?

I took a quick drink of the water, then passed it to Malcom. Everyone had a sip before Sheila put it back away.

"Well, the good news is we do have some beef jerky," Malcom said. "The bad news is that it's Greta's jerky."

Sheila groaned. "It's food, barely."

Malcom passed it around and as soon as I bit into the chunk of meat, I knew why they'd been critical of it. I might as well have been eating rocks.

"It helps if you suck on it a while," Malcom said.

"Taste isn't bad," Kyle said.

"Only because we're starving," Sheila said.

I managed to eat my share, then we each had another sip of water.

"I'll take first watch," Malcom offered.

"No, you and Kyle should sleep," I said. "You two carried Alec all day and we'll need you to do it again if we have to bug out. Sheila and I will take first watch."

"Alright," he said without hesitation.

"You sure, Lola? I could stay up with Sheila," Kyle offered. "We don't both need to sleep at the same time."

"I'm sure," I said.

"You doing okay? I know seeing Tyler had to be hard for you," Kyle said.

"I'll be better when this whole mess is over and Tyler is out of the picture forever," I said.

21

ALEC LOOKED AWFUL. His skin was clammy and pale, his breathing ragged. I walked behind whoever was carrying him, not taking my eyes off him.

He'd pushed me out of the way and taken the super high dose of toxin that was intended for me. I wasn't sure if Tyler's intention had been to kill me or to render me so incapable of fighting back that he could do as he wished. I shuddered at the thought.

Alec had saved me from so much worse than death. A grim thought settled in my mind. Was death the better option than risking losing myself to the mating bond?

I pushed the thought away. I couldn't go there right now. Alec needed me. I was going to get him through this and help him recover. The rest of it could wait. It had to wait.

We approached a rocky hillside that seemed to appear out of nowhere. It didn't match the rest of the landscape and it reminded me far too much of the caves back at Wolf Creek.

Sheila was leading us right for a huge rock that appeared

to be rolled in front of the hill. My whole body tensed and my breathing grew rapid.

"Don't tell me we are going into that cave with the huge boulder to trap us until we die," I said.

Sheila gave me a sympathetic look. "I knew this part might concern you, but give it a minute. I promise it'll be okay."

"I'm not sure it will be," I admitted. My feet were glued to the spot. I wanted to keep moving. Alec needed me, my friends needed me. But I nearly died last time I went into a cave like that.

The only reason I'd been okay in the cave with Alec was because it was shallow and closed on one end. On the other end, it had been fully open. It was more like an overhang than an actual cave.

Sheila placed her hand on the large stone and without effort, it rolled aside.

"Using magic to move it is making it worse, not better," I said.

"You don't have to go in yet. Please, just look."

I forced myself to move. Each step felt robotic and agonizing. I stopped a good ten feet from the entrance. "Happy?"

"A little closer," she said.

I took five small steps and peered into the opening. To my surprise, it wasn't a dark cave. It looked like a window or a short tunnel. Instead of seeing rock and dirt, I saw a neat path that led to a meadow. There was an actual mother-fucking waterfall in the distance. "What the hell?"

"She made a deal with a fae," Sheila said. "They did some of their super special magic for her."

I blinked a few times, ignoring the fact that I'd been told

fae were a myth. Who was I to argue? I was a wolf shifter, which humans thought was myth. "No wonder you're not worried about her being found."

"Yeah, but we shouldn't linger and make that easier," Sheila said. "Go on."

Malcom, with Alec on his back, stepped into the passage. Kyle followed. Sheila waited at the entrance for me. "I have to close it so you have to go."

I nodded, then held my breath and moved forward. As soon as I crossed into the tunnel, my chest felt tight, but I fought through it. After hurried steps, I emerged on the other side, my feet sinking into soft, mossy grass. The spongy ground was a relief for my injured feet. Walking for days in the woods barefoot was a terrible idea. I would never trash talk shoes again.

The meadow we were standing in was like being in another world. Huge, leafy trees swayed in the wind, rainbow-colored birds flitted from tree to tree, and a butterfly flew by. The air smelled different here. Like honeysuckle and lime. You'd never know we just left a mountainous pine forest. Magic was the only explanation. "This is incredible."

"Never snows here, either," Sheila said. "I don't know what she did to win over that fae, but it was worth it."

"She got a hell of a deal," I agreed.

"This way," Shelia led us through the enchanted-fucking-forest, along a well-groomed dirt path.

We walked for a while before a storybook cottage appeared in view. I stared open-mouthed at the brown house with red and white trim and a thatched roof. It almost looked like it was made of gingerbread. "This can't be real."

"Should I be worried about the fact that we're walking

toward a house that looks like it's made of cookies to visit the witch who lives there?" Malcom asked.

"I was thinking the same thing," I said.

"Nobody eat anything," Kyle said.

"No kidding," I agreed.

We approached the home and I marveled at the meticulous landscaping. Rows of flowers in every color of the rainbow surrounded the house. Hummingbirds and fuzzy honeybees busied themselves in the blooms. It was calming and peaceful, and despite the nervous feeling about meeting a powerful outcast witch, I found myself enjoying the beauty of her home.

"Wait here," Sheila said when we reached the stone path that cut through the witch's garden.

I had no problem waiting for her to go first. While she walked to the witch's front door, I checked on Alec again. He didn't look any better, but I didn't think he looked worse, so I guess that was as good as it was going to get right now.

After making sure he was breathing and had a pulse, I set my palm on his forehead. He was burning up. I looked up at Malcom, who was holding Alec like a bride. His expression changed as he read mine.

"What is it?" Malcom asked.

"He's got a fever," I said.

"She's ready for us," Sheila called.

I turned away from Malcom and looked toward the house. Sheila was standing in the doorway, waiting for us.

Malcom walked ahead, cradling Alec in his arms. I lingered behind, waiting for him to get through. Kyle moved next to me. "He's going to get the help he needs now."

"I hope so," I said.

"He's tough, he'll fight through," he assured me.

I reached for Kyle's hand and squeezed. "Thank you, for everything."

"It's my job," he said.

"It's more than that," I said.

He smiled, then walked forward toward the house. I followed him, steeling myself for whatever would happen next.

The interior of the home took the exterior up a notch. It was like walking into a palace. The outside was fairy tale cottage, inside was fairy tale castle. Overstuffed cream-colored couches, vases of flowers on marble tables, pale blue velvet curtains hanging in the windows. Every detail was meticulous and lavish.

The polished wood floors had tastefully placed thick, expensive looking rugs covering main walkways and in the center of rooms. And there were a lot of rooms.

We were standing in a foyer that looked too impossibly large to fit inside the cottage we'd entered. To my right, was a formal dining room with a table long enough for at least a dozen people. To my left was a sitting room. Ahead of me, I saw the hallway splinter into several other rooms.

It was clear the magic of the meadow extended into the house itself. It might as well have been a fucking castle. Sheila led us down the halls, past closed doors, and down a set of stairs.

"You doing okay, Malcom?" I called. He was still carrying an unresponsive Alec.

"I'm good," he grunted.

The staircase seemed to go down forever, taking us deeper

into the ground. There was a damp chill in the air and despite the lights on the wall, it felt like it was getting darker.

"We're not going to a dungeon, are we?" I said, only half joking.

"It'll get weirder," Sheila promised.

"Can't wait," I said.

We finally emerged into a sprawling underground space that resembled a cave far too much for my liking. Stone walls lined the room and the ground was dirt. Lamps flickered, providing some light in the dark room. It was a huge space, but it felt like it was getting smaller by the minute.

Aside from the strangeness of the room itself, the objects in here added to the mystery. Tables covered in bottles and jars with a mix of mysterious tools and instruments lined one wall. Against the other were rows and rows of plants. Orange lamps hummed above the plants, casting the plants in an eerie glow.

In the back of the room, there was a single white door. It opened and a teenager emerged. She was wearing torn jeans and a faded Nirvana tee. Her jet-black hair was cropped short and worn in jagged spikes on top of her head. Around her neck, she had several beaded necklaces that shimmered in the unusual light.

This couldn't be the witch. She looked nearly normal, and she was far too young. The young woman looked up and I noticed her eyes for the first time. They were pure white, no iris, no pupil. Just a bright, nearly florescent white. It was impossible not to stare. I'd never seen anything like it.

"You're the new female alpha, aren't you?" she asked, her empty eyes locked on me. "I wondered when you'd visit me."

I looked around, unsure if she was speaking to me despite the eye contact. "Are you talking to me?"

"No, to the other rudely staring woman," she bit back.

I lowered my eyes. "I'm sorry."

"I'm used to it," she said with a grin. "I just like fucking with people."

"Are you blind?" I asked. "Sorry, that's probably rude to ask."

"It's fine," she said. "I am blind, but not in the way you usually think. I can see with my magic. It's not the same and I miss some details from time to time, but it works well enough for me."

"Is that why they sent you away?" I asked.

"Cedar Coven doesn't like anyone who might make them look weak," she said with disgust. "Bunch of self-righteous assholes."

I liked her. "Their loss."

"Wait, you were part of the Cedar Coven?" Malcom asked.

"Yeah, what's it to you?" she asked.

"Same group who locked in your pack." Malcom lifted his chin in my direction.

"I know where you're going with that but the answer, for now, is no. I'm not going to break any old wards," she said.

"I suppose we'd have to pay you," Kyle said.

"Oh, no, I'd tear down those wards for free just to fuck with those jerks who kicked me out. But we've got bigger problems, don't we?" she said.

"Alec." Why had we not pushed that the second we saw her? I felt awful for getting sidetracked. "He was given a huge dose of the toxin. He's got a fever and he's been out since yesterday. Can you help?"

She swept her arm toward a table that was mostly empty. "Put him down, I'll see what I can do."

22

Malcom and Kyle helped get Alec situated on the table while the young witch looked on.

"Does she have a name?" I whispered to Sheila.

"Star," the witch said without looking up.

"Beautiful name," I said.

"Guess they had big plans for me until my sight was taken. Once my eyes faded, they no longer called me anything." She moved closer to Alec.

"Parents can be awful." We had a lot in common.

Star hummed absentmindedly, her attention elsewhere. She was examining Alec's wounds, her long, thin fingers trailing down his arms, gliding over the cuts on his stomach, then traveled down to his feet.

As far as I could tell, her lack of traditional vision didn't hold her back at all. Her fingers were nimble and sure, and her brow furrowed as she made her assessments.

"He's slipping," she said.

"What do you mean?" Sheila asked.

My chest tightened and I felt like a lead weight fell into the pit of my stomach. "She means he's dying."

"He should already be dead, honestly. Whoever gave him that much toxin didn't intend for him to survive it."

I sucked in a sharp breath. "It wasn't meant for him. It was meant for me."

"Well, I imagine, had the assailant succeeded in striking you, your friends would have had to stop to bury you along the way. His connection with his wolf, and his hunger for life are keeping him alive. I can barely feel your wolf. For a future alpha, you're not as strong as you should be."

Every word about me was accurate. I wasn't as strong as I should be. I wasn't connecting fully with my wolf. If it had been me, I'd be dead. Instead, Alec was hanging by a thread. My throat stung, and my whole body felt heavy with grief. Alec risked everything for me. I didn't even care that it had almost been me instead. If he died, I couldn't live with myself. I'd rather it be me than him. "How do we help him? There has to be a way. Anything. Tell me what to do."

"Well, we can wait and see if his wolf is strong enough to fight this off. It could take days, and he's likely to get worse before he gets better. Or…"

"Or, what?" I asked.

"We can test the antidote on him," she said.

"Is it ready?" Sheila asked.

Star shrugged. "It might be."

"What does that mean?" Malcom blurted out. "It is or it isn't."

"It's not that simple," Star said. "I've been working on it for years, but I've yet to test it on a living shifter."

"Do you think it will work?" I asked.

“It could,” she said.

“Will it cause more harm?” I asked.

“It shouldn’t, but I could be wrong,” she said.

She didn’t strike me as someone who was wrong often, but I didn’t know her well enough to trust my instincts with that.

I walked over to Alec and set my hand on his heart. His breaths were slow and uneven, his chest making a rattling sound with each exertion. I closed my eyes and focused on his wolf. There was a tiny flicker of recognition. My wolf could sense his, but it was so weak. I wasn’t an expert by any means, but I could tell he was dying.

This was Alec. If there was anything we could do to save him, we had to try. I opened my eyes and stepped away from him before turning to face Star. “His wolf won’t last much longer.”

“Are you sure?” Malcom asked.

“She’s right,” Star said. “I no longer see any visions of his future.”

Panic surged through me. “What do you mean?”

Star turned her white eyes on me. “You know what I mean.”

“Does that mean the antidote won’t work?” Sheila asked.

“It means if we don’t do it, he has no chance,” I said.

Star nodded.

“Do it.” The antidote was everything to Alec. He believed in it and I was completely confident that he’d want to try it. “It’s what he would want, anyway.”

“Are you sure, Lola?” Sheila asked.

I nodded.

Star was already standing in front of the table with the

instruments, jars, and tools. She opened a little box and removed a vial holding it up as if it was a sacred object.

In a way, it was. The little vial of antidote was the difference between life and death. And not just for Alec right now. If it worked for him, it would change our world forever.

It has to work. I needed Alec back. He needed to be okay.

"Someone open his mouth," Star said.

Malcom reached Alec first and quickly aided Star in positioning Alec's head. I held my breath as Star tipped the liquid into Alec's mouth.

We all stood around him, watching for any signs of improvement. I had no idea how long it would take for the antidote to work or what to look for as positive signs.

Star walked away, but returned a moment later with a stethoscope in her ears and a pad of paper in her hands. Watching her listen to his heart and make notes was an odd sensation. I realized that Alec would kick himself when he woke for missing the first trial run of the antidote. The thought made me smile. If he woke, *when* he woke, he was going to want all the details.

Malcom and Kyle were pacing the room. Shelia tapped her fingers against her thigh. I had to remind myself to breathe as I kept my eyes locked on Alec. Everything felt like it was moving in slow motion. I just wanted him to wake up.

After what felt like the longest wait of my life, Star finished her assessment and removed the stethoscope from her ears. "His breathing is improving and his heart rate has returned to normal."

I knew it was probably still too early to know for sure if it worked but even this small amount of good news was enough to ease some of the knots in my stomach.

Star walked past me and I took her place at Alec's side. Sheila joined me. "This is going to work."

"I think so, too," I said as I gently removed one of the bandages. With all the dried blood and dirt, it was impossible to tell if it was healing. I looked back at Star. "Do you have any antiseptic or something we can clean these wounds with?"

She grabbed a bottle of rubbing alcohol and some washcloths and walked them over to me. "I'm not used to having to clean wounds on shifters. This'll sting, but it's the best I've got."

I accepted the items from her. "Thanks."

Sheila got to work removing all the makeshift bandages and I poured alcohol onto the cloth. Carefully, I started to clean each wound, checking for any signs that they were healing faster. It was difficult to tell if there was any change in them. It was either too small to notice, or he hadn't yet regained his shifter healing.

After I finished all the cuts and scrapes on his body, I moved to the claw mark on his cheek. I poured fresh alcohol on the towel and carefully dabbed it on the wound.

Alec's eyes snapped open. "Owww. What are you doing to me?"

I dropped the bottle and the cloth, the alcohol splashing out all over my bare feet. "You're awake!"

I threw my arms around his neck, pulling him in to a tight squeeze. Tears streamed down my cheeks and anger mixed with joy. I couldn't imagine what would have happened if I'd lost him. "Why did you do that to me? Why did you push me away? You could have died!"

He grunted and said something into my hair but I was

squeezing so tight, I couldn't hear him. Releasing him, I stepped back. "Please, don't ever do that to me again."

"No promises," he said. "I'll do whatever it takes to keep you safe."

"I'm not worth all that," I said. "What would I do without you?"

"You'd be fine," he said.

"No, I wouldn't," I admitted.

"I'm okay now," he said.

"It should have killed you. Good thing you're stubborn," I teased.

"Wait, where are we?" He looked around. "Star?"

The witch was walking toward him with a glass of water in hand. "Welcome back."

He tried to sit up, then fell back down.

"Don't go too fast," I said. "You just got the first dose of antidote."

Star lifted the glass of water as if making a toast. "Congratulations."

Alec's face lit up. "It works?"

Star nodded.

He laughed, then started coughing. Star offered him the glass and helped him drink.

"It works," he said. Then he turned to me. "I fought your mate. He lost. He was going to break the bond…"

"He lied," I said.

"He didn't hurt you or anything after I was under, did he?" Alec sounded frantic.

My heart raced, thrilled that he was awake, and overwhelmed with emotion at his concern for me. "No. But he got away."

"I'm going to kill him," Alec said as he tried to sit up again.

I pressed gently on his chest. "You need to rest before you try killing anyone."

"She's right." Sheila grabbed Alec's hand and gave it a squeeze. "Besides, you aren't the only one who wants revenge. This guy was already on my shit list for how he treated Lola. I'm not an eye-for-an-eye kind of girl, but I'll make an exception for this asshole."

"You'll have help," Malcom said.

"I'm in," Kyle said.

"Well, before anyone goes off on a man hunt for revenge, the patient needs to recover. He was poisoned. He should be dead. At the very least, let him rest a while," Star said.

"What about the spell?" Alec asked. "Did you break the claim yet?"

"We were a little busy keeping you alive," I said.

"Don't wait on it," he insisted. "It's bad enough that your mate is willing to kill you. We don't need trouble from the royal family, too."

"If you get some sleep, I'll do the spell," Star said. "Deal?"

Alec didn't look fully convinced, but he nodded.

"I'll stay with him," Sheila offered.

"Ready for some magic?" Star asked.

I took a deep breath. My whole life, I'd feared magic. Especially spells cast by witches. In a million years, I never thought I'd agree to have a spell cast on myself. I also never thought I'd have a murderous mate after me or that I'd get the mark of the alpha. "Sure, why not?"

Star grinned. "You don't sound entirely sold, but I'll try to pretend you're excited."

23

"WE HAVE to be outdoors for this spell to work," Star said.

I glanced down at Alec. "Will you be okay?"

"I'm fine. Try not to get attacked or anything while I'm healing," he said.

"As long as there's no surprises waiting for me out there, I should be just fine," I said.

"Ouch." He looked hurt. "One of these days, you'll forgive me."

I hadn't meant to hurt him, the comment came without thought, but I wasn't fully over it yet. Alec's brush with death showed me how important he was and how badly I wanted him in my life. But we weren't done healing the mistrust between us.

Malcom walked over to where I was standing near Alec. "I'll keep an eye on her."

"You might not want that job," I said. "Look what it did to Alec."

"I'll take my chances," he said with a grin.

"I'm far more worried about you than I am about me," I

told Alec.

"You want me to stay with him?" Kyle offered.

I was surprised he was willing to stay behind. His offer showed me how much he trusted Alec, despite his past actions. "Thank you, Kyle."

"Well, this little group is going to make me vomit from all the sweetness," Star said. "Who knew I'd ever meet such sentimental wolf shifters?"

"She's got a point." Malcom punched Alec's arm gently. "It's not like he actually died."

"Sorry to disappoint," Alec said.

"We're going to lose the sun," Star said. "Time for the spell."

I waved to Alec, then followed Star and Malcom back up the long, dark staircase into the upper level of the home. The over-the-top décor wasn't as shocking this time, but it was in stark contrast to our host.

When we got outside, I took a deep breath, and closed my eyes for a moment. The fresh, sweet air was welcome after all the excitement and tension of the last hour. I looked around, appreciating the warm glow of the late afternoon sun. It reflected off the waterfall, making it look like liquid gold.

"It is so beautiful here," I said.

"Thanks," Star said. "I got to give feedback for the landscape, but the house was all Winter's doing."

"Winter?" I asked.

"She's a high fae. Happened to get into a jam in our realm. I wanted a hidden bit of nature where I could pitch a tent. The house was a gift. While I don't recommend making a deal with a fae, I do recommend accepting their thank you gifts. It would have been rude to decline."

The home décor made more sense now. It wasn't indicative of Star's taste because she didn't pick it out. "That's a hell of a gift."

"I'm a very good witch," she said. "And on that note, are you ready for this spell?"

I nodded, my stomach twisting into knots. It didn't feel like I had much of a choice with this. Either I break this claim, or I risk being put to death for the mere crime of being born. Shifter royalty was so fucked up.

"It's safe, right?" Malcom asked.

"She'll be fine. But I have to warn you, I don't have enough blood for two. I was told there was one claim that needed broken." Star narrowed her eyes at Malcom. "Seems they left out the fact that there were two of you."

"I'm not here for the magic," he said.

"You're older, the first born," Star said. "If your father ever took the crown, you'd be next in line. Assuming you kept the claim."

My brow furrowed and I looked over at Malcom. His face contorted into a very confused expression. "What?"

"It could be lucrative for you to keep the claim," Star said.

"I don't want anything to do with him," Malcom spat.

I wasn't sure I believed that Malcom was protected from our father finding him, but I didn't think he was trying to maintain the claim on purpose.

"That's never going to happen, anyway," I assured him, setting my hand on his upper arm. "We're going to stay safe. Together."

"Cute," Star said. "One big, dysfunctional family."

"He's not family," I said quickly. "Our dad, that is. Malcom, is my family."

Malcom looked down at me with the most genuine smile I'd ever seen from him. He lifted his chin. "Thanks, sis."

Warmth spread in my chest. The only family I ever had was my mom and she let me down when I needed her the most. I'd felt that connection with the feral wolves, but Malcom was blood. I didn't realize how badly I'd wanted that kind of connection.

Star whistled. "Seriously. I don't know what's going on with feral shifters, but I've never seen this much goo."

"Goo?" I asked.

"Sentimentality," she said.

"Yeah, we're pretty awful," I agreed. "Maybe we should just do the spell and move on?"

"Please, and thank you," Star said. "There's a gazebo through here that will be perfect."

How about that, there was a white gazebo nestled in a circle of trees. The river that flowed from the waterfall ran around the back of it, making it possibly the most peaceful looking place I'd ever seen. "Do you still have fairies living here? Cause this place is magical."

Star glanced back at me and actually smiled. "It is nice, isn't it? My coven thought I'd die on my own. Imagine if they saw me now."

"I thought it was just wolf shifters who were awful to their young," I said.

"Oh no, there's terrible parents of every kind. Humans, shifters, witches, fae…" She walked up the steps to the gazebo, then stopped in the center. "Alpha girl up here, brother, down there."

"Lola," I said.

"I know," she said. "But I've never met a female alpha so I'm enjoying it."

"I'm not alpha yet," I said. "I just have the mark."

"Your future isn't as set as some I've seen, but you have a chance," she said.

"Well, that's reassuring," I deadpanned.

"It's a good thing when your future isn't set in stone. It means you have the freedom to make choices and those choices matter. If your ending is already written, it doesn't matter. You could go left or right, it won't change. There's power in an open ending," she said.

"How about me?" Malcom asked.

"You should never ask about your future," Star said. "If the information isn't freely given, you don't want to know."

"Well, that's fucking foreboding," he said. "It sounds an awful lot like you're telling me my future is going to suck."

"I'm saying you shouldn't ask. I didn't tell you why," she said.

I had to agree with Malcom, it didn't sound good. But I wasn't going to press the issue after her warning. A subject change seemed best. "So, what's next?"

Star lifted her arms dramatically and black ribbons shot from her fingertips. They widened and grew until they were like long swaths of fabric.

My jaw dropped open as I watched this happen too quickly to realize what was going on. By the time I processed that she was enclosing us in, it was too late.

Everything was dark.

I heard muffled screams outside the gazebo and I knew Malcom was calling for me. My pulse raced and my senses went into overdrive. The air felt still and the fresh scent of the forest was lacking. Instead, I swore I could smell something spicy, like cinnamon. Without the breeze, it felt too warm. I resisted the urge to panic, forcing myself to take slow, steady breaths.

I couldn't see anything in the pitch black of the gazebo. My eyes widened as if I could see better that way. Realizing what I was doing, I blinked a few times, then tried to let my vision adjust. It was still nothing.

"Star? What's going on?" I asked.

"For the spell to work, we need to control the senses," she said.

"You said we needed to be outside," I reminded her.

"I needed you away from distractions. This spell is just as much your energy as it is mine."

"I don't understand," I said.

"Blood magic is dark and dangerous. Too many ways it can go wrong. It's forbidden for a reason," she said.

"You are not making me feel better about this," I said.

"Do you want to break this claim or not?" she asked.

I turned, trying to figure out which direction her voice was coming from. It felt like it was all around me. "I don't think I have a choice."

"You have to want this, or it won't work," she said.

I thought back to what Alec told me about alphas connecting with the king. If I was serious about taking Wolf Creek, I had to go through with this. "I want this."

"Sit." It was a command.

It was more unnerving than I thought it would be to lower myself to the ground without seeing the floor. Star didn't use the typical vision to see things. She used her magic. "Can you see in here?"

"I see enough," she said.

I wanted to ask her more questions to learn more about her and her magic, but now didn't seem like the time. "I'm ready."

"Hands on your knees, mind clear," Star instructed.

I took a breath in and did as she asked. Thoughts of Alec and Tyler flooded my mind. Then, visions of Ace tumbled in. My mom showed up, taking a drag on her cigarette. I cursed under my breath, and tried harder to clear my mind. There was so much I couldn't get out of my head.

"You're not concentrating," Star said. "Push those thoughts away."

"I'm trying," I said through clenched teeth.

"Breathe in, hold it for five seconds, then breathe out," she suggested.

I felt ridiculous, but I tried the breathing pattern. After a few rounds, I actually did find it easier to concentrate.

"Don't panic when you feel me touch your hand. Keep your mind clear," she said.

I continued counting between breaths and when Star's cold hand touched mine, I only flinched rather than freaking out. It felt like she was drawing something on my hand with her fingertip. I tried to ignore it and went back to the breathing.

Star began to chant under her breath. It wasn't any language I was familiar with and it was very hard to keep my mind empty while she was speaking. My count was off, and I struggled to focus.

Suddenly, a flash of light exploded from the center of the gazebo, illuminating the entire structure. In that moment, a massive shadow lunged toward Star. I could see it's teeth and claws coming for her.

Screaming, I leaped from my spot on the floor and I shoved Star aside. The creature made an ear-splitting high-pitched sound. I fell to the ground, wincing in pain. The cry from the creature felt like it was inside my head. I covered my ears and I think I might have screamed but it was too loud to know for sure.

Almost as quickly as it appeared, the creature was gone. The black fabric fell away from the gazebo and Star and I were sitting on the ground. She looked at me with her eyes wide.

"I take it that wasn't supposed to happen," I said.

She shook her head.

"What happened?" Malcom rushed to us and knelt next to me. "Are you alright?" He turned to Star. "What did you do to her?"

"I did the spell but that was not shifter blood. What the fuck kind of game is Alec trying to play? He could have gotten us both killed!" Star stood and faced us, her hands on her hips. She was pissed.

"What are you talking about?" Malcom said. "Alec gave you his blood. You didn't do the spell right."

"No. That was vampire blood. I nearly pulled a vampire soul from it's undead body. I don't want that lurking around my home. You have to go." She glared at us. It was an unsettling sight. "You're a threat to my home. Do you have any idea what that could have done to me?"

"There has to be an explanation." I couldn't believe I was defending Alec, but it didn't make any sense.

"There better be," she said.

24

THE THREE OF us headed back to her basement where Alec, Sheila, and Kyle were gathered. Alec was sitting up now and he looked so much better than when we'd left.

His smiling face didn't last long, though. "What happened?"

"You gave me vampire blood, that's what happened," Star snapped.

"No, I got the blood from Spencer, himself. He handed it to me," Alec said.

"Did you watch him draw the blood from his vein?" Star asked.

Alec's shoulders sagged. "No."

"Fuck, Alec. Such an amateur mistake." Star ran a hand through her cropped hair. "That creature could have killed all of us if I'd completed the spell."

"He played me," Alec said.

"Sounds right," I said bitterly. "Now I know why him and my mom got along so well."

"So now the shunned prince knows about his alpha kid and he knows there's a witch willing to use blood magic against him?" Star sounded pissed. "Are you trying to get all of us killed?"

"For once, I'd like something to go right," I said.

Star tensed. "Who else was with your group?"

"What do you mean?" Alec asked. "Do you sense something?"

"We've got a visitor." Star turned her head toward the staircase.

"Tyler?" Even as I suggested it, I wasn't sure it was possible. I couldn't feel him at all and I'd had hardly any thoughts about him since he took off in the woods.

Malcom, Kyle, and Sheila moved in front of me, pushing me out of the way. I walked around them, lining up next to them. If it was Tyler, I was going to fight him, myself. I couldn't keep letting my friends fight my battles for me.

Footsteps sounded on the stairs. Whoever it was, they were making no effort to hide their entrance. I balled my hands into fists, grateful that they'd already healed from my blows against Tyler.

The figure who emerged from the stairway was not Tyler. I took a step back, physically recoiling from the monster of a man staring out at us.

He was probably seven feet tall and twice as wide as any male I'd ever seen. Between the dark hair, shaggy full beard, and wild expression in his eyes, he looked more animal than man. He made a low, rumbling growl that made even my friends take a step back.

I had no idea who the intruder was or why he was here,

but I wasn't going to let my friends get hurt anymore from my actions. I took a step forward. "Who are you and what do you want?"

I couldn't see his mouth under the tangled beard, but his eyes almost appeared to be smiling.

"Answer us." I kept my tone stronger than I expected.

Out of the corner of my eye, I noticed that Alec was getting up from the table. I glanced over at him. "Sit back down. We've got this."

He shook his head and shuffled over slowly. Each step looked like it caused him pain. "Lola, meet Spencer Lupton, your father."

I turned back to the newcomer, unable to hide my surprise. "What are you doing here?"

"You look just like your mother," he said.

"Never say that again." I now knew my mom had sacrificed everything to try to hide me from this man but I still didn't want to be compared to her. Especially not by him.

"I suppose I expected a warmer welcome," he said.

"You gave my friend vampire blood. You could have gotten us all killed." I took a few steps toward him. "Unless that was your plan. Well, newsflash, it failed. You didn't win."

"Calm down, I wasn't trying to kill you," he said. "I didn't think you actually had a witch who would do the spell."

"Then why did you give him any blood, at all?" I demanded.

"Because I used it as a tracer," he said.

"Fuck me," Alec said. "You tracked the vial."

"Are you here to kill me?" I asked.

"Why would I want to kill you?" I asked.

"Because of the king," I said.

"You think I give a shit about some punishment my brother threw down?" He scoffed. "I served my time. I don't think my kid needs to pay the price for my failure."

"So, why are you here?" Kyle asked as he took a step closer to me.

"I need a favor," he said.

"Why would I help you? Do you have any idea what my mom's life has been like all these years? The extreme steps she went to so I wouldn't be found by you? Not to mention my life? Did you even try to find her or help her?" I didn't even know what kind of a guy he was. For all knew, he treated my mom badly and that's why she fled.

"I didn't even know she was pregnant," he said.

"Would it have changed anything?" I asked.

"No," he admitted. "I'd still have done what I did."

"Then had she stayed with you, both she and I would likely be dead." For the first time, I felt nothing but respect for my mom and her choices.

"Well, I can make it up to you if you do something for me," he said.

I should have known it was too good to be true that he'd want to help me break the claim out of the kindness of his heart.

Sheila, Malcom, and Kyle moved in front of me, blocking me from his view.

"You should go," Alec said. "You're not wanted here."

"This is between me and my progeny," he said.

Malcom stepped forward. "Then you can speak to me and I'll discuss it with her."

I had a better view now of Spencer's reactions. His expression went from anger to confusion to realization in a second. I wasn't going to leave Malcom alone in this. I moved forward, pushing in-between Sheila and Kyle. "Neither of us need you. We'll figure it out without your help."

"There's two of you," Spencer said. "Imagine that. Well, I could use the extra help."

"We don't want your help," Malcom said. "We've managed fine without you."

"Listen, I just pissed off a whole shit ton of vampires to get here and the both kings have to be hot on my tail. You think they're not going to come after you once they realize you exist?" he said.

"How would they know?" I asked. "You didn't know about us."

"If my brother kills me, he'll be your next of kin. So unless you both have mating bonds, he'll connect with you eventually. When he does, he won't hesitate to kill you. You're a threat to him. Just like I was," he said.

"He didn't kill you," Malcom pointed out.

"He couldn't kill me without losing too many alliances. Keeping me alive made him look like he had a heart," Spencer said. "He doesn't have that problem with you."

"So break your claim on us," I said.

"Sure, as soon as you help me," he said.

I growled and glared at the scruffy, giant male in front of me. "I will not be bullied by anyone. I don't care if you are my blood."

"That's the fight I need." He smiled. "You're going to be just fine with this task."

"What's this favor?" Malcom asked.

"You help me overthrow the king. Then you won't even

need the claim broken. You'll be safer than you ever have been in your life," he said.

"No," I blurted out. "I am not going to help you kill someone."

"She'll help," Alec said.

"What?" I stared at him. "I am not committing regicide."

"If he's right and the king is that deranged, breaking the claim might not be enough. If word leaked about who you really were, the king could still kill you," Alec said. He turned to face Spencer. "It doesn't have to be murder, right? You can overthrow a king without that."

"Whatever makes you sleep better at night," he said.

"My mate is trying to kill me, my pack is hunting me down, and you think it's a good time for me to make enemies with the royal family?" I asked.

"You are part of the royal family, like it or not," Spencer said.

I shook my head. "No. You're not family. They are." I gestured to my friends. "We don't get to choose the family we're born into, but I am not going to deprive myself of choosing a better one."

"If she helps you, will you help her in return?" Sheila asked.

I turned to her. "Not you too."

"This could be exactly what we need for you to claim your pack," Sheila said.

"It wouldn't hurt to have help," Kyle added.

"Whose side are all of you on?" I hissed.

"What do you know about your family history?" Spencer asked.

"I learned most of it in the last few weeks," I admitted.

"You know what your grandfather was working on?" Spencer asked.

I nodded.

"You know who financed that?"

"I can guess," I said.

"After my brother got what he wanted in that toxin, he's the one who had the witch curse him. It was supposed to wipe his memory entirely, but his witch wasn't always accurate. Gorgeous, yes; good with spells, not so much," he said. "My brother wanted to make sure nobody else would get the recipe. Which meant that the mind who created it had to be silenced."

"So? He's the one who agreed to create something so awful," I said.

"Yeah, cause your mom was being held as collateral," he said. "She was locked in our family estate for three years while her dad worked in our lab downtown. That's how I met her."

"If you're trying to paint yourself as the good guy while you sat back and did nothing to release my mother from captivity, you're no better than him," I spat.

"You're right. It took me time to figure that out. Once I did, it unraveled everything my brother was doing. I freed your mom and your grandfather. The recipe wasn't erased from his mind, but his sanity was slipping," he said. "As soon as they were out, I tried to take my brother down. I failed."

If what he was saying was true, it made sense that my mom had cracked in Wolf Creek. Living there was a lot like living in captivity.

"Lola, I believe him," Malcom said.

I looked over at him, surprised to see he looked genuine. "You do?

Malcom nodded. "I think maybe you're supposed to help him."

"And just like that, your future is stronger," Star said.

"That's right, you can read the future." I looked at her, hopeful that she could give me some kind of guidance.

"You have choices," she reminded me. "Nothing is set in stone." She lifted her chin toward Malcom. "His was looking bleak, but it just changed. There's hope there now."

"Well, fuck," I said. "Does that mean if I don't help him something bad will happen to Malcom?"

Star shrugged.

I glanced over at Kyle. "What do you think?"

"The new shifter king would be a hell of an ally," he said.

I looked back at the mountain of man in front of me. He was disheveled and worn down. While his size was intimidating, everything else showed that he'd been neglected for a long while.

"You're asking a lot of me," I said. "You're asking that I trust you."

He took a few steps closer to Alec and extended his arm. "Take the blood." Spencer looked back to me. "Use it anytime. No strings attached. But give me a chance."

"If you're in, I'm in," Malcom said.

"I have a needle and a vial," Star offered.

"Do it," Alec said.

"Get enough for two," I said.

I waited until Star filled the vail with Spencer's blood. The room was deathly silent. Everyone's attention was fixed on me, waiting to hear what I'd say.

Star stuck a bright pink band-aid on Spencer's arm, then she nodded to me. She had what she needed. If we did the spell again, it would work, and both Malcom and I would be free of his claim.

"Alright." I said. "But as soon as you break my trust, I'm out."

I had a bad feeling about this, but it wasn't like things could get much worse, could they?

WOLF CHOSEN

MOON CURSED BOOK THREE

PREFACE

Tyler

Moving forward through the dark woods toward Wolf Creek took all my willpower. Every ounce of my being wanted me to turn back. I'd been walking all day, fighting against the pull of my mate.

It felt like I was being ripped in two. My soul was at war with my body, threatening to split from me and find its way to her.

The woman who was the cause of my madness and my pain was also my reason for breathing. I needed her like I needed oxygen.

I wasn't sure when it happened or how I'd let the bond take over so completely. It didn't matter though. It was too late to do anything else other than claim her as mine.

Once I completed the bond, once I felt our souls join, everything would be right with the world. The mark she wore meant nothing. She would bend to me as was her place.

Walking back into Wolf Creek, empty handed, was going

to drive my father into a rage. He never wanted this for me, but he didn't know what it was like. He never felt the pull of the mating bond. It was a connection deeper than blood, an instant loyalty. I'd fought it so hard at first. But the longer she was away from me, and the more I tried to keep her away, the more I needed her.

Lola was the only thing that mattered anymore. Fuck Wolf Creek. Fuck becoming an alpha. I'd burn it all to claim her as my mate.

The worst part of all of this was that there was another male moving in on my mate. And now I knew the body we found in the ruins of my father's house wasn't his. It also meant he'd had help. I wasn't in the place to deal with Kyle's betrayal now. Part of me figured he'd come running back once Lola returned. Then I could make an example out of him.

I couldn't worry about Kyle while I was trying to eliminate the threat on my mate. That feral shifter fucked with the wrong man. With any luck, the toxin I'd given to him did him in.

It was a gamble holding that needle to Lola, but I'd watched the two of them together long enough while tracking them to know he'd take the bait. With him out of the picture, Lola wouldn't have any choice but to give in to the bond.

I cut through the woods until I reached the barrier. A rush of cold shivered down my spine as I entered our territory. I wasn't in a hurry to return home, though. Not yet. As far as my father knew, I was out hunting my mate. He believed I was going to kill her. There was no reason to explain my true intentions. Once she was mine, he'd have no choice but to welcome her to the pack. And she'd have no choice but to yield to me.

A small cottage on the outskirts of town came into view. It was a half mile or so away from the barn where we held ceremonies, making it the farthest structure in Wolf Creek.

Over the years, my father had offered other housing options for our high priestess, but Jenny always turned them down. Something about being out in nature to connect with the elements. I wasn't sure I believed all that, but at this point, I needed advice and I wasn't getting it from my dad.

When I'd had Lola tossed in the caves, I thought our bond would break. It didn't. Instead, it roared to life, stronger and hungrier than before. Jenny had explained that the more you fought a bond, the more it consumed you. If it reached a critical point, even the death of a mate wouldn't quench your longing.

I was there. There was no cure for me. I either had Lola, or I craved her for the rest of my life. That wasn't an option. I would make her mine fully.

A warm glow behind the curtains let me know that Jenny was still awake despite the late hour. I didn't hesitate to knock on her door. She was my only hope for answers.

The door opened quickly, and Jenny greeted me with a knowing smile. "I wondered when you'd arrive."

"Spare me the all-knowing priestess speak," I said. "I need to hear it straight. Nobody knows I'm here and there's no need for show."

Jenny frowned. "You better get inside, then."

I crossed her threshold and was hit by the scent of pachouli and other herbs I couldn't place. Her home was small and cozy, but warm and welcoming. It was a single large room, with a kitchen along the back wall, complete with small table set for two. On my right was a living room with sofa, rocking chair, and coffee table. On the left a bed with a nightstand. I knew the single closed door led to her bathroom. It was far too small for my taste, but Jenny seemed to enjoy her life here.

"Sit," she instructed, gesturing toward the sofa.

I obliged and she took the rocking chair across from me. "You're distressed."

"Please, can you just be Jenny right now?" I'd known Jenny since before she was high priestess. She was friends with my mom and had been the wild streak to my mom's calm. I hated the voice and the show she put on in front of others.

Jenny sighed. "You know I take this job seriously, don't you?"

"I know," I said.

"You know I was chosen by the Moon Goddess, right?"

"I know. Why do you think I'm here?" I demanded.

"Because you can't get your mate to accept you," Jenny said.

I was silent for a moment. "You told me she was distracted by the other male."

"She was," Jenny said.

"You told me that if I got rid of him, she'd find her way to me," I said.

"She will. But he's not dead," Jenny said. "Can you do anything right?"

"I gave him enough toxin to kill a fucking giant. How is he not dead?" I didn't even ask how she knew. That was the thing with Jenny, sometimes she knew shit.

"You don't have to retain this bond," Jenny said. "Lola wants it broken. She'd agree."

"I know. She tried to break it when I found her," I admitted.

"But you won't," Jenny said.

"She must bow to me. I have to break her," I said with a growl.

"Why?" Jenny asked.

"You know why," I said.

"Because of her mark?" Jenny asked.

If word got out that she had the mark of the alpha, and she turned me down, I would lose my pack. I still caught the occasional comment about my dad's lack of mark. The people in this town were so superstitious. They wanted an alpha with the mark. With her as my mate, that mark was just as good on me as it was on her.

That was the one thing my father didn't think about. Our pack wanted an alpha with a mark, but women weren't supposed to get them. The alpha had to be a man. If the mark was on my mate, it might as well be mine. A mated pair were seen as two halves of the same soul. Her mark, was my mark.

"The goddess made a mistake. It was supposed to be on me," I said.

"The goddess doesn't make mistakes," Jenny said.

"Then why put us together in the first place?" I demanded. "She was nothing. A wolf who couldn't shift with a mother who is a disgrace. Why was I paired with her?" Even as I said the words, my stomach tightened with guilt. I was to defend Lola, not say these things about her.

I had given up on trying to hate her, but I wasn't sold on why we were together in the first place. Any other woman would have been more suitable. "Why her?"

"The moon goddess doesn't make mistakes," Jenny repeated.

"You're not helping," I said.

"Look, you want her?" Jenny asked. "Like, for real, willing to do the work, want her?"

"Why else would I be here?" I asked.

"The longer she fights the bond, the stronger it gets. You've already accepted it. She won't have much choice but to do the same soon."

"So, I wait?" I narrowed my eyes. "Tell me something better than to have patience."

"You go to her," Jenny said.

"I tried that," I said.

"You need to be around her, give her a chance to feel your wolf close to hers," Jenny said.

"You want me to shift around her?" I'd done that already and it hadn't made any difference.

"You get her to shift with you. If your wolves run together in harmony, she'll be yours for life. You convince her wolf, she won't have a choice," Jenny said.

Jenny stood and crossed the room. She removed a small box from a cabinet, then resumed her place on the rocking chair.

"What is that?" I asked.

She opened the box and removed a small leather pouch. "This is an herbal mix that witches used to use in the before times. It will force a shift."

I reached out my hand and Jenny set the pouch in my palm. "Am I supposed to throw it at her?"

"Sure. Better yet, add it to food or drink. If you can't get her to shift on her own, this'll do the trick," she said.

I shoved the little pouch in my pocket.

Jenny closed her eyes and held her hands in front of my face. I flinched, then held my breath while she did whatever weird priestess stuff she was doing.

After several long seconds, she lowered her hands and opened her eyes. "If you trust your wolf, he'll lead you right to her. You two are more connected than most of the mated pairs I've met. It shouldn't take you much convincing to get her to complete the bond."

I nodded, then stood. This was my chance. My father was distracted with rebuilding the house and agreed to let me take matters into my own hands. I'd have a few weeks of solitude before he'd care that I wasn't back home.

"Good luck," Jenny said. "May the spirit of the moon be with you."

And just like that, Jenny was back to the priestess talk again. I smiled. "Yeah, thanks."

1

MIST SPRAYED on my face and I closed my eyes, pretending the cool water was helping wash away my anxiety. The roar of the waterfall eased my racing mind, giving me a few blissful moments of peace before the weight of the world came crashing in around me.

My eyes snapped open as I wiped the water from my face. I took a step back, then crossed my arms over my chest. The sun was low in the horizon and my clothes were soaked from standing so close to the waterfall. I was freezing, but that was a small price to pay for a moment of peace.

Star had agreed to let us stay the night at her place, but I had to admit, the thought of fleeing had crossed my mind. It wasn't that I wanted to run from my problems, it was that I was tired of getting swept up in everyone else's. Since when was it my job to help my absentee father with a coup?

I shifted my weight and my feet slipped on the mossy ground, nearly causing me to fall. Finding my balance, I backed away from the edge of the water. At least my sense of self perseveration was strong enough to provide a will to live. That was always good. I recalled when I'd constantly considered ways to end my life in Wolf Creek. At least things weren't that dire. I might be on a suicide mission by making a run against the shifter king, but at least I didn't *want* to die.

Pushing aside the dark thoughts, I turned and walked back toward Star's house. It was easy to sneak out for a few minutes while Star attended to Alec's injuries. I wanted to be with him, to make sure he was healed, but I knew I'd be in the way. Plus, ducking out for a few minutes let me avoid having to speak to my father. I wasn't ready to get to know him any more than I had to.

There was too much to process and too much at risk to move forward without a few moments of reflection.

Not that it helped in any way.

I was still confused. And pissed.

Why had I agreed to help Spencer? I shook my head as I walked. My friends seemed to think that if I helped him, it would benefit my upcoming claim on Wolf Creek. All I could think about was how it delayed the breaking of the mating bond. Again.

In the few hours since Spencer had turned up, my mind had been preoccupied with more than just the prospect of overthrowing the shifter king. I'd found myself constantly worrying about Tyler.

My stomach twisted uncomfortably as my mate made his way into my consciousness again. My emotions were all over the place. One minute, I was worried about him making it back to Wolf Creek safely, the next I was hoping he died before he arrived. It was enough to drive anyone to madness. How much longer was I going to have to face the bond between us? Each time I thought we were moving closer to breaking it, something else prevented the task.

Then there was Alec. For now, I was letting myself take comfort in the fact that he was recovering and that he was safe. Everything else between us would have to wait. Between my father showing up and the mate I couldn't get out of my head, there wasn't room for anything else. Even if I was starting to think my feelings for Alec were far more complex than I originally thought.

I caught sight of Malcom walking toward me. He waved and I returned the gesture. He picked up his pace and met me in the middle of the tall grass, a short walk from Star's home.

"Hey, can we talk?"

We hadn't had a chance to talk since everything went down. At least not just the two of us. As a group, we'd decided we'd get some rest and figure out our next moves in the morning. "Sure, what's up?"

"It's been a long time since I had family," he said.

"I know."

"I need you to know that blood isn't always thicker than water." His expression was dark.

"I think we both know that," I said. "But that's not comforting considering we just found out we're siblings."

"I'm talking about Spencer. He might have contributed to us being alive, but he's not one of us," he said.

Warmth spread through me. *One of us.* He was talking about him and me, as if we were a family. I'd said as much about my friends when I met Spencer, but it was different hearing the sentiment returned.

"He hasn't earned the right," Malcom added.

"Thanks," I said.

Malcom's forehead creased in confusion. "For what?"

"It's nice to have people on my side instead of taking the side with power," I said.

"I've been running my whole life. Even when I settled in at the feral camp, I never thought I'd stay. I kept my few belongings packed at all times," he said. "But you're changing things. Not just for yourself, but for those around you. You'll make a great alpha."

"You have to say nice things to me since you're my brother," I teased. I was trying to be playful, but it was to cover how inadequate I felt. I still couldn't fight well enough, and I wasn't convinced I was the best wolf for the job. I knew I'd be better than Ace, but that wasn't difficult. Most anyone would be better than him.

"You know that's not the reason I believe in you. You're stronger than you think. You stood up to Spencer and your mate. You could have buckled to either of them, simply accepted them blindly. Belonging is a strong motivator. Instead, you stayed true to yourself. You turned them down because you know your own worth. That's fucking brave. And it's exactly what is necessary in a good alpha. You're going to listen to people, and you won't let money or power do the talking," he said.

I considered the way things worked in Wolf Creek. If you made the alpha happy, it meant good things for your family. Hearing Kyle's story solidified it. A child's life was in danger and all Ace cared about was if he could barter something for himself in the transaction.

"You're right," I said. "I don't worry about those things. But I do worry that I'm taking too great a risk by putting everything else off to help Spencer."

"You're not ready," he said. "I mean no disrespect, but you could use the time to learn how to be more wolfy."

I quirked a brow. "Wolfy?"

He grinned. "You heard me. You aren't ready to tackle the challenges in Wolf Creek."

"Yet I'm ready to help a royal take down another?" It didn't seem like it was any less risky than standing up to my former pack. I wasn't sure I was ready for either thing.

"You'll have our help with that endeavor. When you fight an alpha, you must do it alone," he reminded me.

My stomach twisted into knots. "Don't remind me."

The sun had set and it was getting colder by the minute. I shivered, then glanced over at the warm glow coming from the windows at Star's house. "We should go in, it's getting late."

The two of us walked toward the house together, my feet sinking into the soft, mossy earth with each step. If I was going to take on the shifter king, I was going to need a decent pair of shoes. And some clothes. I wondered if Star had anything in my size.

We were greeted by Kyle, Sheila, and Alec when we stepped through the front door. The good news was Alec's color was back to normal and most of his visible injuries were improved. He was healing. I wanted nothing more than to run to him, to make sure he was safe. But his grim expression kept me from acting on my desires. Something was going on.

"What's wrong?" I asked.

"We have a huge problem," Sheila said.

"What's that?" I asked.

"Your father left a little detail out when he got you two to agree to help," Sheila said.

"More like a big fucking detail," Alec said with a growl.

"What detail?" I asked.

"The royal family uses blood magic to protect all their holdings," Sheila said.

"What does that mean?" I asked.

"Similar to what we had at Wolf Creek," Kyle said. "Everything is locked down unless you've got royal blood."

"But how do people who work there get in and out?" I asked.

"More blood magic." Sheila shuddered.

"Pendants containing a drop of royal blood," Spencer said as he walked into the room.

I looked past my friends to see a very different looking Spencer. He'd cleaned up. He was in fresh clothes and his face was clean shaven. His dark hair, which had been matted and unkempt was now a gorgeous pile of glossy curls. I could see why my mom had been attracted to him.

I looked over at Malcom. He had a lot of the same features. Both males had strong jaws, hazel eyes, and dark hair. I never put much thought into Malcom's appearance before, but now that I was looking at him, I realized there was a wave to his short hair. If he grew it out, it would probably curl the same as his father's.

"I told you, the blood magic won't be a problem," Spencer said. "Lola and Malcom are my offspring. They'll be fine."

I turned back to him, then looked over at Alec and Sheila. They both looked furious. "Explain it to me. What makes this any different than Wolf Creek? Sure, it's creepy as fuck, but can't we just give you all some of our blood?"

"It doesn't work that way," Alec said. "You need magic to create a blood pendant and then it ties the person to the location. They could summon us all there, control us, make us do anything as long as we have that blood."

My jaw tensed. That wasn't what I was expecting. I was starting to understand why blood magic wasn't allowed. Taking away free will should never happen. "Can't you just go in and then remove the pendant?"

"It doesn't work that way," Sheila said. "It's a permanent thing. It gets bonded into us. If we pull it off while inside the spelled area, there's likely a curse or punishment waiting for us."

"Death," Spencer said, matter-of-factly. "If anyone with the blood pendant removes it on site, they'll die."

I marched over to Spencer, my eyes narrowed. Heat rushed through me, and I felt like I had electric current in my veins. "When were you going to share this with us? How dare you put my friends' lives at risk. After everything you've already done."

"First of all, I didn't even know you were alive, so spare me the deadbeat dad guilt," Spencer said with a growl.

His tone was menacing, and I tensed but held my ground.

"Second, I never asked your friends for help. I asked you. And your brother was a happy addition," he said.

"That's why you needed us," Malcom said. "You can't do this without blood relatives to help. You weren't counting on the others joining."

"Maybe there's hope for you, after all," Spencer said. "Get your sister in order."

I growled. A low, loud rumbling that felt like it came from my toes. "Nobody gets me in order. We are the ones helping you and we can back out of that at any time."

Spencer lifted a brow. "Did you growl at your future king?"

"Did you talk down to a future alpha?" I snapped. "Because you're not king yet."

Spencer smirked. "You've got a mark. That's why you want to take on your old pack. I've seen wolves fail before. The mark doesn't mean shit."

"And neither does blood," I replied.

Spencer's smile faded. "I failed last time because the friends I had to help me were forced to turn against me. I won't make that mistake again."

"So, you need us," Malcom said.

"I need you," he agreed.

"Then you'll watch your tone," I said.

"Fair enough," he said.

"You can't seriously be considering going?" Sheila said.

"When I agreed to this, I thought you'd have us to help you," Alec said.

"Luckily, you don't get to agree to things on my behalf," I said.

"That's not what I meant," he said. "I know I pushed you to agree. I never would have if I'd known."

"You all keep telling me I need help to take back Wolf Creek. The shifter king isn't too bad as a supporter, right?" I knew Malcom was right and I could feel it in my bones. I wasn't ready to take on Ace. I wasn't sure I was ready for this either, but I had to learn somehow. "If you want to help me, you'll teach me what I need to know to pull this off."

Kyle was standing next to me, but now he took a step closer to Spencer, until he was inches from him. Kyle was a large male, but he wasn't as broad or tall as Spencer. Next to him, I was reminded of just how young and inexperienced we were. Spencer had a few decades on us. He was stronger and faster, even after nineteen years of being imprisoned.

"You will do whatever it takes to ensure she comes back from this alive," Kyle said. "And you will be her second when she challenges for alpha."

"Are you threatening me?" Spencer looked amused.

"I am."

I forgot about the fact that I'd need a second when I challenged Ace. Once I officially challenged him, the challenge had to go on. If I fled before the fight, my second would be accountable. It was a stupid tradition because who would challenge then run? "Kyle, I'm fine. I don't want him as my second, anyway."

The two males didn't seem to notice me. They were too busy staring each other down.

"Seriously, guys?" I took a step closer, intending to get in between them.

Kyle put his arm out to block me. "I need to hear it from him."

Spencer glanced at me. "This is who you spend your time with, daughter?"

"Don't call me that," I said. "You haven't earned it. And yes, Kyle is inner circle."

Spencer scoffed.

"I'll be her second," Malcom said. "We don't need him."

I didn't want Spencer as my second, but I never expected Malcom to step up like that. I wasn't even sure Ace would care if I had a second. He was so bloodthirsty for my demise, he'd likely jump at the chance to finish me without the archaic protocol in place.

"Shit, I'd do it too," Sheila said. "Any of us would, isn't that right, Alec?"

Alec was silent and I knew the reason why he wasn't chiming in. With his mark, he couldn't be a second.

"I know any of you would," I said. "But I doubt Ace is even going to care."

"Well, y'all are being squishy again, aren't you?" Star said.

I hadn't noticed the witch's entrance. "That's what we do, I guess."

"Worst shifters ever," she said.

"Tell me about it," Spencer said.

"For real, though," Malcom said. "Tell us you plan on keeping us alive. That you're not going to sacrifice us for your throne."

"Having you two is beneficial for my rule, why would I want you dead?" Spencer asked. "My brother never had children. His line will end with him. It's got the alphas all riled up. When he dies, it will mean war. Many would rather see an heir to prevent chaos. I think it's the only reason his council was able to talk him into keeping me alive rather than executing me. Technically, they could bring me in to prevent a war."

"I'm breaking the claim when this over," I announced.

"You won't have to," Spencer said.

"I barely even want to be an alpha. You think I want to be queen?" I shook my head.

"Good thing he's the first born," Spencer said, pointing to Malcom.

All the color drained from Malcom's face. I had a feeling he wasn't thrilled with the idea of being in line for the throne, either.

"How about that?" Sheila said. "All these years we've been friends with a prince."

"I've gotta get my throne first," Spencer said.

"If this is going to be the headquarters for the rebellion, my prices are going up," Star said.

"I'll need a resident witch," Spencer offered.

"Is that an official job offer?"

"You'll have protection, power, money…" Spencer let the words hang in the air.

Star pursed her lips and narrowed her eyes. She looked like she was weighing his words carefully. After a long pause, she nodded slowly. "Alright. Fuck it. I'm in. It's probably time to stop hiding from my past."

"Are we all really moving forward with this?" I asked. "After everything?"

"I have no reason to want you dead," Spencer said. "I just need a little help to pull this off."

"If it comes between us or you, we're selling you out," Malcom said.

"I'm fine with that," he said. "You don't know me yet. When you learn a little more about what my brother's been up to all these years, you'll be changing your tune. You know what he did to your mother."

"I know it took you years to stop it and you somehow want a fucking medal for helping her when it was already too late," I said. "What if you hadn't fallen for her? Then what? You let her rot there forever? You're not any better than any of the assholes I grew up with in Wolf Creek."

"I learned my lesson. It just took me a while," Spencer said. "That's why you're going to help me. To prevent others from the same fate as your mother. Or you."

"I'm helping you because I need to buy myself some time," I said.

"If you say so," he said.

"It's getting late," Star said. "We can talk more in the morning."

Spencer grumbled something under his breath, but I didn't pay enough attention to hear what he said. I wasn't in the mood to deal with any more of this. Helping him was a step toward the next part of getting my life back.

I glanced toward Alec, hoping to catch his attention. I wanted a word with him before we turned in for the night. He was chatting with Malcom and the two looked deep in conversation. At least I knew he was recovering from his injuries. Our conversation would have to wait until morning.

"This way," Star called with a lift of her chin.

Reluctantly, I turned away from the others and followed her.

2

I FOLLOWED Star down the long hall, past several doors until we reached a room at the end.

"It's all yours," Star said. "I call it the yellow room."

"Well, that's dubious," I said as I pushed open the door. Everything in the room was an overwhelming shade of yellow. My lips parted. "You weren't joking. I don't think I've ever seen so much yellow in one place before."

The wallpaper was yellow and white striped, the bed was covered in a pale-yellow quilt, and the lampshades were an almost neon lemon color. I stepped into the room, noting the huge yellow and orange rug that covered most of the wood floor. "Your choices or did it come with the house?"

"It came this way. I didn't ask." She walked toward a closet and slid open a mirrored door. "It also came with this."

Inside the closet were men's suits, dress shirts, and ties hung in neat rows. My brow furrowed. "It just showed up in the closet?"

"Maybe Winter thought I'd have a friend over some day. I've learned not to question the fae too deeply," Star said. "The other rooms are the same, but some have womens' clothes. You can investigate more tomorrow if you want. I'm sure your friends will let you explore. I forget which room had which stuff in it. Should have checked before I set everyone up."

"It's totally fine." I honestly didn't care what kind of clothes I had as long as they were clean. It was nice to know I could put something else on, even if it did look like it would be several sizes too big.

"Shower's in the bathroom in the hall. Towels are in the linen closet. Help yourself," she said.

"Thank you for all this," I said. "I know you didn't really want to do this. I hope Alec paid you well."

"He told me how he got the money. I didn't ask him to do that to you," she said.

"I know," I replied.

"But I did ask for the funds. I've been trying to buy my way out of here. I guess it worked out in a way. If your dad actually pulls this shit off, I'll get what I wanted," she said.

I tried not to think about the fact that Alec's turning me over to Ace was all for nothing. We didn't complete the spell, and now Star didn't even need the extra money. I could have avoided that whole week of torture. It was too much. I pushed the thoughts aside.

"Well, it sounds like everyone is going to get what they want." I let out a long breath, leaving all the shit I had to go through unsaid. It was a lot and so much could go wrong along the way.

"You and I both know it's far more complicated than that. We also both know that any time someone gets what they want, it means others get hurt. Take that mating bond of yours for example. You want out. You break the bond with your mate, he lives with the humiliation," Star said. "You get what you want, he pays the price."

"He deserves worse," I said. "That's a terrible example. I want the assholes to get what's coming to them."

"If you do this, many of them will," she said.

My brow furrowed. I recalled that Star could see the future, but she'd withheld the details of her abilities. "You know something, don't you?"

She shook her head. "There's too much in my mind right now. Your future keeps changing. You're connected to more than you realize. The actions of everyone in this house, of everyone in your old pack, and the choices you make will dictate which path comes to fruition."

"But you see something about Tyler." I hated that concern was welling up inside me again. I wanted to be free of him, but the words escaped my lips before I could stop myself.

"I did," she confirmed.

"And?" I was already committed to this. She already heard the worry in my voice.

She stared at me in silence, her expression unreadable. Then I noticed the tiniest flicker of sympathy. It faded quickly. "I can't say. It will complicate things for you."

I bit down on the inside of my cheek to keep myself from begging for answers. It felt like my wolf was clawing at my insides, urging me to press the issue. I shouldn't care. I didn't want to care. But things were complicated with him. I refused to be with him, but I couldn't make all the feelings go away. Would they fade or break once the bond was gone?

"You should rest," Star said. "I'll see you in the morning."

I nodded and maintained my composure until she left. As

soon as the door closed, I fell to the ground, sucking in air as I fought against the overwhelming emotions inside. It was difficult to even determine what was real anymore. I found myself confused and torn about my next steps. Who was I supposed to trust? How was any of this going to get me to where I needed to be?

Taking down a king was bad enough, but it didn't eliminate my previous problem. Tyler was creeping into my mind more often lately. I didn't want to admit it, but the bond was growing more intense. I'd even had a few moments of wondering if there was anything to salvage between us. It wasn't something I'd admit to anyone. It took all my courage to even admit it to myself.

Tyler was a fixture in my thoughts since seeing him again in the woods. Alec had nearly died saving me, but I didn't feel the concern I should. Every time I wondered about Alec, Tyler was there. He wouldn't leave my mind or my heart even though I never asked him to be there.

I pushed him away, trying to clear my mind of all thoughts related to him. My wolf was fighting me, I could feel her conflict. We'd worked this out, hadn't we? *Tyler is no good for us. He's violent and hateful.*

Visions of Tyler injured and vulnerable came to mind. He looked like he was in pain and my heart ached for him. What was wrong with me? He deserved all the bad things that were coming to him.

He tried to kill me. Again. But he was my mate, chosen by the fates.

No. Tyler was never happening.

I thought about Alec, unconscious after taking the dose of toxin meant for me. My wolf seemed to ease a little, as if the memory of how awful Tyler really was, came back. This was where I needed to be. As complicated as things were with Alec, there was something there. And I'd give anything to have him be the only romantic possibility in my consciousness. I wasn't even sure if things with him could be fixed, but despite his poor judgment, he had mostly redeemed himself. He didn't want me dead. And he didn't want to control me.

Tyler is your true mate.

The thought was like an explosion in my mind, removing all other thoughts. I pressed my palms against my eyelids, as I screamed internally. Tyler, and everything about him had to leave me. I couldn't keep doing this. It was getting worse and I was terrified I was going to do something stupid because of the bond.

Panting, head pounding, I leaned my forehead against the floor. I wanted to be free of the bond to Tyler more than anything. I had to break the bond. There was no way I was going to be able to concentrate or focus on what needed done with the bond still in place.

I sat up, eyes wide, terrified at the thoughts in my own head. It was true, though. How was I supposed to move forward when each day made the bond stronger and more difficult to resist?

Tyler wasn't going to break it voluntarily. But maybe there was another way. There had to be another way.

Forcing my breathing back to normal, I collected myself enough to stand. If magic could break a bond between a father and daughter, surely there was something it could do for a mating bond.

I knew not to trust Star. She worked for money, not alliances, but she was letting us stay here. It was possible she'd turn my request down; she might even tell my father since she was going to work for him. None of that mattered if there was the smallest possibility of freedom. At this point, I was willing to do just about anything in exchange for the elimination of my ties to Tyler.

Quietly, I turned the handle and tiptoed down the hall. Earlier, I wanted time to talk to my friends. Right now, I didn't want anyone to talk me out of what I was about to ask. I knew enough about magic to know everything came with a price. I never asked the price of the blood magic to break the claim with Spencer. It seemed important enough to take my chances. This was even greater.

Whatever the price, I had to end this bond.

3

STAR'S HOME was even larger than I realized. I tried the living spaces and peeked into open doors leading to more bedrooms. I found the kitchen and another dining space I hadn't seen at first. Near the back of the house, there was a greenhouse, full of flowers and herbs. The place was stunning and spacious. It was hard to imagine anyone willing to walk away from living here. But along with the home came isolation and solitude.

My feelings about Star were mixed. She was willing to perform dark magic for a price. I'd been warned about witches and their abilities my whole life, but Star was the first I'd met. She'd been kicked out of her coven, much the same way that I'd been ostracized from my pack. We had a lot in common. Both of us were willing to walk the line between right and wrong to get what we wanted.

The house was empty and quiet. I wondered if everyone else was already asleep. I wandered a few more minutes, about to give up, when I spotted the stairs that led to the dungeon like basement.

A shiver ran down my spine as I peered down the ominous steps. I didn't like the thought of going down there, but if Star was there, it could provide more privacy than other parts of the house. I didn't want an audience for what I was going to ask.

You don't cross a witch. Everyone knew that. Though, the example I'd grown up with had been my own grandfather. While the true history was different, and his curse might not have been the result of his direct actions, it was still a warning. Witches could do things with magic that shifters had no power over.

I balled my hands into fists and took a deep breath, steeling myself for the descent. My fear of witches and their magic was less than my fear of being bonded to Tyler for eternity.

The bond was getting stronger, and I needed to stop the connection. I had reached the point of desperation. Anything to break the bond would be worth the risks.

The only light in the basement came from the orange lamps softly buzzing over the rows of herbs. I wondered what made these plants so special that they were grown down here when there was a greenhouse attached to the house upstairs. I wasn't sure I wanted to know.

"Star? Are you down here?" I took a few cautious steps and scanned the space for any signs of another person.

Movement caught my eye and I turned to see Star hunched in front of a table. She pushed a pair of goggles on top of her head and spun around on her stool to face me. "I thought you were going to bed."

"I wanted to ask you a question," I said.

She pulled the goggles off her head and set them on the

table before meeting my gaze. Her expression was impatient. "Yes?"

"I want to know how to break the bond," I said.

"You and your mate have to do it together," she said.

I shook my head. "No. Not the conventional way. He's proven he won't cooperate. There has to be another option."

"Besides his death?" She lifted a brow. "I'm pretty sure if you asked for his head on a platter, you'd have volunteers to take up the task."

"I won't risk my friends' lives," I said. "How would you break it?"

She smirked. "You're asking for magic."

Her words hung in the air between us, my lack of response speaking volumes.

"Mating bonds are handed out by fate," she said. "They can't be broken with normal magic."

"You're not a normal witch," I countered.

"You should go back to your room," Star suggested. "You don't want to follow this rabbit hole."

"I do," I insisted. "I can feel the bond getting stronger. I can still resist for now, but how much longer will I be able to? What happens if he gets me alone and I can't fight it? Will I give in? And then what happens if we do complete the bond? Will I be trapped with him forever? Unable to live my own life?"

My breathing quickened and my chest tightened. The thought of losing my freedom, of having to give up everything I'd worked so hard for, was excruciating.

"Deep breaths," Star said. "I see why this means so much to you."

"I can't go back there and live my life with him. You don't

know what he did to me. You don't know how awful it is to desire him after everything. It's wrong. The moon goddess made a mistake," I said.

"Is this about Alec?" Star asked. "I see the way you look at him."

I swallowed hard. Alec and I were something, weren't we? Maybe friends, maybe something more. I had no idea, and I certainly couldn't wrap my head around it until I was free of my bond to Tyler. "No, this is for me."

Star hummed. "If you go down this path, I can't guarantee what the results will be. I don't think it's worth it."

"Can you break the bond?" I asked.

"Maybe," Star said. "I've never tried. And in all honesty, I think the best I could do would be to break it on one end. He'd still come for you."

"I'll take what I can get. My feelings for him are dangerous. They're going to get me or one of my friends killed," I said.

"You can't afford the spell," she said.

"Name your price." I could have brought up that she never completed the other spell Alec paid her for, but I didn't care. I had to stop feeling this way about Tyler.

"It's not about a tangible price," she said. "It's the price the magic will take. I won't be responsible for what it might cost you."

"I'll take my chances," I said.

"I won't be blamed if this turns out badly," she said.

"It's on me," I said.

"Alright, fine. I'll give it a try." She didn't sound confident. "Take my hands."

I stepped closer and stretched out my hands to hers. Her touch felt like ice, and I nearly pulled away on reflex.

"You sure about this?" She locked her eyes on mine.

I nodded. "Just do it."

After a deep breath, she closed her eyes. I followed, figuring it was a better idea not to watch. My hands began to tingle as what I could only guess was magic moving through me. I felt it travel up my arms and down my spine.

Star mumbled something and I opened one eye to peek at her. Her lips moved slowly, and her forehead was wrinkled in deep concentration.

I squeezed my eyes closed and forced myself to remain calm. It was possible I was making a terrible mistake, but desperation makes us do dangerous things. I was less afraid of Star and her magic than I was of completing the bond with Tyler.

The tingling intensified until it was bordering on painful. I winced, fighting the urge to pull my hands away. Then suddenly, the sensation was gone. I opened my eyes. "Is it over?"

Star looked at me and lowered her hands. "That's the best I can do. I don't think it's permanent. The bond is stronger than I anticipated, but it should give you a break for a few days."

"A few days?" Was that long enough to get through this insane plot with Spencer?

"A *thank you* would be enough," she said.

"You're right. Thank you," I replied.

"You should get some sleep. I heard the others talking and they've got big plans for you in the morning."

"What do you mean?" I asked.

"You wanted to learn how to be a wolf, right? It sounds like they intend to teach you. Fast. Trial by fire sort of shit."

"Wonderful." It was probably what I needed. Especially now with the possible break from the bond for a short time. "How will I know if your spell was successful?"

"Well, I guess you think about your mate and see if you want to kill him or fuck him," she said with a shrug.

I frowned. I tried so hard to avoid thinking about Tyler. The idea of fixating on him wasn't something I was fond of, but it made sense.

She grabbed her goggles and slid them back over her eyes. "Sleep well." Star turned back to her work, clearly done with me.

"Night," I called to her as I headed to the steps. On my walk up, I let my mind wander to Tyler. I thought of the time he'd tossed a black widow spider on me during gym class when we were fourteen. The times he slammed me into lockers, or tripped me in the hall, and cruel comments swirled in my mind. Finally, I thought of the look of complete contempt he'd given me before letting his friends trap me in the cave to die.

By the time I reached the yellow room, I was seething. There was not a single redeeming quality about my mate. Tyler deserved all the bad things that were coming his way. And I was going to bring them to him.

I smiled as I realized that whatever Star had done, it worked. If her spell bought me even a few days of freedom from thinking kindly about my tormenter, I would take it. At this moment, I didn't care if there was a price to pay. I was going to enjoy feeling like I had some control over my emotions for however long it lasted. With any luck, the bond would be broken before this passed. Tyler had to go. One way or another, that bond had to be eliminated permanently.

4

I DIDN'T DREAM. Even after a shower and allowing my thoughts to wander, I didn't once think of Tyler in a positive way. No concern for him. No desire.

For the first time in a while, I felt like myself. It was as if I was waking from a nightmare.

I walked into the kitchen where Sheila and the others were already eating breakfast. It was a bright and welcoming room with windows along one side and a table large enough for eight nestled near the windows. On the counter, several platters were set out, filled with pastries, fruit, scrambled eggs, and sausages. A pot of brewed coffee completed the spread. I wondered how Star got groceries in and who cooked everything.

I took in the sight of my friends seated around the table. Kyle and Malcom were speaking quietly, while Sheila stared into space. Alec was the first to notice me. "Good morning."

"Morning," I said.

"Nice dress," Sheila called.

"This old thing?" I did a spin to show off the men's shirt I was wearing. A tie acted as a belt and the sleeves were rolled up to prevent them from covering my hands. The shirt would have fit most of the male shifters I knew. Which meant it was huge. It did work nicely as a dress, though.

"There's some women's clothes in my room," Sheila offered. "Though, they're all tiny. They fit me, but you might be better off in what you're wearing."

"What a strange thing to be added to the house," I said as I helped myself to a cup of coffee.

"There's a bunch of random stuff in my room if you want to check it out later," Malcom offered.

"How did you sleep?" Kyle asked.

"Great." I made a plate of food and sat down next to Sheila. "Where's Star?"

"No idea. And don't ask me where the food came from. I think the house is enchanted," Sheila said.

"That would explain a lot." Sometimes it was better not to ask too many questions. Besides, I'd already let Star do a spell on me. I was basically jumping all in with the magic thing. What was some enchanted breakfast after everything else?

"What about Spencer?" I took a sip of coffee.

"No idea," Malcom said. "But he knows we need a couple days to work with you before we go running off to challenge his brother."

I recalled Star's warning last night and suddenly, the coffee didn't taste as good as it had. "I take it you have a plan for getting me up to speed?"

"Ideas more than plans," Sheila said in what was probably supposed to be a reassuring tone. She started talking about shifting and using my senses, explaining a system of points, but my focus drifted to Alec.

He looked a lot better than he had yesterday, but he was deliberately staring at his food rather than looking at me. I wanted to ask him how he was feeling, and I wanted to talk about the cave and Tyler and the big, complicated mess between us.

Sheila elbowed me. "Lola?"

"Sorry." I looked over at her. "Can we just take it one step at a time? You tell me where you want me, and I'll be there."

She looked from me over to Alec, then back to me. "Sure." She stood. "Malcom, Kyle, why don't you help me prepare?"

"You need to prepare?" I asked.

"It'll be fine. Just meet us out front when you're done." She glanced between me and Alec again.

"Subtle," I said.

She smirked and waved before walking out of the kitchen. Malcom and Kyle followed her, leaving me and Alec alone for the first time since everything happened.

"How are you feeling?" I asked.

"Better," he said. "Next time I see that mate of yours, I'm going to rip his throat out."

"Please do," I said without hesitation. A flicker of elation rose in my chest. Not a single warm feeling for Tyler came to me. All I could feel was hatred and anger.

"Well, that's nice to hear," he said. "I was starting to worry that you'd let the bond win."

"Not a chance," I said.

"You're really okay with the whole taking down the king thing?" he asked.

"What do I have to lose?" I asked.

"Everything," he said. "Don't do it, Lola."

"I already said I would."

"We could run. I'd run with you," he offered.

"I'm done running," I said. "And you need to be done running too. I know you've been through hell, but you must forgive yourself and let yourself have some joy. You don't have to forget what happened. You don't even have to forgive Wolf Creek. But you should stop casting yourself as the bad guy here. Nothing that happened was your fault."

"I had the mark, and I left my pack. I put myself first." He shook his head. "It cost me everything."

"So, then you rebel by joining a feral pack where the whole motto is every wolf for themselves?" I raised my eyebrows. "You have to admit by now that you formed a community. You brought all those people together. You are an alpha. It just looks different than you thought it would."

"If I stayed..." Alec looked down.

"If you stayed, you'd be dead too. And maybe all the shifters at your camp would be too. They needed a place to go. They needed a leader. They found you," I said.

"This isn't about me," he looked up, locking his eyes on mine. "This is about you."

"Alright. Fine. I'm going to help Spencer because it's the right thing to do. Then, I'm going to kick my old alpha to the curb. If nothing else comes of it, I will break down that barrier and weaken Wolf Creek enough that they can't do what they did to your pack ever again."

"It's the toxin," he said.

"And you have an antidote," I reminded him.

He chuckled. "Yeah, I do."

"Why don't you go work on that with Star? I think Sheila, Malcom, and Kyle have enough planned for helping me train."

Alec's gaze moved to somewhere behind me and a momentary scowl crossed his face.

I turned to see Spencer standing in the entryway. "You're not counting on that group of misfits to help prepare you for breaking into the king's estate, are you?"

"I don't see any other options," I pointed out.

He poured a cup of coffee, then lifted his chin toward Alec. "The witch wants you downstairs."

"Go," I said. "I got this."

Alec hesitated, then stood. There was so much unsaid between us, but I didn't think either of us was clear headed enough to figure out how to say the things we needed to.

Spencer sat down next to me. "You remind me of your mom, you know that?"

I glanced over at him. "I'm not sure that's the compliment you think it is."

"I'll admit, I don't know what she's like now, but you should have seen her before you were born."

"Before you abandoned her?" I countered.

"I made my choice. Your mother made hers. She must have known she was pregnant, otherwise I don't think she'd have left. She would have stayed and fought with me," Spencer said.

"Then she'd be dead too, just like your friends who helped you," I said.

"Maybe," he mused.

"Look, you don't need to do this bonding thing with me. I said I'll help you and my word is good."

"I'm not trying to bond with you. You don't owe me anything and I know that. But you should know about your mom. She was tough as nails. Brilliant and fiercely loyal. She had an energy around her that you could feel. Strength. She wasn't like any woman I ever met," he said.

"She's none of those things anymore," I said bitterly.

"Maybe not, but she passed all those traits to you. I can see it. You have her strength. And you have royal blood. You just need to let yourself lean into your instincts. Trust your intuition. Trust your inner wolf," he said.

"My instincts kept me alive so far, despite the many attempts by others to end my life," I said.

"Good. Now use it to learn how to take the offensive instead of using it as defense."

"What exactly is it that you expect me to do in your plan?" I asked.

"Malcom will be my second," he said. "You get to steal the crown."

My brow furrowed. "You can't be serious. A crown?"

"Malcom is next in line for the throne," he said. "Unless you want to challenge him for it?"

I shook my head. "Fuck no."

"Then he's the natural choice for second," he said.

"So, this is just an alpha challenge on a greater scale?" I asked.

"Basically. If he doesn't play dirty. But that's where you come in. That crown has power. Well, not literal power. It's a hunk of gold. I've never cared for it. But the other shifters, the nobles, and the hangers on, they believe it means something. We have that crown, and we publicly challenge him, he'll have no choice but to fight."

"How did you lose last time? You said your friends turned on you. Why didn't you just challenge him?" I asked.

"I never made it to the throne room," he said. "As soon as I crossed through the front doors, my friends turned on me. My brother was tipped off about my arrival."

"That sucks," I said.

"Yeah," he agreed. "If I had won that day, I would have searched for your mom. You'd have been raised as a princess."

I swallowed. "You didn't even know she was pregnant. You act like you actually cared about her."

He growled. "Don't you dare question my feelings for her. Your mom is my true mate. I wanted a family with her. I wanted forever with her," he said.

I tensed. My mom never told me she'd had a true mate. All this time, she'd been away from him, and she'd quit shifting. Since my dad wasn't dead, she'd have felt that bond all these years. What had that done to her? I was a mess simply being apart from my true mate and we had yet to complete the mating bond. She'd completed the bond, then had to flee. Every day, my very existence had been a reminder of the love she'd lost.

"My mom is broken after everything she's been through." My throat was tight, and I had to stop speaking for fear of breaking down in front of him. He might be my father, but he was still a stranger.

"After we win, I will find a way to heal her. I've never stopped loving her. I never will. Mating bonds are eternal. Chosen by fate. Sacred. She is my other half. Being away from her was the worst part of my punishment. I know I don't deserve your affection, but I hope to at least one day gain your trust," he said.

I nodded once. It was all I had in me. Here was a true mate, trying to get back to his love while I had just taken to magic to break my own bond. Why were the fates so fucking cruel?

5

I WAS GREETED by a trail of rocks outside Star's home that I knew weren't there before. Varied in size, the rocks led away from the front door, out into the soft grass and fading from view as they stretched toward the waterfall.

"What is all this?" I asked.

"My pack might be terrible, but they trained us to connect with our wolves well," Shelia said. "The rocks are markers for each of the steps. As you complete each component, I remove a rock. They aren't really needed, but they're a good visual."

I glanced over at Kyle. "Did you do this?"

"We just ran in the woods when we felt like it," Kyle said. "Pretty sure there was training for Ace's inner circle, but we weren't there yet with Tyler."

I recoiled at the name. I didn't want to think about Tyler at all. Though, I suppose I should be grateful that Ace was lax with his training of his son. How much worse would things have been for me if Tyler was stronger?

"I can see why Wolf Creek needs the toxin to get anything done," Malcom mumbled. "We didn't take away rocks, but we earned a bead every time we reached a new stage. Same concept."

"You're telling me most packs have actual training and Wolf Creek was just a free for all?" Why was I not surprised? It was a good way to keep the majority of the pack weaker.

"Sheila and I talked it. Turns out, we had pretty much the same method to learn how to connect with our wolf," Malcom said.

"And you're both going to run through it," Sheila said, pointing to me and Kyle.

"I know how to connect with my wolf," Kyle said.

"I'm sure it could be improved," Sheila said.

"And this type of training works better with a partner. You two are the newest wolves," Malcom said.

"You can't be much older than me," Kyle said.

"They don't shift at nineteen outside Wolf Creek." I forgot that Kyle didn't know all this. "They shift much younger."

"No shit?"

I nodded. "There's a lot they kept from us."

"Well, who am I to turn down something that will help you?" Kyle said.

"It might help you, too," Sheila said.

Kyle didn't look convinced. "What do you want us to start with?"

"First point is shifting at will. Without the influence of the moon," Sheila said.

Kyle pulled his shirt over his head. "Easy enough."

Nervous flutters filled my stomach. I'd shifted once on my own, during a full moon. I knew it was coming, of course. It made sense that I'd need to learn to shift at will, but it was a big step.

"Alright." I took a deep breath and closed my eyes. *You ready for this?* It was daylight, there was no moon to help, there wasn't a ton of other shifters around. It was just me and my wolf. Well, and Kyle.

When I opened my eyes, Kyle was naked. "You got this, Lola." He shuddered, then doubled over, his body breaking. Bones snapped as he began the change. For a horrible moment, he was all twisted limbs and grunting, then a large gray wolf stood in front of me.

I could feel my wolf responding, calling to me. She wanted to join him. For a moment, I resisted. What if the only way I could shift was if someone else shifted?

"Go ahead, Lola," Malcom urged. "Shift. Quick run, then shift back."

"This is an exercise in control," Sheila explained.

Kyle's wolf paced in front of me, and I could feel his impatience. He wanted me to join him. There was something else there, too. Was it fear? What could Kyle be worried about?

My wolf was clawing at my chest, begging to get free. Right now, I needed to focus on the task at hand. When we were back in human form, I could ask Kyle what was going on. Quickly, I removed the tie and unbuttoned the shirt I was using as a dress.

It didn't take much urging to unleash my wolf. She was impatient, practically knocking me over in her hurry to shift. The movements felt more familiar this time, easier even. My body bent and rippled, the change taking over quickly. A moment of discomfort was quickly replaced by a rush of relief. I was on all fours, feeling the breeze ruffle my fur.

I felt free and at peace, my wolf sending waves of gratitude through me. It was as if she'd been begging to be unleashed and I'd ignored it. But I didn't realize that was how she felt. Now that I was in wolf form, I could sense what she wanted more. I could also sense Kyle better.

The fear was clearer now. It wasn't for him; he was worried about me.

Kyle's wolf took off at a run and I didn't hesitate to join him. After a brief lap around the grass, we returned to where Sheila and Malcolm were waiting. My wolf whined, resisting my desire to return. It was harder than I thought to reign her in. Eventually, she yielded, and I was able to return to my human form. Next to me, Kyle also initiated the change. The two of us stood naked and panting from the exhilaration of running as wolves. Going between the two forms so quickly was more challenging than I anticipated.

"Well done," Sheila said. "I'm impressed. It's one thing to shift and run all night, but the true sign of strength is the ability to shift when needed and return quickly to human form."

"I've never done it quite that quickly before," Kyle said.

I recalled when he'd chased me through the woods. That was a quick turn, but I wasn't going to bring that up. I knew neither of us wanted to go back to the past. Then, I recalled Kyle's concern for me. I couldn't feel it now, in his human form.

I pulled my shirt on, then turned to him. "What are you worried about?"

"What do you mean?" he asked, pausing with one leg in his pants.

"I could feel it. You're afraid for me."

He tugged on his pants. "Of course, I am. You're preparing

to overthrow a monarch and a tyrant. Anything could happen."

"I know," I said. "That's why I have all of you to help me prepare."

Sheila was holding one of the rocks in her hand. "And one rock down. It might be a stupid tradition, but I do love seeing the rocks go away."

"Wouldn't check marks on a list be easier?" I asked.

"Where's the fun in that?" she asked.

"Alright. So, one down, what's next?" I asked.

"Solo shift," she said. "First, you get a friend. Next one is each of you. One at a time."

My stomach twisted into knots. I knew I had to go through the stages and do all the steps. Was I ever going to stop feeling nervous about shifting?

"Kyle first," she said.

"Why did I put my pants back on?" He tugged his jeans off.

"Yeah, you won't need clothes for a while," Malcom said.

Kyle shifted with ease, did a quick loop, then returned to human form. All the while, my wolf begged for release. It seemed that it might be even harder to resist shifting than it was to complete the shift.

When it was my turn, I was surprised that my wolf responded immediately. I shifted, ran a lap, then returned. When I tried to shift back, my wolf fought me. She wasn't ready to be human again. Suddenly, I was running away from my friends, toward the woods, sprinting as fast as possible. My wolf had completely taken over.

Stop. I called to her, trying to reason with her. We had to work together but she was fighting me. Panting, muscles aching, my wolf pushed forward, racing through the trees.

She was elated, pure joy surged through her as anger and fear competed. I needed her to stop, I needed to be in control.

Another wolf ran alongside me now. I could feel Malcom, his wolf called to mine, and she responded, looking over at him. She didn't want to stop. She wanted to run. I burst past Malcom, leaving him behind. I had lost all control.

Fighting against the desires of my wolf, I tried to stop her. Instead, she raced forward, until we were in the tunnel that led away from Star's enchanted forest. If not for the huge rock blocking the way, I think she would have taken us to the woods.

What are you doing?

That's when I felt it. Tyler. He was near. And his wolf was calling to me.

6

MY HEART WAS RACING, and I paced near the tunnel, my whole body tense. My wolf wanted to leave Star's enclave. She wanted to go to Tyler. Was that what she'd run for? Was that why I couldn't control her?

I tried to win over my wolf side, to remind her that Tyler was bad. I'd never felt more divided from my wolf. It was as if I was trapped inside her body, our souls not merging at all. We were strangers. She was in charge, and I was along for the ride.

Fear gripped me, sending icy tendrils through me. I had to change this. I couldn't let my wolf stray from me. We had to be united.

She stepped toward the large rock that enclosed the tunnel and pawed at it. With a whine, she tried to push on the rock.

Stop it. I was screaming internally, desperate to connect with her. It wasn't working. *We need to go back. Our friends are waiting.*

There was no concern for what we'd been working on,

only a sense of urgency to get out of here and find our mate. *No. Not our mate. We broke that bond.*

She growled and pawed at the stone again. This time, she was more aggressive, leaning into it with her whole weight. It still didn't budge.

My pulse was sky high, but with each failed attempt to remove the stone, I felt relief.

You can't do it alone. Go back.

The cry of another wolf sounded behind us and we turned to face three wolves. I could sense my friends in each of their shifted forms. Sheila, Malcom, and Kyle had all come for me.

My wolf growled.

Down, girl. Those are our friends.

Sheila's wolf moved closer. Her fur was like midnight. So black it was almost blue but as she moved into the tunnel, she nearly blended with the shadows.

I could feel her emotions. Concern radiated from her in waves. She stopped a few feet from me and lifted her chin, a clear indication that she wanted me to follow.

My wolf resisted at first, but I was using everything I had to encourage her to go. *Come on. Please.*

She didn't want to leave with our friends. My wolf was only thinking about her mate and how he was out there, waiting for us. It was chilling. A horrible twisted, conflicted feeling of both desire and disdain. *Even if I wanted to go out, it's impossible to move the rock. You won't win this.*

My wolf was furious and I could feel the connection we'd forged slipping even more. She didn't trust me, and she didn't want to connect with me. Being unable to connect with your wolf was every shifter's worst nightmare. How had this happened?

Star's spell came to mind, and I cursed myself for being so stupid. I'd severed the connection to Tyler with my human form, but it seemed to be magnified in my shifted form. Not only that, but I'd risked the connection with my inner wolf.

I wanted to say it wasn't worth it but being able to resist the pull to Tyler in any form was progress. *You know he will cage us if he catches us. We'll never be free.*

My friends yelped, and my wolf turned to look at them. I could feel her resistance fading. *That's it. Back to our friends who care about us. They need us, and we need them.*

She looked back at the barrier, longing tugging deep at my soul. I knew she was desperate to get to Tyler, but the human part of me couldn't feel it at all. My wolf and I were closed off from each other, two separate halves not functioning together at all. I'd broken my connection with my wolf for a chance to free myself from Tyler.

Sheila's wolf was right in front of me now, she sat down, waiting and patient. My wolf was pulled into the calm sensation of her friend's presence, and I could feel her urgency subsiding.

It's time. I encouraged. *We can deal with this later. Just go with your friends.* Finally, my wolf walked forward. Shelia turned and walked toward the others and the four of us exited the tunnel.

We got about halfway to Star's house when my body began to give way. I shivered, then collapsed, unable to make myself move. It was as if my wolf had given up. She wasn't going to walk any farther.

Terrified, I tried to reach out to her, to connect with her. I was met with nothing. No connection, no resistance even, just my human form. It was as if my wolf was gone.

My body began the change, shaking, breaking, reforming. Finally, I was hunched over on all fours, my hands and knees sinking into soft dirt, in human form.

Everything hurt. My head throbbed, my arms and legs ached. It was as if I'd just experienced a beating, not a shift. Cautiously, I pushed myself up to standing and looked at my friends. They were still in their wolf forms, but I could tell they were concerned.

"I'm okay," I lied. "Let's get back, then you can shift."

I was most definitely not okay. I'd lost my connection to my wolf. Worse, I'd felt the pull to Tyler in a more intense way than I ever had before. In the past, I'd been able to resist the bond when my wolf had pushed back. I'd been able to reason with her, explain to her why he was wrong for us. This time, she hadn't cared. She wanted Tyler at all costs.

I was in big trouble. The only thing that kept my wolf from breaking free and running straight to Tyler was the barrier that sealed off Star's home. If that wasn't there, I knew with absolute certainty, I'd be on my way to him now.

Taking careful steps, I walked the rest of the way through the underbrush toward the soft grass where the remaining rocks still stood in wait for me.

All those stages of training that would require me to shift into wolf form now looked like a death sentence. How long could I resist my wolf? What if she broke through that barrier? What if I couldn't even get her to shift in the first place?

I picked up the shirt I'd left in the grass and took my time buttoning it. There was no safe way I could shift after what just happened.

Around me, the sound of cracking bones accompanied my

friends' transformation back into their human forms. They were all silent as they got dressed and I got the sense that they were waiting for me to speak. I wasn't sure how to begin.

"Are you alright?" Sheila was the first to break the silence.

How did I answer that? "I'm not sure."

"What happened?" Malcom asked.

"Maybe she just needs a break," Kyle suggested.

"There's no time for a break. She has to be able to control her wolf," Malcom responded.

"I know, I know." How was I going to explain this? I lost control because my wolf wanted to be with Tyler. My fingernails dug into my palms, and I released fists I didn't know I'd been making. Just the thought of Tyler made my blood boil. I felt no kindness toward him. Yet, my wolf had decided to give up everything to get to him.

Shit.

"I have to see Star," I blurted out.

"You have to get through at least five more exercises," Sheila said. "We don't know how long we've got, and I am not sending you to the king without being able to control your wolf."

"I don't have a choice." I turned before they could say more and bolted toward the house. She'd warned me there would be a price and the bond likely couldn't be broken on both ends. I just didn't expect it meant my wolf would be working against me to get to Tyler.

What good did it do me to try to magically break the bond when it amplified everything my wolf felt? The pull between us in my wolf form was unbearable. Even now, I could sense my wolf's restlessness. She knew her mate was out there, and she was determined to get to him. At least she was still there, so shifting was probably possible. The problem was, it was likely far too dangerous. I couldn't risk shifting again but I had to figure out how to connect with my wolf and regain some control.

"Star?" I called as I took the steps to the creepy basement as fast as I dared. "Hello?"

The darkened space was empty. I should have started with the main house. Frustrated, I raced up the steps and ran from room to room. I finally found Star and Alec in the greenhouse, sitting at a small round table.

They both looked surprised to see me when I stopped in front of them. Alec jumped to his feet, and I got a rush of his emotions. He was concerned but that wasn't all. There was a rage there, too. Something primal and protective. As if he was ready to take on anything that might be coming for me. The sensation was overwhelming. I took a step back, my heart racing.

"What's wrong?" he demanded.

"Nothing, I just need a quick word with Star." I forced a smile on my face.

It took a moment for him to settle down, or reign in his emotions. Once he was calmer, my own emotions began to react. My face felt hot, my body was tingly, desire coursed through me. *Fuck.* Not this again. I should have expected the post-shift libido, but it caught me off guard. Taking a breath, I tried to send all the want and lust away.

Alec's brow furrowed. "Since when do you two have business you can't discuss around me?"

"Girl stuff," Star replied. "You're welcome to stay, but most males aren't interested."

Alec's nose twitched and I could tell he was trying to decide if he should stay.

"Alec, just go, please," I said.

"Grab us some coffee, will you?" Star asked.

He didn't look thrilled, but he headed out of the greenhouse.

"He'll have to make a new pot," Star said.

"Good. Because I have a serious problem," I admitted.

"The bond?"

I walked over to the table and sat down. "When I was in my wolf form, I couldn't control anything. My wolf sensed Tyler beyond the tunnel, and she was desperate to get to him. She shut me out, she was pure instinct."

She clicked her tongue. "The magic of the bond still wants out, it seems."

"What am I supposed to do?" I asked. "I can't afford to lose control of my wolf. I need to be able to shift, to connect."

"What do you mean you can't control your wolf?" Alec stepped back in the room, two cups of coffee in his hands. He passed one to Star, and one to me.

I didn't really want coffee, but I took a sip anyway. It gave me a moment to avoid answering him.

"Lola, what's going on? I know something is wrong. Tell me," he insisted.

I looked over at Star, my expression pleading. She shook her head. There was nothing she could do to help me. I was on my own. The spell she'd done had severed my connection to Tyler while I was in human form, but it was as if all the intensity in my wolf form was magnified to impossible levels. How was I going to do this?

Alec took the coffee cup from me and set it on the table, then he took the chair next to me. "Talk."

"I fucked up," I admitted.

"How?"

"I asked Star to remove the bond. It sort of worked, and sort of made things worse."

"You did what?" Alec turned to Star. "Why would you agree to that?"

"She was desperate." Star shrugged.

"Don't be mad at her. She did me a favor. I asked her for help." I took a deep breath. "The bond was getting stronger. I was feeling sorry for Tyler, and considering what things might be like if I gave in. It was too much."

A dark cloud seemed to have settled around Alec. I could feel anger and jealousy and hate brewing around him as easily as if it were my own emotions. "I'm going to kill him right now. This has to end."

He stood and started walking toward the door.

I jumped up from the table and ran to catch him, grabbing his hand, I pulled him toward me. "Wait. Please, don't go."

"Look what this bond is doing to you, Lola. He has to go." Alec's rage was palpable.

"I can't risk it," I said.

He growled. "Can't risk losing your mate? After everything he's done to you? After everything he did to me? He nearly killed me. I have every right."

"I can't risk losing you, asshole," I said. "I don't give a shit about Tyler. I want him gone. But he nearly killed you last time you two fought."

"I nearly killed him, if you recall. He's the one who played dirty. I can take him," Alec assured me.

"Please don't go." I reached for Alec's face and cupped his cheek. He had a short beard from a few days of not shaving. I rubbed my thumb across his cheekbone and his eyes met mine. In that moment, a thrill shot down my spine. It was an intense, almost electric connection that took my breath away. I gasped and lowered my hand.

My breathing was shallow, still reeling from whatever had passed between Alec and me. His eyes were wide, his lips parted. "You can't kill him, but I can. Unless you can think of another way to get your wolf to cooperate, I don't have a choice. And we both know you can't keep putting this off."

"Not you." I wasn't sure why I was so desperate to keep him safe, but I couldn't stand the thought of anything happening to him. I didn't want any of my friends at risk, but Alec had nearly died to protect me from Tyler.

"If you go slowly, ease into it, you might be able to retrain your wolf, get her to earn your trust," Star offered.

"Would that work?" I wasn't sure if it was possible. Star wasn't a wolf, but it wouldn't surprise me if she knew more about this than I did. It wasn't like I was taught a whole lot about being a wolf shifter growing up.

"It might," Alec said. "If you're with someone your wolf trusts."

"Like you?" I asked.

He nodded. "We can try it. If it fails, I'm going to find Tyler and give him the slow, grueling death he deserves."

"There you are. You alright?" Sheila called as she entered the room. Kyle and Malcom were behind her and all of them wore matching expressions of concern.

I really didn't want to tell everyone about how I'd fucked up with the bond. "I'm okay."

"Well, you two look rather cozy," Sheila teased.

My hand was now on Alec's bicep, and we were inches from each other. I lowered my hand and took a step back.

"She lost control," Malcom said.

"What happened out there?" Kyle asked.

"I think I wasn't focused," I lied.

"Let me try something with her," Alec said.

"She has to figure this out. She can't risk losing control of her wolf if she's going to go for alpha," Malcom said.

I glared at him. He was talking about me as if I wasn't there. "I'm fully aware of what's necessary."

"It's that bond, isn't it?" Kyle asked. "It's getting stronger."

"Is that true?" Sheila asked.

"Look, I will deal with Tyler after we help Spencer. We all agreed that we need his support when I return to Wolf Creek." The whole Tyler thing was driving me crazy, but the thought of sending any of my friends after him was too much. I didn't want them getting hurt because of me.

"I want to try a wolf night," Alec said.

"You sure that's a good idea? Her wolf bolted. She was untamed, wild," Malcom said.

"I wasn't that bad," I said.

"Lola, you were trying to get out. You weren't in control at all," Sheila said.

"One night," Alec said. "If we can't bring the control back, I'm going after Tyler myself."

"If you go after Tyler, I'm going with you," Malcom said.

"You can't. You and Lola have other work to do. Kyle and I can go with Alec," Sheila offered.

"I don't want any of you doing that for me," I said.

"What else are you going to do? You can't kill the bastard and he won't break the bond," Sheila said.

Frustration made my chest feel tight. I wanted to fight my own battles. I wanted to be the one to make Tyler pay for the years of pain he'd caused me, but I didn't want the lifetime of mourning him. "Fine."

"What the fuck is a wolf night? Anyone going to explain for us non-shifters?" Star asked.

I looked over at Alec, wondering the same thing.

"We shift near moonrise and we don't return to human form till dawn. No matter what, no shifting back. It's challenging because we don't usually stay in wolf form that long," Alec said.

"And it's had some adverse effects," Sheila grumbled.

"Like what?" I asked.

"You'll be fine," Alec assured me.

"What adverse effects?" Kyle said.

"Occasionally, there are wolves that don't ever return to human form after a full night as a wolf," Malcom said.

My eyes widened and a chill ran down my spine. Was that possible? Could my wolf take over completely and cause me to be a wolf forever?

"That's an old wives' tale," Alec said.

"You sure about that?" Sheila asked.

"Lola is an alpha. She's strong. She just needs to remind her wolf that she's the one who's in charge," Alec said.

"I can do this." I was determined to fix this. My wolf had to come to her senses.

7

"This is a terrible idea," Kyle said. "We should just go end the Tyler problem."

"Can you guarantee you'll find him before Spencer needs me to go help him? What if he's back in Wolf Creek with the others?" I wanted the bond ended, but it wasn't worth risking my friends. This was my battle, but I wasn't sure how I was going to fight it with the odds stacked against me. Aside from my wolf wanting to run to Tyler, there was that whole problem around killing your mate.

Kyle growled. "I'm supposed to protect you. I can't do that if you're out in the woods with someone else."

"Alec won't let anything happen to her," Sheila said.

"His track record says otherwise," Kyle spat.

"Hey, enough," I said.

"Listen, I know I fucked up, but you have to trust me on this. You're both right. Tyler has to go, but we might not have time right now. You, me, and Shelia can't go with them when they take on the king." Alec wore a wicked grin on his lips.

"That's why you agreed to try this?" I should have known.

"You're going after Tyler while Malcom and I are with Spencer."

"That's actually a good idea," Kyle said.

I didn't want my friends to risk injury for me, but even I had to admit that three of them together was strong odds. I couldn't think of any reason why they shouldn't go after Tyler. The only opposition that came to mind was that I wouldn't get to help them make him pay for all he did to me. I knew I'd be a liability going after him, though. I had no idea how long I'd be free of the bond in human form, and I couldn't actually take him out. Things would be so much less complicated if he'd just let me break the bond.

"Did I hear my name?" Spencer walked into the greenhouse.

"What do you even do all day? Just walk around waiting to join conversations you weren't invited to?" I asked.

He smirked. "You have quite the attitude."

"Well, we're kind of dealing with a crisis that has nothing to do with you," I snapped.

"Good news, you won't have to wait around much longer. We move against my brother tomorrow night," he said.

"She's not ready," Malcom said.

"I don't give a shit. It's our best shot, so we're taking it," he replied.

"What makes that night so important?" Sheila asked.

"It's his birthday. Asshole is bound to have a big, over the top party," Spencer said.

"What if he chooses something low key?" Malcom asked.

"It seems fitting to throw him out on his birthday, don't you think?" Spencer smiled as if entertained by the thought.

"It might be worth waiting. Lola's having an issue with her wolf," Kyle said.

"Star didn't spill the news, did she?" Spencer asked.

My brow furrowed and I looked over at the witch. "What is he talking about?"

"You couldn't let me get past this crisis first?" Star said, turning her blank white eyes on Spencer.

"Keeping you on your toes, I suppose," Spencer said.

"What is it?" I asked.

"I did some spying on the king," Star explained.

"You can do that? Like from here?" Malcom's jaw dropped.

"I can do a lot of things."

"I can see why your coven kicked you out. You don't have normal witch skills," Malcom said.

"That's not helpful," I said.

"I meant it as a sign of respect," Malcom added. "I mean, damn, I'm glad you're on our side."

"Nice save, Malcom," Sheila mumbled.

"So you spied on the king. Like seeing the future kind of stuff?" I asked, trying to return us to the new crisis.

"More like checking out his present movements," she clarified.

"And?" Sheila asked.

"Well, he knows about both of you." She turned her blank gaze on me, then looked over at Malcom.

"How?" I asked.

"Seems we aren't the only ones with a seer on our side," Spencer said. "Chris already set a bounty on both your heads."

It seemed strange to hear the king referred to so casually. Then again, he was my uncle, and I was helping with a plot to take him down. My life had gotten very complicated recently.

"The longer we wait, the riskier the whole thing will get. He knows I'm out and he knows I'll look for the two of you," Spencer said.

"He'll go to Wolf Creek," I said. "They won't know where I am, but could they point out your camp?" A whole new level of concern gripped me. All those feral shifters, living peacefully, were at risk.

"They could," Alec said.

"We can't wait on this." I looked over at Spencer.

"Like I said, we go on his birthday. Whether you're ready or not, we're out of time."

"We'll be ready, won't we, Malcom?" I looked over at my brother, the other piece of this upcoming suicide run.

"Sure, ready." Malcom said. I could see the doubt in his expression.

"Well, I'll leave you all to whatever you were doing. Malcom, Lola, we'll need to go over our plans tomorrow before we leave. I hope like hell you figure out whatever your issue is tonight. If either of you die, it's going to put a damper on my plans." He walked away, then stopped in the doorway, turning back to look at us. "Star, I'm going to need your assistance when you are finished in here."

"Sure, boss," Star said, her tone condescending.

"I kind of hate him." It didn't matter if he was my mom's true mate, or if he was my father.

"We sure we want to help him gain the crown?" Kyle asked.

"From what I heard, he can't be any worse than the current king," Sheila said.

"Not our problem," I said. "We agreed to help and in return, we get what we need."

"Keep telling yourself that," Malcom said.

"You have a better idea?" I asked. "With the guards officially looking for us, and the threat of them going after our friends, we don't have a choice."

"Honestly, I think our moms could have done better," Malcom said.

"He told me my mom is his true mate," I admitted.

Malcom whistled. "That's big."

"It must be killing him to be around you," Sheila said.

"Why?" I asked.

"You likely have a similar scent to your mom. Probably makes him miss her more," she said.

"I can't say I've got a lot of sympathy for him right now," I said.

"It doesn't matter," Kyle cut in. "Forget all the Spencer shit right now. You can't go if you can't connect with your wolf. I don't care what else is at risk. You're a liability to yourself and everyone else if you can't get that fixed."

"He's right," Alec said.

"She needs to try the wolf night with the person she trusts the most out of all of us," Kyle said. "We only get one chance at this."

My pulse raced. I'd already mentally prepared to spend the evening in the woods as a wolf with Alec. The thought of trying it with someone else sent a rush of panic through me. I already didn't love the idea of being a wolf for a whole night. Especially if there was a risk of me being stuck like that.

"He's right," Sheila said. "Lola, you should choose. Any of us can do it with you. It should be who you feel the safest with. Think about who your wolf would want, too. Not just you in human form."

"Well, we all know who my wolf wants right now," I mumbled.

"Lola, it's okay if you feel safer with someone else," Alec said. "I want you to connect with your wolf. It doesn't matter who you do this with as long as it works."

I looked around at the group of friends who were like a family to me. I trusted each of them with my life. It was so different from where I'd started, and it warmed my heart to feel so supported. When I thought about a whole night in the woods, wolf form or human form, there was only one member of the group I could see myself choosing.

After everything we'd been through, and all the ways he'd hurt me, Alec had proven his loyalty. I felt a connection to him I couldn't explain. It wasn't the same as the way I felt around my other friends. I needed to be around him the same way I needed to breathe.

"I'll go with you," I told Alec. "It was your idea, and I do trust you."

He nodded. "I won't let you down."

"While you two are away, I'm going to find out more from Spencer," Malcom said.

"Good luck." Shelia squeezed my hand.

AN AWKWARD SILENCE settled between Alec and I as we traversed the rough terrain. I wasn't sure how far out he wanted to go, but with each step, we were getting farther from the entrance where I'd sensed Tyler. I was grateful for the distance. Especially since I was about to attempt to spend an entire night in wolf form. I had no idea how my wolf was going to respond. Since returning to human form, she'd made herself scarce.

My connection with my wolf had been tenuous from the start, but I thought things were improving. I should never have involved magic in this mating bond. There was only one way forward and that was through my own grit and determination. I had fought my way out of hell my whole life but in the last few weeks, I'd let go of who I was. I was the girl who spit blood back in the face of my attacker. I wasn't the type to take a back seat and watch the world pass me by and I needed to reclaim my identity. But this time, I was going to be able to have a chance when I fought back.

"Thanks for helping me with this," I said, finally breaking the long silence.

"Don't thank me yet. This isn't going to be easy," he said.

"Nothing is ever easy," I pointed out.

"Not for either of us, that's for sure." He stopped walking and looked around.

I took my eyes off him and scanned our surroundings. It was late afternoon, and the shadows were getting longer. The sun had a few more hours of light, but deep in the trees we were already in nearly complete shade.

"Probably as good a place as any to stop." Alec said.

"We just wait till nightfall, then shift?" I asked.

"We can shift whenever. The concept of a wolf night is about prolonged shifting and maintaining control. It's usually done at night to use the moon to our benefit. We won't have that on our side, though."

"So, we just hold off till sunrise?" I asked.

"You'll probably run yourself to sleep. But yeah, the point is to hold out as long as you can," he explained.

Nervous flutters filled my stomach. What if I failed? *No.* I couldn't fail. I wasn't going to give myself that option. I got myself into this mess, and I was going to get myself out.

"Why did you do it?" Alec asked.

"Ask for the magic?"

He nodded.

"You know what a mating bond feels like. Imagine feeling that pull for someone who spent years hurting you," I said.

"I know all that. It's the same thing you've been dealing with, and we had a plan to end it. Why now?"

"It was too much," I admitted. "I was starting to doubt myself."

"You thought you might go to him." Alec's jaw tensed.

I swallowed hard, hating that he was right. "I can't do that."

"I wish you'd let me kill him," Alec said.

"We've been over this, and I don't want to talk about it again. Now isn't the time." I closed my eyes and took a deep breath. Deep inside, I felt my wolf stir. It was as if she was waking from a nap, but she was quickly perking up. I opened my eyes. "Time to shift."

I didn't wait for a response before I stripped off my clothes and took off at a run, calling to my wolf. She responded quickly; the sleepy sensation gone. My body shuddered as it began the change and soon, I was on all fours, feeling the wind in my fur.

8

My wolf was sure of her footing as we raced through the trees. My breathing quickened as we pushed forward. It felt different than last time I'd shifted. It wasn't like the exercises I'd done earlier today, and it wasn't the same as the full moon. There was distance between me and my wolf. We still weren't connecting the way we should. I had to admit, I hoped that once she couldn't sense Tyler, we could return to where we'd left off.

Earlier today, when I had no control, it was because she'd sensed Tyler. Now, I couldn't feel him at all. We were supposed to be one and the same, but there were two sides of our connection. I slowed down, overruling my wolf's desire to continue running. I could feel her hesitation, but she was willing to wait. At least she was responding to me better than earlier.

A rush of relief rolled through me, and I took a deep breath. My wolf whimpered, her disappointment clear.

Remember what he did to us. I always felt a little crazy when I talked to my wolf, but it had helped in the past. *He isn't right for us. He hurt us.*

Sadness, deep and profound, gripped us. It was tangled with regret, desire, and longing. The emotions were intense and confusing, and I pawed at the ground, trying to shake some of the negativity away with movement.

My wolf wanted to understand, but she was struggling. Tyler was connected to us, fated to be our other half. *The fates made a mistake.*

I looked up from the ground and saw Alec's dark gray wolf slowly approaching. My wolf backed up, then held her ground as she realized that Alec wasn't a threat. *He's a friend,* I assured her.

My wolf seemed unwilling to go as far as claiming Alec a friend, but I could tell she was willing to concede that he wasn't a threat. We'd run with him before, but things changed so quickly once I added magic to the mix.

Alec's wolf backed up and lowered his head, as if bowing. I was confused by the action, but my wolf wasn't. She instantly perked up, her hesitation about Alec gone.

There can only be one alpha. I wasn't sure if the thought had come from my human half or my wolf, but I felt like I'd just been doused with ice water. Alec had the mark of an alpha, as did I. If we were a pack, one of us would have to submit.

Alec's wolf had submitted to mine.

My pulse raced. Had he just joined my pack? Or was this just for the sake of our run tonight? I wasn't sure what it meant, but my wolf was no longer interested in sitting still. She wanted to run.

I let out a howl, then Alec's wolf joined in. When I took off at a run, he followed. I didn't need to look back to know he was keeping pace with me. I could sense his emotions as if they were my own. The thrill of the run was clearly radiating from him, but there was more to it. I felt him in a way I hadn't before.

Figuring it was from his wolf's submission, I continued forward. My wolf took the lead running, easily navigating, but not kicking me out as she had earlier. We seemed to be on the same page, running together. I'd never been so relieved in my life. Was it possible we could finally connect the way we should?

We ran a long while, my wolf totally at peace with the freedom. I'd let her take over, trusting her to the point that I didn't even realize where we were headed.

When she stopped in front of the entrance to Star's home, panic gripped me. *No.* I forced her back, making my wolf move away from the cave's entrance. She allowed me to take control but fought me when I tried to leave. *Fuck.*

My wolf sat down and waited.

Alec was next to us, patiently waiting without complaint.

After several long moments, I felt what she'd been waiting for. Tyler.

We could sense him. He wasn't as close as he had been, but he was near. My wolf bounded forward, racing toward the rock that closed us off from the forest. I called her back, struggling to gain any kind of control. She resisted, but her fight wasn't as strong. She was tired from all the running.

This is not going to happen.

I did the only thing I could think of. Using all my willpower, I shifted back into human form. My body broke and reformed, the process agonizing as my wolf struggled to keep me in animal form. In the end, my human side won, and I stood in the cave, facing the rock, totally naked.

"What happened?" Alec asked as he walked toward me, already back in human form.

"She tried to run to him again," I said.

"You sensed him out there?" Alec lifted his chin toward the entrance.

I nodded. "I had more control this time, but in my wolf form, it's too risky. I'm just going to have to wait until the bond is broken."

Rage seemed to explode from Alec, the emotion so raw and powerful, it took my breath away. Whatever had connected us, it was intense.

Alec marched forward and placed his hand on the rock. To my surprise, the stone rolled away, revealing the entrance to the forest beyond.

"What are you doing?" I cried.

"What I should have done the day I returned you to Wolf Creek," he said.

"Alec, wait."

He was already in wolf form again, running away from me.

I knew I couldn't risk shifting, but I couldn't let him go after Tyler on his own. *Fuck.* I had to make a choice. Fast. If I went out there, my wolf could force me to connect with Tyler. Or I could stay in human form and risk letting years of rage get the better of me. As much as I wanted Tyler dead, I couldn't risk being the one to end his life.

With a deep breath, I turned and ran toward Star's house, hoping like hell I'd made the right call. My footsteps were unsteady in human form, I stumbled several times, and was pretty sure my feet and legs were covered in blood when I arrived. None of that mattered. I had to get help.

As much as I wanted to be the one to take care of myself and defend my friends, I knew there were things I couldn't do on my own. Going after my mate, especially with my bond in the state it was in, was one of them.

I burst through the door. "Sheila! Malcom!"

I nearly collided into Sheila as I ran down the hall.

"What's going on?" she demanded. "Where's Alec?"

"He went after Tyler," I said.

"Fuck."

"What's going on?" Malcom and Kyle joined us.

"Alec went after Tyler," Sheila said.

The two males ran past me, not bothering with any other information before they headed out the door.

"Stay here," Sheila said.

"Like hell I will," I snapped.

"At least put some clothes on. You can't risk shifting. You understand me?"

"I know," I said.

"He already went through the entrance, right?" Shelia asked.

I nodded.

"You're going to need these." Star was holding a bundle of clothes in her hands.

I grabbed it from her and tugged on the shorts and tee shirt. She even had a pair of boots for me. They were about a size too big, but it was better than repeating my painful run through the woods barefoot.

"Come on," Sheila said. "I'll stay human with you. It'll help you not shift. Just focus on me."

"Thank you." All I'd ever wanted was to be able to stand up for myself and fight back. It was killing me that I still wasn't there yet. The difference this time was that I wasn't getting the shit beat out of me for trying to do something I wasn't strong enough for. For the first time, I didn't feel sorry for myself. I had friends who were able to help me when I couldn't do it all alone. And I knew I was strong enough to keep getting better.

You are an alpha. I was starting to feel the part, even if I couldn't do everything I wanted to yet. Part of being a good leader was asking for help when you needed it.

Sheila and I headed out. The sun was setting and a cold wind cut through the air. I shivered but I wasn't sure if it was from the cold or the anticipation of what we were about to face down.

Would we find Tyler? Would the others find him before we reached him? I had no idea what to expect. I thought we'd deal with this Tyler thing after we helped my dad. Nothing ever seemed to go as planned.

9

SHELIA and I jogged through the woods, leaping over roots, and ducking under low branches. The way back to the cave felt like an eternity. Neither of us spoke, but the tension hung heavy in the air. As we neared the entry, I realized I wasn't concerned about Tyler at all. At least I had that going for me.

Instead, a weight settled in my stomach as I worried about Alec. I wish I could say I was equally worried about Kyle and Malcom, but I wasn't. All I could think of was that I needed him to be safe.

I told myself it was because last time we'd met Tyler, he'd nearly died, but I had a feeling there was more to it than that. It made me feel guilty. I was a terrible friend. Kyle had broken me out of captivity, and Malcom was literally blood. Why couldn't I worry for them on the same level?

"Stay close," Shelia warned. "If you feel the urge to shift, run. You can't risk completing that bond unless you want to be stuck with him."

"Oh, I'll run." It was good advice. The last thing I needed

was for my wolf to take over and follow Tyler's wolf anywhere.

As we walked into the tunnel, my heart thundered in my chest. I knew we needed to address the Tyler problem, and I wanted him gone, but I couldn't find the anger I once had. Between the lingering mating bond and my concern for Alec, I felt nearly numb. Why couldn't he have just let us break the bond?

I forced myself to recall all the reasons Tyler and I shouldn't retain our bond, finally drawing out some anger. I needed it close to the surface, ready to tap into if my wolf objected.

As soon as we passed through the cave, I could feel him. My wolf clawed inside, desperate to get out. For now, I was in control, able to let my anger drive me. Tyler might be my fated mate, but he was a monster. We were never going to be together. Another force called to me, though, making both my human and wolf halves take note. We could sense the others. Alec, Malcom, and Kyle. Their signatures were just as strong as Tyler's.

I could detect snippets of emotion, but none of it was clear enough to know for certain what they were feeling. All I could tell was that it was intense, but the positive or negative wasn't readable. Panic gripped me. They could be kicking Tyler's ass, or they could be in danger. With the odds, it was far more likely that they were about to end Tyler, but I couldn't take that chance.

I stopped and glanced over at Sheila. "They found him."

"Which way?" Sheila asked.

I paused for a moment, then let instinct take over, moving quickly in the direction that felt right. My wolf was restless, I could sense her desire to break free, but I held fast. There was too much at stake to risk shifting.

It didn't take long before I could sense all my friends more clearly. Their emotions were overwhelming my senses. Frustration, anger, anxiety. These weren't good feelings. "Something's wrong."

Sheila's jaw tensed and she nodded. "Keep going."

I slowed to a walk, taking careful steps as the connection pulled me in closer. Tyler was there too, his emotions unreadable to me. I was grateful that our connection had been severed enough that I couldn't get into his head, but right now, it might have been helpful. My wolf felt like she was pacing, as if reminding me that she would be able to sense him. I fought the urge to shift, bottling it down. *Not now.*

We heard them before we saw them, low growls and aggressive barks. The sounds of angry, impatient wolves. A few more steps and I had them in view. Malcom, Kyle, and Alec were in their wolf forms, circling a tree. My brow furrowed.

"Up there," Sheila whispered.

My gaze moved up the tree until I found Tyler, sitting smugly on a branch. His naked legs dangled above my friends, and he looked pleased with himself. I was even more glad I didn't have to feel his emotions. He was clearly trying to entice the wolves to shift back into human form and climb up to him. But he'd been in the woods a while and it was possible the whole thing was a trap. My friends were smart to maintain wolf form.

But I wasn't a wolf. And I was the exact perfect bait to bring him down. I stepped forward and Sheila grabbed my arm. "What are you doing?"

"Going to flush the asshole out," I said. "Don't worry, I'll let the guys finish him off."

She didn't look convinced, but she released my arm. I took careful steps forward, slowly moving closer to the gathered group. Three large wolves turned to watch me step into view. Alec's wolf growled at me, his message clear, he didn't want me here. I ignored him and stopped below Tyler.

"You're like a frightened child," I spat.

"You're one to talk," he replied. "In your human form because you can't even control your wolf. I felt you earlier. Let her out. She's the smart one."

"Come down, and maybe I will," I said.

Alec's wolf growled, and I could feel his disapproval of everything I was doing and saying. I ignored him, keeping my gaze locked on Tyler.

"You do realize how pathetic you look up in that tree like that," I said.

"Call your boys back and I'll come down. I just want to talk," he said.

"They're staying right here with me. You come down and break the bond and they won't attack you," I countered.

Tyler didn't respond and my friends were getting restless. I turned my attention to the wolves at the base of the tree. "If he's not coming down to break the bond, we have no use for him. Who can knock him down?"

To my surprise, Kyle's light gray wolf was the first to jump at the tree. He landed with all four paws against the trunk, causing the tree to sway. The branches shook and a few pinecones fell to the ground.

I looked up at Tyler and noted that his smug expression

was gone. He was gripping the branch tighter and actually looked a little nervous.

I had no intention of letting Tyler try to break the bond again. He'd proven he couldn't be trusted, but I needed him down from the tree. Then, my friends could do whatever they wanted with him. Any sympathy I had for him was buried deep within my wolf and as long as I didn't shift, I wasn't at risk of having an ounce of compassion for him. The only regret I had was that I couldn't help. The threat of mourning him for the rest of my life was enough to make me hold myself back. It sucked, but the bond had been bad enough.

"Alright, I'll bite," he said, his tone mocking. "Call off your dogs."

I ignored the insult at calling a group of wolf shifters dogs. He was trying to rile me up. He knew that my wolf was more vulnerable to the bond. If I let emotions take over, I'd be at risk of shifting accidentally. There was no way I could risk that. My wolf was ready, I could feel her starting to grow restless. She wanted to shift, which meant, she'd want to go with Tyler. I crossed my arms over my chest and reminded myself I needed to hold back.

"Give him space," I said to my friends.

Their apprehension and anger hung in the air like a cloud. They weren't sure what I was doing, but I hoped once they saw me move out of the way, they'd know Tyler was fair game.

Alec's wolf moved closer to me, as if guarding me. It was comforting to have him so close. Just his presence helped me feel calmer and more relaxed. My wolf seemed more at peace with him nearby and I was able to concentrate better on the moment at hand rather than focusing everything on not shifting.

Malcom and Kyle had moved away from the tree, but both wolves still had all their attention on Tyler while he made his way down.

As soon as his feet hit the ground, he looked over at Kyle. "Nice to see you again, Judas."

"You have no right to talk about betrayal," I snapped.

"I know you're waiting to give the signal for your friends to take me out," he said. "You and me have a connection none of them will ever understand." His upper lip curled in disgust as he turned his gaze on Alec's wolf. "Not even you. You think she's going to be yours? You can't change the fates."

Alec growled and took a few steps toward Tyler. This was it. It was time to end this nightmare. My heart hammered; my palms felt sweaty. Tyler deserved this. He brought all this on himself.

I took a step back, ready to let my friends take over. I wasn't sure if I could watch or if my wolf would force me to change. It might be better for everyone if I wasn't witness even if I wanted to see Tyler meet his end.

"One last thing, love," Tyler said, holding his fist up as if clasping something in his hand.

My brow furrowed. What was he doing?

He took a step toward me, opened his fist, and blew something from his palm. Bits of dirt flew, hitting my face and getting in my eyes. I winced and lifted my hands to block the debris. "What the fuck?"

Coughing, I stumbled back, trying to get away from whatever he'd just blown my way.

"Are you okay?" Sheila asked.

"I think so." My eyes were watering, and I was still coughing, but I wasn't in pain. I looked up just as Tyler was finishing his shift. He took off, running away from our group.

"He's getting away!" I coughed again. "It was a diversion."

"Go!" Sheila shouted. "I've got Lola."

Alec, Kyle, and Malcom bolted after Tyler; the three huge wolves crashed through the woods. I watched until they were out of sight, still rubbing dirt out of my eyes.

"You alright?" Sheila asked again.

"Yeah. What a fucking asshole," I said.

"That was so weird." Sheila shook her head. "Such a coward move."

"It was." My stomach tightened and I winced as a bolt of pain shot into my gut.

"What is it?" Sheila asked.

"I don't know." I felt odd. Suddenly sweaty, and dizzy. I groaned as my muscles tensed. What the fuck was happening?

Without warning, I dropped to the ground, and I realized that I wasn't in control of my own body.

But neither was my wolf. Terror gripped me. "That wasn't just dirt." Panting, I tried to control myself. It was painful to fight the change. Tears streamed down my cheeks.

Sheila knelt next to me. "Lola, can you get up? I'll walk you back to Star's. She can help."

My body began to break, bones cracking and reforming. I screamed. I'd had painful shifts before, but nothing like this. I could feel every inch of me reforming, searing pain radiating across my body. I struggled to remain conscious, my vision going blurry and dark around the edges.

Just as I was about to pass out, the pain eased. I was in my wolf form and only vaguely aware of the fact that I wasn't the one in control anymore.

My wolf howled, calling out to her mate.

"Lola, don't do this," Sheila called.

My wolf gave her a quick glance, then she took off, tearing through the woods, following Tyler's scent.

Stop, stop. You can't do this. Go back, please. Desperation took hold, I begged and pleaded, but my wolf was in charge. There was no reaching her.

My only hope was that my friends would break the bond before I reached Tyler.

10

My wolf could feel Tyler. She was desperate to be with her mate. Reason didn't matter, none of my human emotions mattered, she was determined to reach him.

Every muscle hurt as I fought against my wolf. She was stronger than me and she was fully keeping me out of the discussion. With each footfall, I could feel Tyler getting closer, but I could also sense my friends. *See? They are trying to keep Tyler from us because he's bad for us.* I changed my tactic, hoping the loyalty I could sense for Alec, Malcom, and Kyle could somehow sway her opinion.

My wolf growled, pissed that there was a threat to Tyler. She picked up the pace. Everything I tried seemed to backfire. What was wrong with my wolf? Why had I shifted like that? I'd lost all control, forced to make the change.

Star's warning about magic having a price seemed so long ago. I should know better than to not take chances with magic. The gamble hadn't paid off.

My muscles ached; my lungs burned. I had never moved so

quickly in my life. My wolf was nearing exhaustion, I could feel it. She needed to slow down but she wasn't interested in anything that would prevent her from catching up to her mate.

Finally, we caught up to the others, and raced right past Alec's wolf. He snapped at me, trying to get my attention. *I'm sorry.* Guilt gripped me as I closed in on Tyler. Why had I lost control? If only I'd stayed in human form.

I'd made a lot of mistakes in the last few days, and they were going to cost me everything. My heart was heavy, a contrast to the pure elation surging through my wolf. The dichotomy of emotions was overwhelming, making me feel a little nauseous. What would happen if my wolf got me to break? Would I be happy with Tyler, or would I spend the rest of my life bound to him but hating him?

Tyler's wolf stopped running, my wolf instantly responding to his actions. We were nose to nose, my wolf panting, feeling nothing but pure bliss at being so close to her mate.

Shift back right now. If I were in my human form, tears of frustration would be streaming down my face. Instead, I was trapped in this mix of twisted sensation.

Tyler's wolf nuzzled me, and I started shaking. I wasn't sure if it was my wolf feeling happiness or if it was me feeling terror. The lines between hate and love were blurring more by the second. I could tell he wanted me to follow him. He wanted to leave here and go back to Wolf Creek. It was the last thing I wanted, but it was the happily ever after my wolf craved.

Growls filled the air, sending the hair on my back standing

on end. I glanced behind me to see four wolves, hackles raised, ready to attack.

My wolf moved to defend her mate, blocking Tyler from them. She returned the growl, then snapped her jaws. I fought her, trying to get her to back down. This couldn't be the end. I couldn't abandon my friends and follow Tyler away from here.

Alec's wolf locked his eyes on mine. Even in his wolf form, they were two different colors. Gorgeous, haunting, mesmerizing. Alec's eyes had always seemed to hold power over me, pulling me to him, reminding me of all the feelings I'd had for him. The desire, the connection, the passion. Everything came flooding back to me like a roaring waterfall.

For a brief moment, my wolf stumbled, she let go of her control. I wasn't going to waste my opportunity. I moved away from Tyler and used every ounce of my willpower to force the change.

I was halfway through a painful shift when my wolf seemed to realize what was happening. She was exhausted from the run, and I was able to use that to my advantage to keep her at bay. My bones cracked and reformed, my wolf protesting every movement of my body. I cried out in agony as I pushed to complete the shift. Finally, I overcame her objections and found myself in the fetal position, naked in the dirt.

Everything hurt. My muscles ached, my head pounded, my skin felt hot. I was sweaty but shivering. The world around me spun. I rolled over and threw up in the dirt. After I'd fully emptied my guts, I was able to get my breathing under control. It took more effort than it should have to right myself so I could turn to see what was happening.

Tyler was surrounded, my friends closing in on him. He faced them with teeth bared. I was surprised he was going to try to fight them. His usual plan was to make others fight his battles or run away. I got the sense that they were waiting for me to make the call. After what I'd just pulled, I suppose they were confused. Or maybe they were giving me one last chance to choose Tyler. That was never going to happen. Tyler deserved nothing more than what he gave to me all those years.

Reminded of all the awful things he'd done to me, I pushed myself to standing and immediately fell back to the ground. *Shit.* I needed to help. I needed to face Tyler and end this once and for all. I looked around for anything that might help offer support so I could get up and finish this. To my right, my friends had Tyler surrounded, to my left, was a steep drop off into a deep ravine. I was glad I hadn't been any closer to that during my change back to human.

I crawled toward the wolves, giving myself more space between the drop off before trying to stand again. Nausea rolled in my stomach as I made it to my knees, but I fought against it. Ignoring the pain and double vision, I finally found my feet. Slowly, I walked toward my friends.

"I can't kill you myself, but I can watch as they rip you to pieces, you son of a bitch," I said through gritted teeth.

Tyler whined, his wolf looking up at me with sad, pathetic eyes. As if attempting one last time to pull me in.

My nostrils flared and anger surged. I owed him nothing. "You should have broken the bond when you had the chance."

He moved faster than I anticipated and suddenly, Tyler's wolf was on top of me, knocking me to the ground. His paws on my chest, he pinned me down. His jaws snapped in my face, and I winced, turning away from him. My wolf's sense of loyalty to her mate was bubbling just under the surface. I could feel her desperation to connect with him. She wanted me to shift. She wanted to go with him and complete the bond. I closed my eyes, fighting against her desires.

Tyler's claws pierced my flesh and my eyes snapped open. I cried out. He was trying to get me to connect with him and force a shift. But he'd chosen the wrong tactic. Even my wolf was angry now. He'd hurt us just like he always had. *Like he always will.* My wolf was alert now, her senses mixing with mine, uniting us as one.

She remembered everything.

She remembered how he'd abused us, how he'd sent his friends to torture us, how he'd left us to die. A wicked grin on my lips, I locked my eyes on Tyler's. "You fucked up."

Angry and determined, I screamed as I forced his wolf off me. Adrenaline pumped through my body, masking the pain and discomfort. I was single-mindedly focused on one thing: Tyler had to go. Forever.

It no longer mattered if I had to mourn him. He couldn't be in my life.

Tyler's wolf growled at me, his body tense, poised to attack. My friends moved in closer, and Tyler's wolf snapped at them, sending a clear message. He was going to harm me if they moved closer.

My friends held their ground, but I could feel their eyes on us. They were waiting for an opening. If I wanted Tyler gone by their teeth and claws, I needed to get myself out of the way.

Instead, I closed in on Tyler, facing him myself.

I could hear the warning growls of my friends, but I was acting on pure impulse. The anger and hate were clouding my thoughts, driving me forward. In my weaker human form, it was already risky enough to take on a wolf, but Tyler deserved pain.

I charged him, throwing my shoulder into his side. His wolf stumbled but didn't fall. He turned on me and swiped his claws across my chest.

Hissing in pain, I moved toward the cliff. I knew I couldn't kill him myself, but I might be able to draw him to the edge and push.

Tyler raced after me and caught my feet, making me land face first in the dirt. I rolled to my back and kicked him in the face, then used both feet to push into his side, knocking him to the ground.

Scrambling away on all fours, I got myself some space before attempting to stand. When I did, I turned to engage Tyler again, but this time, I was blocked. Kyle's gray wolf stood in front of me, a warning in his eyes. He growled, low and steady. It wasn't a threatening sound, but I knew he wasn't going to let me pass.

Two more wolves moved in around me. Sheila on my right, Malcom on my left. The three of them blocking me in. "Let me go. I have to end this."

Sheila's wolf snapped at me, then lifted her head toward Tyler. I looked up and saw him circling Alec's dark gray wolf. The two males didn't even seem to notice the rest of us. They were far too engrossed in each other.

Both wolves had teeth bared, their fur was bristled and angry. I swallowed hard. This was exactly what I'd hoped to prevent. I didn't want Alec to take on Tyler alone. What if Tyler hurt him? What if Tyler killed him?

"You have to help him," I said.

The other three wolves didn't move. I took a step forward, and Kyle's wolf nudged me back. I wasn't going anywhere, and they weren't stepping in. Alec was taking on Tyler alone.

11

My chest tightened and I squeezed my hands into fists. I didn't want to watch, but I couldn't tear my eyes away. The two wolves circled each other. They were nearly equally matched. Alec's wolf slightly larger than Tyler's. After their last encounter, I knew Alec was the superior fighter. It didn't surprise me after seeing how Tyler would default to those around him to finish his dirty work.

Even though I was pretty confident that Alec could handle himself, I was still terrified. I didn't want anything to happen to him and I hated that this whole thing was my fault.

No. It wasn't my fault. I was done with self-blame. I gave Tyler the option to break the bond. He brought all this on himself.

To my surprise, my wolf seemed to be backing me up. She was ready to be done with all of this once and for all. I realized I was holding my breath and released it before forcing myself into a steady breathing pattern.

It seemed like an eternity of glaring and snapping and

circling before either wolf made a move. Tyler was the first to break, charging at Alec with his claws raised.

Alec was ready. Jumping, he met Tyler in the air, knocking the other wolf to the ground. Tyler quickly righted himself and attacked again, going in low and managing to swipe Alec's rear side with his claws. I gasped and involuntary took a step forward. Kyle was quick to push me back, knocking me slightly off balance. I didn't realize how unsteady I still was from my ordeal.

I took my eyes off the fight for a few seconds while I regained my footing, and when I looked back up, Tyler was on the ground. He rolled over, righting himself before turning back to Alec. He charged the dark gray wolf, knocking him down. The two creatures rolled together, fighting for dominance. Growls and snapping jaws and slashing claws blurred together as the wolves continued to grapple. Every time Tyler got a blow in, Alec was able to match him.

The fight was taking them further away from us and after a few more blows, they had moved just out of view. I wasn't about to stay in my guarded position and miss out on what was happening. Quickly, I passed between Kyle and Malcom and jogged forward to find the battle.

Suddenly, a wolf rushed me, and before I could react, fangs were around my wrist. Teeth bit into my flesh and I screamed as I tried to pull my arm away.

Tyler had his jaw locked around my arm, sending pain so intense that it knocked the air from my lungs. Gasping and fighting to ignore the pain, I had no choice but to stumble forward as he dragged me.

Alec's wolf appeared in front of me. Hackles raised, he

growled. Tyler's wolf ignored him, continuing to pull me along.

Hot tears streamed down my cheeks as I was dragged forward. I tried to fight back, but moving my arm sent fresh pain and I couldn't get the right angle to land a kick.

"Let me go!" I shouted. What was Tyler thinking? I wasn't going to bend to him, and he was outnumbered. The second he let of go me, he was a dead man.

Ahead, I caught sight of the edge of the ravine. It was a vertical drop at least twenty feet down. What was Tyler doing? Was he going to throw me over? Or pull both of us over the edge?

I yanked on my arm, gasping for air as his teeth bit even deeper into my skin. This was not how I was going down.

We reached the cliff and Tyler finally released my arm. I ran, but he blocked me in, his wolf much faster than my human form. I was inches from a fall that would mean the end of my life. All Tyler had to do was give me a little push.

"Let me go, you fucking sadist," I shouted.

My friends were gathered in front us, careful to keep their distance. Tyler growled. I wasn't sure what Tyler was hoping to gain from this, but he'd successfully gotten his message across to my friends. If they approached, he'd end me. Maybe he'd end himself too, I wasn't sure.

"Back up, all of you." I was cradling my bleeding arm with my uninjured one. Everything hurt but this wasn't the time to let my guard down. I was seconds from death.

In all the times I'd wished for something to take me from Wolf Creek, I never thought I'd be where I was now. I had found friends, I'd experienced happiness, even if it was brief. If I walked away from here, I was going to do everything in my power to make sure deranged, power hungry men like Tyler and his father never hurt anyone again.

There had to be a way to end this, but it might cost me everything. I looked up at Alec and mouthed, *I'm sorry*.

Before I could change my mind, I moved to the side, quickly positioning myself behind Tyler. His head snapped to me, and he turned to face me, but it was too late. Using everything I had in me, I pushed. Tyler's wolf slipped, his back legs the first to go over the edge.

Suddenly, someone grabbed me around the waist and pulled me away from the edge. Two more sets of hands grabbed hold of Tyler's front paws right before he plunged to his death.

"I got you," Sheila said, pulling me into her and away from the cliff.

Kyle and Alec were in their human form, holding on to Tyler's wolf. They dragged him up, then stepped back. Malcom was still in wolf form, waiting in front of Tyler.

"What's going on? Why did they do that?" I demanded.

"They stopped you from a life of mourning that prick. If he fell, his death would have been on your hands," Sheila said. "You're welcome."

"No." Tears stung my eyes. "I can't keep living like this."

"I know," she said. "But you can't kill him. It would drive you mad."

"This is your final chance," Alec said. "Break the bond."

"Tyler, you don't have a choice," Kyle said. "Do the right thing."

Tyler's wolf stared at the two males for a moment. I held my breath, unsure of what was going to happen. I wanted Tyler to pay for all he'd done to me, but the most important thing was that the bond between us be eliminated. If he got to walk away from this, but I was free of him, I would be okay. Maybe.

Tyler's wolf bared his teeth. He didn't seem to like the idea of breaking the bond.

"Tyler, don't," Kyle warned.

The wolf charged forward and Malcom raced forward, knocking Tyler to the ground. Tyler's wolf snapped at him, digging his teeth into Malcom's wolf's shoulder. Malcom yelped but quickly broke free.

Kyle, still in human form, lunged forward and pushed Tyler's wolf. This time, when he went over the edge, nobody caught him.

I turned away, not wanting to watch him fall to his death. The seconds felt like hours, but I felt the moment he took his last breath.

I collapsed to the ground, exhaustion and emptiness spreading through me where the mating bond had once existed.

Sheila wrapped her arms around me. "It's going to be okay now."

I nodded, unable to speak. This was what I wanted, and Tyler deserved everything he got. He didn't deserve the kindness my friends offered him with one last chance to break the bond, yet they'd given it to him and he chose death.

"Let's head back and find some clothes," Sheila suggested as she released me from her embrace.

I stood and looked around at my friends. Everyone was back in human form. All of us were covered in dirt and couldn't hide the fact that we'd just been through hell. I could sense their concern and their sympathy mixed with relief. My bond with Tyler was finally gone for good.

For a fleeting moment, my wolf mourned the loss of her mate. It didn't last long, though. Alec approached and my heart raced at the sight of him. The two of us had been through so much and there was no doubt we had a connection.

Even now, as I should be feeling the pain of Tyler's loss, all I could think about was Alec. It was consuming and intense, a strange overreaction perhaps to the trauma we'd just faced. Typically, after shifting, there was a desire for sex. This wasn't the same thing. I didn't want to hop in bed with Alec, I wanted to connect with him. It had to be the after effect of the trauma.

Alec stopped in front of me and his gorgeous eyes found mine. We stared at each other for several breaths, and then he tangled his hand into my hair, guiding my face closer to his as he leaned closer to me.

Our lips met in an explosion of fire and passion. The sensation of being truly and fully alive spread through me, my whole body alight with possibility. Every inch of me was tingling, my emotions escalating to impossible levels.

I could feel it. All of it. Him, me, us. My heart felt like it might explode from the sheer joy of connecting with him. The other half of my soul.

When he pulled away from the kiss, I gasped as the realization hit me.

Alec wasn't just some guy I was interested in. He was my mate.

12

"How long have you known?" My voice was breathy, coming out as a whisper.

"I suspected during our full moon shift, but I didn't know for sure until just now," he confessed.

"But Tyler…" I knew you could have another chance at a mate if your mate was dead, but it seemed impossible for me to have found a second when so few wolves even found their first.

"He's gone," Alec said.

I knew there were unfinished thoughts in that statement. Alec's mate was also gone. He'd loved deeply and lost tragically. If anyone deserved another chance at happiness, it was him.

Alec caressed the side of my face gently with his thumb. His touch was a balm, soothing and comfortable. I never wanted him to stop.

"What does this mean?" I asked.

"It means that if you'll have me, we can complete the bond," he said.

"But we've already had sex," I said.

"You were fated for someone else then," he said.

"I hate to interrupt the moment," Sheila cut in, "but did I just overhear that correctly? You two are feeling a mating bond?"

"Damn, some shifters have all the luck," Kyle said.

"No kidding," Sheila added.

"Congrats, you two," Malcom said. "But you're going to have to hold off on completing that bond for a bit."

"Why?" I asked. Now that I had the chance to explore what a mating bond with someone I cared about felt like, I wasn't sure I wanted to wait. Plus, my body was already scaling up the lust. I was finding it difficult not to drag Alec to a more secluded place and take him right now.

"He's right," Alec said. "After what you've been through, I want you to have time to sort this out. Plus, there's the matter of your dad and your pack."

I nodded, not thrilled with the idea of waiting, but agreeing that it was the right thing. After everything with Tyler, did I really want to be bonded to anyone?

"We should go back," I said. "It's getting dark."

The walk back to Star's was quiet and it gave me time to think. The bond between Alec and I was new, and it wasn't as intense yet as it had been with Tyler. I knew that would change over time, but I had no idea what would happen if we completed the bond. I wanted my freedom. Would being with Alec make me feel trapped all over again?

The sun had set by the time we returned to Star's house. A rectangle of light illuminated the front door, creating a silhouette of a waiting spectator. I wasn't thrilled that we had an audience for our return. Especially since I was pretty sure it wasn't Star.

Spencer was standing in the doorway sipping a cup of coffee. "I guess you gave up on doing the whole night?"

"The need passed," Malcom said.

"He's dead, then?" Spencer asked.

"He is," Malcom confirmed.

"Good. I need your head in the game," he said.

"Can we not right now?" Things couldn't just be complicated one at a time, could they? I finally have the mating bond cleared up with Tyler, and now I have a new bond, that I might actually want. Instead of getting to figure that out, I had to deal with taking down the shifter king.

"I'm going to take a shower and put clothes on." I walked past Spencer and made my way to one of the bathrooms. Malcom was right, now wasn't the time to figure out my feelings with Alec.

While I washed the dirt out of my hair and soaped up the wounds that had yet to heal, I considered the conversation with Alec. Unlike Tyler, he'd given me the choice.

I froze as doubt crept into my mind. He was giving me an out. Did that mean he wanted out? As quickly as it came, the thought fled. I knew that wasn't true. Alec wanted to be with me as much as I wanted to be with him. I'd spent so many years doubting myself and my abilities. I was used to disappointment and second-guessing. That wasn't who I was anymore. I was going to be an alpha, a leader. I had the ability and I deserved happiness.

It was a different kind of shower pep talk. While growing up, I'd broken down in the shower more times than I'd like to admit. I'd cried there to hide my pain. I'd talked myself into simply surviving. Making it until I was old enough to get out.

Now, I had the power and the capability of setting my standards higher. I no longer needed just to survive, I could start thinking about enjoying my life. I deserved happiness, love, and support. As did all the people in Wolf Creek who couldn't stand up for themselves.

By the time I was finished in the shower, I was feeling renewed. Sure, I was tired from the run, and my emotions were still a messy roller coaster, but I felt like I deserved more than I'd let myself hope for.

Tyler was broken, but his kind of broken caused more damage. Aside from the occasional flicker of sympathy or sadness, mostly I felt relief. I wasn't sure what it said about me that I wasn't mourning my mate. Or feeling guilt about his death. I doubted he'd felt any sensation of loss after trapping me in the cave to die. I wondered if that made me just as terrible as him.

Dressed in one of the random white button-down shirts, I crept from the yellow room into the hall. It was late, and I'd dismissed myself without discussion around any other plans. I wasn't sure if the others were sleeping and didn't want to wake anyone. It had been a big day and shifting took a lot out of us.

The one thing that was different, though, was that I wasn't feeling the same insatiable need for sex. Maybe it was the life-or-death situation that immediately followed the shift. It was a little unsettling, but I wasn't going to argue. It was probably a blessing that I was able to resist Alec tonight while I worked through everything.

Voices carried from the kitchen. I made my way there and found Alec and Kyle sitting at the table. The two males looked like they were having a serious conversation but stopped talking the second they noticed me.

"Should I go?" I asked.

Kyle stood. "Actually, I was just leaving." He walked toward me and stopped right in front of me. "You know I have your back, no matter what."

If that wasn't clear before today, it was crystal clear now. Kyle had sided with me, and defended me, over Tyler. I wasn't sure why it hadn't struck me at how dramatic that was until just now. "I know, today had to be hard for you."

He shook his head. "I thought it might be, but it wasn't. The more distance I got from the abuse of Wolf Creek, the more my eyes were opened."

"I'm lucky to have you," I said.

He gave me a smile and patted my shoulder as he left the kitchen. It was a short conversation, but it spoke volumes. Kyle was a survivor, like me. While he'd been part of the wolves who were accepted, he likely experienced things that were unpleasant. Wolf Creek left its mark on all of us.

I walked over to the table and took the seat across from Alec. I wasn't sure I could trust my libido if I was too close to him. It was still so strange not having a physical response to the shift.

"In case you're wondering, Kyle promised me he'd kill me if I hurt you," Alec said. His tone was serious, but his smile eased the tension.

"Is that so?" I raised my brows. "Should I be concerned that you're going to hurt me?"

He reached his hand across the table and took hold of

mine. "I am going to be making amends for what I did to you for the rest of my life. But I swear to you, I will never do anything to cause you pain again."

Warmth spread from the point of contact, traveling up my arm, across my chest, and down all the way to my center. I sucked in a surprised breath and pulled my hand away.

Alec moved his hand and his brow furrowed, an expression of disappointment on his face.

"It wasn't your words, it was your touch," I admitted. "I don't know how I'm going to wait. Every time we touch, I can feel the desire to complete the bond."

"It'll get stronger the longer we wait," he said. "But you already know that."

"What does this mean for us?" I asked. "You and me, there was always something there, but a bond is so unexpected."

"I know. We have to be the luckiest shifters alive," he said. "I've never met anyone who got a second chance."

"I kept thinking the fates made a mistake when they paired me with Tyler, but what if it was to help me find you?" My cheeks heated. It felt so cheesy to say those words, but they came out before I could think them through.

"I've been wondering that myself," he said. "It sure was a fucked-up way for us to find each other."

I laughed. "That's an understatement."

"I know you've got a lot on your plate now and I'm not going anywhere." Alec reached for my hand again and gave it a quick squeeze before releasing it.

"Thanks."

"Why don't you get some rest. I have a feeling tomorrow is going to be a wild ride," he said.

I couldn't argue with that. Spencer had given us so little

information and I had no idea what to expect. All I knew was that tomorrow I was supposed to steal a crown and depose a king.

My life was so fucking weird.

13

"Lola."

Someone was calling my name but it was way too fucking early for that. I kept my eyes closed, hoping it was my imagination.

"Lola, wake up."

I groaned. I wasn't ready to get up yet. "Go away."

"It's two in the afternoon. You're out of time, princess."

The tone was mocking and I realized it wasn't one of my friends. That made me open my eyes. Spencer was standing near the bed, an impatient look on his face. "About damn time."

"I just went to bed," I whined.

"I let you sleep as long as possible. It's time to get ready," he said. "I guess killing your mate takes a lot out of you."

I sat up and tossed the covers aside. "Are you judging me?"

He lifted a skeptical brow.

"You don't know shit about me and you don't get to judge me. You'd rather see me with an abusive mate than safe and healthy? Fuck you, asshole," I said.

"I didn't say that." He seemed amused by my outburst. "If you'd grown up in my home and anyone harmed you, I'd have killed them myself."

"So what's with the judgy comment?" I asked as I climbed out of the bed.

"You're the one interpreting it as judgy, princess," he said.

"Stop calling me that." I walked past him, toward the door.

"Where you going?"

"I just woke up, where do you think I'm going? I have to pee." I rolled my eyes. This was not the way I expected my day to begin. Spencer waking me and reminding me about Tyler were the last things I wanted. The sooner I helped him, the better. I was looking forward to being done with the favor I promised.

And who was he to judge me then play the concerned parent card all in the span of a few seconds? If he'd actually been worried about me, he could have done something about Tyler.

All he cared about was the throne. And I was the sucker who agreed to help him. I still wasn't sure why I'd agreed to do it, but at least it was nearing the end. Assuming I lived through the whole thing.

I cleaned up in the bathroom, then headed to the kitchen. Was there still coffee this late in the day?

There was coffee, however, there was also Spencer and Malcom waiting for me. The two males were at the table, watching me as I filled a cup. I took a seat near Malcom, opting to avoid being too close to Spencer.

"So, are you finally going to give us some details?" I took a sip of my coffee. It was cold, but it was better than nothing.

Spencer's expression was a little alarming. He was

beaming in an almost insane kind of way. "Oh, I have all the details. I've been dreaming of this day for the last nineteen years. I never imagined I'd have help, but that just makes everything easier. By tonight, I will have the throne and you two will have whatever you want."

"You're that confident that this will go well?" Malcom asked.

"Without a doubt," Spencer said.

"So, where's this crown I'm supposed to take?" I asked.

"The royal residence is in a mansion in the city," he said. "Fifty rooms, hallways for days, and secret passages galore. The whole thing is built for sneaking around. When it was constructed, the thought was for ease of getting in or out."

"Or sneaking in mistresses," Malcom teased.

"That has certainly been done," Spencer said.

"Hey, he's my mom's mate, can we not talk about that?" I asked, surprised that I cared. Sure, my mom had done terrible things, and she'd had her own share of male visitors, but thinking of her being set aside for another woman hurt.

"I didn't say I used them for that," Malcom said.

"Won't your brother know about the tunnels?" I asked.

"Yes, but we're going in the front doors," he said.

"That sounds like a terrible idea," I replied.

"Well, not all of us," he clarified. "Malcom and Star will enter through the front while you and I take a route less traveled."

"How's that going to work? You said your brother knows about us now. And I thought you had to be blood to get in."

"Star is going to mask my scent," Malcom said. "She also said the blood magic won't bother her."

Why was I not surprised that she had a way to bypass

blood magic. The scent thing was different than I expected, though. I lifted my brows. "She can do that?"

"She can do a lot of things," Malcom said.

"Yeah, I'm starting to realize just how scary she is," I added.

"Why would they go in the front?" I asked. "Why not all go in through the back?"

"The entrance is sealed up. Malcom and Star will let us in," Spencer said.

"Wonderful. Sounds like nothing is going to go wrong with this plan," I deadpanned.

"Have a little faith," Spencer said.

I sipped my coffee, taking a moment to bite my tongue. I already agreed to this, so I'd go along and hope we all came out of it alive. I supposed it gave me some distance from Alec to give my mind a break from worrying about mate drama. I thought I wanted to be with Alec, but I was still recovering from everything with Tyler. It was a lot to take in.

Spencer stood. "One of the rooms has to have some pants that fit you. You might want to prepare. We're leaving in an hour."

I nearly spit out my coffee. How was it nearly time to leave already? "I thought you said it was at night?"

"You slept most of the day. We still have to get there," Spencer said.

"It's going to be fine," Malcom said, not taking his eyes off Spencer.

I took a few breaths and as soon as Spencer was out of sight, Malcom leaned in closer to me. "Remember, if it's between us or him, we sell him out so fast it makes his head spin."

"I don't think that's going to be an option if they want us dead, too," I said. "I think our only choice here is to not fuck this up. We're going to have to pull it off."

"You might be right," Malcom agreed. "But I stand by what I said earlier, it's us over him."

I nodded. It was a nice sentiment and it seemed to make Malcom feel better, but I had a feeling it wasn't going to be as easy as all that. "I'm going to get dressed."

I dumped the rest of the cold coffee in the sink, then left the kitchen. I had expected more time to mentally prepare for all of this. If Spencer was to be believed, my role wasn't too dramatic. Once an official alpha challenge was issued, shifter law prevented any harm coming to either side. Although, we were talking the king here. He was shifter law. What made Spencer think his brother would keep his word? Couldn't he just change things on his whim? I knew there were processes and councils and protocol, but I had no idea how much of it would hold up when an actual threat presented itself.

After checking in a few closets, I finally found a stash of clothes that fit me. I was in all black, which seemed appropriate for an evening of breaking and entering. I tried not to think about how strange my life was as I pulled on a leather jacket I found in the back of a closet. It fit surprisingly well. Maybe it was a good sign that things were going to improve. After all, it had been weeks since I'd had properly fitting, clean clothes.

I laced up the boots Star gave me over a pair of men's socks. Okay, so it wasn't perfect, but it was far better than anything else I'd had recently. After a quick brush of my hair, I braided it to keep it out of the way.

"This is where you're hiding."

My heart raced and flutters filled my chest in response to Alec's voice.

I looked up, a smile on my lips. It was such a different feeling and reaction from how I felt whenever I saw Tyler. There wasn't conflict mixed in with the positive emotions.

"Just getting ready to go steal some royal jewels," I said.

"I'm not sure it counts as stealing if they belong to your family and you're not actually planning to keep them," he said.

"That's a good point. I hope you know, I have zero interest in being royal," I said.

"That's a plus in my book." He entered the room and sat down on the bed. Pink throw pillows shifted and Alec pushed them aside. Nobody was staying in the room and the bed was meticulously made with a floral quilt and dozens of pastel pillows.

I moved some of the pillows aside and joined Alec on the bed. He pulled me closer to him and I nestled into his warmth. His presence, his touch, and his scent were calming. I let myself soak in a few moments of him before my libido began to rise.

Frustrated, I jumped off the bed. My wolf protested. Now that Tyler was out of the picture, she was ready to move on. No mourning period necessary. Not that my human half needed it, but it was a surprise after all the trouble my wolf had caused me.

"I better go. Spencer moved up the timeline," I said.

"I know. I came to wish you luck."

"I hate that you can't go with me," I admitted.

"Don't worry, I won't miss out on the main event," he said with a grin.

My brow furrowed. "And what is that?"

"When you claim your pack and take down Ace," he said.

My stomach twisted into knots. "One thing at a time."

14

SPENCER TOUCHED the rock and the stone sealing Star's home moved. I'd seen Sheila and Alec do that, but they had been visiting Star regularly. "Wait, how did you know how to do that?" I looked over at Star. "Did you teach him that?"

"Nope, as far as I know, he's the first to figure it out on his own. I taught Alec and Sheila when we started working together," she said.

"Well? How did you figure it out? And how did you find us in the first place?" They were probably questions I should have asked before, but they wouldn't have changed anything. Plus, I'd been distracted by Alec's injuries, my mating bond, and the fact that my father was a royal. My mind had been a little preoccupied.

"I made a lot of friends with witches while I was living with the vampires. There wasn't much to do, so I learned as much as I could. See this little mark here?" Spencer pointed to a divit in the stone that could have been anything. "The key to get in isn't all that well hidden if you know what you're looking for."

"That just looks like a dent in the rock," Malcom said.

"It's too smooth and it's a near perfect fit for an index finger." Spencer walked through the entrance. Malcom and I followed. Once we were through, the rock rolled back into place.

"And here I thought I was clever. You better win this thing since my secret is out. I can't live here anymore," Star said.

"That doesn't explain how you found us," Malcom said.

"That should be obvious," Spencer said. "We're connected. I was in wolf form most of the time once I broke out. I felt you both any time you shifted. Though, I have to admit, I thought it was just one of you. The fact that you were together helped."

"I told you your magic wore off," I said to Malcom.

"Doesn't matter much now, does it?" he replied.

"Good point," I agreed.

"I thought I felt some lingering spells on you," Star said. "I guess dabbling in magic runs in the family."

"I learned my lesson," I said.

We walked out of the cave into the woods. A chill ran down my spine as I recalled how badly things went last time I'd ventured out here. In the end, I was free of the mating bond. But getting there wasn't easy.

"We just going to walk all the way to… wait, I have no idea where this house even is," Malcom said.

"Eugene," Spencer said. "Our family has properties all over the world, but he seems to like it there."

"That's close, right?" I was still a little fuzzy on where I was geographically. Another thing to add to my list for when this was all over. I was going to spend some serious time with a map to orient myself to the world.

"We'll be there in about four hours," Spencer said. "It's the only reason we can pull this off in time."

"I guess it's good he likes it out here," I said.

"It was our father, your grandfather's, least favorite house," Spencer said. "Growing up, we spent most of our time on the east coast. The packs there were very involved in the monarchy. I think he took up residence here to shut them out."

"Sounds like a stand-up guy," Malcom said.

"I only wish I'd have realized how dangerous he was sooner. If he hadn't directly threatened my mate, I might still be playing his games."

Spencer's words struck a chord with me. The two of us weren't really that different, after all. If not for Tyler, I'd have fled and hidden as a human for the rest of my life.

Instead, I had to fight more than I ever imagined. Not just to get out of the bond, but for myself. I wouldn't have ever shifted. Maybe I'd have even gone insane with time.

A nagging feeling pulled in my gut. Desire for something I wanted my whole life and never saw happening on this large a scale. Power. All those years I tried to fight back, knowing I would fail, I dreamed of being able to simply defend myself.

It wasn't just about defense. It was about claiming my right. As an alpha. As a royal. I just didn't know it.

"I'm glad I didn't sever my bond with you," I said suddenly.

"Oh yeah? Why's that?" Spencer asked.

"Because I deserve all the good things that are coming my way." It felt strange saying that, but it was true. I deserved happiness and respect. I even deserved love.

Tyler wasn't a mistake. He was a lesson.

Alec was my reward.

"You do," Malcom agreed. "And as soon as we win the

throne for our line, I'm going to help you take down that pack of yours."

"We're going to take them down, but I don't want to be the Alpha of Wolf Creek," I said.

Malcom stopped walking. "You don't have to challenge me for the throne. I will gladly pass it off to you if that's what you're thinking."

"I don't want that," I said with a laugh. "The only place I've ever been where I felt like I was home was at camp with you, Sheila, Alec, and all the others."

Spencer stopped walking and turned back to us. "It sounds like you found your pack."

"I did. Malcom didn't." I looked at my brother, understanding him a little better than I had before. "You kept your bags packed. You never shared your story. You never fully belonged. You're meant for something else. Something greater."

"I don't know about something greater," he said with a grin. "If we're being honest, I've been more at peace these last few days than I have my whole life."

"It's okay, I don't mind that you'll take the royal role. I'm going to get rid of Ace and I'm going to free Wolf Creek, but I'm not staying there when it's all done. I'm going home."

"What about Alec?" he asked.

"Did you know he has a mark?" I asked.

"We shifted together a hundred times. Of course I saw his mark," Malcom said.

I looked over at Spencer. "Why would we both have a mark?"

"Because you were marked for each other," he said. "Two halves of the same whole, remember? Nobody talks about it, but when an alpha finds their true mate, they both wear the mark."

"I thought women couldn't get a mark," I said. "How do they even know the male is the one who should rule if they both have one?"

"They don't," Spencer said. "They follow old-fashioned thinking and keep too many secrets."

"That's an understatement," I said. "We weren't even allowed to shift until we were nineteen in Wolf Creek."

"That place is more backward than most packs," Spencer said.

"And I thought witches were bad," Star said. "At least our covens don't care what you have between your legs."

"Witches and shifters have a long history of conflict, but I made a lot of friends with witches during my exile. I think it's time for things to change between us after I take the throne," Spencer said.

I wasn't really listening because I couldn't get the concept of dual marks out of my mind. Was it that same way for true mates for protectors too? Getting a mark from the goddess was rare, and so was finding your true mate. I wondered how often a mated pair like me and Alec happened. Plus, there was the mind-blowing fact that we'd both been fated to someone else when we got our marks. The fates really did work in strange ways.

"My mom doesn't have a mark," I said, suddenly. "Do you or does your brother? Do kings get marks?"

"Sometimes. I don't, and neither does Chris. Our father had a mark, as did our mother. My grandfather didn't and he ruled for sixty years. We aren't chosen for the job by the

Moon Goddess. It's passed down to us and as long as nobody challenges us, we maintain it."

"Sounds like a weak system," I said.

"Perhaps. But shifters like tradition. Only a member of the royal bloodline can throw down an official challenge. It takes a lot more for another line to attempt to take the crown." Spencer shrugged. "It happens every so often, but it's rarely effective."

"That's some fine print, old man," Malcom said.

"You'll be fine," Spencer said. "Usually the challenger is all ego."

"That doesn't make your current bid to challenge the king sound all that impressive," I warned.

Spencer laughed. "I always imagined that if I had kids they'd be little assholes, just like their old man."

I couldn't help but smile. "Well, I guess there's only one way to find out if you're full of shit or you have what it takes."

"So true." Spencer turned and started walking again.

We continued to hike through the woods for a while until I saw a car in the distance. "Is there a road ahead?"

"That's our ride," Spencer said. "And yes, that's a road. You didn't think I walked here from Chicago, did you?"

"I didn't really think about it at all," I admitted. It was an older grey sedan that looked like it had seen better days. There was nothing impressive about it, but as long as it got us there, I wasn't going to complain.

"Well, I'm glad we'll get to take a break from walking," Malcom said.

I climbed into the back seat of the car with Star, hoping it would provide me with a little more time to think. Malcom sat in the passenger seat next to Spencer.

The car rattled a little when the engine came to life, but it eased once we got going. Hopefully, it would hold out long enough for us to make it to the party.

We drove along a gravel and dirt road, the car vibrating and bumping, a cloud of dust following in our wake.

The whole group was silent for a while and Spencer looked like he was concentrating hard on driving.

"We need to pull over," Star said.

"You're not going to throw up, are you?" Spencer asked as he slowed the car.

"No, but I realized I need Malcom back here. I might as well start working on making his scent."

Spencer stopped the car. "Go ahead."

I didn't love the idea of sitting up front, but three crammed in the back was far worse. Especially since one of the party was a huge male wolf shifter. Malcom would probably take up two of the seats back here. He was going to be just as uncomfortable in the back as I was in the front.

I opened the door and stepped out of the car, going around the back to get to the passenger side. Malcom intercepted me, resting his hand on my arm for a moment. "If he does anything weird or anything feels off, you signal for me."

I nodded. Malcom didn't trust Spencer. I wasn't sure I did, either, but I didn't doubt our mission. Maybe I should have been questioning things more.

The two of us continued by. Malcom got into the back seat and I reluctantly took the front seat.

Nothing like a few hours next to your estranged father.

Spencer got us back on the road. It felt like he was driving fast, but I didn't have a whole lot of experience in cars.

Anything was faster than walking, which was my typical mode of transportation.

"When we get inside, I'll point you in the right direction for the crown and I'll be heading to the throne room," Spencer said.

"I'm not going to have to crawl under lasers or cut a circle in a glass case to get the crown out, am I?" I asked.

"You've seen too many movies," he said with a laugh.

"It isn't just sitting out is it?" I asked skeptically.

"No, but it's not exactly locked up," Spencer said.

"Elaborate?"

"Chris keeps it in his closet in his bedroom," Spencer said.

I pictured my tiny closet growing up. I didn't own a lot, but if I wanted to hide something in there, I could have buried it in a pile of dirty laundry. If he's got a large collection of clothing and other things, it might be difficult to find. "Is it well organized?"

"I don't think you'll have a problem finding it," he said.

The dirt road gave way to asphalt and the car got a lot quieter. The vibrations eased and I relaxed my shoulders a bit. Spencer drove past barns and sprawling fields of green. There were less trees here, but I could still see the familiar forest in the distance.

Before long, we were on a freeway, filled with cars. The sun was low in the sky. It was early evening already. My stomach was in knots. Each passing moment was taking us closer to the craziest thing I'd ever done.

Spencer was on his second attempt to overthrow his brother, nineteen years after the first. Most of us didn't go around challenging kings or even alphas. Here I was assisting in the first, and determined to succeed with the second.

"Why now?" It suddenly hit me that Spencer had waited nineteen years for this. Why hadn't he broken out sooner? Why bother trying to overthrow his brother again when he could just flee and live on a tropical island somewhere?

"What do you mean?" Spencer asked.

"Why did you wait so long to break out? And why do you even care who the king is? They locked you up and let him do whatever he wanted. Why take it over for yourself?"

"Why do you care about the people in your old pack?" He asked.

"That's not the same. I get the feeling you could have escaped years ago. Why didn't you?" I asked.

"Honestly, I gave up. Your mother left me when she found out what I planned to do. I thought she wanted out," he said. "I made friends with witches and vampires, I built a new life. I figured nobody missed me or cared. So many people I thought were my friends stood by and did nothing after I failed. I was in a dark place for a long time."

"What changed?" I asked.

He glanced over at me. "Your friend found me. Alec."

"And he convinced you that the shifter king was terrible?" I didn't hide my skepticism.

"He told me I had a daughter," he said. "Being a father was something worth fighting for."

15

"WOW," Star said. "Now I know where you got your cheesy shifter love fest from."

"I guess so," I said. "I certainly didn't learn it from my mom."

"Tell me about her," Spencer said. "You said she's not like she used to be."

"You don't want to know," I said.

"That bad?" he asked.

I hummed, not trusting myself to open my mouth and speak. My childhood had been miserable all around. Much of it could have been avoided had I been cared for by a parent.

"Well, Malcom should be all set," Star announced.

"You're sure?" Malcom asked.

"Pretty sure," she said.

"Guess we'll find out when I try to walk in the front door," Malcom said.

"I'm sure Star has you covered. Besides, she'll be with you and I have a feeling she can handle herself and take care of you," I said.

“That’s the truth,” Star said.

The drive felt less tense for a while as conversation turned in other directions. Star shared about her training as a witch, and Spencer shared about what vampires were really like.

Both conversations were very eye opening. I’d been so closed off from the rest of the supernatural world, but it turned out it might not be as scary as I feared. Of course there were bad vampires and witches, but there were also bad shifters. Hell, humans did terrible things to each other even without magic.

All the tension returned the second Spencer turned the car into a residential area. Streetlights lined the dark road and massive houses with sprawling yards appeared every so often. We were going up in elevation, the road winding in a spiral. The farther we went along the road, the more sparse the homes were.

“We’re close,” Star said. “I can feel it.”

“You can feel the king?” Malcom asked.

“I feel shifters,” she said. “First it was only humans. Now, I can sense the wolves.”

“It’s the house on the top,” Spencer said. “It used to be nothing around here. Lots of open space. Great for shifting and running. I think it’s why my dad wasn’t fond of this place. It was a little too built up and populated for his taste.”

“How does he run with all these houses?” They did have much larger yards than anything I’d seen in Wolf Creek, but it wasn’t enough to hide wolves running. Plus, there were so few trees. It looked like a terrible area to run.

“Was it all cleared out?” Malcom asked. “Where are the trees?”

“It’s a little unnatural feeling,” I added.

"It's the humans you're sensing," Star said. "They're the absence of magic. It makes things feel like a void. It's uncomfortable for many of us. It's why most supernaturals live in cities populated with many of our kind or in the hidden enclaves like where you grew up."

"That's it, up ahead." Spencer pulled the car over.

I looked at the house on the top of the hill. It stretched across enough space to be a dozen houses. A large semicircle driveway lined in white lights led up to a front entry. A row of cars snaked its way up, dropping passengers at the front doors before the cars drove away.

In the center of the driveway was an island of grass, complete with an ostentatious fountain. Everything about the home cried excess. It was the opposite of most of the shifters I'd grown up around. Sure, Ace's house was large and he had nice things, but it was a shack compared to this monstrosity.

"What now?" I asked.

"Now, you and I hand over the car. We're walking the rest of the way." Spencer opened his door and stepped out.

I removed my seat belt and exited the car. Malcom and Star got out of the back and closed the doors behind them.

"Guess we'll see you soon," Malcom said.

"Be careful," I warned.

He pulled me in for a quick embrace. "You too."

I watched as Malcom and Star drove away. "You think we can really pull this off?"

"We don't have much of a choice," Spencer said. "Come on. We might as well get it over with."

The house looked even bigger as we approached. I thought I'd be nervous, but the closer we got, the less worried I was. At least for myself. My goals had changed and I was far more concerned about Malcom and Star than I was for myself.

I wanted to help Spencer do this, but I was more interested in moving on from here. I had big plans and this was a step I needed to take. With a goal of liberating Wolf Creek rather than taking over, I was going to need the support of powerful wolves more than ever. I didn't know how to break the barrier, but I figured Star did. If she didn't have the skills, Spencer would probably be able to help. Assuming he came out of tonight alive.

I was finally starting to see how it was all connected. There was a reason I was doing all this. In all the years of wondering why I'd suffered so much, I was finally finding purpose. Don't get me wrong, I don't think it's okay that I had to go through hell, but I was going to wear my past like a badge of honor. No more fear.

Chin held high, I followed Spencer past an eight-car garage. A secondary driveway was lined with a dozen cars. Shifters in tuxedos were leaning against the cars, smoking cigarettes as they conversed. None of them noticed us. And if they did, they didn't care. I got the feeling these weren't guests. Drivers, maybe?

We continued around the side of the building and stopped at a door that probably led to one of the many garages. Spencer peeked in the window, his body tensed. I held my breath, worried I was going to give us away if I made any sound. Spencer's shoulders eased, and he turned the handle. To my surprise, the door opened easily.

"Seriously?" I whispered. "No locks?"

"You underestimate my brother's hubris. And his ability to monitor every inch of this place," he said.

"I guess that works to our advantage," I said.

"Come on." Spencer walked through the door and I followed. We were in the massive garage, complete with a collection of cars that was impressive even to someone who knew nothing about cars. Several sports cars, a few huge SUVs, and even a limousine. It was excessive even for a house of this scale. Who would have time to drive all these?

"You sure you're not doing this for the perks?" I teased, gesturing to the cars.

"Those were brought here from other places. My dad was really into cars. Something he and my brother had in common," Spencer said.

"Not you?" I was surprised.

Spencer looked around, then pointed to a bay at the back. "Those were mine." Six motorcycles, all covered in bags, sat abandoned and neglected.

"Daredevil type," I said. "Good to see your death wish extends beyond challenging the king. Way to stay on brand."

He chuckled. "No more dangerous than the way my brother drives."

We crept between the vehicles, toward an indescript back corner. Spencer began to run his fingers over the wall and I caught sight of a seam. This wasn't a solid wall. It was one of the passages he'd told me about. After a few more movements of his hands, Spencer must have found what he was looking for. The wall slid aside, revealing a passageway.

Now, I was feeling the nerves. We were a step closer to the reason we were here. So far, it had been creeping around. Now, it was getting far more real.

The tunnel beyond was pitch black. I took a deep breath as

I followed Spencer inside. The door closed behind us. There was no turning back now.

Hands extended in front of me, I inched forward, listening to Spencer's near silent footfalls. My eyes adjusted a little, but it didn't help much. I still couldn't see my hands in front of me.

"You sure you know where you're going?" I asked. "Didn't you say you only visited this place once?"

"You're fine, deep breaths," he said.

I rolled my eyes despite the fact that he couldn't see my frustration. The longer we walked, the more it felt like the walls were closing in around me. Which was possible since I couldn't actually see the walls.

There was no way of knowing if Spencer was directly in front of me or if he'd taken off at a run. My only guide was that I could still hear him. As that thought flickered inside me, I realized that wasn't entirely true. I could feel him.

Much the same way I could connect with my friends' emotions, I could feel Spencer's. They were tangled with my own thoughts, so I didn't notice at first. A mixture of excitement, fear, and a hint of doubt.

I really, really hoped the doubt was coming from me and not from him. We were all counting on him to pull this off. "Do you think Malcom is okay?"

"I hope so. He's the one who has to let me out on the other end," he said.

"What about me?" I asked.

"Your exit won't be sealed. I still have a few friends on the inside," he said.

"That's news to me," I said. "Why did you need to involve me and Malcom if you've got help?"

"I told you, if they got caught, they'd be killed. You can't be killed as easily," Spencer said.

"That's comforting," I said.

"It should be. Once I have Chris in a corner, and the other nobles bow to me, my friends in wait will help us."

"Seems like a big part of the plan you left out," I grumbled.

"It doesn't matter for what you need to do. And if we don't succeed, they'll never reveal themselves," he said.

"Why couldn't they open the entrance you need?" I asked.

"Because it's in the throne room. I have a feeling Spencer is aware of that tunnel and has it checked regularly. Especially since I used the tunnels to get to him last time," Spencer said.

"So we're using the same method that failed last time?" That was not reassuring.

"I improved on the plan," Spencer assured me.

Suddenly, I walked right into him, nearly knocking me to the ground. "What the fuck?"

"Shhh," Spencer warned.

"Why'd you stop without warning?" I hissed.

"We're here."

My eyes widened. "Here?"

"Step back a little, let me check." Spencer turned on the light on his cell phone.

"Why didn't we use that from the beginning?" The tunnel was illuminated and I glanced around, my eyes narrowed against the sudden bright light. The walls around us were brick and the ground was cement. I was pretty sure I saw a rat scurry away from the light. My stomach churned. What else was in here?

"Didn't want to draw attention." He took a few steps forward, then turned the light off.

"Stand back. I'm going to open it. If for some reason, it's occupied, we'll need to run," he said.

"That wasn't part of the plan," I mumbled. Seemed there was a lot unsaid when this was initially discussed.

"We're close to finishing this. Eyes on the prize, Lola. Get in, get the crown, find your way to the throne room. With that crown in your hands, nobody should mess with you," he said. "Just act like you're delivering it to the king if anyone sees you."

"More details that would have been nice before," I said.

"I'll take that into advisement for our next heist," he said.

"Great," I mumbled.

"Here we go," he whispered.

A door opened the same way the one had appeared in the garage. I held my breath as I tried to get a peek into the room beyond. My eyes weren't used to the light and they watered a little. In the chamber beyond the doorway, I saw a canopy bed, a sitting area around a fireplace, and a bearskin rug. I wrinkled my nose. Who had a bearskin rug?

"Looks clear," Spencer whispered.

I stepped forward, my whole body feeling like it was on overdrive. I was hyper alert, everything seeming to be firing at once.

"Good luck," Spencer said.

The door closed behind me. I was alone in the shifter king's bedroom with the goal of stealing his crown. After allowing myself a moment to let that sink in, I started looking around for the closet. The sooner I got this over with, the better.

"Where did you come from?" A smooth, cold male voice said.

My breath caught and I turned slowly to face the source of the words. A man who could almost be mistaken for Spencer's twin walked into the room. He was dressed in a perfectly tailored suit that fit him like a glove. Dark curls, dark eyes, strong chin, straight white teeth in a lecherous grin. He was handsome in a way that sent off alarm bells. Even if I didn't know he was the shifter king and my uncle, I would have fled had I met him in other circumstances. Everything about him screamed predator.

"You must be my birthday present," he said with a growl. "A little early. The party won't be over till well after midnight."

Oh. My. God. He thought I was here to fuck him. I held back the bile that rose to my throat and forced a smile. *Fuck.* Internally, I was screaming. I had to find a way out of this.

"It was supposed to be a surprise," I said, feeling dirty all over at the rouse. "I was instructed to surprise you after the party. I'm not ready yet and you are going to ruin your surprise, you naughty boy." My skin was crawling and I wanted to scrub my own mouth out with soap.

He held his hands up in front of him. "Okay, I can take a hint. I'll pretend I didn't see you."

I smiled with what I hoped was a playful expression. "Have fun at your party, your highness."

His eyes moved up and down my body, taking every inch of me in. He hadn't touched me, but I felt completely violated by his gaze.

"I have a feeling the party won't be nearly as fun as the afterparty with you later," he said. "Maybe I'll even bring a friend and we can make it a group event."

"You're the birthday boy," I said.

He kept his eyes on me while he walked to the side of the

room. He opened a door that I could see led to his closet. I only got a glimpse as he stepped in, grabbed something, and stepped out.

He closed the door, then walked over to me. I tensed, and fear gripped my chest. If he touched me, I was going to blow this whole thing.

The king took a deep inhale. "You're a wolf shifter. They usually send me human girls."

"Birthdays are special occasions," I said, hoping my voice wasn't as shaky as I felt.

"I look forward to the end of the party," he said.

I smiled, keeping my mouth closed for fear of saying something I shouldn't.

"I'll see you soon, little wolf," he called.

My stomach clenched and I felt like I'd been punched in the gut. It was the same thing Tyler had called me. The nickname used to make me feel small and powerless. I forced myself to remain as still as a statue as the shifter king leered at me.

Finally, he walked out of the room, closing the door and sealing me in. I waited for several long seconds, my heart pounding in my chest, worried that he'd turn around and decide to sample his supposed birthday present before the end of the party.

Moments passed, and the door remained closed. I finally blew out a breath. My whole body was shaking. I was so tired of powerful men who thought they could do anything they wanted. I was so tired of playing their games to keep them from harming me.

Things needed to change. Not just for me. Not just for Wolf Creek. All of it. I thought about Sheila's mark and how she'd been barred from her life's purpose because she had a vagina. It was the same for most female shifters. We were secondary, designed to help bolster the males around us. I was done with it. Done with feeling small.

Jaw clenched, fueled by pure rage, I stomped over to the closet and opened the door. Things were going to change. Starting now.

16

THE SHIFTER KING'S closet was no joke. I'd seen smaller houses. A row of drawers and shelves divided the space in half, creating two separate chambers. The walls on either side were lined with rows of suits and clothes on hangers. Two crystal chandeliers sparkled above me, one on each half of the space. At the rear of the closet, I saw an arched doorway leading to a dark space that wasn't lit by the same switch I'd used to turn on the chandeliers. I had a feeling that was where I needed to be.

I walked past the clothes toward the doorway. As soon as I passed through, lights flickered to life. My jaw dropped. I was staring at glass shelves lined with jewelry on black velvet cushions. Huge diamond necklaces, gold chains, rings with stones of every color. None of this should be so easily accessible. He seriously left a strange woman in his room with all this behind a simple door?

Hubris did not begin to define it. This was plain stupid.

In the center of the spread of gems and gold sat a surprisingly plain gold crown. It was simple and compared to the sparkling stones and jewels around it, it was a little bit of a letdown.

As Spencer had said, though, it was symbolic. I supposed it was one of those cases where age and sentimentality made something more valuable. I picked up the crown, half expecting an alarm to sound like in the movies.

Nothing happened.

Seriously? I was a little disappointed, though I had to admit, I was relieved. I didn't want to end up trapped in here by a door slamming down or lasers suddenly appearing.

So far, Spencer's plan was working. Aside from the unforeseen interaction with his brother.

I looped my arm though the crown and carried it out of the closet. When I reached the bedroom door, I recalled Spencer's suggestion that I pretend I'm delivering the crown. With a sigh, I repositioned my hands so I was holding it with more care. I felt ridiculous, but I'd already had one uncomfortable run in and it was possible I'd encounter more people.

As soon as I stepped out of the bedroom into the hall, I froze, realizing I had no idea where the throne room was. *Fuck.* We should have spent a lot more time going over these details.

I chose a direction and walked. The hallway was empty, and I passed by a few doors until I reached a staircase. I could hear sound coming from below. While I didn't want to run into people, there was a better chance that I was going in the right direction if I followed the sound.

Slowly, I descended the stairs until I reached the bottom. A dozen people turned and stared at me. *Shit.* I was in a kitchen, full of people in chef coats and matching uniforms.

"Can we help you?" A tall male in a white chef coat asked.

"Um, I'm supposed to deliver this." I lifted the crown.

"Who are you?" he demanded.

Well, there goes my contribution to the plan. All eyes were on me, expectantly waiting for my response.

"I told you, Monica, you need to change into your uniform before you begin working." A plump, younger woman with dark hair stepped forward. "Come on. You're going to get yourself fired before you even get your first paycheck."

The woman took hold of my upper arm and guided me through the kitchen. Everyone around us seemed unbothered by me anymore. They went back to calling out ingredients, filling trays with food, and bustling around the kitchen.

Nobody cared that a woman in regular clothes was walking around carrying the royal crown.

My guide led me to a small storage room. There was a rack of uniforms and a hamper full of dirty clothes. She closed the door, then turned to me. "What are you doing? Trying to get yourself killed?"

"Just delivering the crown," I said, not sure what else to say.

She rolled her eyes. "You're going to get all of us busted. It only takes one to let him know there are dissenters. You need to be more careful."

"Oh, yeah, that," I said. Apparently, she was one of my dad's helpers. But I got the sense she didn't have any clue who I was. "How much do you know?"

She raised an eyebrow. "You know better than to discuss anything here." She shoved a uniform at me. "Put this on."

I would blend in better dressed like an employee. Why wasn't that part of the original plan? I was going to have a serious talk with Spencer when we were finished with this about his lack of direction. I set the crown down on a pile of saran wrapped linens. Quickly, I removed my clothes and pulled on the navy-blue dress. It was a little big, but the other woman tied the belt around the back for me tight enough to cinch everything in.

"Thanks," I said, picking the crown back up.

"Don't fuck this up," she warned. "We can't keep living like this. We all need this."

I nodded, feeling a sense of responsibility to her even though we just met.

She left the room without another word, leaving me alone with the crown, surrounded by laundry. Mentally, I kicked myself for not asking where the throne room was. *Dammit.* I was terrible at this.

Figuring I'd play the new girl role if I needed to ask for directions, I left the storage room. The noise of the kitchen was behind me, and several employees in their matching uniforms walked past me carrying trays of food and glasses of champagne.

I followed them, my pulse racing as I moved forward. The sound of the kitchen faded, soon replaced by lively piano music and muted conversation.

I emerged into a ballroom, full of people. Little tables dotted the edges of the room and a glass ceiling above highlighted the waning moon.

Everyone was elegantly dressed and not a single person looked in my direction. I made my way toward the wall, moving forward through the ballroom, scanning for any signs of Chris, Spencer, or Malcom.

I was supposed to be in the throne room and this certainly wasn't that room. There was no throne in sight. Shit, there weren't even any chairs in here. Just high tables and a few bars where guests could grab a cocktail.

A set of double doors caught my attention. Fogged glass was inset into dark wood and they looked expensive and formal. That had to be a good sign.

I headed straight for the doors, hoping I was making the right choice. Just as I neared the doors, they opened, two huge males in tuxedos propped against each. A woman in a floor-length black sequined gown stepped between them. She clapped her hands. "Attention, everyone."

The music stopped and the chatter of conversation died down. I stood rooted to the spot, about ten feet from the doors. Slowly, I stepped closer to the wall, hoping to blend in more.

"It is time to pay our respects to the king. The throne room is now open." She gestured toward the open room behind her, then turned and walked inside. The males holding the doors maintained their position. I got the sense that they were not guests. They looked a lot more like guards.

Whispered conversation resumed as the guests pushed forward toward the open doors. Slowly, I weaved my way into the crowd, this time aiming for the center rather than the edges. I moved with the others, as if riding a current, past the guards and through the open double doors.

There was no mistaking this room was the throne room. The moment I entered, I was struck with pure opulence. Gold wallpaper, deep purple carpet, crystal chandeliers, and a raised dais in the rear, complete with an ornate, massive throne. Atop the throne sat the man I'd interacted with in his bedroom. Chris Lupton, the shifter king, himself.

I scanned the room, hoping to catch a glimpse of Spencer, Malcom or Star. In all the crowd, they should be easy to find. None of us had been in formal dress and I wasn't seeing anyone who stood out.

Where were they? Had something happened?

I waited in the middle of the crowd, not waiting to reveal that I had the crown sooner than I had to. The whole point was to use it as leverage for Spencer's alpha challenge. At this point, I was worried Chris would notice it and demand it brought to him before Spencer got to say his piece. What would happen when he recognized me as the woman from his room? He'd know I took the crown and followed him here.

With each passing second, I got more nervous. I looked around the room, wondering if there was a place I could hide the crown for now. In this dress, I could blend in well enough to probably hide in plain sight.

"Friends, this year is an extra special birthday," the king called.

Everyone went silent.

Fuck. I was stuck here. Out of options. Where was Spencer?

"As you know, my treacherous brother violated his exile by leaving the city of Chicago."

The crowd mumbled and hissed sounds of dissent. I bit down on the inside of my cheek to keep myself from saying anything.

Chris stood. "Since he has fled, I can't punish him. But I found an acceptable substitute." He nodded to someone and a door opened.

A pair of guards walked through, each of them gripping the upper arms of a woman bound in chains. I sucked in a breath and nearly dropped the crown in my hands.

They had my mother.

17

Chris rose from his throne and walked to the edge of the dais. He looked so fucking pleased with himself. "Friends, I give you my treacherous brother's true mate. She fled years ago, abandoning him. Honestly, that should tell you everything you need to know about him. Even his own mate didn't want him."

The shifters around me laughed. Some of them politely, nervously, but they all participated. My blood boiled and I gripped the crown tighter, feeling anger roared inside me.

My wolf was clawing at my chest, desperate to get out. She wanted to shred the shifter king to pieces. How dare he humiliate my mother like that? And how dare he put in a dig like that about true mates. The whole system was fucked. If someone wanted out, they should be allowed out.

The problem was, I don't think my mom wanted to be away from her mate. I got the sense that all her choices had been to protect me. It wasn't right. She wasn't supposed to be involved in this.

Where the fuck was Spencer? He needed to act. My mom

was dragged up to the dais. Her red hair hung in a matted mess in front of her eyes, her clothes were baggy and dirty. Everything about her made her look as pathetic and desperate as I remembered. Except now I knew better. She'd let herself be driven to madness out of desperation.

The gathered shifters continued to laugh. Some of them yelled insults. A few even threw things at her. Internally, I was seething. My wolf paced, more unsettled and angry than I'd ever felt her. This wasn't something we should have to endure. My mother shouldn't be here. Her life, and my life should be so different than it was.

What if she'd continued to shift? What if she'd taught me? Would Spencer have busted out and come for both of us? Or would I have never lived to see my nineteenth birthday?

There were so many questions but none of them mattered. I couldn't change the past. All I could do was be ready to offer the crown as soon as Spencer challenged the king.

"There's more, my friends!" The Shifter King lifted his hands in the air, effectively calming the jeering crowd. "I have two more surprises."

I held my breath, waiting for his words, terrified he was going to threaten to harm my mom. I wasn't going to be able to stay hidden in the crowd much longer. If he threatened her and Spencer wasn't here, I didn't have a choice. I would have to act. But what could I do? The king was surrounded by guards. What chance did I have to save my mom from him?

The doors burst open again and all eyes turned to see more guards with more prisoners.

My heart felt like it stopped and everything seemed to move in slow motion. Spencer and Malcom were being led into the room, their wrists bound in chains, a guard on each side.

They were marched up the dais and made to stand next to my mom. Both males looked unsteady on their feet, groggy and unfocused. Their expressions were blank and passive and neither of them appeared to be looking for me. What had they done to them?

Cries of surprise led to excited conversation through the crowd. Most of the shifters probably recognized Spencer. What the fuck was I supposed to do now? I couldn't leave them there, but if I acted, I would join them.

Someone grabbed my arm and I jumped, only barely managing to stifle a scream. "Shh." Star was by my side, her expression frantic.

"What happened?" I hissed.

"They grabbed them both as soon as Spencer came out of the secret passage," she said. "Dosed them both with that fucking toxin."

"Shit. What are we going to do?" I asked.

"I have the antidote, but I can't give it to them while they're on display," she said.

"You think they'll take them to a holding cell or something?" I asked.

"How would I know?" she whispered.

"Good point," I said. "We play it by ear, then."

Star and I waited silently for the king to speak. His eyes scanned the gathered shifters and he looked pleased. He was enjoying the confusion and excitement he'd caused.

It felt like the most impossibly long wait before he lifted his arm, the gesture extinguishing the sound around me. The room was deathly silent, everyone focused on the show unfolding before them.

"I had intended to use my brother's mate to lure him out of hiding, but the cocky bastard came to me before I even told anyone I'd snagged her." He shoved Spencer, causing my father to tumble and nearly fall to the ground.

My brow furrowed and my chest felt tight. Laughter filled the room again, the king's smile wide as he relished the humiliation he was dishing out.

Spencer had been so strong previously. The toxin wasn't just a way to eliminate shifting, it did terrible things to your body. When I'd had it, I was weak and could hardly concentrate. There were whole days I couldn't remember what happened to me. The worst part was it took time to wear off. Without that antidote, we weren't going to get any help from them for a while.

This was so bad. Our plan had no alternate. Spencer had been so confident that it would work correctly. Shit. I really should have put more effort into this. Everything about it was doomed from the start. It was less of a plan and more of a suicide run. I'd been far too distracted by everything else to really take notice.

"Since it is my birthday, I thought some spectacular entertainment would be in order." The king was grinning like a lunatic. "My assistant suggested fire eaters and circus performers, but an execution sounds so much more fun, doesn't it?"

The crowd erupted in cheers and applause. I'd never heard such unanimous support of something so bloodthirsty. My heart raced and my face felt hot. I looked around at the blurred mass of screaming shifters. The doors opened again, this time, a male walked in carrying a huge axe.

He was going to kill my family. Right now.

"Stop!" I shouted. My cries went unheard amid the chaos. I pushed my way forward, gripping the crown with one hand, holding it by my side. "Stop!"

Shifters shoved me and glared at me as I made my way toward the dais. They didn't like that someone else was moving closer to the gruesome main event.

Finally, I reached the front and I cried out again. "Stop this right now!"

Nobody on the stage even looked my way. It was impossibly loud and the man with the axe was climbing the dais, the weapon over his head like a trophy. The crowd roared its approval.

I had no choice. Moving as fast as I could, I reached the side of the dais where the stairs were. Quickly, I climbed up. The king and his guards noticed me now, all of them turning their attention to me.

"I thought you were going to wait in my room," Chris called, barely audible over the din. "Role play as my royal crown bearer is it?"

My upper lip curled in disgust. "Let them go."

His brow furrowed in confusion. "I'm sorry, it sounds like you were trying to give me an order. I don't know what you were told, but I'm not into that. I'm always the one in charge. In and out of the bedroom."

"First of all, gross. Second of all, I don't think I want you to be in charge anymore," I said.

The cheers had died down as the crowd noticed that

something was going on. The king's guards took a few steps toward me, but he held out his hand, stopping their progress.

"Are you challenging me?" He looked amused.

Was that what I was doing? I was done with these sick, twisted men in power. I was done being the damsel in distress. And I supposed there were worse ways to go than trying to save my parents and my brother. "Yeah, I am."

I held up the crown. "I challenge you for the crown."

Gasps and mummers rolled through the audience. They were loving every second of the drama.

"You're cute, but you can't. Only a royal can challenge a royal." The king waved his hand lazily. "Take her away. I'll deal with her later."

"Don't you lay one hand on me," I said.

To my surprise, the guards paused, confused by my words and my tone. I sounded more commanding than I ever had in my life and I was not about to apologize for it or back down. This was it. I had to do this.

"I'm your niece. Spencer Lupton is my father. And I am going to strip you of your crown."

18

"I'll give you one chance to walk away from this," the king said, his tone deadly.

Spencer's punishment already made my life forfeit. Even if they let me walk away tonight, I'd be hunted until they killed me. Aside from being ready to claim my true power, I wanted to live.

That had been it my whole life. Everything I'd done, everything I'd survived, had been a battle to stay alive. I wasn't about to lose now.

I was going to defeat this asshole.

I didn't ask for it, but the burden fell on me.

"Choose forms," I demanded.

He raised a brow. "You're really going through with this?"

"You really wanted to fuck your niece, you sick asshole," I said.

"I didn't know you were my niece," he said.

"You didn't know anything about me yet you were ready to engage in sex with me? Men like you give all men a bad name," I said.

"No, sweetheart. Men like me make the world go round. We get what we want when we want because that is our birthright."

"Are you going to accept the challenge or are you surrendering now?" I locked my eyes on his, unblinking, unwilling to back down.

He tried to mask his surprise, but he wasn't successful. I could feel his anger and confusion. There was something else there too that felt a little bit like fear.

I wasn't certain it was coming from him, but I hoped it was. He should be afraid. I had a decade of being the punching bag in my pack to help me prepare for this. I kept myself fit and I tried to teach myself to fight. I fought back whenever I could, I had lots of practice. The difference was, I wasn't a wolf then. I was weaker, slower, smaller.

Now, I had found my wolf. She was fired up. She was ready. And we were going to work together as a team to save my family.

"Choose. Your. Form." I kept staring, daring him to back down.

"You're from Wolf Creek, right?" he asked.

"I'm from nowhere special," I said.

He smirked. "You just started to learn how to shift recently and I know your alpha keeps you all weak on purpose. You do this, I'm not holding back. You might not make it to surrender before your body gives out."

"I'll take my chances."

"Alright. We shift. We fight as wolves," he said.

My wolf practically leaped for joy. She wanted out now and she was ready. It was true that we hadn't had training the way others had, but I was scrappy and she was strong. When we were in synch, there was no telling what we could do. I had faith that we'd come out of this alive.

"We're taking this party outside," the king called.

The audience cheered and flooded toward the doors out of the throne room.

One of the guards grabbed my arm. "This way."

"Don't touch me again." I pulled my arm away.

He grinned, showing several missing teeth. "Next time I touch you it'll be to drag your lifeless body away."

I scowled. "I hope you're prepared to go down with your asshole boss."

He laughed and walked away. I glanced around. Everyone was distracted with the change of scenery. Guards still held on to my family, but even they were looking at the crowd rather than their charges.

I bolted over to them. Malcolm was the nearest to me so I stopped in front of him. "Hey, Malcom. You okay?"

His head lolled to the side and his eyes were glassy and unfocused. "Lola?"

"Yeah, it's me. It's going to be okay. I'm going to get you out of this." I wanted to say more, to comfort him, but he wasn't going to remember this anyway.

The guard holding Malcom pulled on him. "Get outta here. You're not supposed to be talking to them."

I glared at him. "You are a monster, you know that?"

He leaned closer to me, his teeth bared. "You better not lose. Good luck."

I took a startled step back, unsure if his words were a threat or meant as encouragement. His tone made it so they could go either way. Was it possible he was one of the people working with Spencer?

"Ladies first," a voice called.

I glanced behind me and saw the king smiling at me. I rolled my eyes. He was such a sorry excuse for a ruler. Just another bully like Ace.

"Don't worry, little wolf, I'll have your family brought out to watch you take your last breaths," he said.

The reaction my wolf had to his taunting was visceral and almost painful, I had to hold her down to keep her from shifting right here. She wanted out. She wanted blood.

I walked forward, leaving the dais. Most of the crowd had dispersed but I followed the lingering few out the doors, through the ballroom, and into an open courtyard.

The crowd parted for me and I walked into the center of a circle of onlookers. We were surrounded by the home on all four sides. It made the air feel unnaturally still. I stood in the middle of a huge square of pavestone. To the side were chairs and trees with a few tables around. The center was wide open with the exception of a fountain on one end. It appeared to be a mermaid with water coming out of her head. Everything about the decor here was over the top to the point of being cheesy rather than impressive. I wondered if that's why my paternal grandfather had avoided this place or if the decor choices were made under the recent occupant.

A moment later, the crowd parted again and Chris Lupton, the shifter king himself, walked into the circle. The gathered shifters cheered and whooped, making their final bid of allegiance to the candidate they thought would win. I didn't blame them. I was nobody and I was so much smaller than my opponent.

He'd had years of shifting and fighting under his belt. I was new to everything. There was a good possibility I wouldn't live past tonight, but I refused to fully acknowledge that. I sent the thought away, determined to tempt fate again.

I'd done it so many times before, what made tonight different? I'd lived through injuries that should have killed me and when I'd been trapped in a cave to die, I'd emerged stronger than ever. Okay, fine, I was at death's door a few days ago and my wolf saved me, but that experience brought me my wolf. With her, I was capable of anything. I knew I had yet to even touch on what was possible when we connected.

The king began to strip his clothes, tossing them to the side, near the crowd. I wasn't thrilled with the idea of walking around naked in front of so many people but that was likely what he was counting on. It wasn't like I hadn't been naked in front of lots of people I'd just rather keep my clothes on. I could play his game. It was just skin.

I unbuttoned the uniform I was wearing and let it fall to the ground before kicking it aside. Out of the corner of my eye, I noticed a commotion in the crowd. I turned to see Spencer, Malcom, and my mom being shoved front and center to watch. None of them looked like they were aware of anything happening around them. They weren't even going to remember this when it was over. Maybe that was a good thing. However this went down, Spencer was going to be pissed that his plan failed.

The guards holding my family looked distracted already and the fight hadn't even started. I considered trying to make a run for it. Should I grab them and take off? Realistically, I wasn't going to be able to pull that off. And honestly, I wasn't sure I wanted to. For once, I wanted to stand on my own and face the bully. Another familiar face caught my attention and I smiled as I realized that Star had managed to get right next to my family. I knew she'd get that antidote into them if possible.

I turned my attention back to the king. He was so busy encouraging his adoring fans that he hadn't noticed I was distracted for a moment. While I'd been checking out the crowd, he'd been getting then to cheer for him. It was a little pathetic how much he seemed to need the adoration and support.

My lips curled into a smile as a dark thought struck me. How adoring would they be if an unknown female shifter kicked his ass?

An unusually small male shifter broke from the group and walked over to the king. His whole demeanor was timid and shy. My brow furrowed as I watched him approach the much larger male.

Chris's expression was just as curious as my own. The smaller shifter said something, then pointed to me. The king looked up at me as if seeing me for the first time.

"You're sure?" he asked.

The small shifter nodded.

"Come on, start the fight!" someone called from the now quiet crowd.

The Shifter King glared at me, his eyes dropping to my hip. "You have a mark?"

"Yes." There was no denying it. I was naked and it wasn't like I was hiding it. Honestly, I was surprised the king took so long to notice. "If you'd spent less time being a peacock, you might have noticed sooner."

"That mark doesn't mean anything," he said.

"Sure," I said. "Of course not. Kings aren't given marks since they inherit the crown with blood or some bullshit."

"The old king had the mark," a woman's voice called.

I turned and saw the woman who'd helped me earlier. She was still in her uniform, standing out among the guests in their party finery.

"The king should be an alpha," she said. "You have always been and always will be a fraud."

"You think because she has the mark she should be king?" Chris laughed. "Just because my father had the mark, didn't mean anything. Neither of his children had the mark. It proves nothing."

"It proves that the Moon Goddess knew that neither of you were fit for the job," he said.

A pair of guards closed in on the woman but she held her chin high.

"Leave her alone!" I called.

"She's right," the king said. "Let her watch her hopes and dreams bleed out in front of her. Then we'll add her to the execution line up."

Chris turned his gaze back to me. "It's funny, tonight I thought I'd be executing your mom. Instead, I get to wipe out your entire family. And you are the opening act."

His body shuddered and he doubled over as he began the change. Fur sprouted along his skin, his bones cracked and broke, his limbs in unnatural directions.

My wolf howled internally, ready for release. I let her take over, guiding me through the change.

19

THE SHIFTER KING'S wolf was impressive. His fur was a pale gray with black markings and he was just as large as the other powerful males I'd seen. While I was confident in my wolf's abilities, I was at a disadvantage based on size. Unless I found a way to use that.

My wolf was practically vibrating with pent-up anger. She wanted to make the larger wolf pay for what he'd done to Spencer, Malcom, and Mom. She wanted to make him pay for enabling shifters like Ace to continue their abuse of power. I wanted to humiliate him.

The two of us seemed to be on the same page. Equal partners, our minds working together as two halves of the same whole. We'd only shifted a few times, but we'd never been this connected. We were finally working together as we should.

The king's wolf circled me, his strides long and confident. He moved slowly, the muscles in his back and shoulders rippling with his motions. Each step was intentional and focused. I could tell he was trying to intimidate me. That was not going to happen.

Sure, I might go down tonight, but I was going to make him work for it. Best case, I took him down. My wolf's chest was full of hopeful, excited flutters at the thought of victory. It was the only solution she saw. She was right, I needed to get on board with the optimism. Match her fire. *Fine. We win this, then.*

I thought back to one of my few conversations with Spencer. What had he said about my instincts? My mind whirred, trying to recall the only fatherly advice he'd given me.

Suddenly, it came crashing back to me. He told me to trust my wolf. That I needed to start going on the offensive instead of always reacting. That was my whole life. I didn't start anything, I defended myself. I never fought to win. I fought to survive.

I wasn't going to get out of this unless I was trying to win. Which meant, I needed to attack first.

Baring my teeth, I growled and tensed before launching myself forward, claws out. I landed on the king's back, digging into his flesh, using every ounce of my strength to pull him down.

He twisted, throwing me from him. I hit the ground hard, knocking the wind from my lungs. In the past, I might have stayed down, or hesitated. But my wolf took over, getting me up to face my opponent without pause. *Instinct.* I needed to rely more on it. More letting my wolf take point when she had the upper hand, and my human side kicking in when it served us better. That was the only way this was going to work.

The king lunged forward, but I'd had years of experience dodging attacks. I moved out of the way quickly enough that it sent him flat on his face, coming up empty handed.

He growled and snapped his jaws, turning toward me in a heartbeat. This time, his blow was successful and he managed to knock me to the ground. His wolf had me pinned and a flicker of panic rose inside me. My wolf squashed the feeling down. She bit the other wolf's shoulder, digging her teeth in until we tasted blood.

With a howl, he loosened his position enough that I was able to shimmy away. *You attack, I'll defend.* My wolf seemed to be in agreement. I released my hold, letting her take over the fight. She charged just as the king moved forward. I saw that he was going to have the upper hand and I took over, changing our position just enough that we avoided most of the impact. It was enough to throw our attacker off guard and I quickly relinquished control back to my wolf side.

She swiped her claws across the king's face. He lunged forward, managing to return the action. It felt like my face was on fire from the cuts but I'd been through worse. I growled. *Come at me, asshole.*

The king was hesitating, waiting for something. I wanted to react instead of take charge, but I remembered our strategy and I passed off control again. My wolf leaped into the air, landing on top of the king again. This time, when he tried to throw us, we hung on, rolling with him.

My wolf bit him again, making the king yelp as we rolled together across the courtyard. When he tried to gain control and pin us, I took over, using my skills to shift our weight and prevent us from getting under him.

When we stopped rolling, my wolf was on top. I growled down at him. The king snapped his jaws at me and wiggled under my hold. He was larger and stronger and I knew I couldn't out match him until he was more tired or a lot more injured.

Before he could turn the tables, I jumped off of him, giving us some space before he could charge us again. As the king righted himself, he moved a lot more slowly. He wasn't as cocky as he had been when we started.

I waited, staring him down, daring him to charge. I could do this for hours. Short attacks and lots of dodging his blows. There was a possibility I could wear him down enough to beat him.

The king paced in front of me, his wolf keeping his gaze on me. He looked confused. Pissed, but confused. A rush of devious joy shivered through me. I'd caused him to question his tactics and rethink his strategy.

He didn't have a strategy.

Once again, I didn't know if the thought was mine or my wolf, but it rang true. He didn't think he'd have any trouble with me. His whole plan was brute strength and physical dominance. He wasn't counting on someone agile who could outmaneuver him.

His body tensed and I knew he was going for it, but his position was off. I almost missed it, but the human side of me caught the adjustment he made and I knew he was going to feign his attack. He was trying to use my own game against me.

Quickly, I moved just as he changed his angle, and his teeth grazed my back rather than striking true. Passing the baton back to my wolf, I let her veer around and go in for another attack. She swiped her claws along his side as we passed, digging in deep.

He howled in agony but my wolf didn't relent. She pivoted and returned, striking another blow to his face.

The king was dazed and unprepared for our agility. He couldn't move as fast as my wolf. As soon as he adjusted, we were back at him, teeth or claws at the ready.

We knew we weren't strong enough to hold him down or break him the same way he could do to us, so our attacks had to be different. Instead of playing into power and trying to be flashy, we were relentless and quick. Each attack in and out.

The king's wolf struck back a few times. He even managed to pin us again. But every time, we wiggled out and got him again.

I was starting to feel exhaustion kick in and my movements were growing slower. If we didn't wear him down soon, we were going to be in trouble.

The king was limping now, but he wasn't done yet. In a move I didn't see coming, he charged us, knocking my wolf to the ground. I gasped and let out a yelp as we landed, my head hitting the stone. My vision blurred, and I felt a little nauseous. That was a major blow and I wasn't sure I was going to be able to get up right away.

We were in a tight spot, claws digging into our chest, flat against the ground. The king's wolf growled, teeth bared. He leaned closer and I was terrified he was going to rip my wolf's throat out.

My wolf seemed to growl internally. As if she was mad at me. Just as I was about to snap back at her in my head, I realized I'd slipped up. I was letting the human part take the lead. Usually if we were pinned, I could get us out, but right now, the human part of me was fuzzy and injured.

I relinquished control, letting my wolf take charge. *Get us out of this.*

With a movement that caused searing pain, my wolf twisted. The king's claws tore through our skin, but with another movement, one of his paws was off and my wolf pushed on until we were back in control. The king's wolf was under us and now our claws were digging into his chest.

I felt the tension ease from the wolf below us. He was tired and it was as if all the fight was suddenly gone. We could end this right now. All we had to do was bite his neck or some other equally horrifying thing.

This was what we signed up for. We wanted the power, we wanted to make the bad guy pay. The problem was, I didn't want to become the thing I hated. I wanted to stand up for others and defend myself. I didn't want to hurt others.

I growled, showing my teeth. It didn't have to end this way. There was another way out. He could surrender. He could go into exile. Death wasn't the only option.

Was he going to take the chance or was he going to make me do it?

My wolf was impatient. She was worried we were being too soft. Or that he was faking to earn sympathy. *Just a little longer.*

I had to figure this out. I wanted this. I wanted to win. But I didn't want to be like him.

Suddenly, his body began to shudder, bones cracked, and he yelled in agony. I leaped off him just before the fur gave way to flesh.

A few minutes later, a broken, bloody, pathetic looking old man was hunched over on all fours, panting. He looked up at me and I could see the rage and embarrassment in his expression.

I was still in my wolf form, which meant, I had not yielded.

At least I listened enough in history class to understand how an alpha challenge worked. It was odd that while so many other things had seemed trivial, understanding this had seemed vital.

Maybe this was why.

Maybe I always wanted to defeat the alpha and reclaim the power that had been stripped from me.

I growled, taking a few steps toward my opponent. While he had shifted back into his weaker human form, he was still in play unless he formally yielded. I wasn't going to be tricked into a draw. I had to be in wolf form until I either killed him or he surrendered.

The king rose to his knees. The deep slashes on his sides were already healing, but he was in for a long, painful night. He turned his gaze on me, still taking in deep breaths.

Killing him might have been more merciful. He didn't deserve mercy and I didn't deserve to have his death on my hands.

I growled again. *Submit.*

The king looked around at the spectators. I'd forgotten they were there. Risking a quick glance, I realized they were all silent. Nobody spoke. Nobody laughed. Nobody cheered.

They were witnessing the fall of a king.

When he turned to look at me again, I saw the defeat in his eyes. He lowered his head. "I submit."

I growled, a warning. He needed to say it louder and he needed to make it clear. I took a step forward, letting my wolf tense and threaten him with everything I had left.

He flinched but he understood. "I submit. I surrender. Long live the queen."

20

Silence had never been so overwhelming. Nobody in the gathered group said a word. There was no movement, no wind, no anything.

I lifted my chin, hoping I didn't look as exhausted and relieved as I felt.

Then, his words hit me.

Queen.

That was how it worked, but I hadn't thought that through. I wanted the power, I wanted to win. But I'd said I didn't want to be queen. Even if it was exactly what I knew I needed.

Once, being a part of the feral shifters would have been enough. Now, queen was what I needed. The whole system was broken. The only way to repair it was from the top.

I turned toward movement and noticed that Spencer and Malcom were fighting their restraints. I padded over to them, still in wolf form and growled at the guards.

"She wants you to release them," Star said.

The guards looked from her over to their fallen king. He didn't lift his head. I growled again.

"Release them. On order of your queen," Star said.

To my surprise, the guards did as ordered. Spencer and Malcom rubbed at their wrists. My mother didn't react. She looked like she was still in a toxin induced stupor. How much had they given her?

My wolf was tired. She was ready to let the human side take over. I glanced back at the disgraced king. Dethroned by a nineteen-year-old nobody. Elation mingled with surprise, making me feel both powerful and terrified. When I'd come here, I wasn't expecting any of this. I had claimed far more than I anticipated, but deep down, it felt right.

Siting back, I let my wolf guide us through the change. My body shivered, then rippled as bones reformed and my body twisted from wolf to woman. The change was easy this time, the minor pain was over before I had time to react.

I rose from my crouched position and looked out into the faces staring at me. I was probably supposed to say or do something, but I wasn't sure if there was a specific protocol and I was afraid I'd fuck it up.

Spencer joined me in the center and he grabbed my hand, then lifted it in the air. "I present your queen."

The silence broke with an explosion of cheers and hollers. The crowd applauded and reacted as if I was the one they'd been waiting for their whole lives. I was sure some of it was an act, but in the moment, it didn't matter. My heart felt full and I relished the moment of celebration.

I'd come from nothing. I'd held no power. I wanted to show them all. In my wildest dreams, I never thought this was how I'd accomplish my revenge.

I lowered my arm, still holding Spencer's hand. Leaning close to him so only he could hear me, I spoke, "I'm sorry I challenged him."

Spencer smiled. "Don't ever apologize for that. I never wanted to be king. I just thought it was the only option. Now, you need to figure out what you're going to do with him."

I glanced over at my uncle. Without his cocky grin and entourage, he no longer looked impressive. He had pulled on his clothes and was staring at me. "What's your sentence, your highness?"

I looked at Spencer. "What would you do?"

"Exile sounds like a good punishment," he said.

"You can't exile me, you have no authority," Chris spat.

"There's always execution." Malcom joined us, the housekeeper who had helped me by his side.

"Exile sounds like a good choice," Chris added quickly.

"Don't ever let me see you again," I said. "I don't care where you go or what you do, but if you ever come near me, my friends, or my family, I will take my brother's suggestion."

A couple of guards appeared on either side of the former king. "You want us to get rid of him?"

"Wow, nobody liked you, did they?" I asked. "I mean, I'm grateful they're ready to switch sides, but it goes to show how bad you were at your job."

One of the guards was fighting against a smile. "We're happy to remove the trash for you, your highness."

"Please do," I said.

They hauled him away, presumably taking him off the grounds. I was proud of myself for holding back and not killing him and I hoped he was smart enough to keep his distance.

"Thought you might want these, your highness," the housekeeper woman held up my black pants, shirt, and jacket that I'd abandoned in the storage closet.

"Thank you," I said. "Seriously. For everything." I pulled on my clothes, grateful for the warmth.

She smiled. "We waited a long time for someone to stand up to him."

"What's your name?" I asked.

"Claire," she said.

"Do you like your job, Claire?" I asked.

She laughed. "I'm pretty sure I got myself fired tonight."

"I think your boss is the only one who got fired tonight," Malcom said.

"What are you good at, Claire?" I asked.

Her smile faded and she looked down at her hands.

"What's wrong?" My brow furrowed. Had I offended her?

She looked up. "I had a mark once. I was meant to be a protector. I'm not sure if I'm good at it, because they didn't let me try."

"Do you want to try?" I asked.

She shrugged. "Maybe."

"My friend Sheila had a mark too," I said. "You'll have to meet her."

"You're queen now, Lola," Spencer said. "You'll need your own close guard. Sheila and Kyle can't do it alone."

My lips parted as I considered his words. I hadn't just inherited a title, it was a job with lots of working parts. "You're right." I turned to Claire. "If you're interested, I'd love to have you."

"I'll consider it," she said.

"What do you want to do about the rest of these people?" Malcom asked. "Should we send them home?"

"It is all set up for a party in there," Claire offered.

I grinned. "Well, we shouldn't let a good party go to waste."

"Everyone back inside. We've got a coronation to celebrate!" Malcom called.

The gathered shifters cheered again and headed back to the house. My head was spinning from how quickly everything had changed.

"Claire, would you be willing to take my mom inside and help her get comfortable?" My mom was the only one who didn't appear to have recovered from the toxin yet. Or it was all the drugs and everything else she'd done over the years finally catching up to her.

Claire nodded. "Of course. I'll take care of her."

I watched my mom led away by the near stranger. It was an odd sight. My mom had yet to even acknowledge that she was aware of my presence. My chest tightened. It hurt that she wasn't part of this but helping her was going to take time.

The problem now was what I was supposed to do next. Was I going to be attacked the moment I walked into that building? It was possible my victory was going to be very short lived.

"Was he really that hated?" I asked. "None of these shifters seem to care that there's a new leader."

"Close your eyes," Spencer instructed.

I lifted a confused brow.

"Just do it," he commanded.

With a sigh, I closed my eyes.

"Now, clear your mind, and think about the energy and emotions you can feel. Simply feel."

I took a deep breath and tried to not worry about all the things that had just happened. After a few breaths, new sensations began to flood into my head. Fear and joy, pain and pleasure, happiness and sorrow. A million emotions and a million connections. My eyes snapped open. "What was that?"

"It's all the alphas. You are connected to them. With practice, you'll be able to use that power for good." He shrugged. "Or evil, I suppose. Depending on what kind of ruler you are."

"They can't go against you," Malcom said. "The only one who can challenge the king or queen is a blood relative. They physically can't fight you. They don't have much of a choice other than to follow you."

"That sounds like a terrible system," I said. "What if I go nuts and abuse my power?"

"Then I'll have to challenge you," Malcom teased.

"I'm serious," I said.

"There are ways around it, but they aren't easy. It's why Chris's lack of an heir was such a big deal," Spencer explained.

"Guess you better have a few kids so if you are drunk with power, they can take you out," Malcom said.

I elbowed him. "I'm not ready to think about kids, thank you. But I do wish Alec was here. And Sheila and Kyle. They should be here."

"I can make that happen," Star said. "Wanna give me your car keys?"

"Give my keys to the blind witch?" Spencer said. "I don't think so."

"That's insulting. You know I have ways of seeing without my eyes." Star set her hands on her hips.

"I'll go. You stay and make sure Lola doesn't go challenging anyone else tonight." Malcom stepped toward me and pulled me into a hug. "I'm proud of you."

I squeezed him tight. "Thank you. You're going to help me with this, right?"

"Till the end," he said. "You're stuck with me now."

I laughed as I released him. "Lucky me."

21

Most of the guests found their way back into the house and I was left standing outside with Spencer, Star, and a few lingering males in security uniforms.

"You don't need to stand out here with me," I said.

"We do, we swore to protect the king. That means we stay to protect you," one of them said.

I looked at Star. "Is that blood magic still binding everyone here?"

"Yeah," she said. "It's holding strong."

"I don't want it to," I said.

The guards shifted uncomfortably. "The blood magic has always been used for security. It's how we stopped the last attempt. No offense." He nodded to Spencer. "You know we were all pulling for you."

Spencer growled. "I lost friends that day."

"We all did," another guard added. "We all gave up on ever seeing the king's reign end that day as well."

"I'm not going to rule that way," I said.

"It's going to take me a few weeks to get rid of all the blood magic," Star said. "But I can disable enough tonight so that our friends can step foot on the property at least."

"That's a start," I said.

"Wait, does that mean I've got the job?" Star asked. "I had an agreement with your old man, not you. He was supposed to be king tonight."

"Foiled again, were you, Spencer?" One of the guards asked with a smirk.

I bit down on my lip to keep from laughing. It was kind of funny.

"Are you kidding? I won tonight. Chris is gone, and I don't have to do the work of a king." Spencer grinned.

"What about your mate?" I asked.

Spencer's smile faded. "She's far worse than I expected."

"I tried to tell you," I said.

"How long were they giving her the toxin?" he asked. "I've never seen a shifter who was given it for such a long time."

My eyes widened and my jaw dropped. Was that what she'd been taking? "She was always popping pills. I never asked what it was. I didn't know…"

"You think she did it on purpose?" Spencer was shocked.

"She was adamant that I not shift. Terrified you'd find me. What if she got hold of the toxin and dosed herself to keep from shifting?" I wasn't sure why the thought hadn't crossed my mind before. When I'd experienced the toxin, I'd been a wreck. No wonder my mom couldn't keep her shit together.

"She's going to need a major detox. And a lot of antidote," Star said. "I don't know if it'll work, but I'll see what I can do to help her."

"Thank you," I said.

Star let out an exaggerated sigh. "I guess I'm on the clock

already. Tearing down blood spells and saving your mom. My salary better be really high."

I laughed. "I don't know how any of that works but I will make sure you get top dollar."

"I've been away a long time, but I'm sure I can help you figure out the transition to the job," Spencer offered. "But right now, I want to go with Star and check on your mom."

I nodded. "Go."

Star and Spencer walked toward the house, leaving me with the group of guards. There were four of them, standing a few feet from me, waiting silently.

"You all want to keep doing this?" I asked.

They nodded.

"Well, if you're going to be following me around, we're going to have to drop some of the formality and get to know each other."

The guard that spoke earlier smiled. He took a step forward. He was a huge shifter with a close-trimmed black beard and cropped black hair. "I'm James, Your Highness."

"Nice to meet you James, I'm Lola. You don't need to use the title," I said. It felt weird and I wondered if I'd ever get used to it.

"Yeah, I do," he said. "But I'll save it for when other people are around."

"Alright," I said.

The other guards introduced themselves and I could feel some of the tension easing from them. We were going to be spending a lot of time together and it was nice to start to get to know them.

"James, Malaki, Ruben, and Cole," I said, pointing to each of them in turn.

They smiled and nodded. "You got it," James said.

"Well, gentlemen, should we head in and see what everyone else is up to?" I asked.

"After you, Lola," James said.

I took a deep breath and marched forward. Music and flashing lights greeted us in the ballroom. They really had gone full swing into the party. Shifters in blue uniforms carried trays of food, bartenders poured drinks at stations set up in the corners, and nearly everyone was dancing.

I was by far the most underdressed person at the party, but I was certain nobody was going to say anything. Shifters waved and called to me, some of them bowing or using my newfound title as I weaved between the crowd. With the adrenaline wearing off, I was starting to feel stiff and sore from the fight.

My wounds would heal with time, but it was going to hurt until they did. My uncle had not held back in his attacks.

After I walked around the room a few times, I asked James if there was a place I could freshen up. My guards were quick to surround me and lead me away from the noise of the party.

Shifters knew how to celebrate, and I was pretty sure they'd continue late into the night whether I was there or not.

We walked down a hall lined with landscape paintings and past a library overflowing with books. I paused to take it in. The shelves were two stories high, complete with sliding ladder. I had a feeling my uncle never opened a single book.

I resumed walking, telling myself I could ask for a tour later when there weren't a whole ton of shifters having a party a few rooms away. Finally, my entourage stopped in front of a door.

"This is a guest suite," James said.

"Thank you." Everything ached and the healing wounds felt tight every time I moved, irritating them. I needed to get them cleaned and I needed to rest.

"Can you let my friends know where I am?" I asked.

James nodded. "I'll stay at your door. Cole will find your friends."

"Alright." James must be the leader. I was sure there was some kind of hierarchy. There was so much for me to learn but most of it was going to have to wait.

I let myself into the room and found a light switch on the wall near the door. When I flipped it on, I gasped. Much like my uncle's room, every inch of this room screamed luxury. A fireplace was inset to the wall on my right. A couch and two chairs formed a horseshoe facing it. In front of me was a four-poster bed with plush bedding and a dozen pillows. Several expensive looking rugs were strategically placed around the room. On either side of the room were arched doorways. I caught a glimpse of a bathroom beyond one and a closet beyond the other.

I shook my head as I made my way to the bathroom. I was never going to get used to this.

Carefully, I peeled my clothes off my injured and dirty body. The fabric stuck to the drying blood and I winced as I pulled it from my wounds. They were healing, but most of the injuries were deeper than I was used to. Sleep would probably help speed it up.

There was so much I needed to figure out, so much I needed to learn about my new role, but exhaustion was setting in.

I stepped into the huge shower and turned on the dual shower heads. Water came at me from both directions and I stood there, soaking in the warmth and breathing in the steam. Okay, so maybe I could get used to a shower like this.

Reluctantly, I finished washing up and turned off the water. I didn't have a plan for what I was going to do next, but the last time I'd had a plan, it had failed spectacularly. Maybe things went better for me when I followed my instincts and didn't overthink everything.

I dried off and walked over to the closet, hoping I'd find something to wear. To my surprise, it was stocked with several varieties and sizes of pajamas. I supposed that made sense for a guest room. I found a pair of flannel pants and a button up shirt and put them on. If I had to return to the party, I'd look pretty strange, but I was hoping I could hide out here the rest of the night.

A knock sounded on the door and I quickly finished buttoning my top before heading over to it. Opening the door a crack, I peeked out.

James filled the whole opening. "You have a visitor, your highness."

I winced at the title, but he'd warned me he'd use it in front of others. I opened the door wider, expecting to see Spencer or Star. Instead, I was greeted by the exact person I wanted to see more than anyone else.

"Do I need to bow?" Alec asked.

I smiled and laughed. "That depends. Does the king have to bow to the queen?"

Alec lifted a brow. "Are you proposing to me?"

I shrugged. "Not yet. But there are other things I'd like to do with you."

James cleared his throat.

My eyes widened. I forgot he was there. I grabbed Alec's

shirt and pulled him into the room. Someone, probably James, closed the door for us.

"How the fuck did you come here with the plan to help steal a crown and end up taking the crown for yourself?" Alec asked.

"It's been a wild night," I said.

"I heard. Malcom filled us in." He slid his arm around my waist and pulled me close. "You are such a badass."

"You're not intimidated, are you?" I teased.

"I'm turned on," he admitted.

"Good, cause I have plans for you." I stood on my tiptoes and pressed my lips to his.

He pulled away. "Wait."

I stepped away from his embrace and crossed my arms over my chest, hurt. My cheeks flushed with embarrassment. How had I read all those signals wrong?

"Before we go any further, I want you to be sure. Once we do this, the bond will be complete," he said.

Flutters filled my chest and the concern eased. He was giving me one last chance to turn him down. I could overthink this for the rest of my life, or I could let my instincts take control.

Every piece of me was desperate to feel his touch. My wolf was practically begging me to pull his clothes off right now. My instincts had no doubts. Alec was my true mate. The one I was meant to have.

"I've never been more sure about anything," I said.

22

I'D FELT a pull toward Alec since we met, but I struggled to let him in. Now, every inch of me was drawing us closer. Desperate to feel his skin against mine, I slid my hands under his shirt and up his bare chest. It was as if my very soul was waking, urging me forward to complete the bond with him.

Alec quickly pulled his shirt over his head and tossed it aside. His mouth claimed mine in the most hungry, intense kiss I'd ever felt. My body responded, heat growing low in my belly, wetness already spreading between my legs. I kissed him back, hard and fast and a little sloppy as I tried to also undo the buttons I'd just fastened.

His fingers joined mine, the two of us unwilling to break the connection to stop and take my shirt off. We were moving backward, closer to the bed, as we continued the attempt to remove my clothes.

Alec pulled away, breaking the kiss. I wined, desperate to feel his lips on mine again. With a growl, Alec pulled the fabric of my shirt apart, buttons popping as they gave way.

Finally free of the shirt, I tossed it aside and took the

opportunity to remove my pants. I looked up at my mate. “Why are your pants still on?”

He smirked. “That’s an excellent question.”

“Off. Now.”

He slowly worked the top button before lowering the zipper painstakingly slow. Frustration built, and I growled. “Hurry up before I tear them off.”

Pants still around his hips, he lunged forward, grabbing me and planting his lips on mine once again. He kissed me hard, slipping his tongue in. I moaned into his mouth, my tongue finding his and matching it stroke for stroke.

I wasn’t going to forget about those pants, though. I reached down and slid them from his hips as low as I could before breaking from the kiss.

“What are you waiting for?” I was panting.

Alec’s eyes were heavy with lust and I knew he wanted me as much as I wanted him, but he was hesitating.

“What’s wrong?” I demanded.

He stepped out of his pants, leaving only his boxers between me and what I really wanted. And from the tent in those, I knew he was just as ready as I was.

“Last chance,” he warned. “We can’t undo a mating bond.”

“Will you stop?” I asked. “I want you. I am choosing you. I was going to choose you over my mate without feeling a bond between us. I want to be with you.”

He grinned. “I want to be with you, too. But the choice needed to be yours. After everything you’ve been through, I need you to know your choices matter. You have the power to control your own life.”

I took a step closer to him. “I am the shifter queen. I’ve

never had more power or more choice in my whole life and I still choose you. I'd choose you every time."

"The shifter queen and a feral wolf," he shook his head, "who'd have seen that coming?"

"How about the shifter queen and her king?" I rose to my toes and softly kissed his cheek.

Alec shivered, then he slid a hand around my waist. "You know I'll have your back for the rest our lives."

"Is that what this is all about?" I asked. "You're still trying to atone for what you did?"

"I'm never going to forgive myself for that," he said.

"Alright. Tomorrow we'll go fix that. You and me, we face my old pack, together. But right now, I don't want to think about them. I want to think about your hands on my body and your lips on mine."

I hooked my fingers under the waistband of his boxers and pulled. He didn't object. Once he stepped out of them, I grabbed his hand and led him to the bed.

The kisses were gentle this time, slow, passionate, full of emotions that neither of us could ever define. We tumbled onto the bed together, wrapped in each other's arms, our bodies intertwined as one.

Hands caressed skin, fingers ran through hair, lips trailed kisses everywhere. This was so different from the other times we'd been together. Our other experiences had been hungry and tense. This wasn't the same. It was deeper, slower, more intentional. Not that there was anything wrong with hard and fast; I liked that too, but this wasn't that.

Alec settled between my open thighs, his hardness pressing right outside my entrance. My fingers trailed along his back, feeling the movement of his muscles as he kissed my neck. His lips moved to my chest, before his tongue found each of my nipples in turn. I gasped as he licked and sucked each of the sensitive nubs. My hips lifted and lowered in anticipation as he worshiped my body with his mouth.

Breathing fast, the need to have him inside me was overwhelming. I reached down and stroked his shaft, causing him to pause. He groaned and adjusted his position, so it was easier for me to reach him. I moved my hand faster.

"Lola, I can't wait anymore," he said, breathless.

"Then don't." I released him and lifted my hips, encouraging him to enter.

His eyes met mine and I marveled at how gorgeous they were. I was never going to get tired of staring into his eyes. And I would get to do it for the rest of our lives.

Slowly, Alec lowered his mouth to mine. As he kissed me, I felt the tip of his cock press into me. It was slow at first, as if he was still expecting me to tell him to stop. I grabbed his ass and pulled him to me, sending his full length inside.

I gasped and lifted my hips involuntarily, taking him all in. Something roared to life inside me, an overwhelmingly intense emotion that felt nearly as good as an orgasm. I knew it was the mating bond, working whatever magic it was that would connect us forever. I threaded my hands into his hair and deepened the kiss. His thrusts picked up speed, the two of us finding an easy rhythm.

As we each neared climax, Alec bit down on my shoulder. I gasped, pain and pleasure mixing as the bond completed. Rapture exploded inside me, the climax so intense my vision blurred. Alec grunted as he tightened inside me, finding his climax. Panting, he rested his head on my chest, the two of us gasping and recovering from the most amazing orgasm possible. Every inch of my skin tingled as it continued to roll through me in ripples. It took several minutes for it to subside enough for me to return to normal breathing. Alec rolled off and the two of us snuggled together in the bed.

He kissed my forehead. "I think I'm the luckiest shifter alive."

"I think we both are," I agreed.

"You do realize this is the first time we've had sex indoors," he said.

"And we didn't break the bed this time," I added.

"I think we're going to need to try again." He leaped on top of me. "Maybe we can break it this time."

I laughed. "I'm up for the challenge."

23

I WOKE to the sound of knocking. My eyelids fluttered open as a warm pair of arms pulled me tighter. A smile spread on my lips as the events of last night came flooding into my mind.

Of course, the good memories of three rounds of fucking fantastic sex with Alec were followed by the memory of the challenge. I sat up, nearly elbowing Alec in the process.

"What's wrong?" His voice was groggy.

"I beat the shifter king last night," I said.

He chuckled. "Yeah, you're the queen. We already knew that."

"Right, but that means there are people expecting things from me." I had ideas. Big ideas. Things I wanted to change, but I wasn't sure what the protocols were or what hoops I'd need to jump through. Spencer had said he'd help.

I glanced at the clock on the bedside table. It was ten in the morning. *Holy shit.* They must have ended the party without me and nobody bothered us all night.

I guess there were perks to being the shifter queen.

The knock sounded again and I scrambled off the bed,

grabbing a blanket to use as a makeshift toga to get me to the door. I opened it a crack and peeked out.

"Good morning, your highness. Today starts your transition to the throne." Spencer looked well rested and happy. Something I wasn't sure I'd ever seen before.

"Um, what does a girl have to do to get an audience with the queen?" A familiar voice called.

Sheila pushed past Spencer, a wide smile on her lips. "Morning, Sunshine. Anything interesting happen last night? I mean, besides taking down the monarchy or the patriarchy or something like that."

"Of course, I have the fight of my life and snag a rather impressive title and you're only interested in sex," I teased.

"I'm not going to deny any of that," she said as she pushed the door a bit wider.

"I really don't need the details." Kyle looked away as he came into view, acting as if he hadn't seen me naked dozens of times before.

"I agree with him," Spencer said. "I only need to know the facts."

"Wow, this is a lot before clothes," I said.

"Or breakfast," Alec said as he joined me at the door. He didn't bother with a blanket.

"I suppose that answers that question," Spencer said.

"Fucking finally!" Sheila squealed. "I knew it. I called it before either of you figured it out."

Alec pulled me in close and planted a kiss on my head. "She's officially off the market."

"Hey, I have a girlfriend," Sheila said.

"Alright, so now we got that out of the way. Can we get a few minutes to get dressed?" I asked.

"Oh, no, I am not leaving you two alone in there again. Last night Alec told me he was going to check on you and that he'd come back for the rest of us. He kept you to himself all night," Sheila said.

James, who had been quietly observing the conversation, cleared his throat. "If the queen desires, we can send someone out to do some shopping."

"Wait, clean clothes?" I asked. "I can make that happen?"

James looked both a little confused and amused. "Yes, it would be one of the more tame requests we've had over the years."

"Yes, please. Jeans, tee-shirts, and for the love of the Moon Goddess some clean underwear." I couldn't believe my luck. Getting clothes that actually fit and actually belonged to me was a luxury I was never going to take for granted again.

It took a few minutes of promising I wasn't going to spend the rest of the day in the room to get my friends to let me close the door to go find something to wear. I had to admit, the thought was tempting, but we had other things we needed to take care of.

I found a new pair of pajamas from the massive closet since the pair I had on last night was in pieces on the floor. Alec pulled on the clothes he'd worn last night, then the two of us emerged from the room to the onslaught of waiting shifters.

It wasn't just my friends in the hallway. In addition to them and my guards, there were several shifters in the blue uniforms I'd seen on kitchen staff last night, and a handful of shifters who looked like they belonged in a human conference room. They were wearing suits and shiny shoes and all of them had their hair meticulously combed back with far too much product.

I wrinkled my nose. Who were all these people and why were they waiting outside my bedroom? I suddenly wished I did have something more formal to wear than borrowed flannel pajamas.

"Your father's council insisted on meeting with you this morning," Spencer said, unable to keep the contempt out of his tone.

That explained the stuffy looking shifters in suits. "And the others?"

"Your house staff. They run this place and will attend to your needs while you're here," Spencer said.

"It's lovely to meet you all, but you really don't need to be here," I said.

"It's vital that we get started right away, your highness," One of the members of the council said.

I glared at him, then returned my gaze to the staff I had been speaking to. "Please know that if any of you are here against your will, my friend is working to break the blood magic. As soon as it's gone, I'll let you know."

They all looked at me with wide eyes and open mouths.

"Nobody should ever be trapped someplace they don't want to be," I added. "It won't hurt my feelings, I swear."

"I'm not sure that's the best thing for your safety," another council member said.

I turned to look at the group of males who were probably used to getting their way. "I will meet with you soon. But not until I've had breakfast and some time to speak alone with my friends first."

The man who had spoken up cleared his throat, then

bowed his head. "As you wish, your highness. We will wait in the great hall for you until you are ready."

The group didn't look pleased as they walked away, leaving me with my friends, guards, and a handful of staff. I returned my attention to them. "For real, though. I keep my promises."

"Told you Claire was telling the truth," an older woman with white hair said to her companions. She looked at me. "If there's nothing more for us, we'll get back to work."

I nodded. "Find me if you need anything."

She smiled, then herded the group away from me.

Now that the extra people were gone, I looked at who remained. The guards weren't going anywhere, so this was probably about as close to private as I was going to get. Besides, I couldn't wait to ask this question any longer. "Where's my mom? How's she doing?"

"I'm not sure," Spencer said.

"What do you mean? I thought you were going to her last night?" I asked.

"I did, and she was in bad shape. She didn't even know who I was." He shook his head.

My chest tightened. "Where is she now?"

"Star's been with her all night," Malcom said. "She said she figured you'd understand if she tried to help her first then dealt with the rest of the blood magic."

I felt a little guilty after what I'd just told the house staff, but I wanted my mom to be okay. I wasn't sure I'd ever seen her the way she should be. I had no idea how long she's been using that toxin to self-medicate.

"I'd like to see her," I said.

Spencer nodded. "I'll take you to her."

"We'll see to finding some breakfast," Kyle suggested.

"Yeah, we'll be wherever the food is when you're ready to find us," Sheila said.

"Do you want company?" Alec asked.

I stretched out my hand and he took it. The two of us silently followed Spencer. I didn't need to look behind me to know that my guards were following me. It was one of those things I was going to have to get used to, I supposed.

"Have you seen her this morning?" I asked.

"Not yet," Spencer said.

"You think Star can help her?" I asked Alec.

"If anyone has a chance, it's her," Alec said. "She figured out an antidote to that toxin. And you've seen what else she can do."

That was part of my concern. What if Star hadn't been able to help my mom? If she couldn't, I wasn't sure anyone else could.

As we continued down hallways lined with doors, and up a few flights of stairs, I considered what I would even say to her. Everything in my mind about my mom was so full of conflict. I wanted to help her, but she was also such a source of pain for me. She might not have been in control, but why did she have to do that to herself in the first place? Why did she flee to Wolf Creek of all places? Why hadn't she found another way to protect me? I didn't know if hearing her side of the story would even matter. I wasn't sure it could fully repair what we'd lost. Yet, I wanted her to have a chance at happiness if I could help her find it.

Spencer's movements were tense and robotic. He had to be feeling just as much anxiety as I was. Although, he had happy memories with my mom. He would recall her as the way she was, which meant he was in for a shock when he saw her. I wasn't sure which of us had it worse. I witnessed her descent into madness. For him it came as a surprise.

"This is it," Spencer said as he stopped in front of a door. We were in another wing of the sprawling home and I wondered what the design purpose was for having random bedrooms spread throughout the place.

Spencer knocked on the door and Alec squeezed my hand. I got a rush of emotion from him. Encouragement, support, sympathy, all of it rolling from him into me like a warm caress. I'd sensed his feelings before, but this was far more intense. That mating bond was no joke. We were supposed to be able to feel each other even when we were apart.

The door swung open and Star greeted us. She had dark circles under her eyes and looked more pale than usual. "Hey."

"Rough night?" Alec asked.

"You have no idea," she said. "You thought your detox was rough. She's got decades of toxin to sweat out."

"How is she?" I asked.

"She's not through it yet. She needs more time," Star said. "I don't think you should see her yet."

Disappointment made my stomach tighten. "I understand."

"What about me?" Spencer asked.

Star shook her head. "It's not pretty and she's embarrassed. I think having witnesses will keep her from breaking the hold."

"Does she remember me?" Spencer asked, desperation in his tone.

"She hasn't mentioned you," Star said. "I'm sorry."

"How much longer?" he asked.

"I've never done this before," she admitted.

"It's okay, Star. We'll check back later." I smiled at her. "Thank you. Sincerely. Thank you."

She nodded and closed the door. My shoulders fell. That was not what I expected, but I would give her the time to do what needed done.

"Your friends are in the third floor dining room if you'd like to join them," James said.

"Let's go," I said. "We'll feel better after some food."

"You told me she was bad," Spencer said. "But I didn't realize how bad it was. She was like this your whole childhood?"

"Most of it," I said. "I have a few happy memories, but she got worse each year until she simply stopped even caring for me at all."

Spencer shook his head. "I had no idea you were alive. I would have broken out immediately if I'd known."

"They might have killed you. And me," I said. "Like you said, you didn't know."

"I never even tried," he said.

My brow furrowed. "What do you mean?"

"I could have felt for a connection between her and I. But I was worried that if I went to her, my brother would find her and make an example of her. He couldn't kill me until he had an heir. He would have taken his anger out on her," he said.

"Don't do this to yourself," I said. "You know we can't change the past."

"I'm going to be there for you and Malcom. Whatever you need," he said.

"I appreciate that." I let go of Alec's hand and moved closer to Spencer. Our relationship was new, untested, but he was trying. And there was no harm in me trying as well. I wrapped my arms around him, giving him a hug.

Spencer tensed as if he wasn't sure how to respond. Then he relaxed and threw his arms around me, pulling me closer.

In all my fantasies about how my life would play out, I never once thought I'd know who my dad was, let alone be able to give him a hug. When we released each other, we were both smiling. I'd come a long way from the sad girl in Wolf Creek. The thought of my old home reminded me. I had some unfinished business to attend to. "Come on. We've got a big day."

24

BREAKFAST with my friends felt familiar and safe. Sheila, Malcom, and Kyle had mostly waited to eat until we arrived. The guards stood outside the room, and at my instance, the staff was willing to leave the food and let us serve ourselves.

To my friends' credit, they all steered the topic of conversation toward random things that were unrelated to our current situation. It was as if they knew I needed a little break before I had to figure out how to do the job I'd committed to when I took down the old king.

We ate till we were all stuffed and laughed at Malcom's stories about trying to learn how to fix a car and accidentally setting it on fire. Tears streamed down my cheeks as I pictured Mario's face. "I bet he never let you near his car again."

"Only if I'm trying to fix it. Driving I'm fine with. It's when you give me tools that it causes an issue."

"I'll keep that in mind," I said.

"Your highness," a male voice said.

I turned and saw one of my guards. Malaki, I think.

He was holding a few shopping bags. "We got you some options. And a few different sizes. I forgot to ask."

I pushed my chair away from the table and accepted the bags. "I'm sure it's better than what I have. Thank you so much."

"I don't know. I've got boys. I don't know what ladies are wearing. My wife lives in leggings and my old tees," he said.

"That sounds perfectly reasonable," I said, then I turned to Alec. "You have any old t-shirts around I can steal?"

"Forgot to pack my bags before I came," he said.

I looked at the bags of clothes, then back at Malaki. "I'm sure I'll be just fine with what you brought."

"Guess the party's over," Malcom said.

"He's right. You can't really blow off the council for much longer," Spencer said.

I sighed. "Tell me about them. They worked for my uncle, right? The old king? Don't I get my own council?"

"Yeah, you can. But before you dismiss them outright, I might give them a chance. Some of them worked for your grandfather. They might be helpful," Spencer said. "I can sit with you for a while if you'd like my advice."

"Can you be on the council?" I asked. "And them?" I inclined my head to my friends.

"If I have to be your next in line, I'd like to see what these old guys have to say," Malcom said.

"What about the rest of you?" I asked.

"I'm not sure that's really my thing," Sheila said.

"I'm a protector, not a politician," Kyle said.

"I'm the arm candy and I'm cool with that," Alec teased. "But I'll help however you need me."

"All of you are the reason I'm still alive," I said.

"Meet with the council first, see what you think. Fire them all, keep them all, add to it... the choice is yours."

"I'm not used to having so many choices," I reminded him.

"It'll get easier," he assured me.

I lifted the shopping bags. "First, I should find something that isn't pajamas. Malcom, Alec, Spencer, you want to meet me at the council meeting place, um wherever that is, in ten minutes?"

They nodded and I headed out of the room, pausing in front of my guards. "Know a place nearby I can change before going to see the council?"

James nodded. "Follow me."

We ended up in another bedroom. This time, though, all the furniture was covered in fabric and the closet wasn't stocked. It hadn't been used in a long time. I wondered how much of this house was like this. There had to be a lot of unoccupied rooms. It was far too large for any one family.

I didn't waste time exploring, though. I wanted to get this meeting over with so I could move on to other things. No matter where my thoughts went, I continued to return to two things. My mom, and Wolf Creek.

I couldn't do anything about my mom right now, and I knew I couldn't move on until I made my peace with my old home.

Dressed in jeans that fit surprisingly well, a long sleeve tee, and fresh underwear, I let myself out of the bedroom. James was waiting for me outside.

"Can we come grab the rest of the clothes later?" I asked.

"I'll have someone take them to your room," he said. "If you like your accommodations from last night, that is. Because we can find you a new room if you'd rather."

"It's fine. I'm not even sure how long I'll be staying here," I said.

"This has been the primary residence of the royal family for so long now, I nearly forgot you had other options," he said.

"It's not that, it's more that it feels strange to simply fight someone, then move into their house," I said.

"Spencer Lupton is your father, correct?" James asked.

I nodded.

"May I speak my mind?" he asked.

"Of course," I said.

"If your father hadn't been exiled, you'd likely have been raised here. If not here, at another holding, with regular visits. You or your brother would have been raised to inherit the throne. You'd have tutors and training for your future role. You'd have attended parties and ceremonies, and likely shadowed your uncle until he gave you a position with responsibilities to help you learn and prepare. All that was stripped from you when your father tried to take the throne," he said.

I swallowed. Spencer had mentioned something similar but with far less detail. I wondered what that would have been like. Would I have been raised to take over if Spencer had ignored his bother's actions and married my mom? Would she have been accepted into their family and in turn, allowed me to be accepted?

There was no way of knowing what might have been. All I had was how things were.

"Maybe," I said. "I guess we'll never know."

"The thing that gets me is the fact that had you been raised as the next heir, the throne would have bypassed your father and gone right to you." James chuckled. "It's almost like fate had a plan for you."

When I'd been paired with Tyler, I thought fate was out to get me. Now, through the trials of fleeing him, I was on a path nobody could have ever dreamed. Perhaps James had a point. Maybe fate already had a plan for me.

"Thanks, James," I said.

He nodded. "Come on. I'll take you to the council."

When we arrived, Spencer, Malcom, and Alec were already waiting for me. I realized that none of us were at our best. I hadn't even brushed my hair today and there were pink scars where my injuries from last night had yet to heal. My entourage of my father, brother, and mate, were in the same clothes they'd worn last night and all of them looked like they could use a few days to do nothing but sleep.

As soon as possible, I wanted to make sure we all got the rest we needed. Unfortunately, I had a few things I wanted to discuss with this council and we weren't going to be able to rest yet.

"They're waiting for us," Spencer said.

"Let's do this," I said.

The four of us stepped through the double doors and the members of the council rose when they saw us. They had been seated at a long wood table, with a dozen chairs. At one end of the table there was a chair twice the size of the others. A crackling fire glowed in a wood fireplace behind it. The floor was dark wood and a red and gold rug sat under the long table. The chandeliers above the table were made of antlers, a very different aesthetic from the crystal I'd seen in the other parts of the home.

"Thank you for waiting," I said, trying to sound more calm and commanding than I felt in the moment.

"Of course, your highness," one of the men said.

I walked to the larger chair and sat down. The gathered males took their seats. One side of the table was my family, on the other, the four males who made up my predecessor's council. It was an odd arrangement, but if Spencer thought it was worth hearing what they had to say, I'd give it a chance.

"We are honored that you're willing to meet with us," the male closest to me said. He was balding and his face was creased with lines. I wondered if he had served for my grandfather.

"Should we begin with introductions?" Spencer asked.

"Please," I said.

"I'll begin," Spencer offered. "Spencer Lupton, father of the queen."

"Guess that's me next," Malcom said. "Malcom… shit, do I take your last name now?" He looked at Spencer.

"If you'd like," Spencer offered.

"I'll think on it," he said. "I'm Malcom."

"He's my brother," I added, before he could quantify with how much blood we shared. That didn't matter to me.

"I'm Alec. The queen's true mate," Alec added.

"Your turn," I said to the council.

They went down the row, the older male with the lined face was Horace. Next to him was a pale male with red hair, the color close to my own. His name was Dean. The last two were brothers, both with gray hair, Franklin and Jack.

"Your highness, I speak for the entire council when I say, thank you," Dean said with a smile. "We've been waiting so long for something to change. When your father failed, we feared we'd have to wait for your uncle to have children. But he never did."

"I thought I wouldn't live to see another ruler," Franklin said.

"Are you all bound here by the blood magic as well?" I asked.

They nodded.

I'd assumed they were like my uncle. Men who sought power and enjoyed pushing others around. I glanced over at Spencer. "You knew this?"

He nodded. "Remember those friends on the inside?"

"I'm starting to think it would have been easier to point out those who wanted my uncle to stay in power," I said.

"They were few and they've already been sent away," Jack said. "We took the liberty of cleaning house for you last night. I hope we didn't overstep."

"I figured you needed the rest," Spencer said.

"You will be safe here. All the remaining staff and guards are loyal," Dean added.

"What about the blood magic keeping them here?" I asked.

"It was set up so they can leave, but they can't return," Jack said.

"I want all the staff to have a choice to leave if they wish," I said.

"No problem," Dean said.

"Before we discuss all those things, there are a few items regarding the transition from the old king to your rule," Horace said. "Do you mind if we proceed with that?"

"Sure. What do we need to do?" I asked.

"We'd need to officially announce your rule, and the departure of your predecessor," Horace explained.

"I would think the word is out," I said. "Wouldn't the alphas know by now?"

"Oh, no. A change in rule has a strict protocol for announcements. The guests are forbidden to speak your name until we've informed all the alphas," Franklin said.

There was a lot of ceremony and protocol I never knew existed, but it made me happy to hear.

"How is that announcement made, exactly?" I asked.

"You'll call all the alphas for a meeting. There you'll greet them as the queen," Horace explained.

"That's all just ceremonial, though, right?" I asked.

"Are you wondering if you're already the queen?" Spencer asked.

"Pretty much," I said.

"Yes, but it's a long-standing tradition and I'd caution you against choosing that as the first change during your reign," he said.

"I'm not thinking of changing it," I said. "I'm wondering if I can pay a visit to my old pack before we send out the official word."

"Oh, I see. You'd like to share the good news with them first. Yes, that could be arranged," Horace said.

"I'm sure that's exactly what she has in mind," Alec said, not hiding his sarcasm. "We get to come with you, right?"

"I wouldn't have you miss it for the world," I replied.

25

Wolf Creek was ready to greet the royal family when we arrived. The entire pack turned out, everyone gathered in front of the barn as requested.

I could see them waiting as we approached, careful to keep myself hidden from view behind the guards and accompanying council. I didn't tell them why I wanted to return here, and I was certain they were expecting some kind of happy reunion.

Alec was already seething with rage, the emotion far more intense than it should be. My wolf clawed at my chest, wanting to get out to comfort her mate. That's when I realized I wasn't just sensing Alec's emotions, I was feeling his inner wolf. And he was pissed.

My wolf was distracted by her mate. Her feelings toward Wolf Creek secondary to his discomfort. It was interesting that Alec's hate toward Wolf Creek was two-fold. I could feel his personal vendetta against my old pack mixed with a need to protect and defend his mate. In a strange way, it was kind of sweet.

"Let me take lead on this," I said to him as we neared the pack.

"I'll try," he said.

After everything we'd been through, my old pack deserved to feel exactly the kind of pain they'd dished out. But the more I thought about what punishment they deserved, the less I thought death would be enough.

Tyler was gone, despite our attempts to give him another chance. He'd made his choice. In his death, he'd been spared the humiliation of a mate rejecting him and he would never see the pack he was sure he'd rule handed to someone else.

Ace's punishment would be different. Death was too easy and ran the risk of making him a martyr. I wasn't naive enough to think that generations of males who were used to unquestioned power would simply bow to a female monarch. We had a lot of work ahead of us to right the wrongs. For every story like mine, there were a dozen more. Sheila and Clara had both been stripped of their right to a position granted by the Moon Goddess herself. How many others had suffered at the wrath of weak men who wanted to maintain power?

Ace would be an example. Weakened, stripped of his power. I needed him to survive as a warning and a sign of what was to come rather than a reason for shifters to rise up against me.

He wasn't being punished for being sexist, he was being punished for abusing all the members of his pack. I wanted to make sure that was clear.

My guards stopped, leaving a gap between our group and the leaders of my former pack. Ace and his favorites were gathered at the front, behind them were a few hundred shifters who called Wolf Creek home.

Ace lowered his head into a bow. "Welcome, your majesty. Thank you for gracing us with your presence."

I touched the arms of the guards in front of me, indicating that I wanted them to step aside. They parted, allowing me and Alec to pass.

I stood in front of Ace, my head held high. He lifted his head and caught sight of me. His eyes widened and his jaw dropped. All the color drained from his face. "You."

"That is no way to address your queen," Alec said.

"That's impossible. You should be dead," he said. "Tyler went after you."

"Someone is threatening the queen's life?" James asked.

I looked over at my guard. "He's already been dealt with."

"He can't hurt me anymore," I added as I looked back at Ace.

The alpha dropped to his knees. "You killed him?"

"He chose death instead of breaking the bond," I said. "I believe you also wished death on me."

Ace shook his head. "No. I would never. How is this even possible?"

"I challenged the king. And I won." The words tasted like victory.

"Your highness, I am loyal to the crown," he said.

"No, you're loyal to yourself." I let the words hang in the air. Nobody said a word. The gathered shifters had moved a little closer and I knew everyone was waiting to see what I said.

"You failed your son, you failed your family, you failed

your pack. As a father, as an alpha, your job was to protect. Instead, you terrorized."

"No, I raised a strong family and a strong pack. I did not fail," he spat.

"Strength is not demonstrated through fear. You are a disgrace." My tone was calm but my words biting. I never thought I'd get to stand up to Ace, let alone point out all the hurt he'd caused. I know I wasn't alone, even if I felt like it growing up. Everyone under Ace's control, which was all of Wolf Creek, was hurting. We were trapped, unable to live our lives as we wished.

"Ace Grant, I strip you of your title and your role as alpha of Wolf Creek," I said.

"No, you can't do that. You can't. I earned this." He stood, his hands balled into fists.

For a moment, I thought he might charge me. My guards moved closer and Alec stood in front of me.

Ace took a step back and Alec's tension eased. He stepped aside, but stayed right next to me.

"You stole the title," I said. "You didn't work for it. You didn't earn it. You didn't prove anything to gain it."

"He doesn't even have a mark," someone shouted from behind. The gathered shifters cheered in response.

"Send him to the caves!" Another voice called. The cheers grew even wilder.

I smirked, knowing I had been correct. I was never alone here, we were all prisoners.

"Please no, have mercy," Ace said. "I already lost my son. Isn't that enough?"

"You don't want to be trapped in the caves?" I had no

intention of sending him there, but I had to admit I was enjoying hearing him beg.

"I didn't betray anyone. It's not a fitting punishment," he said.

"I'll bite," I said. "What do you think a fitting punishment is for someone who trapped his pack, prevented them from leaving, and worked with witches to keep them from shifting?"

He stuttered a few syllables but didn't get a word out.

"There's also the matter of the pack next door. Which you and your inner circle murdered with use of an illegal substance," I added.

"The toxin isn't illegal," he said.

I shrugged. "It is now."

"It wasn't - the king, he approved. He knew. I had his blessing to expand our territory. He wanted more toxin," Ace pleaded.

"You killed innocents. Hundreds of people who were living their lives," Alec said. "Each of them should be here now."

I tensed, hating that the act that eliminated Alec's pack was endorsed by a member of my own family.

Someone grabbed my hand and I turned to see Malcom. He pulled me close so he could lean near my ear to whisper. "Blood means nothing, remember that. What he did is not a reflection on either of us."

I smiled and nodded, grateful that he was here with me and that he understood what had caused my hesitation. He was right. As shifters we were taught that pack was like family, but Ace had never instilled that here.

I glanced around at my friends, silently standing around

me to support me. Sheila and Kyle were with my guards, Malcom and Alec by my side. Spencer was standing to the side, watching with an approving expression. He nodded, as if encouraging me to continue.

"Ace Grant, I strip you of your title, and I exile you and your inner circle from Wolf Creek. You will never again hold status as an alpha or be part of any other inner circle. You will live out the rest of your days as feral wolves, forbidden to join a pack. If you violate these terms, you will all be executed."

Three of my guards stepped forward. James remained by my side while the others closed in around Ace and his closest friends. They were finished in Wolf Creek.

Ace took gasping breaths and his eyes widened in terror. I'd given him the worst possible punishment. He needed the adoration, the ability to drive fear into others. Without his place of power, he'd have nothing. If I executed him, he'd claim he was the hero until the end.

Mummers from the gathered shifters grew slowly as the sentence was repeated among the crowd. Eventually, they gave way to applause.

Kyle took a step forward, walking over to Ace. I had no idea what he was going to say, but I knew he needed some closure here too. He whispered something to Ace, then backed away, a smile on his lips.

Ace looked pissed but he didn't retaliate. I wasn't sure what Kyle said, but it wasn't my place. He'd been hurt by Wolf Creek under Ace's rule as much as I had. Kyle had done things he shouldn't, but he'd always tried to balance the good when possible. What could he have accomplished if he wasn't walking the line between pleasing Ace for his sister's sake and doing the right thing?

"Well, this wasn't what I expected when you said you wanted to visit your old pack," Horace said.

"I wasn't sure you'd approve," I admitted.

"If it were me, I'd have a couple of guards escort him to his home and give him an hour to pack. Then, I'd kick his ass out." Horace took a deep breath. "That toxin has been the black mark on my time of service. I would be honored if you'd allow me to help you destroy it."

"I'd like that," I said.

"Guards, escort him to his home. Check the roster for his inner circle, past and present. Kick them all out." For once, the strict rules and lists for who was considered the alpha's inner circle worked to my benefit. All packs had to keep records. As long as Ace has been in power, he's kept track. The positions were valued but there were shifters who'd turned them down. Everyone knew working for Ace meant good things for your family, but it might cost you everything.

A pair of my guards escorted Ace away. Several members of his inner circle followed him. Wolf Creek deserved a chance at peace.

To my surprise, Viki, Ace's wife approached me. She had yellow and purple bruises on her face, nearly healed by her shifter blood, but still visible.

"Did he do that to you?" I asked.

"It doesn't matter," she said. "I wanted to ask if I can stay here. Independent of Ace. I'm not listed as inner circle, but I am married to the brute."

"The priestess is the only one who can issue a divorce," Kyle said.

"I didn't exile you," I said. "Only inner circle."

She smiled. "I'll speak to Jenny. Thank you, Lola."

"You do know that most feral wolves are nothing like our camp," Alec said, a touch of darkness in his tone. "None of them are going to survive long."

"I know," I said. "I worry it's not enough punishment for what they did."

"It's perfect," Alec said. "The longer they survive, they more they'll wish you'd killed them."

We were silent for a moment and watched until Ace and his crew were out of sight. "What next?" Alec asked.

"I'm not sure," I admitted. "I want to take down the barrier, but I'll need Star's help for that."

Spencer walked over to me. "You did good. But you're missing one thing."

"What's that?" I asked.

"A pack must have an alpha," he said.

"You want the job?" I said with a laugh.

"No, but you can ask who wants the position and set up a challenge if there are multiple takers or you can appoint someone," he said.

"That's correct," Franklin said. "In the absence of an alpha, the king, er, queen, has the authority."

With a smile, I stepped closer to the gathered crowd. I wondered if that's why they were still gathered. That or they wanted me to make some other kind of speech. Appointing a new alpha would probably be good enough to appease them.

"Hello, citizens of Wolf Creek," I said. "I know most of you know me. I grew up here, even if you avoided looking at me or pretended I didn't exist." The words stung a little, but they were true.

A few of the people in the front shifted their weight uncomfortably.

"Wolf Creek was never the family we were told it was. We were never a strong pack. We were a pack locked away from the rest of the world, run with fear and deceit." I looked at the familiar faces. Fellow students, people I'd seen in shops and walking around town my whole life. I knew these people, even if they'd been told they couldn't be kind to me.

"Wolf Creek should be a place we're proud of. It should be a place where everyone can thrive, and learn, and grow. And none of you should be trapped here. Did you know that outside our border, shifters have their first shift as early as thirteen?"

A few startled sounds and whispers rolled through the crowd.

"There was so much hidden from us, but that doesn't mean things can't change," I said. "Wolf Creek has an unusual history that's flawed, but ours. You need a leader who can take you from what we were to the amazing pack we can be."

Everyone's eyes were glued to me, and I could sense the rising anticipation in the group. There was only one person who could take on Wolf Creek successfully.

"Kyle Sinclair, I'd like you to be the next alpha," I said.

Kyle blinked a few times before stepping closer to me. "Seriously? I'm a protector, not an alpha."

"You're both," I said. "And you're exactly what Wolf Creek needs. Someone who cares about them, and will guide them, while letting them find their unique place in the real world."

"Yeah, Kyle!" Someone shouted.

"I didn't hear him accept yet," a woman pointed out.

"What do you say?" I asked.

"What do they say?" He asked, looking out to the gathered shifters. "Anyone object?"

We waited, looking around for any signs that someone else wanted to claim the position for themselves. Nobody spoke.

"Alright," Kyle said. "I'll do my best."

"Wolf Creek, I give you your new alpha." I gestured to Kyle.

The shifters charged forward, surrounding us as they cheered and hollered. Kyle was lifted into the air on a pair of shoulders and carried around the field. Instead of tension, I felt relief, joy, and peace coming from the shifters all around us.

Kyle would have his hands full here, but if anyone could get Wolf Creek where it needed to be, it was him.

26

WHILE MY OLD pack was busy peppering Kyle with questions, I took Alec aside. "You doing okay?"

"Yeah," he said. "I know Kyle's going to deal with this mess well."

"And you and I get to deal with the bigger mess," I said. "If my uncle was authorizing Wolf Creek's use of the toxin to take out their neighbors, what else don't we know?"

"I know Spencer said to give them a chance, but you sure you want a council that enabled that behavior to stick around?" Alec asked.

He had a very good point. "I'm not sure I do want them around. But I do think we need to learn from them and find out what has been going on for the last few decades."

"You're not out of the woods yet. You're a walking target, you know that, right?" Alec asked.

"I know. I wish I wasn't used to it," I said. "But at least I'm not alone this time. I've got you, Sheila and Malcom. And the four of us can work together to figure out who we can and can't trust."

"They're good shifters. Even before Malcom shared his story, I got the sense I could trust him. And Sheila has never let me down."

"Don't discount yourself in this," I added. "I know I can do this because I have you by my side."

He laughed. "It's sweet that you're trying so hard, but you'd be just fine without me. Don't get me wrong, you're stuck with me now, but you are the one the world needs to watch out for."

"Says the guy who helped find the antidote to the toxin and turned a group of feral shifters into a pack," I teased. "We're going to make a hell of a team."

I caught sight of Spencer walking toward us out of the corner of my eye. He was holding a cell phone in his hand and his expression was odd. He wasn't worried or scared, but he wasn't happy either. Something was going on.

"What is it?" I asked, turning toward him.

"Star just called. Your mom is asking for you. She's awake. Star says she's for real awake. No more toxin," Spencer said.

My stomach twisted into knots and nervous flutters filled my chest. This was what we were hoping for but what was going to come of it?

"We should go," Alec said.

"I'll talk to Kyle." I jogged over to where Kyle was standing. He was holding hands with his little sister and his mom was by his side. You didn't need shifter emotion reading abilities to feel the pride radiating from her.

As I approached, the attention turned from him to me. Some of the shifters bowed while others stared at me. There was a mixture of awe and confusion coming from them and I didn't blame them. They'd had a lot of change thrown at them today.

"Can I borrow you for a minute?" I asked.

"Of course," Kyle said. "Excuse me."

Kyle followed me away from the group. "What's up?"

"I have to head back. Will you be okay here?" I asked.

"Sure," he said.

"I should also apologize for throwing this on you. You really are the best possible person for the role," I said.

"I never would have asked for it," he said.

"I know. That's part of why you're perfect."

"You'll come back soon, right? I mean, I did swear to protect you. I feel bad that I'm leaving you," he said.

"You're not leaving me. I'm the one doing the leaving. Besides, alphas report directly to the ruler, right? So you're still helping me."

"We're going to tear down the barrier, right?" he asked.

"I'm going to get Star on it as soon as possible," I said.

"She's got all that blood magic to deal with first," he said.

"I'll find out if she has any friends. Maybe it's time for us to repair the wounds between us and the witches."

"You are going to be one hell of a queen," he said.

I stood on my tip toes and threw my arms around his shoulders, pulling him into an embrace. "You're going to be one hell of an alpha."

He hugged me back. "Be careful, okay?"

"You, too." I stepped away. "I'll be in touch soon."

He nodded. "I'll be okay."

"I know you will," I said.

"So will you, you know. You were born for this."

I smiled at my friend. We'd been through a lot together in a short time and I knew the bond we'd forged would keep us as friends for the rest of our lives. You don't go through what we did and not connect on a deeper level.

Kyle returned to his pack, and I walked over to my waiting entourage. "Malcom, would you be willing to stay with Kyle a few days? Just so he has someone loyal here."

"Of course," he said. "Now, go. See your mom. Kyle's got this but just in case, he's got me."

The drive back to the house felt like an eternity. After a few failed attempts at conversation we all settled into silence. The hours ticked by, most of us too exhausted or too overwhelmed to say anything.

"She's going to be fine," Alec said, squeezing my hand.

I looked over at him. The two of us were in the back seat while Spencer sat in the front next to James, who was driving. I was glad we didn't have council members or other guards in the car with us.

"Star got all that toxin out of me," Alec reminded me.

"She said she was awake." It was hard to imagine what I might be walking into. "I don't know what I'm supposed to say when I see her."

"You'll know when we get there," he assured me.

When we arrived, Alec went to find Sheila and I followed Spencer back to the room where my mom was waiting for us. My footsteps felt heavy as we neared the doorway.

"I'll wait here," Spencer said when we arrived.

"You sure? You can come in with me if you want," I said.

"She asked for you," he said. "I haven't been around the last nineteen years."

"Alright." I took a deep breath before turning the doorknob. When I entered the room, I was met by a person I had only seen in fleeting memories. My mother didn't look the way she had when I last saw her in Wolf Creek. There wasn't a cloud of smoke curling from her lips, her hair wasn't tangled and in a frizzy bun. Even the dark circles under her eyes were gone.

I hardly recognized the stunning woman with bright red hair and sparkling green eyes staring at me. "Mom?"

She smiled, and her eyes filled with tears. "Lola, I'm so sorry."

My eyes burned and I swallowed against a lump in my throat. It took everything I had not to break down right there. I couldn't speak for fear of losing it completely.

My mom took a step forward and extended her arms. I hesitated for a moment. This was the woman who had given up on raising me, or so I thought. She'd shut me out when I needed her the most. Yet, the very thing that had caused her madness was the way she'd tried to protect me.

She lowered her arms. "I should have done more to help you. I thought I could handle small doses of the toxin."

"I know," I said. "I know why you did it and I know why you fled and I know you meant well."

"Your friend told me about your mate and everything you've been through," she said. "I never meant for any of that to happen."

"You knew a wolf who didn't shift would go mad," I said.

"I had a plan, before I lost myself but none of that matters. I would take it back if I could," she said.

My mom was a different person. This wasn't the woman

I'd known most of my life. She was the faded childhood memory of the woman who read me stories and waded into the creek with me looking for fish. I supposed she'd always been there, but she'd been lost, overtaken by the toxin and the other cocktail of substances she used to mask the pain.

"Spencer is here," I said.

"I know, I can feel him."

"Yet, you aren't running to him," I said, unable to keep the accusation out of my tone. After years of various men in and out of her bedroom, I was a little surprised I'd come before her true mate.

"I left him to protect you. If you asked me to choose, it would be you." She offered a weak smile. "I know it doesn't seem like it, but I did try. I just failed spectacularly."

Now the tears slide down my cheeks. I wiped them away with my fingertips. "You don't have to try so hard anymore. We're safe now."

She chuckled. "It was supposed to be me saving you. But it looks like you saved us all."

"Not without failing a few times along the way," I admitted.

"That's okay. As long as you kept fighting. I'll admit, I lost the fight. I'm not sure when I gave in. But I wasn't as strong as I thought I was," she said.

"You had a lot going against you," I said.

"I know you don't really need a mother anymore, but I'd like to be part of your life at least a little," she said.

I stepped forward and threw my arms around her. "I still need my mother."

She squeezed me and the two of us cried together. We had

a lot of work to do to repair what had been broken between us, but there wasn't anything that couldn't be fixed in time.

Once we both settled, we eased from the hug and I took a step back. I wiped the tears from my face and took a few breaths. "Do you want to see him?"

"Spencer?" she asked.

I nodded.

"I do," she said.

"I'll send him in. We can talk more later."

"I hear you found your mate," she said. "A second one. Star said he's a perfect match and that you're happy."

"I did. I can't wait for you to meet him." There was so much ahead of us. It was like I had to get to know her all over again. I walked toward the door.

"Lola," she called.

I turned to look, the door already cracked open. "Yeah?"

"I am so proud of you."

I smiled. "Thanks, mom."

When I stepped into the hall, I found Spencer pacing like a nervous wreck. He stopped and looked up at me expectantly. "How is she?"

"She's good," I said. "She wants to see you."

He sucked in a breath and his eyes widened. He looked nervous.

"Go on," I encouraged.

It was a strange thing, watching my father taking cautious steps toward the door where my mother was waiting to see him. Lots of families were complicated and mine was full of extra complication. With time, though, I was hoping we could begin to heal and get to know each other. I felt like I'd been given a second chance. With my family, with my mate, with my life.

It turned out, I was stronger than I thought. While I knew I didn't deserve what I'd been through, I was damn proud of how far I'd come. I fought for this and I deserved all the happiness coming my way.

EPILOGUE

THE ENTIRE HOUSEHOLD was buzzing as they finished preparations for the Solstice celebration. The longest night of the year happened to fall on a full moon, which meant one party of epic proportions.

I took a deep breath as I prepared to greet the guests. While having the alphas of the packs for visits had almost become routine, this gathering was different.

Alec took hold of my hand. "You're going to be great. Nothing bad is going to happen. This is what you've been working so hard for the last year."

He was right, of course. And he'd been by my side for every step. I was truly grateful to have such a strong and supportive leader by my side. We'd found a balance in the last year, working together to improve pack relations and begin the process for positive change for all shifters.

Tonight we took that a step further. While we'd been working to break down the years of animosity between us and the witches, our alliance was still in its infancy.

Shifter and witches both held sacred connections to the

full moon and the solstice. It was my insane plan to invite the heads of the covens and the alphas to one party.

There had been some pushback, of course, but things seemed to be improving. Tonight was going to determine the fate of all our hard work.

When I opened the door to exit my room, I found Spencer waiting in the hall with my mom.

"You match," I pointed out. Spencer had tucked a lavender handkerchief into the pocket of his tux. It was the exact shade of my mother's gown.

"It was Spencer's idea," my mom said.

I smiled. It was nice to see her happy and well. We'd done a lot to repair our relationship and things were good between us.

"Everyone who accepted the invitation has arrived. So far, they all appear happy to be here," Spencer said.

I wanted to feel relieved at that remark, but the night was young. "I hope it stays that way."

"We've worked hard on this, I think we can expect this night to be mentioned as the turning point in shifter-witch relations," he said.

"You've worked so hard on this," I said. "Thank you."

Spencer, in addition to helping me learn how to navigate my role as queen, had taken point in reaching out to the covens. We wouldn't be here tonight if not for him. His unlikely friendships during exile had given him a unique perspective and opportunity to start conversations.

"I never thought I'd live to see the day," Spencer said. "But with humans encroaching on our territories, and discovering more of us every day, we're going to need the support."

I nodded. That was a whole other issue I wasn't ready to dive into. "One thing at a time."

The four of us walked away from my room, toward the outdoor gardens where the party was set up. We'd moved back to the east coast, where there was a greater number of shifters. It was freezing outside, but we'd set up heaters for the witches. Most shifters weren't bothered by the cold.

"How's the wedding planning coming?" my mom asked.

My cheeks heated. There had been a lot of pressure on us to make our partnership official. Without a wedding, Alec couldn't hold the title of king. I wanted him to gain that title, but we'd had a lot going on.

"We have a date," Alec offered. "Make sure you don't have any plans for the Summer Solstice."

"Even if I had plans, I'd drop them to be there for you," she said.

Sometimes, it was still hard to accept that she was recovered and that she really would be there for me. But I was getting better at it. We both were. "Thanks."

The four of us paused at the entryway to the gardens. James, the guard who had been with me since the very beginning stepped forward. "You ready for us to announce you, your highness?"

"Let's do this," I said.

Alec squeezed my hand. "You're going to be great tonight."

I rose to my toes and gave him a kiss on the cheek. "As long as you're by my side, I can do anything."

James stepped into the garden and announced us. The four of us followed him, greeted by applause. Nervous flutters filled my chest and for a moment, I felt like an imposter. Who was I to be queen? Who was I to think I could do all these things?

I caught sight of Malcom, Kyle, Sheila, and Star waiting for me at the front of the gathered group. Sheila cupped her hands around her mouth and whooped.

The fear passed. I didn't have the answers for everything, but I had support and help when I needed it. I would continue to do the best I could, and I would continue to rely on my friends to help me be the best queen possible.

THANK you for reading Wolf Chosen! Want to stay up to date on upcoming releases, bonus scenes, and deals? Click Here to Sign Up For My Newsletter

ALSO BY ALEXIS CALDER

ABOUT THE AUTHOR

Alexis Calder writes sassy heroines and sexy heroes with a sprinkle of sarcasm. She lives in the Rockies and drinks far too much coffee and just the right amount of wine.

Printed in Great Britain
by Amazon